The Katres' Summer

Book Three of the Soul-Linked Saga
by
Laura Jo Phillips

ISBN-13: 978-1468162844
ISBN-10: 1468162845

Cover Background Image: Hubble Space Telescope image, captured on February 4, 2004, of the dust cloud surrounding the star V838 Monocerotis. Credit to United States National Aeronautics and Space Administration (NASA), the Hubble Heritage Team, the Association of Universities for Research in Astronomy (AURA), and the Space Telescope Science Institute (STScI). We express deep appreciation to the dedicated scientists, engineers, and technicians associated with bringing this and so many other stunning Hubble Space Telescope images to the public for these many years. You have shown us the glory and the beauty of the Cosmos and, in doing so, have enriched the human Mind, stirred the human Heart, and lifted the human Soul.

DEDICATION

As always...

For my husband, best friend, constant companion and partner in fantastic, amazing, star-reaching dreams and fantasies. Thank you for sharing your life, mind and imagination with me. Once again, and always, I never could have done this, and had so much fun doing it, without you.

For Mom, Grandma, and Great-Grandma---Thank you all for the creativity you passed along to me, as well as the heart to do something with it. There is a little bit of each of you in these books, just as there is a little bit of each of you in me.

The Bearens' Hope

Book Four of the Soul-Linked Saga

by

Laura Jo Phillips

Available Spring 2012

A sneak peek
will be available to read online soon.
Look for it at:
www.laurajophillips.com

Chapter 1

Summer Whitney browsed through book titles, already knowing what was there, but hoping that one might inspire her imagination for new ideas.

Advanced Logistical Issues in Interstellar Naval Combat, Introduction to Metaspacial Fusion Plasma Physics for Naval Engineers, The Xarthax-Arkellian Wars: A Strategic History, A Comparative Ecological Profile of Tau-Ceti II and Epsilon Indi IV, Mineralogy and Gemology in the Thousand Worlds with Emphasis on Echthaww and Jasan, Issues in Intellectual Psychometrics for Highly Able Adults....

That last one caught her attention and she opened it up and began scanning the table of contents. After a few moments she sighed inwardly and put it back in its place on her mental shelf.

"What good is it to remember every word of every book I've ever read if I've never read anything helpful?" she wondered. *"Now, something entitled* How to Escape From A Slave Compound In the Middle of Nowhere On An Unfamiliar Planet, ***that*** *would be helpful."*

More than anything, Summer wanted to stand up and pace her cold, bare little cell. She wanted to beat her fists against the locked metal door, yell and cry and beg to be released. She had never thrown a tantrum of any sort, but she wanted to now, and would have if there hadn't been a security camera trained on her every single moment she was alone in her cell. Nothing in her life had prepared her for the past long year of captivity, and she was certain that she would have lost her mind long ago if not for her father. Every time she needed a boost of courage, and that had happened quite frequently over the past year, she told herself to think like Father. What would Father do? How would Father act? What would Father think?

The soft snick of the electronic lock being released on her cell door warned her that the night was over. She focused for a moment on the control node for the mass of microscopic nano-bots that had been injected into her brain so many months earlier, and sent it a reactivation order.

The ability to control computers with her mind was something she had played with since she was a child. She had never dreamed how important it would become to her sanity. Even so, the Controller had a firm grip on her brain by the time she realized it was there, so it had taken her months to wrest control of her brain away from it, and to gain control of the nano-bots at the same time. It would have been easier to disable them altogether, but she had quickly come to realize that she needed them.

By then she had become familiar with the physical tasks the Keepers put her and her fellow prisoners through on a daily basis. There was no way she could ever force herself to stand in one position for hours at a time with no sign of movement, or to push herself through the long, strenuous sessions of physical exercise each day without collapsing on the floor in exhaustion. Only the Controller could force her physical body to act and react as the Keepers expected. So, disabling it was not an option. Instead, she worked to gain control of the Controller, and eventually, she had succeeded.

The door to her cell opened and the familiar face of Keeper Tesla stepped in. "Stand," Tesla ordered the Controller, not unkindly.

The nano-bots in Summer's brain instantly complied with the order and Summer felt her body sit up on the hard, narrow shelf that served as her bed, swing her legs over the side and stand. Keeper Tesla stepped forward and swept Summer's long, black hair back away from her face.

"After you feed this morning you will not attend training with the others," the woman said. "Instead, you will go to the groomers. You have been purchased."

Shock radiated through Summer like a wave of ice. She was glad the nano-bots were in control; otherwise she would have certainly given herself away.

Keeper Tesla continued speaking as she removed the short, coarse night shift from Summer's immobile body and replaced it with an equally short, slightly less coarse day shift. "Once the groomers are finished, you will be packaged and transferred to the Office to await final shipment."

Keeper Tesla tossed the night shift onto the bed and stood before Summer once more. "I'm not sure why I am telling you this," she said. "I might as well be talking to a post."

Not for the first time Summer wondered why it was that the Keepers didn't seem to know that she was still herself inside her head. She had examined the nano-bots and their software very carefully many times, and she knew that they were specifically designed to keep her mental capacities whole and untouched while they took over her physical body.

Summer pondered the question even as the Controller obeyed Keeper Tesla's commands and moved her body out of the cell and down the hall to the cafeteria. Summer had, on several occasions, tested the

Controllers on her fellow prisoners. She could only do it when she was in close proximity to them, and that didn't happen often. Over the course of several months she had been able to examine the Controllers on about a dozen of the other women. Each of them had Controllers that were different from her own. Their Controllers took over their minds completely. Those women could not even think a thought that the Controller did not tell them to think. Just thinking of that would have made Summer shudder if the Controller hadn't been in charge. But, something inside of Summer told her that those women were still there. They were prisoners deep inside their own minds, but they still existed. If the Controllers in their brains were disabled or removed, they would be released. She knew it. She just wasn't sure how such a thing could be done without causing permanent brain damage.

But her own Controller was different. It wasn't because of her ability to control computer processors, either. It was different in many ways from the one used on her fellow prisoners. She was both relieved and frightened by that knowledge. In her experience, being singled out was rarely a good thing.

Maxim Katre forced himself to stop pacing and leaned against the side of the ground-car instead. He folded his arms across his chest, exerting all of his self-control to remain motionless when his body wanted nothing more than to continue its restless pacing. He gazed up the busy street toward the spaceport while he waited for his brothers to return, trying yet again to understand his own feelings.

For months now he had felt as though he had an itch he couldn't scratch. There was something nagging at him, an almost constant urge to do...*something*. But he did not know what. Several times over the past few months he had even caught himself leaping from his bed out of a sound sleep, instantly ready for battle.

He had, of course, discussed his feelings with his brothers and had been disturbed to learn that they, too, were having strange feelings and impulses. Theirs were not quite as intense as his own were, but strong enough to have them on edge nearly as much as he was. They all wanted to put it down to the intense grief they felt over the recent deaths in their family. But none of them could deny that the strange feelings had begun a year earlier, about the same time as Arima Saige Lobo had arrived. The loss of their family members had occurred a full three months after that.

Maxim's attention was drawn by the sight of a white ground-truck pulling into traffic from a parking lot beneath the building across the street from where he stood. He watched as the vehicle entered traffic, then stopped at the corner briefly before turning off of the main thoroughfare and out of sight.

There was nothing outwardly disturbing or significant about the vehicle. It was an ordinary ground-truck like thousands of others in the small city of Badia surrounding the spaceport. He wondered why it had caught his attention and could come up with no logical explanation.

Suddenly he had that nagging, need-to-do-something feeling again, stronger than ever. His hands clenched into fists and he found himself pacing the sidewalk again without having made a conscious decision to do so. This was getting to be ridiculous. Perhaps he needed to go to a Healer. If Riata were still alive, he would have already gone to her. But then, Riata had known things about the Jasani that no other Healer knew.

As he paced, Maxim's gaze kept returning to the tall building across the street that the white ground-truck had pulled out of. He had the strangest urge to cross the street and enter the building. He shook his head at himself.

"Maxim, would you open the trunk please?" Ranim asked.

Maxim turned to see his brothers approaching him on the sidewalk, both of them loaded down with large boxes. Maxim smiled briefly as he moved to open the trunk for them.

When their cousin, Princess Nahoa-Arima Lariah Dracon, had discovered that her long awaited order of new clothes and toys for her daughters and the Lobos' new daughters had finally reached Jasan, she had been very excited. When she had then learned that delivery from town to the ranch would be delayed another week, she had been so disappointed that Maxim and his brothers had instantly offered to drive into town to collect the order themselves. Anything was better than seeing the sadness in Lariah's eyes, even driving four hours each direction.

As Lonim and Ranim loaded the boxes into the trunk, Maxim wondered if they would have room enough for everything. Perhaps they should have borrowed Pater's ground-truck, he thought. In the end they had to tie a few boxes to the roof, but they managed to get it all into, or onto, the ground-car. As Maxim finished tying off the last box to insure it did not fall off during the trip back to the ranch, he noticed that both of his younger brothers were staring at the same building across the street that had caught his attention earlier. He again considered crossing the street and going into the building. He sighed. Perhaps all three of them needed to see a Healer.

"That's done," he said, to get his brothers' attention. They both turned to him with expressions of confusion and frustration on their faces. To see emotions on Ran's face was not unexpected, but to see them on Loni was a shock. Loni rarely allowed his feelings to show.

"Let's get these home to Lariah," Maxim said. Loni and Ran nodded and turned their backs on the building, the set of their shoulders telling Maxim that it was as difficult for them as it was for him. On impulse, he climbed into the driver's seat of the ground-car. He usually let Ran do the driving, but he thought it might help him to keep his mind from wandering for awhile. Besides, doing nothing when he had an almost constant urge to do *something* was beginning to drive him stir-crazy.

"Controller, open eyes."

Summer's eyes opened and she found herself staring at a smallish man with almost delicate features and soft brown eyes. There was something downright scary about those eyes, in spite of their ordinary color. Summer didn't know what it was exactly that tipped her off, but she knew that this mild looking man was very dangerous.

"Controller, follow me," the man said abruptly before turning and walking away. Summer's body followed him obediently as he led her out of a small, cold room that appeared to be a janitor's store room, then down a long, dimly lit hallway. He stepped into an elevator, waited for her to enter, and pushed a button. Summer felt her stomach lurch as the tiny service elevator shot upward. Seconds later the elevator stopped and the doors slid open.

Summer's body followed the man as he led the way down another long hallway, this one brightly lit, carpeted, and dotted with several closed doors. There was even art on the walls, though Summer was unable to turn her head or eyes to look at any of it.

The man reached the end of the hallway and entered the door there which had the name *Lio Perry* stenciled on it in gold letters. There was nothing else on the door; no company name, no title, no address. Just the name. Summer followed the man through the door which he closed behind her. He then led the way across what appeared to be a very luxurious waiting room to a set of large, ornate double doors with gold-colored door knobs. He opened one of them and stepped inside, then waited for Summer to follow, closing the door firmly behind her.

"Stop," he said. Summer's body stopped at once while her mind took in the opulent, but sparsely furnished office. The man walked around her slowly, examining her carefully in a way that made her feel both nervous and disgusted.

"So, Miss Summer Whitney," he said, his smooth voice filled with dark humor and menacing innuendo. "How does it feel to be locked inside your own mind?"

If Summer could have, she would have gasped in shock. As it was, of course, she could not react physically at all.

The man grinned at her. A decidedly unpleasant expression that made Summer hope that she would not be under this man's power for very long.

"Yes, I know that you have a different type of Controller, and I know what it does, and what it does not do," he said. "I find it extraordinarily amusing. You and my toy are the only two females to have earned the Prime Controller. So far."

Now this was information that Summer found interesting.

"You have one because you are a *berezi,* of course," he said. "My toy has one because I wished it." He smiled again, an expression that Summer was already learning to detest. "It is truly a pity that I have strict orders to keep you in your current...pristine...condition. I believe I would find you amusing for a day or two."

A high, insistent beeping sounded from somewhere behind Summer. An expression of irritation crossed the man's face. He walked away, presumably to answer the beeping noise. Summer could not see him, but she had no trouble hearing him.

"Yes," he said coolly.

"I'm sorry to bother you Mr. Perry," said a male voice speaking quickly. "You asked me to remind you about the meeting this afternoon."

"So I did. Inform the board that I will be there soon and I expect them to wait."

"Yes Sir, Mr. Perry," the man replied at once.

Summer heard a soft click, indicating he had closed the connection, then the sound of footsteps as the man returned to stand in front of her again.

"I'm afraid I have business to attend to now," he said. "However, you are not due to be shipped out until tomorrow evening, so I will at least have a few hours to enjoy your company tonight."

He smiled that nasty smile again and Summer knew that no matter what, she had to find a way to escape this office before he returned from his meeting.

"Controller, follow," he said abruptly. The Controller immediately obeyed, moving Summer's body across the large office to a screened area in the far corner. As Summer stepped around the screen and into the small alcove beyond, she was again glad that the Controller was in charge. Otherwise, she wasn't sure how she would have reacted to the sight that greeted her.

Standing in the corner was a woman with shiny silver skin. She was dressed in a tiny bra top and short skirt made of some type of shiny black material, and torturously high, shiny black shoes. The woman was standing on one foot with one leg held straight out in front of her at hip height, both arms held straight out at her sides, wavering slightly as the Controller continually adjusted her balance on the skinny heel of the shoe. The expression on the woman's face was one of utter joy, but the tears of pain streaming down her silver face to drip onto the shiny black fabric of her top belied the fixed smile.

Summer had never seen a more horrific sight in her life. The worst thing about it was the knowledge that this woman was, like herself, still aware inside of that parody of herself.

"Summer Whitney, meet my toy, once called Darleen Flowers," the man said genially as though introducing the two women at a party. "Toy, this is Summer Whitney." The man laughed, a high, cold sound. "Rather, her name *now* is Summer Whitney. Who knows what her new owner may wish to call her?"

The man paused as though awaiting some type of response, but as neither Summer nor the silver woman, Darleen, could possibly reply, the silence stretched out for several moments. Finally the man sighed.

"Controller, over here," he said, pointing to a spot on the floor directly opposite Darleen. Summer's body obediently moved to the spot indicated, facing Darleen Flowers.

"Now ladies, you two get acquainted won't you?" he said with a chuckle. "I have a meeting to attend, but when I return, we will, I think, have us some fun."

The man left the alcove, laughing at his own sick humor. Summer listened carefully to the sounds he made as he opened a drawer in his desk, riffled some papers around and then closed something that sounded like a briefcase. Then she heard the door open and close softly before the metallic rattle of a lock being engaged.

Summer wasted no time. She immediately sent a deactivation order to her Controller and took a deep breath as her body relaxed. She then reached out with her mind to examine the nano-bots in the other woman's brain, and was excited to discover that the man had not lied. She did indeed have the same Controller that Summer had.

She stepped closer to the woman and raised one finger to her lips in a warning to be quiet, shocked anew at this closer look of her. Hoping Darleen would obey her request for quiet, she gave the Controller a soft order.

"Controller, fully release subject," she said, then held her breath as she waited to see if it would work.

During the months she had been held captive she had observed that new Keepers had to use the word "Controller" a few times when first giving orders to each woman's Controller. After that, the Controllers appeared to recognize their voice and respond to their commands without them having to say "Controller" first. Since none of the women with the other type of Controller were able to speak, there was never any danger of them commanding their own Controller, or that of a fellow prisoner.

She was relieved when Darleen's body immediately complied with the order and the woman's face relaxed, her leg lowered slowly to the floor, and her arms went down to her sides. She looked at Summer, her eyes wide with surprise and hope.

"How?" she asked. Then she shook her head. "Never mind that, get us out of here before he comes back."

"Do you have any idea how long he will be gone?" Summer asked as the woman slowly bent to remove the horrible shoes from her feet before carefully straightening her ankles so that her feet were flat on the floor, her face a mask of pain.

"No, not really," the woman replied with a breathless gasp as she stood up and tried to stretch her aching muscles. "Could be an hour, could be five. I never know when he will come or go, and I'm never able to predict it."

"Is your name really Darleen?" Summer asked.

"Yes," the woman replied. "Darleen Flowers. Are you really Summer Whitney?"

"Yes."

"I've heard your name before," Darleen said.

"You have?"

"Yes, I've heard Lio say your name a few times when talking on the vox or the vid. He always refers to you as a *berezi*, though I don't know what that means."

"Neither do I, but I think I better find out," Summer replied. "Are you ready to get out of here now?"

Darleen took one step, then another, moving slowly due to the pain in her joints that had become a constant part of her life over the previous year. "Yes, I think so," she said. "But I think it would be better to call for help first. If anyone sees us, they will probably bring us straight back here."

"I agree, but I don't want to risk using the vid terminal. There might be security protocols installed. A vox would be safer," Summer said.

Darleen pointed to an end table next to a big cushy arm chair where Lio liked to sit while he ordered the Controller to put her body through painful contortions. He found her pain and humiliation endlessly amusing.

Summer hurried across the small, screened-in alcove, her heart suddenly racing at how close she was to escape. She snatched up the vox and slapped it to her ear just as she heard the door lock rattle.

She hurried back to the spot Lio had placed her in, and brushed her hair behind her shoulders the way it had been when Lio left. She started to reactivate the nano-bots in her brain when she realized that Darleen was not back in her place. Instead, she was standing near the edge of the screen where it opened into a doorway, holding a carved statuette over her head.

Summer's heart seemed to stop beating as she realized what Darleen meant to do and, at the same time, that it was too late to stop her. Even now she could hear the door swing shut, then a soft thunk as Lio put something heavy on his desk.

"Where the hell is that damn vox?" he muttered amidst the sound of papers shuffling and desk drawers opening and closing.

It's in my ear, Summer thought with growing fear and horror. Just as she began to slip over the edge into full panic, she asked herself, *What would Father do?*

Hell, Summer thought, *that's easy. Father would fight.*

Summer looked around the enclosure for something she could use as a weapon. All she saw was a thick, black rod leaning against the wall in a corner so she rushed across the alcove for it. The moment she picked it up she realized that it was a Maarkezi Pain Baton.

She had never actually seen one outside of a book, but because of her eidetic memory, she recognized it instantly for what it was. The Maarkezi Pain Baton caused every nerve ending in the body to produce instant pain. The level of pain was controlled by the dial, but even at its lowest setting it was said to be excruciating. The most insidious thing about it was that it artificially stimulated the nerve endings without causing any real damage, which prevented the victim from escaping the pain by passing out. The Maarkezi Pain Baton was outlawed on almost every planet in the Thousand Worlds, and for good reason.

Summer turned the object in her hand slightly, noting that the dial was set at ten, the highest setting. She looked up and saw that Darleen's eyes were glued to the baton, an expression of mingled fear and hatred on her silver face. Summer started to dial the baton down, but changed her mind and left it where it was. She had no idea how strong Lio was, but even though he was a small man, he was still bigger than either of them, and they would not have more than one chance at surprising him.

She hurried over to where Darleen stood, her ears straining for sounds from beyond the screen. It was hard to hear over the thundering of her own heart, but she thought she heard his footsteps against the marble floor as he crossed the large office toward them. Summer tightened her grip on the baton and set her feet. She had never performed a violent act in all of her life, but she meant to walk out of this room a free woman, and she would do whatever she had to in order to make that happen.

Only this was much larger, with a thick needle and a metal reservoir instead of the usual clear plastic.

Darleen pulled the injector out of the case and held it out for Summer to see. Summer knew what it was. She hadn't seen one before, but she still knew. She looked Darleen in the eye for a long moment, then nodded slowly.

"Yes, if that's what it takes, then that's what we must do," she said firmly, though her lips felt numb with shock at her decision.

Darleen crawled over to Lio, grasped his head by the hair and roughly turned it until the back of his neck was exposed. She placed the end of the thick needle against his flesh and pushed hard until it penetrated the skin, then she depressed the plunger and injected the Controller nano-bots into him. She withdrew the needle with a little grunt of satisfaction.

"How long does that take to start working?" Summer asked, still holding the baton against Lio's shoulder, though it was on the lowest setting now.

"I don't really know," Darleen said as she struggled painfully back to her feet. "I've seen a lot of women come through here over the past year, but I don't think any of them had the same Controller you and I have. Besides which, they already had their Controllers by the time they got here."

"Then how did you know how to do that?"

"Lio likes to talk."

Taking the hint, Summer didn't ask more about it. She really didn't need to know the details of what had been done to Darleen. The condition of the woman's body was more than enough information.

Summer felt torn. She didn't want to continue to subject the man to the torture of the pain baton but at the same time, she could take no chance that he would do anything to interrupt their escape.

"I suppose we should call for help now," Summer said.

"Yes, I think that would be a good idea," Darleen agreed. "I don't think anyone will come in here without Lio's permission, but you never know."

"I have the vox, but I don't even know where we are, let alone who to call," Summer said.

"We are in Badia, I know that much for certain," Darleen replied. "I think we are close to the spaceport because I hear shuttles coming and going sometimes when Lio leaves the window open, but I don't know the address, or even how big the building is that we are standing in."

"Do you know of anyone specific we can call for help?" Summer asked hopefully.

Darleen hesitated. She knew who the best people were to call, and she knew they had the power to get help to them faster than anyone else on Jasan. At the same time, she knew that those people had reason to want her either dead, or in prison for the remainder of her life.

Well, she thought, death and imprisonment were both preferable over what she had endured the last year.

Unfortunately, she had no idea how to reach either the Dracons or the Lobos. She doubted very much that Lio had their private vox numbers stored in his directory. Besides, they were at least four hours away. She didn't think they could count on being undiscovered for that long. Eventually someone was going to come looking for Lio, and since he was supposed to be at a meeting, that would probably happen sooner rather than later.

"Try asking the vox to connect you with Emergency Services," Darleen suggested. "I know I've heard Lio mention your name, and I think that the Dracon Princes have been searching for you particularly, so give them your name when you call, but don't mention mine."

"Why not?" Summer asked.

"The Dracons and the Lobos have reason to dislike me," Darleen replied. "Good reason."

Summer's eyes narrowed angrily. The idea that they would not receive help because someone didn't like Darleen was infuriating. She was very surprised, therefore, when Darleen chuckled softly.

"I appreciate your outrage on my behalf," Darleen said. "But I promise you, they have very good reason for their feelings toward me, whatever they may be."

Summer shook her head and decided to let it go. Now was not the time for what her mother used to call a *confession session*. She reached up and tapped the vox in her ear to activate it.

"Directory assistance," said a mechanical voice.

"Emergency Services please," Summer said.

"One moment." Summer was prepared for a long wait and was surprised when a real voice spoke in her ear a few seconds later.

"Badia Emergency Services, how may I be of assistance?" said what sounded like a very young male voice.

"My name is Summer Whitney and I have been abducted and held against my will," Summer began.

"Excuse me, Miss," the voice interrupted. "Did you say your name is Summer Whitney?"

"Yes, I did," Summer replied. She opened her mouth to continue when the voice interrupted again.

"Your name is on our priority sheet, Miss Whitney. If you will hold for one moment, I will put you through directly to Prince Dracon."

"I don't have a lot of time," Summer said. "We could be discovered at any moment."

"Don't worry Miss Whitney, I have already recorded your exact location and notified local authorities. Two Tactical Teams are being dispatched to your location immediately."

"Thank you," Summer replied with relief.

"You are welcome, Miss Whitney," the voice replied. "Please give me just a few moments and I will have you connected to the High Prince."

Chapter 4

Faron Lobo sat holding his eldest daughter, Varia, in his arms. Varia was currently sleeping, which was a relief to the entire household. The baby was only three months old, but she had a set of lungs on her that rivaled High Prince Garen's for both capacity and sheer volume. Faron smiled as he wrapped a lock of her dark blue hair around his finger. She looked so angelic. When she was asleep.

His vox beeped softly in his ear and he reached up to tap it. "Yes?" he said, keeping his voice low so as not to awaken Varia.

"The Princes are unavailable and I am taking calls in their stead," he said. "You are speaking with Faron Lobo, Prime Guardian. I have full authority to act on their behalf."

Faron's eyes widened with surprise and excitement as he listened to the Emergency Services operator. "Excellent, patch me through," he said.

He looked up and met his youngest brother's questioning gaze. "Ban, call the Katres and tell them Summer Whitney has been located and they need to reach her at all speed," he said, then rattled off the address the operator had given him. "Extreme measures may be taken to secure her."

Ban was talking to the Katres before Faron was finished speaking, but Faron knew he heard every word he'd said. A moment later his vox beeped again and he tapped it.

"Faron Lobo here," he said.

"My name is Summer Whitney," Summer began again.

"I know, Miss Whitney," Faron interrupted. Summer was wondering if she would ever get to finish a sentence, then decided she was being ridiculous. If they wanted to help without long explanations, then she should be glad, not frustrated.

"I have already been informed of your location, Miss Whitney. There are ground troops on their way to you, but it may take them a few minutes to arrive. Are you safe for the moment?"

"Yes, I think so," Summer replied. "We are in a locked office in a big building, and I don't think anyone will come in, but I don't know for sure."

"We have contacted a high ranking male-set who just happen to be in Badia right now and they are already on their way to you. They will probably reach you before the troops. What is your condition?"

Summer had to think about that for a moment. It had been a very long time since anyone had asked her how she was. "I'm okay, but there is a woman here with me who will need medical attention," she said.

"Shall I contact Emergency Medical Services for her?" Faron asked.

"One moment please," Summer replied. She placed her hand over the vox and whispered to Darleen. "Do you want Emergency Med Services now?"

Darleen wasn't sure how to answer that question. Over the past year, she had often wondered if it would be possible to reverse any of the things that Lio had done to her body. Whenever she thought about it, only one face ever came to mind, though she could never understand why. The old man everyone called Doc, who worked on the Dracons' ranch taking care of livestock and pets, had never impressed her much on any of the handful of occasions she had met him. But for some strange reason, she felt that he was the only real chance she had for returning to any semblance of normal.

As Doc's craggy, white mustached face rose up in her mind, she realized that Summer was still waiting for an answer. Darleen shook her head. No, she did not need emergency medical aid. Nor did she think that Doc, who was a huge fan of Princess Lariah Dracon, would ever consent to help the woman who had aided in the abduction of both Lariah, and the Lobos' Arima, Saige.

"No thanks," Summer said into the vox. "We just want out of here."

"The male-set on their way to you is about 4 minutes out. Their names are Maxim, Lonim and Ranim Katre."

"All right," Summer said.

"Keep the vox with you in case you get moved so we can track it," Faron warned.

"I will," Summer replied. "Thank you." She tapped the vox to disconnect and turned to look at Darleen. "They will be here in a few minutes."

"I would like to find something to cover up with before our rescuers arrive," Darleen said. Summer heard the nervousness in the woman's voice and didn't blame her for it.

"I saw a coat rack when I came in," Summer said. "There was something big and black on it. You might try looking there."

"Thanks," Darleen replied. She limped hurriedly out of the alcove and Summer turned her attention back to Lio. She suddenly realized that the man was no longer conscious, which was a relief. She turned the pain baton off and started to put it down on the floor, but decided it would be wiser to hang on to it just in case Lio awoke.

Summer rose to her feet just as Darleen came back into the alcove wearing a long black cloak. “How’s this?” she asked.

Summer’s first inclination was to say it was fine, but knowing how important it would be for herself to be covered were she in Darleen’s position, she decided to treat it with more seriousness. She eyed the cloak carefully, noting that it nearly reached the floor, the fabric heavy enough to completely conceal Darleen from her shoulders to her bare, silver feet. She walked around Darleen and discovered that the cloak had a deep hood attached which she lifted up and slid over the back of Darleen’s shiny silver head. Darleen felt the hood and reached up with a soft “oh.” She hadn’t noticed the hood before and was very pleased with it. Summer walked back around until she stood in front of Darleen once more and smiled.

“With the hood up, it covers you completely,” she said.

“Good,” Darleen replied softly.

“Darleen, do you know if there is a way to remove that polymer coating on your skin?”

Darleen’s expression did not change, but Summer saw the fear in her eyes. “I’m not sure,” she said. “Lio told me that there was, and that it was easy to do, but who knows if that is true?”

“That is the first thing we will be asking him when we have control of him then,” Summer said. The look of gratitude on Darleen’s face made Summer uncomfortable so she changed the subject.

“Lets find something to tie this creep up with in case he wakes up before help arrives,” she said.

Lio’s eyes opened. “Wha...?” he mumbled, reaching up with one hand to touch the side of his head.

“Controller, stop movement,” Darleen said, her voice harsh with sudden fear. Lio’s arm froze in mid-air, much to Darleen and Summer’s relief. Summer reached out with her mind to the nano-bots in Lio’s brain and discovered that, so far, they had only marginal control. Enough to allow them to control his gross motor functions, but little more. It was enough.

Summer turned to Darleen. “It’s okay,” she said, trying to reassure the other woman. “The Controller is just getting hold, but it is enough already that he can’t move unless we allow it.”

Darleen nodded and forced herself to relax and take a breath. The sight of Lio’s mud brown eyes opening had frightened her. All he had to do was say a word and she would be under his control again. She shuddered at the thought.

"What is it?" Summer asked.

"I just don't want him to be able to control me again," Darleen replied in a low voice.

"Well, let me fix that," Summer said. She reached out to place one hand on Darleen's shoulder and closed her eyes. After a few moments, her eyes opened and she smiled.

"I have disabled your Controller's voice command protocols," she explained. "Until we find a way to remove or disable the Controller completely, that will prevent anyone from being able to use it to control you."

Darleen was surprised to feel tears burn her eyes. She never cried. Not ever. Tears of pain when she had no control over herself didn't count. "I don't know how you did that, but thank you," she whispered, unable to speak normally around the lump in her throat.

"It's just a thing I've been able to do since I was a child," Summer replied with a shrug. "It's not really a big deal, but you are very welcome, Darleen."

She looked down at Lio where he lay, arm still raised half way to his head. Anger rolled through her at the man who had so cruelly abused the woman standing beside her.

"Controller, stand," she ordered. Lio's body instantly obeyed and rose to its feet. Since the Controller did not yet have full control over the his brain, his facial expressions were still his own to control. Summer was surprised to see nothing but fury in Lio's eyes and face. No fear, no horror. Just fury.

"If you two know what's good for you, you will release me at once," he said, surprising Summer again. She had not thought he would be able to talk, but then, she had not ordered the Controller to prevent it either.

"Right, because so far, you being in control has been so good for us," she said. "Now, do us a favor will you? Shut up."

Lio's eyes blazed with anger, then widened in surprise. It seemed obvious that he had tried to speak, and discovered he couldn't. The Controller had obeyed Summer's command for him to shut up.

There was a part of Summer that was very happy to see this horrid, evil little man getting a taste of his own medicine. At the same time, there was another part of her that was appalled at what she was doing. But, this time, she didn't have to ask herself what Father would do. She understood that this was a high stakes game, and she could not afford to be squeamish.

She reached out to the nano-bots in Lio's brain and discovered they had gotten a little further along. "Is there a way to remove this silver skin from Darleen's body without causing her harm?" she asked.

Lio nodded.

"What is it?" she demanded.

Lio's lips remained pressed tightly together. Summer reached for the nano-bots again, and realized that the ability to control his brain and body to the extent required to force him to answer questions against his will would take longer to develop.

"Don't worry, Darleen," she said. "In another couple of hours he won't have any choice but to answer our questions."

Darleen nodded, but she had pulled the hood of the cloak further forward so that her face was hidden, and Summer could not see her expression.

Suddenly a deep, loud roar sounded from somewhere in the building. It was so loud that Summer thought she could feel the floor vibrate beneath her feet from it. Darleen jumped, then stepped forward and gripped Summer's arms tightly.

"I can't go through it again," she said in a hoarse whisper. "I mean it, I would rather be dead. I cannot let him, or anyone, have control over me like that again."

"Its okay Darleen," Summer replied. "Nobody can control you now, remember?"

"Test it," Darleen demanded.

"Controller, sit down," Summer ordered.

Darleen relaxed when nothing happened to her, but Lio suddenly dropped to a sitting position on the floor beside them. Darleen's grip on Summer's arms loosened. There was another roar, followed by a third. Whatever, or whoever was roaring, Summer had a feeling they were getting closer.

"Darleen, stay here and keep an eye on him," she said. "I will go find out what's going on. Don't come out until I tell you to, okay?"

Darleen nodded, then backed deeper into the alcove until she blended into the dark shadows, though she kept her eyes trained on Lio.

Summer reached for the pain baton. She closed her eyes for a moment and mentally pulled up the information she had read on the weapon, including the various ways to use it. She opened her eyes, set her jaw and gripped the baton in both hands in the prescribed manner after turning the dial all the way back up to ten. She looked once more toward Darleen, then Lio, before stepping out of the screened in alcove.

She was in full agreement with Darleen. She would not go back, would not be a prisoner again. She would rather be dead. But that did not mean she wanted to die. Only that she would fight to the very end if need be.

Chapter 5

Maxim Katre drove the ground-car up onto the curb and was already throwing his door open as the car skidded to a stop. He flung himself out of the vehicle and raced for the entrance of the very building that he had been watching a short time earlier from across the street, Loni and Ran right behind him. He pushed through the door and found himself face to face with a pair of human guards barring his way.

"You will move," Maxim said softly.

The guard on the left smirked at him. "Why should we? You have no business here. Leave now."

"I am the Commander of Intelligence and Covert Operations for the Jasani Combined Military Forces," Maxim said, his voice a deep, rumbling growl. The man's eyes widened. "If you do not step aside immediately, you will be eviscerated where you stand." Maxim grinned, baring his sharp, white teeth. "It will be messy."

The man stepped aside, quickly waving the other guard back out of the way as well.

Maxim was still growling softly as he ran across the lobby toward the bank of elevators, sliding to a stop on the marble floors as he reached for the door leading into the stairwell. He had no intention of waiting for an elevator when they could run up the stairs far more quickly than it could carry them.

According to the information provided by Emergency Services, the vox call from Summer Whitney had originated from the top floor of this fifteen-story building in the southwest corner. Maxim and his brothers raced up the stairs to the fifteenth floor. They moved so fast that, had a human been in the stairwell, they would have seen little more than three odd blurs that came and went too fast for the human eye to identify.

Moments later Maxim pushed through the heavy metal door with the numeral 15 painted on it. He stepped into a long, tastefully decorated hallway. He had one brief moment to take in the thick carpeting, soft lighting and expensive art on the walls before the scent of sun warmed grass and spring wildflowers filled his senses.

His mating fangs burst through his gums and his cock hardened instantly, even as adrenaline flooded his body at the sharp scent of fear mingled with the other scents. The scent of their Arima. Behind him, he heard Loni and Ran react as they caught the scents as well.

Maxim fought against his body's instinctive reactions. He was able to prevent himself from shifting into his katrenca alter-form, but he could not prevent the loud roar of fear and anger that burst from him. Moments later, Loni and Ran roared as well, causing the art on the walls to vibrate, such was the depth of their feelings. Maxim turned and was relieved to note that neither of his brothers had succumbed to the urge to transform. The three of them stood together for long moments, struggling to regain control of themselves.

Much to his own shock and bewilderment, Maxim was not altogether happy with this turn of events. He understood as well as any Clan Jasani what a miracle it was for them to have found their Arima. And he knew that he should feel nothing but excitement and anticipation over it. But he didn't.

He took a long deep breath in an effort to calm himself. Loni and Ran followed his example and they all felt their shoulders relax. They were once again in control of themselves, but only barely. They had to find their Arima quickly. Whether Maxim was pleased with the knowledge that they were about to meet their Arima or not, their bodies were insisting they hurry to her at once, and there was no denying the strength of that instinctive need.

Maxim turned and began stalking up the hall, following the invisible scent trail until they reached a closed door at the end. He paused to get his bearings and realized they were in the southwest corner. Either Summer Whitney, or another woman behind this door, was their Arima. He was glad to know that he would not have to shirk his duty in rescuing Miss Whitney in order to find their Arima.

He opened the door and entered what was clearly a large reception area. It took only a moment to discern that the room was vacant, so they crossed to the next door.

Maxim reached out and tried the doorknob, but it was locked. He sent a tendril of air magic into the lock, building the pressure inside of it enough to break the mechanism. A moment later he tried the knob again. It now turned freely and he pushed the door open slowly.

At first glance the room appeared empty, so he stepped inside, his brothers fanning out on either side of him. The office was quite large and sparsely furnished. There was an expansive executive desk to the right, a couple of chairs and a table to the left, and a screened off area in the far corner, leaving a large expanse of white marble flooring in the center of the room.

That must be where the woman is, he thought as he took a step forward.

"Stop."

Maxim stopped, astonished by the sight of the woman who stepped out from behind the screen, a baton held expertly in her hands as she walked toward them. The woman moved with a willowy grace that all of the Katre brothers found extremely attractive, and they all swallowed hard at the brief glimpse they got of her long, straight, glossy black hair before she swept it back behind her.

She stopped several yards away from them in the center of a wide expanse of empty floor, giving herself plenty of room to move around in if she was forced to fight. Maxim instantly felt admiration and respect for the woman as she raised the baton into a classic defense/attack position and set her feet, turning her body at a slight angle to them. She was obviously ready to take on all three Katres if necessary, and he sensed she would fight to the death. His heart swelled with pride. This was their Arima, and she was stunning.

She was tall for a woman, which suited them as they were very tall themselves. She was very slender, with long arms and legs that were delicately sculpted with lean muscle. She had chocolate brown eyes that tilted up at the corners, giving her an exotic appearance. Her nose was straight with a small bump in the middle of it, her lips full and pink, her neck long and graceful. She wore a shapeless shift made of some thick, rough fabric which hid much of her figure, but that did not detract from their overall impression. To them, she was unbelievably beautiful in her courage and grace, as well as her features.

"Are you Summer Whitney?" Maxim asked.

"That depends on who is asking," the woman replied. Maxim could not hear the slightest trace of fear in the woman's voice, but he could smell it in her scent. His admiration grew, outpacing his initial reluctance.

"I am Maxim Katre," he replied. "These are my brothers, Lonim and Ranim."

Summer relaxed her stance only a little. These were the men she had been told were coming to rescue her, but there was something about them that bothered her. She had the oddest feeling about them, as though she knew them somehow, even though she had never laid eyes on them in her life.

These men were tall, lean, muscular and strikingly beautiful with their golden cat's eyes and wild golden hair that reminded her of a lion's mane. They were almost identical triplets, but Summer was not surprised by that.

She had done a lot of research on Clan Jasani before deciding to become a Candidate Bride, usually called a Candy Bride for short. Lots of women just signed a bridal contract, sight unseen, since the Candy Bride route was more expensive and time consuming. Summer had spent nearly a year waiting for an opening at Bride House. But, expense aside, it seemed wiser to her to travel to Jasan and stay at Bride House for the allotted six months and meet several Clan Jasani before selecting a male-set to marry. While waiting, she had dug up every bit of information she could find on the Clan Jasani, what little there was of it. She knew that they were a race of males, that they were always born in sets of three, and that one woman was always married to one set of three brothers, called a male-set.

That all seemed so long ago now. Her one big adventure, to go to Jasan, select a male-set and marry them. She had been so excited about it, so sure it was the answer to her loneliness, and her need for family. But it hadn't quite worked out the way she had planned.

Summer sighed and yanked herself back to the moment, and the subject at hand. Which was, why did she feel an instant connection to these three males? She studied them carefully, noting that they had one distinguishing characteristic. Each of them had a long lock of hair pulled forward over their right shoulders which hung nearly to their waists, and each lock was a different color.

Maxim's was black, Lonim's a dark, deep red, and Ranim's was white. She wondered briefly if they dyed the hair that color so that people could more easily distinguish them from one another. She shook her head. What difference did it make and why would she care? Why would she even wonder about it? There were, after all, a few more important issues to deal with at the moment.

"Yes, I am Summer Whitney," she said, finally answering Maxim's question.

"We have searched for you, and the other women who have been abducted, for many months, Miss Whitney. Have you been held here for all of this time?" Maxim asked.

"No," she replied. "I only just arrived here today. About an hour ago I think."

Maxim's eyes narrowed. "Were you brought here in a white ground-truck?"

Summer shrugged and relaxed her hold on the pain baton. "I don't know," she said. "I was put into a wooden crate for the trip and I never saw anything until the woman who brought me here opened it up in a closet a few floors below. I think it was a janitor closet. She took the crate with her and locked the door, leaving me there. A little while later, the man whose office this is, Lio Perry, brought me up here."

"The woman who brought you here, did she have short brown hair and a round face?" Maxim asked.

Summer nodded. "Yes, she did. She was wearing a white jacket and a blue shirt. Did you see her?"

"Yes," Maxim replied. "I saw her drive out of the parking garage as she left this building about an hour ago. I was standing across the street when I saw her."

Summer sighed. "Too bad," she said. "I was kind of hoping she was still here."

"Why?" Ranim asked curiously.

"Because the compound where I've been held for the past year is also holding about twenty-five other women," Summer explained. "I have no idea where it is, but one way or another, I will find it, and I will release those women."

Maxim bowed low to her, as did Loni and Ran. "Your goal is worthy, Summer Whitney," he said solemnly. "We will be pleased to aid you in your quest to free your fellow captives. However, for now, we must complete our rescue of you."

Summer smiled, an expression which lit up her entire face and caused the Katres to all but gasp at her beauty. Summer was completely unaware of the effect she was having on them. She was just happy to be rescued, and to know she would have help rescuing the other women.

"All right, follow me," she said as she turned and walked back to the screened alcove in the corner of the office. Maxim and Loni followed while Ran stayed behind to guard the door.

Whatever Maxim expected to see when he stepped into the alcove, it was not the sight that greeted him. On the floor sat a middle aged human male wearing an expression of outraged anger on his face. In the corner stood a female concealed in a long black cape, her face hidden deep beneath the cape's hood. But he did not need to see the woman to recognize her scent.

He hissed angrily as he stared at the hooded figure. "Step forward and reveal yourself, Darleen Flowers, betrayer and false friend," he said with contempt. "There is no use in hiding yourself. You will evade justice no longer."

Summer spun around, her eyes flashing angrily. "Do not speak to her in such a manner," she snapped. "She has told me that there are those who do not like her, and she said it was for a good reason. But whatever the reason, whatever she did, this woman has suffered more than you can imagine and you will not lay a finger on her, nor will you threaten her."

Maxim was surprised, distressed, and more than a little offended by Summer's defense of the woman responsible for so many crimes against people he cared about. Nor was he particularly pleased that she would take sides with a woman such as Darleen Flowers against him. She was their Arima. Arimas should not take sides against their own Rami.

He took a slow deep breath and reminded himself that she did not yet know she was their Arima. Besides, he told himself, after all she had been through, it was normal for her to be a little irrational.

"I will neither harm, nor threaten Darleen Flowers," he said at last, then tried to change the subject. "Who is this man?"

"Lio Perry, the man I told you about," Summer replied, perfectly willing to set aside the discussion concerning Darleen until later. She did not know what the woman had done, but whatever it was, it appeared to have been serious judging by Maxim Katre's response.

"We will have the security officers take him into custody then," Maxim said. He turned his head slightly. "I believe I hear them coming now."

Summer bristled. "You will not," she said flatly. "He stays with me."

Maxim frowned. Would this woman contradict everything he said? It was one thing to be strong and capable. Another to be argumentative and unreasonable. "Why would you want this man to remain with you?" he asked.

Summer opened her mouth to explain, then decided it might not be a good idea. What if these men decided that injecting Lio with the Controller was wrong, and took him away from her? She needed the knowledge in his head too much to allow that to happen. She considered the problem for a moment, trying to dredge up some reason that would convince them to let her retain custody of Lio without actually telling them the truth.

Her Mother was a Sentient Species Specialist and had written many books on the subject, all of which Summer had read. She took a moment to flip rapidly through several of those books in her mind until she hit on something she thought might work.

"I claim this man as my captive," she said boldly. "I defeated him in honorable combat, and he is mine to do with as I wish." Summer almost winced at that stretching of the truth. They hadn't actually engaged in battle, conking him over the head from behind with a statuette probably couldn't be considered honorable, and she hadn't even been the one to do it. But, at this point, she didn't really care about splitting a few hairs.

"You claim Right of Capture?" Loni asked with no trace of emotion to indicate what he thought about it.

"Yes," Summer replied, wondering how she knew that Loni was surprised by her claim when his expression had not changed by so much as the flicker of an eyelash.

"You must claim Warrior Rights before you can claim Right of Capture," Maxim said.

"Then I claim Warrior Rights," Summer said, though she cringed inwardly. The idea of herself as a warrior was laughable. All she knew of war and combat was what she had read in Father's library. There had been a lot of books, but reading did not make a warrior.

Maxim was aware of several races whose women were warriors, and he was also aware that many Earth women chose to be warriors. Summer had certainly handled the pain baton with easy familiarity, and her ready stance when she had greeted them had spoken of one who knew how to handle herself in a fight. He had never heard of a Clan Jasani female warrior, aside from Saige Lobo. But even though Saige was warrior-like, she was always kind and agreeable with her male-set, the Lobos. She did not argue with them at every turn. But Summer was not Jasani, he reminded himself. At least, not yet. And to deny her Warrior Rights out of pique would be petty.

"I recognize your claim of Warrior Rights, and honor your Right of Capture," he said finally.

Summer nearly sighed with relief, but bit it back in time. She could not show these men any sign of weakness or they would walk all over her. She wasn't sure how she knew that, but she knew it.

A thought occurred to her and she spoke before taking time to think it over further. "I also claim this woman, Darleen Flowers, as mine to protect."

"On what grounds do you claim her?" Maxim asked, fighting to hold back an angry growl. Already he regretted giving into her on the issue of Warrior Rights. It was apparent that this was a female who would always want more than was offered. He was beginning to understand his initial dismay at finding their Arima. He had always worried that he and his brothers would end up in an unhappy relationship as their fathers had. Now it seemed he'd had good reason for his concerns.

Summer had not been ready for the question but as soon as he asked it the answer came to her. "On two grounds," she replied. "First, I saved her life. Therefore it is mine to protect, if I wish, from this day forward. Second, she joined me in battle as a fellow warrior. She guarded my back, and I hers."

Maxim grimaced. Her first reason could be argued, but the grounds of Battle Bond could not be ignored or denied. Such bonds were inviolate.

Maxim glanced at his brother who did no more than blink his eyes, but Maxim understood his brother was thinking as he was. There was no honorable way to deny her in this. After a long moment, Maxim and Loni raised their left fists to their right shoulders in the traditional warrior salute, and bowed. "We honor your Battle Bond with Darleen Flowers," Maxim said reluctantly.

"Thank you," Summer replied, feeling a little uncomfortable with all of the bowing as she had no idea how she was supposed to respond to it.

"However, I must point out that our Princes have authority to reverse our decision," Maxim warned. "Under normal circumstances they would not deny a Battle Bond, but they have a personal reason for their feelings against Darleen Flowers."

"I will deal with that when I get to it," Summer said, suddenly feeling very tired.

At that moment there was a loud commotion from beyond the screen. Summer raised the pain baton back into fighting position and set her feet in a combat stance without even thinking about it.

"Be calm," Maxim said. "It is our own people arriving to aid in your rescue."

Summer lowered the baton but did not fully relax. There had been a hint of something in Maxim's tone that bothered her. Sarcasm? she wondered. But no, that made no sense. She shook her head. It was probably her imagination, and if it wasn't, she was just too anxious to figure it out right now.

"If you will wait here for a short time, I will speak with them," Maxim said.

"Okay," Summer replied. All she wanted to do at the moment was sit down, but she remained where she was until both Maxim and Lonim had left the alcove. As soon as they were gone, she walked across the alcove to Lio's chair and nearly fell into it.

Darleen hurried over and started to lower herself to her knees on the floor in front of the chair. Summer placed a hand on Darleen's arm to stop her. "No, don't do that," she said softly. "There is no need to cause yourself more pain."

Darleen nodded with some relief. "Are you all right, Summer?" she whispered.

"Yes," Summer replied. "I think I've had a few too many adrenaline rushes this morning is all." Summer glanced over her shoulder to be sure they were alone, then lowered her voice to a soft whisper. "I need to get a better mental on his Controller. I don't want the Katres to know what we did."

Darleen nodded. "All right, go ahead and I'll keep watch," she whispered back.

Summer closed her eyes to aid in her concentration and reached for the nano-bots in Lio's brain. She was relieved to find that they had progressed a great deal since the last time she'd checked. They should be able to ask him about Darleen's skin by now. But first she had to reprogram the Controller to accept her mental commands.

A few minutes later, Summer was satisfied that she could mentally control Lio's Controller as easily as she could the Controller in her own brain. Lio was standing up now, and the expression on his face was one of calm acceptance rather than anger, due to Summer's silent commands. She wasn't sure how she was going to explain the man's obedience to her, but she would worry about that later. One thing at a time, she told herself as she prepared to face Maxim once more.

Chapter 6

Maxim stalked out of the alcove, across the office and into the reception area with Loni following silently behind him. Ran was standing near the door speaking with a young Falcoran male-set unfamiliar to Maxim. As he approached, the Falcorans bowed to him and introduced themselves. Once the introductions were complete, Maxim got down to business.

"Summer Whitney is in the next room with another female and the male who was apparently in charge of this operation," he said without preamble. "We will transport them to the Dracons' ranch immediately. Please call for a VTOL to land on the roof, one with sufficient space to transport the six of us. I will also need someone to drive our ground-car to the ranch. The packages it contains belong to Princess Lariah."

The lead Falcoran glanced at his youngest brother who turned and stepped out into the hallway to carry out Maxim's orders.

"I believe that it would be best to detain all personnel in this building for questioning on site," Maxim continued. "Call in a forensics team for this office. Have the results of all findings reported to me as soon as they are available."

"Yes, Lord Commander," the Falcoran replied with another short bow. The youngest Falcoran returned and addressed Maxim directly.

"Your VTOL will land on the roof within ten minutes, Lord Commander," he said.

"Thank you," Maxim replied. "How many men do you have with you?"

"Two teams consisting of ten human males each, highly trained and reliable, as well as one young Gryphon male-set who are still in training," the lead Falcoran replied, "

"Please select one of your best men to post inside this door until we depart," Maxim said. "We have a few things to discuss among ourselves. Nothing in this office is to be touched until the forensics team arrives."

Again the youngest Falcoran left, returning seconds later with a stony faced human soldier in full combat gear and carrying a wicked looking high capacity blaster, who took up position several feet away from the Clan Jasani. Maxim nodded in approval and the Falcorans left to order the rest of their men. Maxim waited until he heard the men disperse, then he gestured to his brothers and stepped out into the now empty hallway.

"What's going on?" Ran asked. "I can tell you are irritated about something."

"Our Arima is perhaps not all that we could wish her to be," Maxim said, forcing his voice to calm. He wasn't sure whether he was more angry than disappointed, or the other way around.

"Why would you say such a thing?" Ran asked in surprise.

"She is argumentative, opinionated and demanding," Maxim replied.

"I find that difficult to believe," Ran said carefully, not wishing to contradict his eldest brother directly.

"You were not in there," Maxim bit out. "Loni, do you agree with my assessment?"

Loni lifted one brow just slightly. "Perhaps," he said.

"Perhaps?" Maxim growled. "Did you not hear her take sides with Darleen Flowers against us? Did you not hear her demand regarding the human male? Why would she want that man close to her? By her own words he held Darleen Flowers captive, and herself as well, yet she wishes to protect him and demanded Warrior Rights to do it."

"You did grant her request," Loni pointed out calmly.

"What choice did I have? She made a valid point and I could not in honor deny her, and well you know it."

Loni lifted one shoulder in a shrug. "That is true."

Ran shook his head in confusion. Darleen Flowers was here? Summer had demanded Warrior Rights? What was going on here? Several questions rose to mind, but as it was, the most important issue was their Arima, and why Maxim was so angry at her.

"This makes no sense," he said. "My mating fangs descended and so did yours. She is our Arima. She is made for us, as we are made for her. How can she be as you say?"

"She is human," Maxim snapped. "That is in itself enough explanation."

"Our royal cousin, Princess Nahoa-Arima Lariah was raised on Earth, as was Arima Saige Lobo," Ran pointed out reasonably.

"Obviously they were raised somewhat differently than Summer Whitney," Maxim replied. "We will not tell her she is our Arima," he said.

Ran was so shocked by Maxim's pronouncement that he gasped aloud. "Maxim, with all respect, I disagree with you in this. She is our Arima, and that is no small thing. We are blessed to have been chosen for this honor. Besides that, as you well know, if we do not accept her, we forfeit all hope of family."

"You wish to walk away from her after one meeting?" Loni asked. As always, there was very little in Loni's voice to indicate his feelings in the matter. He might have been asking if Maxim wanted ice in his juice.

Maxim opened his mouth to reply, then closed it. He knew that he had a bit of a temper, more so of late than ever. He was also aware that when he was angry he had a tendency to act first and think later, the direct opposite of his middle brother, Loni. This was far too important a matter for his temper to determine. He bowed his head and forced himself to reconsider the situation. His brothers stood silently, allowing him time to rethink things. Finally he lifted his head and met his brothers' gazes with his own.

"I have promised Miss Whitney our aid in locating the slave compound where she was held, and I will, of course, keep my word. We will spend time with her, and, perhaps, we will learn she is different from the impression she has made so far. If that is so, I will reconsider my decision on the matter. Until then, we will not tell her, or anyone else, that she is our Arima."

Ran opened his mouth to argue but one stern look from Maxim stopped him. He knew his brother in this mood, and discussion would not improve things.

"Very well," he agreed unwillingly, promising himself that at the first opportunity, he would get Loni aside and find out what had really happened in that alcove.

"I will abide by your decision," Loni said. Something in his voice earned him a sharp look from Maxim.

"You do not agree with me in this?"

"The woman has been held captive for an entire year," he pointed out. Maxim waited, but Loni had no more to say. A stab of guilt hit him. He had not considered that fact in his judgment of her. He wondered if he should rethink things again, but decided to stick with his decision. They would wait and see what this Summer Whitney was really like. He would not lock himself, and his brothers, to a woman he did not care for, Arima or not. If he renounced her, he was sentencing himself and his brothers to a life without a mate or children. But, he reasoned, they had managed without those things for 500 years. They could continue to do so if necessary.

Chapter 7

Za-Linq was displeased.

He had made a surprise trip down to this abominable planet in order to have a special meeting with the human, Lio Perry. He had even gone so far as to have a transport pad installed in the warehouse office specifically for this time period since he knew the human was having a *board meeting* at this time, in this place. Za-Linq was not completely sure what a *board meeting* was, but so far as he had been able to tell from his surveillance vids, it was the human equivalent of a brood *tzeak*, only without the blood letting.

He had meant this visit to be a pleasant surprise for Lio, to let him know that the Jasani slave routes were going to be fully restored to their previous configuration. It had taken a full year of careful maneuvering and extreme vigilance on his part to get Xaqana-Ti to agree to this after Za-Queg's failures. And now, at the moment of his first real accomplishment as *Zang-Lide*, Leg-Leader, of his own ship, here he stood, waiting on a human.

There was a soft, almost hesitant knock on the office door. Za-Linq scented the fear of the human on the other side of the door, and was slightly appeased by it.

"Enter," he said coolly, smiling at the instant increase in fear scent.

The door opened slowly and the human male who worked as assistant to Lio Perry stuck his head into the room while keeping his feet outside of it.

"I am sorry, Mr. Za-Linq, Sir," the man said, speaking quickly as was his habit, "but I'm afraid Mr. Perry has not yet arrived. I have sent a runner to his office to let him know that you are here, and that he should arrive in all haste."

Za-Linq felt a frisson of worry. "Is it normal for Lio to be late to his own meetings?"

The human swallowed and dropped his eyes nervously, clearly searching for the best way to word his response. "Mr. Perry is a busy man, Mr. Za-Linq, Sir, as I am certain you are, and he often has interruptions that cause a brief delay in his arrival. But I am certain that the moment he is made aware that you are awaiting him he will come as fast as he is able."

"When you hear from your runner, inform me at once," Za-Linq ordered.

"Of course Mr. Za-Linq, Sir, absolutely, at once," the man promised before pulling his head back and closing the door.

Za-Linq stared at the closed door for a long moment as he considered returning to his ship. While it was true that Lio had not known he was being paid a surprise visit, it still made Za-Linq angry to be kept waiting. It would serve the arrogant human right if Za-Linq were to replace him.

Za-Linq toyed with the idea, not for the first time. And, again not for the first time, decided to continue honoring Za-Queg's request to allow the human to retain his position. If it had not been for Za-Linq's admiration for his elder brood brother, he would have destroyed the human as a matter of course when he agreed to accept Za-Queg's ship and position. In fact, that same admiration was the only reason Za-Linq had accepted the position at all. He had not been Xaqana-Ti's first choice, nor the second, or even the twenty-second.

True, there were many who would love to have Za-Queg's ship, position, and territory, but, according to Xanti custom, along with the good, came the bad. Za-Queg had left a large mark on Xaqana-Ti's web, and his punishment had not removed that mark. Therefore, whoever took over his position, also took on responsibility for the mark's removal.

Again a frisson of worry ran through him. He did not know why Lio was late to his own meeting, but now that he was here, it would be wiser to stay until he found out. Thinking about his responsibility for Za-Queg's mistakes reminded him that he could not afford to make any of his own. Not that he needed the reminder.

Chapter 8

Summer wasn't sure how she felt about being taken to the home of the Dracon Princes. She knew that they had been searching for her in particular, though she did not know why, and she also knew that they had a problem with Darleen, also a fuzzy issue. No matter what the reasons were, what she really wanted to do was get time alone with Darleen and Lio so she could ask him how to remove the silver coating on Darleen's skin, and where the slave compound was located. But, as Darleen had pointed out to her before they had boarded the VTOL with the Katres, learning the location of the compound wasn't going to be enough. They could not get there and raid the place on their own. For that, they were going to need help.

Summer was hoping that the Princes would offer the help she needed. She had no reason to think they would, but it was the only hope she had at the moment. The Katres had offered their help, but their initial warmth toward her had cooled dramatically. She wasn't sure why, and she didn't really have the energy to figure it out. She just knew that she could feel them in some strange way, and that they did not seem to like her very much. Particularly the eldest brother, Maxim. She could feel his anger toward her pouring off of him from where he sat on the other side of the small aircraft cabin, though his expression appeared calm and neutral.

That actually bothered her more than she thought it should. She told herself it was absurd. Why should she care what those men thought of her? After all that she had been through over the past year, the last thing she needed to think about was men. Especially men who didn't like her.

She pushed her hurt feelings aside and focused on her current goals, which were finding the slave compound, getting someone to help her free the women being held there, and doing it all without letting anyone know they had injected a Controller into Lio's brain.

The flight from Badia to the ranch had been short, barely half an hour in the high speed VTOL. It had also been virtually silent. None of the Katres had spoken a word during the trip, and neither had she, Darleen or, of course, Lio. Summer had hoped for a few moments to speak with Darleen privately before they reached their destination, but that had not been possible. Now, as she stepped off the VTOL with Darleen close by her side, and Lio marching right behind her, she began to feel nervous about meeting these Princes. She knew nothing about them, and was suddenly worried that they would take Darleen from her in spite of the Katres' acknowledgment of her Battle Bond.

She was distracted by the sight of a large man approaching them from the edge of the field they had landed in, and Maxim moving ahead of their group to meet him. For the first time, Summer realized that she was still wearing the ugly, coarse shift that Keeper Tesla had put on her that morning, and nothing else. Her feet were bare and the thick, blue grass was cold and wet beneath them. There was also a cold breeze blowing and the skies were dark with clouds. She folded her arms in front of her, shivering with the cold as she glanced at Darleen worriedly.

Her feet were bare as well, but at least she had the cloak to cover her. Summer had seen Darleen without that cloak and knew that she was very thin, her eyes sunken, her bones sticking out all over. Summer did not think the other woman had enough physical reserves to fight off a cold or a chill, so she was doubly thankful for the cloak that covered her, providing some protection from the wind.

In contrast, Summer was in the best physical shape of her life. The forced exercise and diet provided by the Keepers at the slave compound was intended to make the women healthy, beautiful and desirable to prospective owners. Clearly Lio had no such intentions with Darleen.

Summer glanced down and saw that Darleen's silver feet flashed briefly with each limping step she took. Well, there was no help for it. She hoped these people would have enough compassion not to mention it.

Faron Lobo watched the party disembark from the air transport. Maxim first, then Loni, then a tall woman with long black hair. She was followed by a figure cloaked in black, then a human male. Last was Ran, who hopped out of the pilot cockpit and walked a few yards behind the group of humans.

There was something odd going on, Faron thought. Maxim did not glance behind him even once to check on the women, nor did he walk at a pace that they could hope to match. Faron lifted a hand to call Maxim forward. As Maxim picked up his pace, Faron glanced at the women again and noted that the one with the long black hair was wearing no more than a short dress, and was obviously quite cold.

Maxim stopped before Faron and bowed. "I greet you Lord Protector," he said.

"Is the woman with the dark hair Summer Whitney?" Faron asked.

Maxim stilled. Faron's lack of return greeting indicated his extreme displeasure, and the question told him the subject, if not the reason.

"Yes," Maxim replied, moderating his tone carefully. Faron Lobo was a friend, but he was also High Lord Protector, a rank exceeded only by the Dracon Princes themselves.

"Why is it that you have not done her the courtesy of providing her with some warm clothing or a wrap? It is quite cold and the woman is all but bare."

Maxim turned around and looked at the group approaching them, noticing for the first time that Summer was indeed cold, and barely dressed. His anger and disappointment in her as their Arima was no excuse for ignoring her basic needs.

As he watched, Ran whipped off his own jacket, hurried forward and laid it across Summer's shoulders. Summer looked up at him in gratitude as she pulled the oversized garment around her. Even as tall as she was, Ran's jacket reached her knees.

Maxim turned back to Faron, shame written clearly on his face. "That was thoughtless and careless of me," he admitted.

Faron studied Maxim carefully. "You are extremely upset," he noted.

Maxim nodded but offered no explanation.

"I have sent for a ground-car to take us to our home," Faron said. Maxim looked at him in surprise. "Our Princes are currently in an important meeting and unavailable. I will handle this matter on their behalf."

"Very well," Maxim said. "You should be aware that the cloaked figure is Darleen Flowers."

Faron's eyes narrowed as he turned his eyes again to the group still walking slowly toward them. He watched the cloaked figure for a long moment, then turned his eyes back to Maxim.

"What has been done to her?" he asked.

Maxim was annoyed by the question. "I have done nothing to her," he said. "I have not even seen her without the cloak."

"I meant no accusation, Maxim," Faron said, puzzled by Maxim's behavior. "Clearly something dreadful has been done to her. I only asked if you knew what."

Maxim was confused. He turned around again and, for the first time, took a moment to really look at the cloaked figure. Even with the cloak concealing her, it was obvious that the woman was very thin; her shoulders were sharp against the cloth, and barely wider than her head. Her limping, stumbling gait indicated both injury and weakness, and brought his attention to the bright flash of silver beneath the cloak at each step. For a moment he thought she was wearing silver shoes, but his eyesight was quite good, and it took him only a moment to realize that her feet were bare, and that it was her skin that was silver.

He again felt a stab of guilt. How was it that he had not noticed what was so obvious? But he knew the answer to his own question. He would have noticed had he bothered to look, but he hadn't.

"Miss Whitney said that she was Lio Perry's prisoner for a year," Maxim said. "She also indicated that Darleen Flowers had suffered horribly, and demanded that I not harm or threaten her."

"Lio Perry?" Faron asked.

"The human male following Miss Whitney like a trained *squilik*," he replied, struggling to keep the petulance out of his voice.

Faron realized a lot more was going on between the Katres and the humans they escorted than he knew. But now was neither the time nor the place for a long discussion.

"We shall talk more later," he said to Maxim just as the rest of the party reached them.

"Miss Whitney," Faron said, bowing to the woman wearing Ran's jacket, her bare feet nearly as blue as the grass she stood upon. "I am Faron Lobo. I believe you have met my Arima, Saige, once named Saige Taylor."

Summer's eyes brightened. "Yes, I remember her from the *Cosmic Glory*," she said. "I am not familiar with the term *Arima* though."

Faron smiled. "It is of no matter at this time," he said as Ric arrived with a ground-car. "We will have time to talk when we are someplace warm and dry, and you have had some time to rest." He turned to the cloaked figure. "Darleen Flowers," he said. "As you may know, there are serious criminal charges against you. However, I am aware that you have been held prisoner this past year and I understand that your suffering during that time has been great. Therefore, we shall set the other matters aside for now, and bid you welcome."

Maxim knew that Faron was correct in his handling of Darleen Flowers, and wondered at himself that he had not paid more attention to either woman's physical condition. He was truly ashamed of himself for that. He had allowed his emotions to cloud his judgment, a juvenile mistake. And an unacceptable one.

He turned and looked at Loni, whose face wore its usual placid mask, then he glanced at Ran who, in contrast, was an open book. Ran's pupils were thin slits against the gold of his eyes, an indication of real anger.

Maxim knew the anger was directed at him. He acknowledged that he deserved at least part of it. There was no excuse for his neglect of the women's health and comfort. But, even so, he was not ready to change his mind about Summer Whitney.

Chapter 9

By the time Lio's assistant knocked on the door for the second time, Za-Linq was nearly ready to practice his skills at *xafla* with the man. Za-Queg had been the acknowledged champion at clean-slice, but Za-Linq had not been far behind his predecessor in the game.

"Enter," he snapped impatiently.

The door opened and again the assistant stuck his head into the room. The scent of fear was pouring off of the man and Za-Linq prepared himself for bad news.

"The runner did not return, Mr. Za-Linq, Sir," the man said nervously. "So I took a run down to the office myself and the entire building is crawling with Jasani troops. I don't know what's going on, but I thought you would want to know at least that much so I came right back to tell you."

A wave of dread ran through Za-Linq. He simply could not afford a disaster at this time. He had just gotten into his Ruling Female's good graces after a year of hard work.

Za-Linq took a deep breath and ordered himself to think. There were many reasons why the Jasani could be at that building, all but one of them having nothing whatsoever to do with himself or the Xanti slave operation. It was logical to assume that Lio was simply lying low until the Jasani left the building.

Yes, Za-Linq thought, that was the logical thing to assume. However, the safest thing to assume, the *wisest* thing to assume, was that Lio had made a mistake and brought the Jasani down upon himself. In that case, the best course of action for Za-Linq was to destroy Lio before the Jasani had a chance to learn more from him than whatever they already knew.

Za-Linq glanced at the assistant who was still waiting at the door for further orders. He briefly considered putting the man in charge, then discarded the idea. The man was certainly more respectful than Lio had been, but he did not appear to have the proper leadership qualities. Of course, it was difficult to tell such things with humans. Well, that was a decision for a later time.

"Dismiss the men waiting for Lio," he said. "Then secure the warehouse and go home. I will contact you directly for further orders when I am ready."

"Yes Sir, Mr. Za-Linq, as you wish," the man said quickly before pulling his head back and shutting the door.

Za-Linq stepped onto the transport pad and pressed the button on his wrist band, taking a calming breath in preparation for the disorienting sensation this method of travel always caused him. A moment later he blinked in confusion to find himself still standing in the warehouse office. He pressed the button on his wristband again, and again he remained where he was.

Za-Linq calmly reached for the emergency location device around his neck and activated it. He then settled down to wait the half hour or so it would take for his retrieval. While he waited, he carefully considered the question of how many pieces he should carve his chief engineer into. There were valid points of argument for several different numbers, some favoring odd, others even, so there really was a lot to consider. Nevertheless, he was certain that by the time he was once again aboard his own ship he would have made his decision, and would be fully prepared to commence the festivities.

Chapter 10

Summer sat in a soft chair in the corner of the guest room she had been led to once they had arrived at the Lobos' home. There had been a lot of raised brows and a few angry stares when she had insisted that both Darleen and Lio remain with her in the same room, but she didn't really care what they thought of her. Once upon a time she would have. Very much, in fact. But not any more. Her likeability was the least of her concerns.

She glanced up at Lio where he stood facing the wall in another corner of the bedroom, and thought about the information she had finally been able to get out of him. He had not known the exact coordinates for the slave compound, but had provided directions on how to reach it by ground-car. He had also revealed that Darleen's polymer skin could be easily and safely removed by use of a tool he kept in his desk drawer. Unfortunately, she had no way of getting back to his office to retrieve it, and the way the Katres were now behaving toward her, she didn't think they would agree to have it brought to them.

Every time she thought about the Katres something in her chest hurt. She couldn't figure out why they disliked her so much. Perhaps it was because of Darleen and Lio, and her insistence on keeping them close to her. If that was the case, she thought, then she had no use for them. She had her reasons, and had they bothered to ask her, she would not have lied to them in spite of her decision to keep the knowledge of Lio's Controller hidden. But they had not asked.

Darleen opened the bathroom door a crack, peeked out to be sure that Summer was alone, then opened it wider and stepped into the bedroom. She now wore a plain black shirt and a pair of black cotton pants that tied at the waist. The clothes had been brought to them by an older woman who told Summer that they belonged to Saige Lobo.

Summer herself wore nearly the same outfit, except hers was gray. She didn't care what color or style the clothing was. It was the first time she had felt clothed in a year and she loved it.

"Feel better after your shower?" Summer asked as Darleen crossed the room and sat on the edge of the bed.

"Yes, I do," Darleen said. "You?"

"Much," Summer replied. "Are you ready to eat?"

"There is food?" Darleen asked, her voice barely above a whisper. Summer easily read the hope and the hunger on the woman's face.

"Yes, I was waiting for you so we could eat together," Summer replied as she got up and went to the dresser near the door to pick up a large tray covered with a white cloth. She carried the tray back to the table next to the chair she had been sitting on and set it down.

"Come on," she said to Darleen, waving her to the other chair before removing the cloth with a flourish.

There was hot soup, sandwiches, and a pitcher of juice, along with some fruit and small iced cakes. It was the first time either woman had seen real food since their captivity. While it was true that Summer's Keepers had fed her, what she had eaten day after day was a watery gruel-like mixture. It had no substance, no texture and no taste, but was clearly full of vitamins and nutrients or she would not be so healthy. She had no idea what Lio had fed Darleen but whatever it was, it had not been nearly enough. Both women had a difficult time restraining themselves from grabbing at the food and gulping it down. As it was, Summer was glad that Darleen was the only one who was there to witness her eating this first meal.

As much as they wanted to devour every morsel on the tray, neither of them could do it. They were too full to eat another bite in no time at all, a result of having too little food for too long. When they were finished, Summer prepared a plate for Lio consisting of a sandwich and a bowl of the soup. She carried it over to him, and, using her mind only, ordered the Controller to make him sit on the floor. She placed the dishes on the floor in front of him, then ordered him to eat the food and not to spill any of it. When she was certain he was following her silent instructions, she returned to her seat at the table.

Darleen was glaring balefully at Lio's back, and Summer didn't blame her, but she could not treat Lio as Lio had treated Darleen. What Lio had done to Darleen was both inhuman and inhumane. He might not deserve to be treated better than he had treated Darleen, but Summer could not, would not, lower herself that far for any reason.

"Lio said that there is a deionization tool in his desk at the office that will cause the silver coating on you to simply fall off," Summer said. She had Darleen's instant attention, as she had hoped.

"Is there a way to do it without the tool?" she asked.

Good question, Summer thought. She silently sent the question to the Controller in Lio's brain.

"I believe that there is another way to effect deionization without the tool," Lio said. "But I do not know what it is."

"We will just have to find a doctor to ask, or a scientist," Summer said.

"Yes, I suppose so," Darleen replied softly.

"He also told me how to get to the slave compound from Badia, via ground-car," Summer said. "Unfortunately he does not know the coordinates, we are no longer in Badia, and we don't have a ground-car."

"The Katres promised to help," Darleen pointed out, her voice very low as though she were almost afraid to speak. Summer realized that Darleen had been very subdued ever since they had entered the house.

"What is it Darleen?" she asked quietly.

Darleen dropped her eyes to her lap. "I don't want to tell you this, but you are going to hear it soon anyway, and I think it would be better if I told you myself."

"Okay," Summer said, keeping her voice gentle as she watched the other woman carefully. She was so thin, and so weak in spite of the hot food. Summer did not want her to over stress herself.

"I did a very bad thing, Summer," Darleen said. "I hurt three women simply because I was angry at one of them, and one of those three women was Saige Lobo." Darleen shook her head slightly. "Yet, here I sit in her home, wearing her clothes and eating her food."

Summer wasn't sure what to say. She didn't know what Darleen had done in the past, or what kind of person she had been. She only knew *this* Darleen, and she had only known her for a couple of hours. A couple of hours in which Darleen had helped her to disable Lio, injected him with the Controller, and agreed to follow her lead without question in a mission to release their fellow captives, even though she knew nothing about Summer at all. Summer would return that loyalty. They had not known each other very long, but in the short time since they'd met, they had formed a strong bond. In all of this world, Darleen was the closest thing she had to a friend, and the only person she felt was truly on her side.

She opened her mouth to say so when a knock on the bedroom door interrupted her. She reached over and patted Darleen on the hand gently, then got up to answer the door.

"If you are ready, the Lobos will see you now Miss Whitney," said the woman who had delivered their food and clothing.

"Thank you," Summer replied. "Give us one moment please."

"Certainly," the woman replied. Summer closed the door and turned to face Darleen.

"Ready?" she asked.

Darleen stood up and crossed the room to the bed, picked up the black cloak and wrapped it around herself. She pulled the hood up and forward so that her face was hidden in its depths.

"I'm ready," she said when she was fully concealed.

Summer sent a silent command to Lio's Controller. Lio put down his spoon, stood up, turned and walked toward Summer. Summer took a deep breath, pushed her hair back behind her, and reached for the doorknob.

After leading the trio through the large house, the woman stopped at a set of carved wooden doors and opened one before standing aside. Summer took a moment to ask herself how Father would handle himself in this situation, squared her shoulders, and stepped into a large room that contained a long, gleaming wood table lined with many chairs. It was obviously a meeting room, though the chairs seemed overly large to her. A familiar woman with short brown hair and light green eyes rose from her seat near the far end of the table and hurried forward to great Summer, a smile on her face.

"I am so glad you have been found," she said, wrapping Summer in a quick hug. "Come in and sit," she said, urging Summer toward a chair at the end of the table. Summer started to sit down when she noticed that all eyes in the room were directed at something behind her. She turned around to see Darleen standing there, still covered in her cloak, Lio at her side.

Summer turned back to face the people sitting at the table and looked at each face one by one. Maxim Katre was all but glaring at her, Lonim's face held no expression at all, and Ran looked uncomfortable. The other men she did not know, but they looked suspicious, as did Saige. Summer bristled angrily.

"Why do I feel as though we are on trial here?" she demanded. "We have done nothing wrong, unless you believe that being held captive and enslaved for the past year is a crime. If that is the case, state your punishment and send us on our way. We have more important things to do than appease a bunch of people we do not even know."

Faron rose from his seat at the opposite end of the table. "Of course you are not on trial, Miss Whitney," he said. "If you will please be seated, we will explain the reason for our feelings."

Summer didn't want to sit, but she didn't see that she had much choice. She could walk out easily enough, that was true, unless they decided to physically stop her, and she didn't think they would. But she needed to free those other women, and she would need the help of powerful men like these to do it.

She blew out a breath in frustration and sat in the chair.

"Miss Flowers, you may be seated also," Faron said. Summer looked over her shoulder to see Darleen's hooded head shake.

"She prefers to stand right now if you don't mind," Summer said coolly.

Faron sat down in his chair once more, and Saige returned to her seat at the far end of the table as well.

"The most important issue here is your captivity, and what you can tell us about those who held you, and where you were held," Faron began. "But, before we get to that, we apparently must first explore the more volatile issue of Miss Flowers."

Summer noticed the quick glare Saige sent Faron and wondered at it. Personally, she agreed with Faron about the importance of the first issue, but clearly the two of them were outnumbered.

"I do not know what she did," Summer admitted, "so I'm afraid I am not equipped to discuss it."

"How long have you known Miss Flowers?" Faron asked.

Summer shrugged. "Since this morning," she replied.

Maxim's brows rose in surprise, but the wave of resentment and anger she felt from him did not lessen.

"Then it makes sense that you do not know her past," Faron said reasonably. "She assisted in the kidnapping of three women, one of whom was killed."

Summer heard a sharp intake of breath from behind her, as did every other person in the room apparently, as all eyes went to Darleen.

"First, a diversion was created whereby a fuel tanker was sabotaged to crash into the Dracon Prince's home. Aboard that tanker were two male-sets, one of whom were the younger brothers to the Katres."

Ah, Summer thought. That explained some of their anger.

"They were able to divert the tanker away from the Princes' home, but it did crash and destroy our house. As it was empty at the time, no one was hurt. However, it was an unpleasant situation, and only because of the strength of the Princes' magic were the male-sets on board the tanker able to eject and escape an otherwise certain death."

Summer clenched her fists together beneath the table. This was already far worse than anything she had imagined, and they hadn't even gotten to Darleen yet.

"During the diversion, Miss Flowers, who had pretended a friendship with the Princess for many months, used her familiarity with the ranch, and the ranch hands' familiarity with her, to approach the house and lure the women outside the protected area by shooting the Princess's dog. The Princess was nearly due to deliver her triplets at that time. When the women exited the garden, they were each shot with a tranquilizer and tossed into the trunk of Miss Flower's ground-car by the two men she had with her."

Summer wanted to turn and look at Darleen, to see if what this man was saying was true, but she didn't. She did not move at all. Somehow, she already knew that Faron Lobo would not lie.

"Miss Flowers then drove off the property, which, due to the size of the ranch, took about an hour. A short distance from the ranch she pulled over and had the men remove the women from the trunk and drop them on the ground nearby. She then taunted the women, whom she believed to be still paralyzed from the drug they were given, gave her men some final instructions, then got into her car and left them with the two men.

"The women who were abducted were Princess Lariah, and Saige. There was a third woman taken as well, only because she happened to be having lunch with Saige and the Princess at the time. Her name was Riata, an Alverian Empath and Healer who was very important to the Jasani people. She was also the most pure and gentle being I have ever had the privilege to know. However, Miss Flowers let her men know, more than once, that she did not care in the least what they did to the Alverian, but that the other two were wanted unharmed. Regarding Riata, the men apparently took her at her word, as they carelessly dropped her on a stone outcropping which broke her back and killed her. They did not, however, follow her instructions regarding Saige and Lariah, because no sooner did Miss Flowers leave than they attempted to assault Saige. Luckily, Saige is an expert in *tiketa*, and Riata had Healed her from the drug before they were removed from the trunk. She killed one of the men, and disabled the other. Then Miss Flowers' employer, a Xanti, arrived and shot Saige with an energy weapon, nearly killing her. His intent was to take both women off-planet, and had our Princes not arrived at that moment, they, and the six daughters they have since borne, would be lost to us now."

Faron paused a moment, looked over Summer's shoulder at Darleen, then back to Summer. "That is the story of what Darleen did, and why there is such animosity at this table for her."

Summer looked down at the table before her, thinking hard. When she looked up again, she kept her eyes on Faron Lobo.

"Do you know what a Controller is?" she asked. There was a rustling around the table.

"Yes, we do," Faron replied. "We recovered one from the scene when Saige was rescued after her abduction from the *Cosmic Glory*. Our scientists have determined that it is very advanced nano-technology that works as a control interface for the human brain. That is all we know of it."

Summer glanced at Saige in surprise. "So you were abducted from the liner as well?" she asked.

Saige nodded.

"You have no idea how lucky you are to have been rescued," she said. "I was not so lucky." She looked back at Faron. "Your scientists are good. They have it exactly right. *Control interface for the human brain* is a very good description. I have one, so I am intimately familiar with it."

The effect of her statement on those at the table was immediate. They were shocked, horrified, and offended, all emotions Summer agreed with completely. She noticed that the Katres looked particularly upset by her announcement, though she did not understand why.

"How is it that you escaped?" Faron asked.

"I have an ability to control computers with my mind. Turn them on, turn them off, give simple commands. It's a type of telekinesis specific to computers, or computerized technology. The nano-bots that the Controller is made up of fall into that category. Because of that, I was eventually able to take control of the central processing node for the nano-bots injected into me, which gave me control of the Controller."

"Unfortunately, even though I had control of the Controller, I was in the middle of nowhere on a strange planet and locked in a tiny cell every night, as were about two dozen other women," she continued. "There was no way for me to escape, no opportunity to call for help. I had to let the nano-bots remain in my brain and release control of the Controller to the Keepers in order to prevent discovery.

"This morning I was told that I had been purchased. Being treated like a mindless robot is one thing. Being told you've been bought, like a pair of shoes or an eggplant, is just...indescribable. I knew then that I had to escape before they took me off of Jasan.

"I was taken to Badia, to Lio Perry's office. That's where I first saw Darleen, and discovered that she had the same type of Controller that I have. Because of that, I was able to release her when Lio left the office for a meeting."

Summer looked straight into Faron's eyes. "You have no idea what this women has been put through over the past year. Frankly, neither do I, but I have a good idea. If it is your desire to see her punished, believe me when I tell you she has been. Severely."

Summer blinked rapidly and cleared her throat. "After I released us, Lio returned to his office for his vox. By that time I had his vox, but I hadn't had a chance to use it to call for help yet. So, we were forced to attack him."

Summer hesitated. She had not planned to tell these people what she and Darleen had done to Lio, but she now realized she had no choice. There was no logical explanation for his obedience to her other than the simple truth.

"Darleen knew where he kept another Controller like the one we have, so we injected him with it. He has a lot of information in that sick little brain of his, and I mean to get it out and use it."

"So that is why you claimed Right of Capture?" Maxim asked.

"Yes," Summer replied.

"What is it you plan to do with the information you extract from him?" Maxim asked.

"I intend to find, and free, every single woman who has been injected with one of these Controllers," she declared, "no matter what type of Controller they have."

"There are different types?" Faron asked.

"Yes, as far as I can tell, there are two," Summer replied. "The first one subverts the subject's mind completely. They are unable to think, speak or act without a direct order which the Controller complies with. The other type is what I have, and what Darleen has. Our Controllers leave our minds alone. We are locked inside, able to think and feel, aware each moment of what is happening to us. But we have no control over our own bodies. The Controller responds to verbal orders, and we are helpless to prevent it."

"That's the most horrific thing I have ever heard," Saige said softly.

"I agree," Summer said. "According to Lio, only two people have what he calls the *Prime Controller*. Myself and Darleen. And now him, so I suppose that makes three."

"What did you do to your Controller, and Darleen's, to prevent them from working?" Faron asked.

"I've disabled their ability to accept verbal commands."

"Can you do this for the other women?" Faron asked.

"No, I can't," Summer said. "I tried on several of the other women at the slave compound with me, but it didn't work. Their Controllers are not the same. But, I really believe that those women are still inside their own minds somewhere. Not conscious, as Darleen and I were, or even as Lio is now, but there nevertheless. If a way can be found to disable their controllers, then maybe that's all it will take for them to return them to normal."

"What if nothing can be done for those women?" Saige asked. "What if they remain mental vegetables for the rest of their lives?"

Summer sighed. "That would be sad," she said softly. "But at the same time, whether they are aware or not, they should not be owned and used by others. They deserve rescue and release, and I will find a way to make that happen for them, regardless of their mental state."

"What of Darleen?" Saige asked.

"I don't know," she replied. "I know that what Darleen did was wrong, but I also have an idea of what price she paid this past year."

"We do not," Saige pointed out.

Summer turned and looked up at Darleen. She could not see the other woman's face, but she knew that Darleen could see her. "It's up to you," she said softly.

"Before I do this, I wish to say something," Darleen said in a shaky voice. "I did not know that Riata lost her life that day, nor was I aware that the Xanti were involved. I do not say that as an excuse. There is no excuse for what I did, nor do I ask, or expect, a pardon for my crimes.

"I ask only that I be allowed to assist Summer Whitney in her quest to release the other women, and to bring their captors to justice. Once that task is complete, I will willingly return here to face justice for my actions against Saige, Lariah, and Riata."

With that said, Darleen reached up and flipped back the hood of her cloak.

While everyone in the room was trying to adjust themselves to the sight of a bald, silver skinned, malnourished and scarred Darleen Flowers, she released the fastenings on the cloak and let it fall to the floor. It helped that she was wearing clothing now so that the majority of her body was covered, but it was still difficult for her to stand there in front of those people and let them stare at what she had become.

After a long moment of shocked silence, Summer rose from her chair, knelt to pick up the cloak, and wrapped it gently around Darleen's shoulders. She helped Darleen refasten it, then pulled the hood back up for her.

"This man. Did that.. To you?" Faron asked, his voice rough and growly. Summer looked up in surprise to see that all of the men had glowing eyes. Darleen nodded, a small movement of the hood.

Faron began to rise from his seat, but Saige reached out a hand and stayed him. "Easy my love," she said softly. "Summer needs that vermin alive, remember?"

Faron dropped back into his seat, but it was several minutes before the tension in the room began to subside. Summer waited quietly, watching the male Jasani warily until their eyes returned to normal.

Faron turned to Saige. "*Amada*, what does your heart tell you?"

Saige stood and walked slowly around the table until she stood only a few feet away from Darleen, with nobody else between them. She stared for a time at the cloak enshrouded figure, then turned her gaze on Summer. After only a few moments, she turned and stared at Lio. She grimaced almost at once and took a step back.

"This man's heart is so dark and disgusting that I feel dirty just from looking at it," she announced. She turned to look at Summer. "Summer's heart is a pure and shining light," she said with a smile before turning to Darleen. "Darleen's heart is not pure, but neither is it evil."

Saige turned to face Faron. "I ask for a few moments to meditate," she said.

Faron nodded. "Of course," he replied.

Saige returned to her seat at the table, folded her hands in her lap and closed her eyes. After only a few seconds the meeting room fell away and she found herself in the familiar gray fog that always surrounded her when she met with Riata, her Spirit Guide.

"I greet you Saige Lobo," Riata said softly as she stepped from the swirling wisps of gray.

Saige smiled at the Alverian, the short orange feathers on her head bright even in the gray fog. "I greet you, Riata," Saige replied with a bow. "It is good to see you again."

"I would congratulate you on the birth of your daughters," Riata said. "I am most happy for you."

Saige's smile widened, happiness flooding her at the thought of her babies. She was the luckiest of women.

"I must ask for your counsel," Saige said, her smile fading.

"I already know of what you would speak," Riata said. "I am afraid there is little time, so I will answer your questions before you ask them."

Saige frowned. "Little time for what?"

"Patience," Riata urged gently. "Saige, I would ask you, do you know how many spans of seasons I dwelt on the plane of the living?"

"No," Saige replied, uncertain what the question had to do with anything.

"I lived just over 700 Standard years," Riata said. Saige nearly gasped aloud in shock. "My time to move on was upon me," Riata continued. "If it had not happened the way it did, it would have happened another way."

"You wish me to forgive Darleen for her role in your death," Saige guessed.

"In part," Riata replied. "I also wish you to forgive yourself."

Saige felt tears threaten. "If I had not pretended to be paralyzed when they removed us from the trunk...."

"Then we would have all perished," Riata interrupted. "Yourself and Lariah, as well as her unborn daughters. This I know for truth Saige Lobo. All things happen for a reason."

Saige remained silent for a time, considering what Riata had said. "Why is it important that I forgive Darleen?" she asked.

"It takes great power to Heal," Riata said. "Power that can harm, or kill, as easily as Heal. If you hold anger in your heart when you attempt to Heal, the results of your efforts could easily be quite different than you intend."

"You are saying that I need to Heal Darleen?" Saige asked.

"You must Heal all of those who have been befouled by this device of the Xanti, and you must begin with Summer, Darleen and, yes, even Lio Perry."

"But I do not know how to Heal," Saige said worriedly. "I have tried and tried this past year since you passed your gift to me, and I have failed."

"All things happen in their own time, Saige Lobo," Riata said. "Now is the time for you to Heal. Place your hands on Summer first and you will understand," Riata said. "There is no more time for explanations."

"All right, but please, before you go, can you tell me if Summer is the Mind you spoke to me of?" Saige asked.

Riata only smiled her gentle smile and bowed before fading slowly until all that was left for Saige to see was the gray fog. She sighed, then closed her eyes, focusing on returning to the meeting room.

When she opened her eyes again she saw Faron staring at her expectantly, but she was filled with a sense of urgency and knew that there was no time to explain what had happened. She stood quickly and walked back around the table to Summer, placing her hands gently on the other woman's shoulders. She closed her eyes and emptied her mind, hoping that whatever was supposed to happen would just come to her.

And it did. Suddenly she sensed the intricate web of the nano-bots woven throughout Summer's brain as they moved busily to and fro. The mental image of them made her skin crawl, but she maintained contact, wondering what it was she was supposed to be looking for. Then she saw it. Saige nearly gasped aloud, but controlled herself and focused on the tiny program hidden from the nano-bots themselves in the control node. She reached out with some part of herself and destroyed it in a bright flash, uncertain exactly how she had done it.

She spent another few moments checking to be certain she had gotten all of it, then removed her hands from Summer's shoulders and turned quickly to Darleen. Without thinking she placed her hands on Darleen's shoulders, feeling the woman stiffen beneath her palms, but too focused to worry about it. She found what she was looking for more quickly this time, and again destroyed it in a bright flash of mental energy. Another moment to be sure she had not missed anything and she reopened her eyes and stepped back from Darleen. She turned to Lio and, with some reluctance, placed her hands on his shoulders. She reminded herself that, evil as the man was, his knowledge was important, and he needed to be alive for them to gain any use from him.

Again she quickly found what she was looking for and destroyed it, and again she spent a moment searching for further problems. This time she found something, buried deep within the man's flesh near his shoulder. Only this time she could not destroy it, though she tried.

With a growing sense of urgency she removed her hands and her mind from Lio and turned to Ban. "He has an explosive in him, like those men in the ground-car," she said quickly. "I can't neutralize it, and I think it's being activated now, or will be soon."

Ban was on his feet and moving toward Lio before Saige finished speaking. He held up one hand and did a partial shift, his hand transforming from human flesh to the fur covered, razor clawed paw of his loboenca. He raised one claw and glanced at Saige who pointed at a spot just beneath Lio's shoulder.

Ban sliced into the flesh without hesitation, then reached in and withdrew a small, flashing red device. Realizing that the device had already been activated, Ban, Faron and Dav all focused their magic on it, encasing it in a cube of solid air. That done, Ban raced for the doors at the far end of the room that opened onto a deck. Dav followed him, and opened a deep pit in the soil beyond using earth magic. Ban dropped the cube into the pit and together he and Dav replaced the soil and tamped it down. Only then did the Lobos remove the shell of air around the device.

Chapter 11

The Lobos and the Katres all had good enough hearing that, for them, the muted bang was clear, though Summer and Darleen heard nothing. It was obvious that the explosive had not been strong enough to do much more than destroy the person it was implanted in, and anything else in its immediate proximity. It would have caused damage to their newly built home, and perhaps would have killed, or seriously injured, Darleen and Summer since they were both so close to Lio.

"Apparently the Xanti are aware that Lio has been compromised," Faron said. "The question is, what will they destroy next?"

"The slave compound," Summer gasped.

"Do you know where it is?" Faron asked.

"Not really," she replied with frustration. "Lio was only able to give me directions on how to get to it via ground-car from Badia."

Faron jerked his chin at Dav, who hurried over to Summer, took her gently by the elbow and guided her to a quiet corner of the room. It would only take a few moments for Dav to determine the location of the compound from the driving directions Summer gave him.

Faron turned to Ran. "Contact the air field, tell them to prepare the VTOL for flight immediately," he said. Ran tapped the vox in his ear and began speaking into it as Faron turned to Maxim. "We cannot accompany you, much as we would like. With the Dracons gone, security for Lariah, Saige and their daughters is our responsibility."

Maxim was already on his feet. He bowed quickly to Faron, then turned to Loni. "Call the bunk-house and tell whichever male-set is currently off-duty to get out to the VTOL now," he ordered. Loni nodded and stepped away to make his call as Summer approached.

"Dav said that the compound is only about twenty minutes from here in the VTOL," she said. "He's calling it in to the pilot now."

Maxim looked at Summer for a long moment, his face unreadable. "I think it would be helpful if you turned over control of Lio Perry to one of us. He may be of some use to us."

Summer shook her head. "I can't do that," she said.

"Must you argue with me at every turn?" Maxim snapped, his pupils thinning with anger.

The entire room fell silent and Summer took a cautionary step backward. Everyone in the room was shocked at Maxim's outburst, including Maxim himself.

"I apologize," he said stiffly. "There was no reason for me to speak to you in such a manner."

Summer was torn between hurt and anger. But, she reminded herself, the women still being held at the slave compound took precedence over everything else at the moment. She clenched her fists, but forced herself to speak calmly.

"I was not arguing with you," she said. "I am simply unable to do what you asked. It is not possible, or if it is, I haven't yet figured out how to do it."

Maxim bowed. "Again, I apologize," he said, deeply embarrassed, and a little confused, by his own behavior.

Summer wanted very much to ask Maxim why he disliked her so much. She also wanted to know why it mattered to her. But all of that would have to wait.

"I accept your apology, of course," she said briskly. "I agree that Lio may have information that would be helpful, and I spent a year in that compound, so I think he and I should go along."

An instant objection rose to Maxim's lips, but this time he paused to consider before speaking. "I am sure it would be helpful if you and Lio came along, Miss Whitney," he said, forcing himself to sound as reasonable as possible. "But there is a limited amount of space in the VTOL. We will want to bring all of the women being held there back with us, and if there are as many as you think, there may only be just enough room for them as it is."

Summer nodded reluctantly. What he said made sense. She only wished.... She reached up and touched the vox in her ear. She had forgotten to remove it after calling for help earlier.

"I still have Lio's vox," she said. "Maxim, please, let me know as soon as you can if the other women are all right."

"I promise, you will be kept informed," he said, unable to deny her this small request. Everything else aside, she had spent an entire year as a captive, and all she wanted was the safe release of her fellow captives. Information on their well being was a small thing to ask.

"Thank you so much," Summer said fervently. She requested the vox's code from the device and gave it to Maxim. He entered it into his own directory, then bowed shortly.

"We will return with all of them," he promised before turning and hurrying out of the meeting room, Ran and Loni right behind him.

Chapter 12

Suddenly the meeting room was quiet.

"Come and sit down with us," Saige invited Summer and Darleen.

"Thank you," Summer said, taking Saige up on her offer at once. She suddenly felt very tired again. So much excitement and commotion after a year of enforced calm was taking its toll on her. She took the seat where Maxim had sat, and Darleen took the chair next to her.

"What was it that you did when you put your hands on us?" Summer asked Saige.

"There was a program and explosive in the Controller, hidden even from the nano-bots, which, if activated, would cause it to self-destruct," Saige replied.

Summer gasped and Darleen's hands flew up to the back of her head. "Don't worry," Saige said quickly, "I've deactivated it in all three of you."

"How?" Summer asked. Even with her ability to control the nano-bots she had not found anything like that herself. But, as Saige had said, it was hidden from the nano-bots as well.

"Its kind of a long story," Saige said.

"We have time," Summer pointed out.

"Very well, but first, Darleen, I would like to call Doc and ask him to come and check you over," Saige said. "Would you agree to that?"

Darleen stilled. Doc. She always thought of him whenever she imagined her body being returned to some semblance of normal, but she had not believed she would ever have the opportunity to see him again. "Do you think he would agree to help me?" she asked.

"That will not be a problem," Faron replied. "Are you agreeable then? We don't have another physician available at hand, and you are in need of medical attention."

"Doc?" Summer asked.

"He is the ranch veterinarian," Darleen said, though there was no hint of sarcasm or belittlement in her tone.

Summer frowned, but Saige shook her head. "Doc is far more than a vet," she said. "He does look after animals, but that is his choice. He is an excellent physician as well."

Darleen had not known that, but she was, somehow, not surprised by it. "Yes of course, I would be most grateful if he would agree to see me," she said.

Faron smiled and stood up. "I will call him now, if you ladies will excuse us," he said. "I will also ask Lessie to bring you refreshments."

"Thank you," Saige said, her eyes bright with love as she watched Faron, Dav and Ban leave the meeting room.

Summer smiled to see the expression on Saige's face. The woman she had met on board the *Cosmic Glory* had been distantly friendly, but withdrawn and a little sad. This Saige glowed with happiness.

Saige turned back to Summer and Darleen. "I know that what I am about to tell you will sound far-fetched, but please try to keep an open mind. I promise you, it's all true."

"Don't worry about that," Summer said wryly, "enough has happened to me of late that I seriously doubt that I would seriously doubt anything you say."

Saige grinned, then her smile faded as she considered how much she should actually tell Summer. There were some things that she thought best left unsaid for the time being. She did not want Summer to feel as though she was required to live up to a prophecy. Either she was the *Mind* Riata had spoken of, or she was not. That decision made, she cleared her throat and began.

"Riata, as Faron mentioned, was an Alverian Empath and Healer. When she died, she passed her gift of Healing to me. Later, she came to me in a dream and told me that she had been selected to be my Spirit Guide. She said that she would help me with certain things when she was able."

"What is a Spirit Guide?" Summer asked.

"Good question, and not one that anyone seems to have a specific answer for," Saige replied. "I think it just means that she will help me out now and then, like she did today."

"She helped you today?" Summer asked.

"Yes," Saige said. "When I sat down here and closed my eyes I called to her and she came to me. She told me two things. The first thing was that her time on the plane of the living had already been near an end at the time of her passing, and that I needed to forgive Darleen, and myself for it."

"Forgive yourself?" Darleen asked in surprise. "Why should you feel responsible?"

"I suppose I feel like I should have acted sooner than I did," Saige said vaguely. "It doesn't matter. The other thing was, she said I needed to put my hands on all three of you, beginning with you, Summer, and that I needed to do it quickly. When I did, I discovered the self-destruct program."

"But how? How did you find it?" Summer asked. "I can control the nano-bots, and I have even been able to examine their programming to some extent. But I never saw anything like that."

"I'm not really sure," Saige replied. "I only know that it's the first manifestation of the Healing power Riata gave me. Even though she passed her gift to me, until now I have never been able to use it. But when I put my hands on you three, I knew that I had finally found at least one way to use that power."

A thought occurred to Summer. "I wonder if you would be able to heal the other women," she said with barely controlled excitement. "The ones with the other type of Controller."

"I don't know," Saige replied. "Riata told me that I must Heal them, so I will certainly try. You said that their minds were completely gone?"

Summer nodded. Then shook her head. Then shrugged. "I honestly don't know," she said finally. "The nano-bots in their brains are different. They completely control the entire brain and body. As far as I can tell, the women who have them are just...not there any more. If I disabled them, I think the physical body would just collapse and die." Sumer sighed. "At the same time, I can't help but feel as though those women are still there, deep inside their own minds. I don't think they are conscious of what is happening to them, certainly not like I was, or Darleen. I think it's more like they are in a deep sleep."

"If taking the control of the nano-bots away won't help, I don't see what I can do," Saige said.

"I can control computers to a certain extent," Summer said. "So I could probably turn the nano-bots off. But I think that's all I could do. You have the power of Healing within you. I think you could do a lot more."

Saige thought for a few moments. "Perhaps we need to work together on this," she said. "If you can turn off the Controllers, then perhaps I could heal whatever damage they have caused."

"I don't want to risk these women's lives with experiments," Summer said. "But unless we try, they won't really have lives at all."

A soft knock at the door interrupted them, followed by the housekeeper with a tray of snacks and drinks.

"Thank you, Lessie," Saige said as the woman placed the tray on the meeting table and began unloading it.

"You're most welcome, Mrs. Saige," Lessie replied with a smile. "Mr. Faron asked that I tell you Doc will be here in a few minutes."

"Okay, Lessie," Saige replied. "Could you show him in here when he arrives?"

"Yes ma'am," Lessie said as she picked up her empty tray and left the room.

After a long silence Saige looked at Darleen. She couldn't really see the woman as the hood was pulled so far forward that it effectively hid her. Saige remembered the first time she had met Darleen, and how beautiful she had been with her long silky hair, perfect features and sexy body. From the brief look she had seen earlier of Darleen, there was nothing about her now that resembled the beauty she had been a year earlier.

"Darleen," Saige began hesitantly, "we only met twice, and neither occasion was good. But in spite of everything, I want you to know that I am sorry for what happened to you."

"Thank you for that, Saige," Darleen said. "I am not really sure why you would care what happened to me after what I did, but I appreciate it."

"Darleen, I don't know what was done to you, but your current condition tells its own story. Nobody deserves whatever you went through."

Darleen's head turned slowly towards where Lio still stood at the far end of the room, all but forgotten by Summer and Saige. After a long moment, Darleen turned back to Saige.

"May I ask you a question?" she said.

"Certainly," Saige replied.

"When you said that my heart was not pure, but not evil, was that true?"

"Yes, it was true," Saige replied. "I have been given a gift which allows me to see the hearts of those around me."

"Are you sure that there is no evil in my heart?" Darleen asked. Saige realized that this was not a casual question. Darleen was very concerned about this.

"If you had asked me an hour ago whether I thought you intended Riata, or any of us, to die that day, I would have said yes," Saige said. "But now, after looking into your heart, I know that is not true. The heart of a murderer is black. The heart of one who has a hand in the death of another is also black and it is not a blackness that fades with time. You have done things in your life that were not always right, but you have never done anything with evil intent. If you had, there would be blackness in your heart that would never leave you."

Darleen did not appear to react to what Saige had said, but Saige had sharp hearing now, and she heard the soft sigh of relief that escaped the dark hood.

"Darleen, I don't mean to be rude, but I would like to ask you something if you don't mind?" she said.

"Of course Saige," Darleen replied. "You may ask me anything you like."

"It appears to me that you have changed a great deal in the past year," Saige said. "Have you?"

"Perhaps," Darleen said. "I don't know if I've changed so much as I have a new set of priorities." Darleen paused a moment as though considering what she was about to say. "I spent an entire year locked inside my own head," she continued. "That's a lot of time with nothing to do other than search for memories to help you forget where you are, and what is happening to you. It didn't take very long to realize that my entire life was boring, monotonous and shallow. I don't have one single memory that is happy enough, sad enough, or exciting enough that I would ever want to relive it in my own mind. So I promised myself that, if I ever got free, I would find something worthwhile to do. It didn't matter what. Just something. So that if I ever end up stuck in my own head again, I will at least have something to remember that is worth remembering."

"That sounds like an admirable goal for anyone to have," said a gruff voice from the doorway.

Saige had known Doc was there the instant he had stepped into the hallway because of her sharp loboenca senses. Summer and Darleen, however, had not known, and they both jumped when he spoke.

"I apologize," Doc said. "I didn't mean to sneak up and startle y'all like that."

"Its okay, Doc," Saige said. "Doc, this is Summer Whitney, and I believe you've met Darleen Flowers. Ladies, this is Doc."

"Nice to meet you," Summer said politely while she took in the craggy faced man. With his white hair and mustache and faded jeans, he didn't really look much like any doctor she had ever seen. She didn't want to be impolite, but she couldn't help but feel skeptical of the man's abilities. Darleen was in bad shape and she didn't need someone poking and prodding at her who didn't know what he was doing.

Doc smiled, his blue eyes crinkling with silent laughter. "Your feelings are written all over your face Miss Whitney," he said. Summer blushed but Doc raised a hand. "Oh no, don't be embarrassed," he said. "I know I don't look much like a doctor, but I assure you, I know a thing or two." Doc then turned to Darleen's black cloaked and hooded figure.

Doc looked at her for a long moment. "Miss Flowers, would you mind putting your hood back so I can get a glimpse of what we're up against?" he asked.

Darleen flinched slightly, but she reached up and pushed the hood back as Doc had asked. Doc's eyes widened in surprise, then narrowed in fury. His gaze went to where Lio stood at the back of the room. "This the man that done this to you?" he asked.

Darleen nodded. Before Summer could even think to stop him, Doc crossed the floor to Lio, doubled up one fist and punched the man square in the jaw. Since Summer had ordered him to stand in that place and not move, Lio's head jerked with the blow, then sprang back into place, but there was no other sign of movement or reaction.

Doc turned to face the women who were all staring at him in surprise. "I apologize, ladies," he said in his rough voice. "I just couldn't help myself."

"Not a problem," Summer said with a shrug. "One good punch in the jaw is the least he deserves for what he's done to Darleen."

Doc nodded and turned his attention back to Darleen, who was sitting motionless, her eyes glued to the table in front of her.

"Miss Flowers, I'm not gonna pretend I'm happy with what you did last year, but I am gonna tell you that, after what I just overheard, I think you deserve a second chance. And even if I didn't, I would still do my very best to treat you medically. So, if you think you can trust me, come on with me to the med-lab and lets us see what we can do for you."

"All right," Darleen said softly. Summer was surprised to feel Darleen's cold hand reach over beneath the table and grasp her own.

"Do you want me to come with you?" she asked as she gave Darleen's thin hand a careful squeeze.

"Yes, if you don't mind."

"Of course not," Summer replied. She stood up, still holding Darleen's hand. "Saige, do you mind if I leave Lio here? I don't want him tagging along for this."

"Are you positive he can't just walk away?" Saige asked. "Maybe we should post some guards on him. I do have three babies in the house now."

Summer reached out with her mind to Lio's Controller. "I'm positive," she said after checking it carefully. "But there is no reason to take any risks with your children. Posting guards on him can't hurt."

"Good." Saige closed her eyes and fell silent for a long moment. She smiled and opened her eyes. "Faron is sending a young male-set to keep an eye on him while you go with Doc. I need to check on my daughters."

Summer smiled. "You just talked to Faron with your mind, didn't you?"

"Yes, I have that ability," Saige replied. "Sometimes it comes in very handy with three Rami to keep tabs on."

"I bet it does," Summer said with a grin. She turned back to Lio and sent his Controller orders to keep him standing in the corner, face to the wall, until she returned. Then she and Darleen followed Doc out of the meeting room.

Chapter 13

Lio was furious. And in shock. And his jaw hurt. Damned old man. When he got free of this Controller, that old man was going to pay for that punch.

Lio turned his mind back to the puzzle of how he was going to get out of his current situation. He knew that it was impossible to do. Few knew that better than he did. Except that the *berezi* had found a way out. And if she could do it, then he could as well. There was nothing a female could do that Lio Perry could not do.

As he stood staring at the wall inside the home of the Lobos, he racked his brain trying to figure out how the *berezi* had overcome the Controller. He had heard her tell the others that she could control it with her mind, but that had to be a lie. He'd never heard of anyone able to do such a thing. It was ridiculous. Ludicrous. Impossible. It was also something he knew he could not do himself. Therefore, she had lied, and there was another way around the Controller that she had found and did not want to reveal. Yes, that made sense. Females were so sneaky, so under-handed. Never trust a female. He knew that.

His nose itched and he wanted to scratch it but his hand refused to obey him. Just like the rest of his body refused to obey him. This was the fault of that damn *berezi*. And Darleen. That damn Darleen. When he got out of this, he was going to make them both pay and pay and pay for this.

Lio worked himself into a mental temper tantrum so intense that, for a time, he saw only a red haze instead of the wall before him. The worst part about having a temper tantrum when you couldn't move was that you couldn't burn off the adrenaline with physical activity. So it took a lot longer than usual for the tantrum to cool.

When it did cool, Lio again tried to think. There had to be a way out of this. There just had to be. He felt a twinge in his shoulder where that disgusting Jasani shifter had cut him open, and remembered his shock when the man had removed the skin-bomb. Of course he knew about the skin-bombs. Hell, he'd even implanted a few of them himself on new employees. It wasn't a big deal. A quick little pinch with an injector device the Xanti had designed, and the victim never even knew it was there. Who had implanted one on him, he wondered, and when? It made him angry that he'd had one and hadn't known it.

It had to be that damn Za-Linq, he thought. He didn't like Za-Linq. There was something about him that set off Lio's warning bells. Za-Queg had set off his warning bells too, but Za-Queg had been right up front about his own underhandedness and deceit. Lio understood that, and respected it. Za-Linq, on the other hand, tried to pretend everything was on the up and up, and that he wasn't really working for himself.

Yes, Lio decided, it had to be Za-Linq. Probably did it while I was sleeping. If Za-Queg had done it, Lio thought, he would have done it while Lio was wide awake and knew about it. Like the time he'd planted the tracking device in the back of Lio's ear, not long after they'd started working together.

Lio thought about that device now, wondering if it were possible that Za-Linq was aware of it. Or even if it still worked. Probably, he decided. Xanti technology was quite good. But it certainly would not work from inside the Dracons' ranch. They'd tried every single device they could come up with but no matter what they did, the moment a listening device, or a remote imager, or a transponder, or anything else was on Dracon land, it stopped transmitting.

Not that any of it mattered since Za-Linq had detonated the skin bomb which, unfortunately for Lio, worked fine as it was a receiver rather than a transmitter. Which meant Za-Linq knew Lio was in Jasani custody. And that the office had been compromised. Lio didn't really blame the Xanti for detonating the device. It was what he would have done. What bothered him about it was that now the Xanti thought he was safely dead, which meant they wouldn't be bothered about trying to free him from Jasani hands. If there was a way for him to let the Xanti know he was still alive, then maybe someone would try to free him. Of course, they might just try to kill him. Again. But it was, at least, a chance.

Chapter 14

Summer and Darleen followed Doc outside the Lobo's house and across a wide, graveled path to a long, low building. He unlocked the door and stepped aside to allow them to enter first, reaching in to flip the lights on for them before entering and closing the door behind them.

"This is all new," Darleen commented softly.

"Yes, a lot has changed over the past year," Doc agreed easily as he moved across the med-lab, flipping on machines and lights as he went. "Since it was discovered that the Xanti were involved in matters, the Jasani Military has increased its readiness. And since the only two Arimas known to exist, along with the only six Jasani daughters, all live here on this ranch, there is a heightened military presence here as well. Bunkhouses, kitchens, armories, training facilities and this med-lab, along with a larger med-center in the valley, have been built to accommodate the increased guards and security measures that have been set up."

Doc pulled on a white cotton smock over his clothes, then scrubbed and gloved his hands while he spoke. When he was finished he gestured to Darleen. "If you'll get up there on the table we'll see what we can do."

Darleen moved to sit on the exam table, the black cloak still covering her from the neck down.

"According to Lio, there is a tool in his office that will remove this polymer coating in one step," Summer said. "He called it a *deionizer.*"

Doc raised one brow, then stepped up to the exam table. "I need to remove this," he said to Darleen, touching the cloak lightly with his fingers.

Darleen nodded and reached up for the fastenings, but Doc was faster. "I'll get it," he said. Darleen lowered her hands. The cloak slipped down her shoulders when Doc released the fastenings, pooling around her on the table. Doc reached for one of Darleen's hands and lifted it up toward the light so he could see it better.

"You sure that man can't lie to you?" Doc asked Summer.

"I'm sure," Summer replied. Doc nodded and lowered Darleen's hand back to her lap before releasing it.

"Guess we'll find out," he said as he crossed the room and began opening and closing drawers. He finally found whatever he was searching for and returned to Darleen with a small metal object in his hand. "Whether this works or not, it won't hurt, nor will it harm you," he said.

Darleen shrugged. "I don't care if it hurts, I just want it to work."

Doc smiled. "If it doesn't, we'll just have someone get that tool from Lio's office."

Darleen's eyes brightened. She hadn't thought of that. Summer had, but had dismissed the idea because she didn't think the Katres would be willing to do it for them.

Doc placed the metal object gently against the skin at the back of Darleen's neck and pushed a tiny switch. As promised, Darleen felt nothing. Not a shock, sting, or pinch. Nothing at all. Except that suddenly her skin felt lighter. The tight sensation that she had felt for so long she had become used to it, was gone. She looked down at her hand and gasped to see her own, normal skin tone instead of the hated silver.

"Thank you," she breathed softly as she raised both hands and turned them over as though hardly daring to believe they were a normal skin tone now. There were long thin strips of dull gray polymer on the floor and table, but none of it clung to Darleen's skin any more.

"You are very welcome," Doc said. Summer glanced at Doc's face and was surprised to see an expression in his eyes that had nothing to do with the feelings of a doctor for a patient.

"Now, let's see what else we can do here," he said, his tone suddenly brusque. "I noticed you have a limp."

"Yes," Darleen said, dropping her eyes to her lap. "My hip has been dislocated a few times. It doesn't seem to want to go back into place any more."

"That shouldn't be too difficult to fix," Doc said. "Anything else? I assume you would like to have your hair follicles reactivated?"

Darleen raised one hand to her head, then dropped it. "You can do that?" she asked.

"Yes," Doc replied. "Its easy enough, and I can even accelerate growth a little. It does tend to sting a bit though. I suggest we start with your head and not worry about the rest, at least for now. And we might be able to do something about the scarring too. I don't say we can get rid of it, but I think we can reduce its appearance some. If you want."

Darleen nodded eagerly. "That would be wonderful," she said. She dropped her eyes to her lap again. "There are...a few other things," she said haltingly.

Doc's eyes flew to her face, hearing the shame in Darleen's voice. "What things?" he asked.

Darleen hesitated, but he couldn't help her if she didn't tell him. "Piercings," she said, her voice barely above a whisper. Doc's jaw clenched tightly.

"I don't expect you to be able to...fix...the damage," Darleen continued, her eyes still on her lap. "But if you could remove the...the metal...from...my body, I would be grateful."

Doc's eyes blazed angrily, but his voice remained gentle. "I will remove the metal immediately," he said. "And I will do my best with any damage."

Darleen heaved a sigh of relief, but still kept her eyes on her lap. She just couldn't bring herself to look into Doc's eyes. She was too ashamed of what had been done to her.

Summer felt a helpless mix of anger and disgust at this new revelation of what Lio had done to Darleen. She stepped up to the table, reached out and placed a finger lightly beneath Darleen's chin. "Look at me, please," she asked.

Darleen raised her eyes and looked at Summer. "What was done to you is not a reflection on you, Darleen," she said. "You have nothing to be ashamed of. It is not your fault."

Darleen wasn't so sure about that. She had often thought that the past year had been her punishment for things she had done in the past, but she wasn't going to admit that right now. Not in front of Doc. Instead she just nodded. "Thank you, Summer."

Summer smiled. "Now, I am going to leave you here in Doc's capable hands," she said. "You do not need an audience for what is to come. Unless you want me to stay. If you do, I will."

Darleen glanced quickly at Doc, then back to Summer. "No thanks, Summer. I'll think I'll be okay now," Darleen said. "I'll see you later."

Summer leaned forward and wrapped her arms around Darleen in a spontaneous hug, and she was very pleased when Darleen hugged her back.

"You take good care of my friend Doc, you hear?" she said.

"Don't you worry any, Miss Whitney," Doc said. "We'll have her back to her beautiful self in no time."

"No," Darleen said sharply. Summer and Doc both looked at her in surprise. "I don't want to be beautiful," she said earnestly. "I'm done with beautiful. I just want to look normal enough that people don't stare."

Summer wasn't sure how to respond to that so she patted Darleen lightly on the hand and left, closing the door behind her.

Chapter 16

After leaving the med-lab Summer crossed the gravel path and reentered the Lobos' house, uncertain exactly where she should go.

"How's it going with Darleen?" Saige asked as she stepped into the hall. "I was just coming to check on you."

"Doc got the silver skin off, so she's a normal color now. That's the best part." Summer hesitated. She didn't think it was her place to reveal the more private things Darleen had said. "She's more comfortable with Doc now, so I left to give her some privacy while Doc works on some other things."

Saige nodded, though she looked a little ill. "He did a lot of bad things to her, didn't he?"

"Yes, he really did," Summer replied.

"You have no way of knowing this, but the last time I saw her, Darleen Flowers was the most beautiful woman I had ever seen," Saige said.

"Really?" Summer asked, surprised. It was difficult to imagine the emaciated, bald, scarred and beaten woman she knew as beautiful.

"Yes," Saige replied. "She was also selfish, manipulative and mean."

"I suppose that the changes to Darleen's interior are as great as the ones to her exterior," Summer said with a faint smile. "She just said that she was done with beautiful. She only wants to look normal."

"Then you are correct," Saige said.

"Have you heard anything from the Katres yet?" Summer asked.

"No, you?" Saige asked as she turned around and led the way back up the hall.

"Nothing," Summer replied as she followed Saige into a cozy little sitting room. "But then, the Katres don't much like me, so maybe Maxim won't keep his word."

Saige waved Summer to a chair by the fireplace and took another for herself. There was a tray on a table beside Saige's chair and she poured two cups of coffee from it and offered one to Summer.

"I noticed Maxim's behavior toward you was a little strained," Saige said. "I've never seen him like that before. Did something happen?"

Summer sipped the coffee gratefully. It had been a very long time since she had tasted coffee. "This is delicious," she said. "Thank you so much."

Saige smiled. "One of the many luxuries of Jasan is that there is no shortage of coffee."

"You probably shouldn't have told me that," Summer replied with a grin. She took another sip, then sighed. "I don't know what happened," she said, answering Saige's question about Maxim. "They seemed to like me okay at first, then they didn't." Summer shrugged as though the entire subject didn't bother her as much as it really did.

"Well, maybe if you tell me what happened, I can help you figure it out," Saige suggested.

Summer hesitated, but figured why not? Saige was married to three men. She had to have a better understanding of them than Summer did. Maybe she could explain what Maxim's problem was.

With that hopeful thought in mind, Summer told Saige everything that had happened from the time the Katres had entered Lio's office. Since she had an eidetic memory, she was able to relate every word exactly as it had been spoken. When she was finished, Saige refreshed their coffee while she mulled over everything Summer had told her.

"I'm sorry Summer, but honestly, I don't get it either," she said. "Maybe my guys will understand it. If you don't mind me telling them, of course."

"I don't mind," Summer replied, trying to hide her disappointment.

"Speaking of changed personalities," Saige said, "you've changed a bit yourself over the past year. I don't imagine it was any easier for you than it was for Darleen."

"I think it was far easier for me than Darleen," Summer objected. "I was treated like an unthinking, unfeeling object, and I was forced to respond to physical commands as though I were a robot. But I was not tortured, beaten, starved or mutilated as Darleen was."

"But?" Saige prompted.

"But, yes, it changed me. I used to work really hard to make people like me. I hid my intelligence and pretended to be happy and bubbly so that I would fit in more easily with other people. Fitting in has always been very important to me."

"Why?" Saige asked, then shook her head. "I apologize," she said. "that came out more rudely than was meant. It's just that I was always a bit of an outcast myself as a child, and I understand it can be difficult. I'm just curious as to why it was so important for you to fit in."

Summer took another sip of her coffee as she thought about Saige's question and how to answer it. She didn't know why, but she felt as though there was almost a kinship between herself and Saige. Perhaps because she had met her on the *Cosmic Glory* before she'd been abducted, she thought. Saige's face was the first familiar one she had seen since then.

"Loneliness," she said finally. "My parents are wonderful people, but they are both wildly intelligent and extremely prominent, with demanding careers. Until I reached school age, we traveled all of the time, so I never had the opportunity to play with other children. I would sit with them at the dinner table and listen to them talk, but I never understood anything they said so I couldn't join in their conversations. So I read every book Mother had written, which was dozens, and every book Father brought into the house, which was hundreds, just so that I could understand and join in their talks.

"That's when I discovered that I had an eidetic memory. I remembered every single word I had read, and understood a large percentage of it. I was five years old at the time, and it was a big mistake. All of that knowledge in a five year old made me much different from other children my age. I ended up even lonelier than before, even after we settled down and I started going to school. I could understand my parent's conversations, but there wasn't another child my age that wanted anything to do with me. I was just too strange.

"When I was ten years old, Father was transferred to another base, so I had a chance to start over in a new school with children who didn't know anything about me. I'd watched the other children for years, so I knew what traits other kids liked, and accepted as normal, and those they didn't. I used that knowledge to create a new persona for myself. And it worked. I made friends, and for the first time, I had a social life. The only problem was, my parents did not like the new me at all. It created a rift between us that exists even now."

"That's a shame," Saige said. "Didn't they understand why you did what you did?"

"Oh yes, they understood," Summer replied. "They just didn't agree with it. They wanted me to be true to myself." Summer rolled her eyes. "That's what they said, but what they really wanted was for me to excel academically so that I could follow in at least one of their footsteps, if not both."

"So you deliberately got lower grades in school?" Saige asked, surprised that anyone would go that far to have a social life.

"Yes, I did," Summer admitted. "It was dumb of me, I realize that, but at the time, it was more important to be accepted than it was to get good grades." She shrugged. "Now it all seems so silly to me. I've spent my life being someone I'm not, and I didn't realize the magnitude of that until, like Darleen, I was forced to live within my own mind and examine myself and my life."

"It came at a high price," Saige said.

"Yes, and that makes it that much more important. Right now, I don't really care so much what anyone thinks of me. All I care about is finding and freeing all of the other women, no matter where in the galaxy they may be."

"While you are at it, please remember that you have a lot of people on your side," Saige said. "People who have the resources to aid you. You are not alone in your desire to see these women freed, and to prevent more from being abducted."

"That's wonderful to know, Saige," Summer replied enthusiastically. "Knowing where other women might be is one thing. Getting to them, and releasing them is another, and I wasn't sure how I was going to manage that."

"That's not going to be a problem," Saige said. "If you can find out where they are, we will help with the rest of it."

Summer was so excited she nearly jumped up to go find Lio and start questioning him about the locations of other slave compounds. But she restrained herself. Now was not the time and besides, there was already one raid taking place. As she took another sip of her cooling coffee, something Saige said finally registered

"Saige, are women still being abducted off of passenger liners?" she asked.

"We aren't sure," Saige replied. "In the past year no passengers have gone missing from any liner or ship to dock at the Jasani skyport. As far as we can tell."

"As far as you can tell?" Summer asked.

"We can only compare records. If the records are altered, there is no way for us to know that. We have instituted a lot of precautions and warned all of the owners of passenger liners, as well as the captains and even the governments of every planet we have any kind of relation with. So either the Xanti are staying away from Jasani bound transports, or they are altering the records."

"And there is no way for you to know for sure one way or another?"

"Not that we have been able to figure out," Saige replied. "Worse, we cannot do anything about ships outside of Jasani space. There is no way of knowing how many women are being abducted from ships going to other worlds."

"Then the only real solution is to destroy the organization behind the abductions," Summer said.

"Yes, and until now, we haven't been able to find a scrap of information to get us started on that," Saige said. "Now, because of you, that has changed."

Summer hoped that she would be as much help as Saige seemed to think she would be. She started to tell Saige that when her vox beeped softly in her ear. She reached up to tap it.

"Summer here," she said.

"Miss Whitney, this is Maxim. I am afraid I have some bad news for you."

Chapter 17

Slater Sugetku was worried.

He leaned down to sniff the contents of the daily meat bucket left for him at the bottom of the path, and sighed. The meat was not rancid, but it was not far from it. Well, he thought, it was better than nothing at all. He picked up the bucket and headed back up the slope to his little stone house.

He stood in front of it for a moment, but decided he really did not want to go inside. Instead, he walked around to the back and climbed up to the roof. He set the meat bucket down carefully so that it would not fall off, then settled himself in his usual spot so that he had a view of the village in the distance.

Things had not gone quite as he had expected this past year, and he wasn't really sure how or when it started going bad. It had just snuck up on him.

First, there was the matter of Xi-Kung. In the beginning, he and the Xanti had stuck close to each other, working together to fulfill their plans for Onddo, trusting only each other. Slater admitted to himself that he had enjoyed that time. Even though he hadn't truly trusted Xi-Kung, he had experienced a camaraderie with the Xanti that he had never experienced with anyone else.

Slater had never had any close friends as a youngling, had never concerned himself much with social matters. Partly because it was not in the Narrasti nature to be social until they reached breeding age, and partly because it had never occurred to him to try to make a friend. His thoughts and dreams had always been centered on his own advancement, his own personal glory.

Just when he was becoming accustomed to having someone to plan and work with on a regular basis, things had changed. Xi-Kung began to spend more and more time alone with Magoa, and less time with Slater. When Slater had asked Xi-Kung about it, Xi-Kung had seemed surprised. He had reminded Slater that it was part of their plan for one of them to get close to Magoa, and that they had agreed it should be Xi-Kung. Slater had nodded in silent agreement, though he did not remember any such plan. Even now, many months later, he still wasn't sure if Xi-Kung had lied, or if his own memory was faulty.

Not that it mattered, Slater decided as the darkness grew thicker and the village lights began to come on. He rarely saw Xi-Kung any more, and had not spoken with him in many weeks. When he did see the Xanti, he was always in the company of Magoa. That bothered Slater a great deal since Xi-Kung was the only one who knew Slater's secret.

The other thing that bothered Slater was the way people treated him. He had imagined that being a mighty sugea, the only sugea in thousands of years, would earn him instant respect and power. He had even dared to hope that he would eventually supplant Magoa as the leader of their people. But it hadn't turned out that way at all.

Instead, people avoided him. They had granted him a stone hut located at the far edge of the village, which Slater had, at first, thought to be a sign of their respect for him. Then he had realized that none of the people ever came near that area, and in fact, went far out of their way to avoid it, and him. The only time anyone ever came close to his dwelling was once each evening when they sent someone to deliver a pail of meat to him. He never saw who delivered it, but from the scents he picked up when he went down the short path from his hut to the main road where his food was left for him, it was rarely the same person twice.

Slater had not understood why he was feared, but not revered, and had asked Xi-Kung about it on one of the rare occasions when they met and spoke. Xi-Kung had explained that the racial memories that his fellow Narrasti had of the sugea were not all that pleasant. The sugea had been arrogant, demanding and cruel leaders over the rest of the Narrasti in ancient times. Of course Slater knew that, or pretended to anyway. He wasn't really sure that he remembered quite that much about the sugea. Mostly, he just knew that they had been great. But, when he told Xi-Kung that he still did not understand, the Xanti had explained that none of the Narrasti on Onddo wanted to see a return of the sugea and their ways. They preferred Magoa, who ruled with a gentle hand in comparison, in spite of the large numbers of people he had sent to the exterminators in an effort to cleanse their gene pool.

Another thing that disturbed Slater was the lightening speed at which his people absorbed the technological advances that the Xanti were pouring into the village. It had taken him years to learn a fraction of what the villagers had already learned. Of course, he reminded himself, they had teachers. He had been alone, trying to learn things as he went with no help from anyone. He doubted that any of his fellow Narrasti could have done better than he had under the same circumstances.

That was when Slater started watching the village from his roof. The first time he climbed up and studied the distant village he had been surprised. There were a lot more buildings, there were definitely a lot more lights, and the sound of ground-cars and air transports was an almost constant hum. Before long he began to get the impression that the recently primitive villagers were rapidly approaching his own level of knowledge, and that had bothered him greatly, though he wasn't sure why.

After awhile the changes in the village seemed to slow and he wondered if it was because they had stopped, or if it was because he just could not see them from his distant perch. So, under cover of darkness, he had transformed himself into a generic, unknown Narrasti, and sneaked down to the village in an effort to get a better idea of what was happening.

He had been stunned to discover that the village was no longer a village. It now resembled a highly technological town, its citizens no longer wandering aimlessly, shoulders slumped, heads down. Now the people walked with a purpose, head up, eyes sharp, steps determined.

Aside from a few primitive decorations or badges, his people had not worn clothing in centuries. Now, everyone was fully dressed in clothing made from modern fabrics and materials, including boots, belts and even hats. Most of the people he saw carried weapons. Not the stone axes and wooden cudgels of a year past, but sleek hand lasers and energy pistols.

And there were other changes too. Rather than living in stone lined crèches in the ground, there were now row after neat row of houses built along paved streets where ground-cars came and went at all hours. Instead of training fields, there were now large, climate controlled buildings where masses of Narrasti were taught everything from reading and writing Standard, to weapons training, engineering and even pilot training, as well as a host of other subjects too varied for Slater to grasp all at once. By the time Slater had returned to his own tiny stone hut, his mind had been whirling with all that he had seen and heard.

It was true that the original plan between himself and Xi-Kung had been to bring the Narrasti on Onddo into the current technological age and, eventually, harness them as a fighting force against the Jasani. But never in his wildest imaginings had Slater thought such a thing could be done with such speed and at such a scope. He had been so dizzy with what he had seen, so confused by how it had happened so quickly, that it had taken him days to absorb it all.

Now, here he sat on his roof again, trying to figure out where his place was in all of this. He leaned toward the meat bucket, and wrinkled his nose. He didn't want to eat it, but he needed the sustenance.

Suddenly, it dawned on him that one of the most obvious changes in his fellow Narrasti was not the clothes, or the houses, or the technology. No, the most obvious change was that they all looked healthy and well-fed. Slater thought about that for a little while, finally realizing that he had not seen any food lines at all when he had been down there. In fact, now that he thought about it, he had actually passed by several restaurants. Being the galaxy wide traveler that he now was, Slater knew what a restaurant was, but there had never been such a thing on Onddo before. How was it that there were now several of them?

He pondered that puzzle for a little while before remembering that he had also seen a couple of food synthesizer markets. Again, there had never been such a thing on Onddo before. Why had it not stood out more clearly to him? He decided it was because the village resembled a small town on just about any other planet in the galaxy except Onddo, and such things were common in small towns.

As soon as he realized that the villagers had food synthesizers, he also realized he was being treated quite poorly indeed. They had access to such glorious food and still brought him only rancid meat. He considered transforming into his sugea and fire strafing the entire village for their insolence. But in order to do that, he needed energy.

Slater curled his lip at the pail of meat before him, then sighed once more. Whether he strafed the village or not, he had to eat, and as that was all he had, it would have to do. He started to reach for the bucket, then decided to transform into his sugea first. Perhaps the sugea would not mind the taste as much as he did in his usual form.

Glad to have a good reason to shift into his sugea, Slater did so at once. The moment the sugea got a whiff of the meat in the pail it knew the food was drugged. A moment later, it also sensed the stealthy approach of several dozen villagers.

Slater was stunned to realize that the villagers meant to kill him, and that the drugs, had he consumed them, would have made him easy prey. If Slater had still been in his usual form, he might have stood frozen with surprise and indecision long enough for the villagers to reach him. Luckily, the sugea was in charge and instantly took flight. It took one short turn around the village and spit fire at its would-be attackers before pointing its nose to the west and racing away so quickly that not even the newly trained fighter pilots in their shiny new air jets could follow.

Chapter 18

Summer felt the blood drain from her face. “Bad news?” she asked, surprised that her voice sounded almost normal.

“Yes,” Maxim replied. “Do you know a woman named Tesla?”

“Yes, she’s a Keeper,” Summer replied. “Why?”

She heard Maxim hesitate. Or maybe she felt it. She wasn’t sure. “Please tell me.”

“When we arrived, most of the inhabitants were already deceased,” Maxim said.

“Dead?” Summer gasped, hardly able to believe that was really what he’d said. “They’re all dead?”

“No, not all,” Maxim said. “There was a group of women in a room at the end of one hallway. Three women with Controllers, and this Tesla, who was apparently protecting her charges from the other Keepers.”

“Are you saying that there are only four women left alive in the entire compound?”

“I’m sorry,” Maxim said, “but yes. As far as we can tell, the Keepers went into the cells and killed the prisoners, then sat down on the floor and killed themselves. Except for this one woman. She is wounded and currently unconscious. We are bringing her and the surviving prisoners back with us, along with the remains of the other prisoners.”

“Thank you,” Summer said.

Maxim cleared his throat. “We will arrive back at the ranch in a few minutes.”

“All right,” Summer said. “Thank you for letting me know.”

“You are welcome, Miss Whitney,” Maxim said.

The connection closed and Summer looked up to see Saige holding a square of white cloth out to her. Summer frowned in confusion, not understanding the meaning of the gesture at first. Then she felt the tears on her cheeks and reached for the handkerchief.

“Thanks,” she said.

“Not good news,” Saige said.

“No,” Summer replied. “There were at least two dozen women being held there besides myself. Maybe more. Only three still live. And one woman who was a guard.”

“Did Maxim tell you what happened?” Saige asked.

"He said that the Keepers killed the prisoners, then killed themselves. All except one, Keeper Tesla, who apparently was able to save three prisoners."

"Sounds like Xanti work," Faron said from the doorway. "I think that when the bodies of the Keepers are checked, there will be something implanted in them that caused their actions."

"I don't know much about the Xanti," Summer said, "but I know enough to know I hate them."

"Nobody knows much about the Xanti," Saige said. "At least, nobody who's willing to admit it to us."

"I wonder if Lio worked directly with the Xanti," Summer said. "He was apparently somewhat high up in this slave ring organization."

"If you ask him, will he tell you honestly?" Faron asked with barely suppressed excitement. They had been trying for months to gather information on the Xanti, and had come up virtually empty handed. It had been very frustrating for everyone. Apparently, the Xanti had been a deep mystery for centuries. Even millennia. There were many worlds who, like themselves, knew *of* the Xanti. But none seemed to know anything *about* the Xanti.

"Yes, he will be truthful," Summer replied. "He has no control whatsoever over anything he does or says."

"Lets go ask him then," Faron said eagerly. "No, wait," he said, changing his mind. "We should do this right. Let me get things setup so that we can record everything he says. I'd like to have Eldar Hamat there as well."

"Let's not forget that this has been a very long day for both Summer and Darleen," Saige pointed out gently to her Rami. "I think you should set this up for tomorrow, and let the women have a good night's sleep first."

"Of course, *amada*, you are correct," Faron said. "I apologize for getting carried away, Miss Whitney."

"Please, call me Summer," Summer said. "And there is no need to apologize. I'm as anxious as you are to learn whatever Lio has in that twisted head of his. But right now, I want to see the women the Katres bring back from the compound, and find out more about what happened there tonight."

"They should be arriving at any moment," Faron said. "I suggest we go over to the med-lab, as that is where the women will be taken as soon as they arrive."

"Okay," Summer said, putting her cup down and rising to her feet. Saige stood up too, though not quite as quickly.

"Give me just a moment to check on the babies, and then I will be right with you."

Faron leaned over to kiss Saige lightly on the lips, the expression on his face as he gazed at Saige nearly bringing tears to Summer's eyes. What would it be like, she wondered, to have someone look at me like that?

Summer dropped her eyes and turned away from the private moment. She didn't think it was possible for anyone to like her for her true self. But she was not going to go back to pretending.

"Shall we?" Faron asked a moment later.

Summer looked up, saw that Saige was already gone and nodded before following Faron back out of the house. As they stepped outside and moved onto the graveled path, Summer heard the sounds of approaching footsteps and looked up to see the Katres, each of them carrying a woman as they hurried toward the med-lab. Saige recognized the women as fellow prisoners, and though she didn't know their names, had never spoken to them, and knew nothing about them, she could not help feeling a strong sense of camaraderie when she saw them.

Faron opened the door to the med-lab for them, but Saige held back, letting them enter before her. As they passed they each nodded to her briefly. Summer felt something inside of her warm at the acknowledgement, and that irritated her. She shook her head at herself and started to follow them inside when she saw another man coming toward her carrying another woman in his arms. The man was not familiar, but the woman was. It was Keeper Tesla.

Summer was surprised that she felt no real animosity for the woman who had helped keep her prisoner for so long. But, the truth was that of all of the Keepers, Tesla had been the kindest in her own way. And now Summer knew that she had done her best to save at least three of her charges. For that alone, Summer could not hate the woman.

Summer waited for the man carrying Tesla to enter the building ahead of her before following after. The quiet med-lab she had been in a short time earlier with Doc and Darleen was now crowded and noisy. Summer stayed in the back of the room near the wall and watched the activity. After a moment, Darleen made her way through the bustle to stand beside her.

Summer smiled when she saw that Darleen was no longer wearing the hood of her cloak pulled up. Her skin was a normal tone, and there was already a light fuzz of pale blond hair on her head. Best of all, some of the tension had left Darleen's face. She looked almost relaxed.

"You look beautiful," Summer said.

"No, I don't," Darleen replied, running one hand over the short hair on her head. "But I don't mind the way I look now. Its strange, but I think I'm happier with my fuzz than I was with my hair when it was long and perfect."

"Well, I think you're beautiful with your fuzz," Summer said stoutly, "and I never saw you before, so how you used to look doesn't count with me."

One corner of Darleen's mouth turned up in a tiny, almost smile. "I think Doc worked a miracle," she said. Summer caught something in Darleen's voice that hinted at more than a doctor-patient feeling, but she pretended not to notice it. She would not tease Darleen. Not after all she had been through. She'd heard the same note in Doc's voice earlier, and if Darleen felt the same, all the better. As far as she was concerned, Darleen deserved any happiness she could get.

Summer turned back to watch the controlled activity in the med-lab. "These are the only four people left alive from the compound where I was," she told Darleen.

"Yes, Doc told me," Darleen said. "I'm so sorry. Those women don't appear to be harmed, so that's something."

Summer looked over at the three prisoners where they sat on chairs against the wall. They looked like life-size dolls with vacant eyes and motionless bodies, and she shuddered to think how close she had been to having that happen to her.

"I wonder why it is that I got a different Controller," she said, voicing aloud the question she had wondered about for so long.

"Because you are *berezi*," Darleen replied matter-of-factly.

"Excuse me, but did you just say that Summer is *berezi*?" Faron asked from where he stood a few feet away from them. Both women looked at him with startled eyes. "I apologize," he said. "I didn't mean to eavesdrop, but the word *berezi* caught my attention."

"Yes," Darleen replied. "I don't know what it means, but I heard Lio refer to her as a *berezi* many times."

"That's right," Summer added. "He told me this morning that I was *berezi*, and he said that was why I have the same Controller Darleen has," Summer added. "But I don't know what it means. Do you?"

"Yes, I do know what it means," Faron said. "I am not sure now is the right time to explain it though."

Summer frowned and opened her mouth to argue when Saige arrived. Summer turned to her instead. "Saige, do you know what the word *berezi* means?" she asked.

"Yes, I do," Saige replied slowly as she looked from Summer to Faron and back again. "Why do you ask?"

Summer blew out a frustrated breath. What was the big deal? she wondered. She just wanted to know the meaning of the word and there weren't any Jasani dictionaries handy. She opened her mouth to answer Saige's question when Faron held up one hand to stop her.

"There is no need," he said. "I will tell you. *Berezi* is an ancient Jasani word that is now used to describe a woman who has the potential to become an Arima to a Jasani male-set. We believe that the Xanti have discovered a way to identify these rare and most important females, and are marking them specifically for abduction."

"What is an Arima?" Summer asked.

Faron looked to Saige, then, reluctantly, turned back to Summer. "An Arima is...."

"Stop," Maxim interrupted imperiously. Faron turned and glared at him.

"I apologize," Maxim said quickly. "But I would request that you not explain the meaning of *Arima* to Miss Whitney at this time."

Faron stared at Maxim for a long moment in complete surprise. He was about to give the eldest Katre a hard dressing down for his presumption when the truth finally hit him.

"Oh," he said, unable to think of anything further to say. Saige, however, had no such problem.

"Is Summer your Arima?" she demanded, her light green eyes sparking with outrage.

"Yes, Arima Lobo," Maxim admitted. "She is."

"She's your Arima and you have not only failed to tell her that, but your treatment of her has been abominable." Saige growled.

"Now, *amada*," Faron said gently, trying to intervene.

Saige glanced at Faron, then turned her gaze back to Maxim. "Are you ashamed of her because she was held prisoner for a year?"

Maxim's eyes widened in shock. "Of course not," he replied. "Such a thought never occurred to me."

"Wait," Summer interrupted. "I don't understand any of this. What is an Arima? Why are you so angry, Saige? And what has it got to do with Maxim?"

Saige opened her mouth to answer, but a look from Faron stopped her. She closed her mouth with a snap, folded her arms in front of herself and glared at Maxim.

"This is a subject that is best discussed in private between you, and the Katres," Faron said. "I do not think this is either the time or the place for it."

"Nor do I," Doc interjected. "I'm trying to save this woman's life over here and all of the shouting is not helping my concentration. And if Miss Flowers doesn't mind, I could use another hand."

"You want me to help you?" Darleen asked in surprise.

"Yes, please," Doc said. "So long as you aren't squeamish that is."

"No, I'm not squeamish," Darleen said as she hurried forward, giving Maxim Katre a wide berth on her way to the exam table.

Summer sent silent thanks to Doc, then turned to Saige. "I think Faron is correct," she said. "Now is not the time. Those women sitting over there are more important right now."

Saige turned to look at the women the Katres had brought from the slave compound, the anger leaving her expression.

"You're right," she said. "Let's see if we can help them."

Summer nodded and they crossed the room to where the three women sat, each of them dressed in the same rough shift that Summer had worn, staring blankly ahead.

"Can you get them to stand up?" Saige asked doubtfully. This close-up view of the women made her feel slightly ill. Their eyes were so empty and cold, like looking into a dead person's eyes.

Summer grimaced. She really did not like doing this. "Controller, stand," she said in a firm tone. All three women stood up in perfect synchronization, like three parts of one mechanism.

"That's just creepy," Saige said.

"I know," Summer said. "Can you help them?"

"I don't know, but I will try," Saige said. She stepped forward and reached out to the woman on the end, placing her hands gently on the woman's shoulders and closing her eyes.

A few seconds later she removed her hands from the woman's shoulders, took a few steps back and bent over, her arms crossed in front of her as she gasped quietly. Faron rushed to her side and lifted her into his arms, pulling her close against his chest. Saige turned her face into Faron's shoulder and he turned around, hiding her from the concerned eyes of the others in the room.

"Shhh, *amada*," he crooned to her softly. "It's going to be all right. We will care for these women, I promise you that."

It wasn't long before the door burst open and Dav and Ban rushed in, their eyes almost frantic as they hurried to Faron's side, surrounding Saige completely. Summer watched as all three men stroked and soothed Saige, whispering to her softly in an effort to calm her.

She wanted that, Summer realized with surprise. Not just a family, as she had told herself when she'd first decided to come to Jasan. No, she wanted much more than that. She wanted to be loved exactly the way the Lobos so obviously loved Saige. But, she was no longer willing to pretend to be someone other than herself, and experience had taught her that her true self was not likeable. No one liked the real Summer Whitney.

No, she amended silently. That's not true. Saige seems to like me, and Darleen as well. Its nice being liked without having to pretend to be someone else, she thought. It's not the same as being loved, but it's better than nothing. Perhaps it will be enough.

After a few more minutes Faron lowered Saige to her feet. She crossed the room to the sink and splashed water on her face, then used a towel to dry herself before turning around.

"I apologize," she said quietly. "That was just...difficult."

"Is there no hope at all?" Summer asked.

"Oh, there is plenty of hope," Saige said quickly. "I really think we can do this if we work together."

"So why were you so upset?" Summer asked with a confused frown.

Saige shuddered. "Because Rebecca...that is that woman's name...Rebecca is trapped in her own subconscious mind, and it's having a nightmare. A nightmare she cannot wake up from, and that is slowly driving her insane. Just spending a few moments in her nightmare with her was almost more than I could stand."

Saige turned to Doc, who had paused in what he was doing to listen to her. "Doc, I am very concerned that suddenly awaking from their nightmares might push these poor women over the edge."

"You want to sedate them?" he asked.

"Not a lot. Just enough to dull reality for them."

"I think that's a wise idea," he said. He turned to check on his patient, then walked over to the drug cabinet and unlocked it. A few moments later he returned with an injector.

"I'll just give her a little of this," he said as he swabbed Rebecca's arm. "It won't do more than dull her senses a bit. If she seems to need more when she awakens, then we can give her a little more."

"Good," Saige said with relief. "Summer, I really don't know how I know this, but the Controller has caused damage to the part of their brains that allows them to wake up. They are essentially in a deep dream state, and have been for however long the Controllers have been in them. I can Heal that part of their brain, but the Controller will immediately work to destroy what I Heal."

"So, as soon as you Heal them, I need to deactivate the Controller," Summer said.

"Yes," Saige replied. "The problem is going to be timing. You were correct when you worried that stopping the Controller would kill them. It will. Almost at once. It controls their breathing, their heart beat, everything. We have to Heal the damage, then shut down the Controller almost simultaneously."

"Okay," Summer said. "Let me get in there first. I need to mentally get hold of the central processing node so that when you are finished, I can try to shut the whole system down."

"All right," Saige said. "Go ahead. Let me know when you're ready."

Summer placed one hand on Rebecca's shoulder to help her get a stronger connection with the Controller. It only took her a few moments to find what she needed. When she was certain she was ready, she reached over and tapped Saige, unwilling to break her concentration by speaking aloud.

Almost at once she sensed Saige join her inside of Rebecca's mind. It was a surprise, but she managed to hang onto the Controller in spite of it. She sensed something pure, bright and clean flash through Rebecca's brain, then felt a sudden tap on her arm. She immediately deactivated the central processing node, ruthlessly destroying every tendril of the Controller with a hard, mental slam of power that she hadn't even known she was capable of.

She felt her knees weaken and she started to slump to the floor, knowing she was going to land hard but helpless to stop herself. Strong arms caught her before she hit and picked her up, cradling her against a broad chest. She forced her eyes to open and looked up, confused to see Maxim's face. She had a moment to wonder why he had bothered to catch her before darkness closed in.

Chapter 19

"No, she needs to rest first," Maxim was saying as Summer swam up out of the darkness. She struggled to open her eyes and was stunned to find herself surrounded by all three of the Katre brothers. Ran and Loni were both watching her carefully, their eyes never wavering from her face, though Maxim was looking over his shoulder at whomever he was talking to.

"I'm okay," Summer said "you can put me down now."

Maxim turned to look at her for a long moment, his face unreadable. "Very well," he said and lowered her slowly to her feet, waiting to be sure that she was standing firmly on her own before releasing her. He then stepped back so that she could see both Saige and Darleen standing there, gazing at her worriedly.

"Did it work?" Summer asked. "How is Rebecca?"

Saige smiled. "Yes, it worked. Rebecca is a little groggy and confused, but I think she'll be fine. How are you?"

"I'm not sure," Summer replied. "I don't know what I did exactly, but it took a lot more energy than anything I've ever done before. I think I destroyed the Controller though."

"Really?" Saige said eagerly. "Do you mean it's completely gone, or merely disabled?"

"I don't know," Summer replied. "If there's any part of it still active, I can probably connect to it and see how much of it is still there. But if it's destroyed, there won't be anything for me to connect to. Do you want me to try?"

As soon as she asked the question, Summer felt Maxim's instant *No* as clearly as if he'd shouted it. But he was standing right in front of her and he had not so much as twitched, let alone spoken. Summer stared at him in surprised confusion for a long moment before turning back to Saige.

"I don't think it's a good idea for you to do any more tonight," Saige was saying. "I keep forgetting what you've already been through today, you and Darleen both, and I apologize for that."

"But what about the other two women?" Summer asked. "I don't want them to suffer any more than they have to."

Again she felt a negative response from Maxim, but, as before, he had not moved a fraction. She frowned at him, wondering what was going on, then set it aside for the more immediate concern.

She turned back to Saige only to find that Doc had joined them. "Miss Whitney, you expended a great amount of mental energy just now, and that takes a toll. Take my advice and give yourself some time to rest up a bit before you try it again. If you cause yourself harm, then nobody is going to be able to help these women. They'll be okay for another day or so. They made it this long, another day won't matter to them."

Summer opened her mouth to argue further, but Doc held up a hand. "I also think it would be best to observe Miss Rebecca for awhile, make sure that whatever you and Saige did doesn't have a bad effect on her."

Summer couldn't argue with that and from the smug expression on Doc's face, he knew it. "Fine, I know I'm being manipulated, but honestly I am too tired to argue further."

"Saige, would you mind if I used a different guest room so that Summer can sleep without me waking her when I go in?" Darleen asked. "I want to stay and help Doc with this patient."

"Of course not," Saige replied. "I will ask Lessie to prepare the room next to Summer's. Would that work?"

"That would be wonderful, thank you," Darleen replied. She turned to Summer. "Do you want me to walk back to the room with you?"

"No, I'll be fine," Summer replied.

"We will accompany her," Maxim announced, much to Summer's surprise.

"Okay," she agreed reluctantly, not wanting to start an argument when he seemed to be feeling nice toward her for a change, though she was irritated by his imperious tone. "But first I need to find Lio."

"Why?" Maxim asked.

Maxim's demanding tone caused Summer's defenses to flutter, but she was just too worn out to argue with the man. "Because if I don't tell him to lay down and go to sleep, he will stand in that corner all night long," she explained as patiently as she could.

"I don't see the problem with that," Maxim replied testily.

Summer frowned. "Look, I know the man is horrible, and that what he did to Darleen was evil, and that he deserves to pay for that. But *I* am not evil, nor is it up to me to determine what his punishment should be for his crimes. I admit that injecting him with a Controller was wrong, and if necessary I will pay the price for that. But I did it because we need him, or rather, we need the knowledge inside his head. We all do. I did not do it so that I could torture him."

Something about the set of Maxim's features softened just a little bit. "Nor would I ask you to torture him," he said. "I apologize for my rudeness. We will escort you to him so that you can do what you must. Then we will see you to your room."

Summer didn't think she needed three big men to escort her around the house, but she had no wish to break this small peace between herself and Maxim so she just nodded. "Okay, thank you," she said.

She spent another few moments saying goodnight to Darleen, setting up a time to meet with Saige to heal the other two women, and agreeing to attend Faron's interrogation of Lio the next day before finally leaving the med-lab with the Katres. It wasn't until much later, after she was snuggled up warm and cozy in bed, almost asleep, that she realized nobody had ever gotten around to telling her what an Arima was.

Chapter 20

Maxim stood staring at the door for a long time after Summer went inside and closed it, deep in thought. Loni and Ran waited patiently, deep in their own thoughts as well. Finally he turned, looked at his brothers and sighed.

"Let's talk," he said. He turned and led the way back up the hallway and out of the Lobos' home, then down the gravel path toward the air field. It had been a very long and eventful day, but the sun had set hours before and it was drawing to a close. The air was clear and cold, though it didn't bother the Katres. They enjoyed the cold.

When Maxim was certain that they were alone, and that there was nobody close enough to eavesdrop on them, he stopped and turned to face his brothers. "I am confused about Summer," he admitted. "I cannot make up my mind about her."

"I do not understand the problem," Ran said, relieved to have this chance to discuss the matter. "She is beautiful, intelligent, and honorable. Why is it you don't like her?"

Maxim clenched his jaw tightly as though fighting to hold back words. "I just want to be certain about her," he said finally. "She said a few things earlier that bothered me. Though I understand her reasons now, I am not yet convinced of her character. I do not want us to jump into something that we will be stuck with for the rest of our lives."

"She is our Arima," Ran said. "We are *supposed* to be with her for the rest of our lives. I also think she is the reason we have been so unsettled this past year."

Maxim's jaw clenched tighter, but he nodded in agreement. He had realized that as well.

"Maxim is worried that she will be like Mara," Loni said. Ran turned to his middle brother in surprise.

"But she is nothing at all like Mara," Ran argued. "Why would such an idea even occur to you?"

"You weren't there this morning," Maxim said. "You didn't hear her."

"Loni?" Ran asked.

"I did not get the same impression as Maxim," Loni admitted. "However, I do not disagree with his decision to take care in this. We have seen the result of a bad choice."

Ran shook his head. "That's true, though I don't like admitting it," he said. "But this is different. Summer is different. She is our Arima. Made for us as we are made for her."

"Made for us, but raised on Earth," Maxim argued. "No, Ran," he said when his youngest brother started to argue further. "I know how you feel, and I understand it. But there are things that you do not know. Things that neither of you know. For now, we will go slowly in this matter."

"What things do we not know?" Loni asked.

"Things of which I cannot speak until I know more," Maxim said.

"If these things concer Summer, we should be made aware of them," Loni said calmly, though something in his tone warned Maxim that he was very serious.

"No, I know nothing more of her than either of you. And that is the point. I wish us to know her better, to make a careful decision and not be led by either fate or our hormones."

"Then you speak of our parents," Loni said.

"No," Maxim said. "I speak of Mara."

It was Ran's turn to clench his jaw. "You've had a thorn in your paw about something with her ever since the accident, Maxim," he said. "When are you going to tell us what's going on?"

"When I have something to tell," Maxim replied shortly. He turned and paced away from his brothers, then turned back. "I'm sorry," he said. "I cannot say more until I am sure."

Chapter 21

Summer slept late the next morning and, when she awoke, she was disoriented for a few moments. It was her first morning awaking in a real bed, with a mattress and blankets, warm and comfortable, in such a long time that she had nearly forgotten what it felt like. When Lessie brought her a tray loaded with hot food and a carafe of coffee she thought she'd died and gone to heaven. She actually had to pinch herself to prove she wasn't dreaming.

The only problem was that, almost from the moment she opened her eyes, she sensed the Katres. They were not close by, but they weren't too far away either. She did not sense any specific emotions from them, but she had the feeling that they were busy with something serious, though she had no idea what.

Nor did she care, she told herself firmly as she reached for the coffee carafe. She had just had her first sip of coffee when there was a knock at her door.

"Come on in," she called after checking to make sure she was decently covered. She was wearing an oversized t-shirt and a pair of shorts, presumably belonging to Saige.

The door opened and Darleen poked her head in before opening the door all the way and stepping inside. "I've got a surprise for you," she said.

"A surprise?" Summer asked, just as a young man followed Darleen into the room lugging several suitcases. Very familiar suitcases.

"*Gardez donc!*" Summer exclaimed. "My luggage! That's my luggage! How?"

"Apparently the Katres contacted the security chief over at the spaceport and told them to send your luggage, and mine too," Darleen replied. "It just arrived a little while ago."

"That was thoughtful of them," Summer said, mildly surprised by the gesture. "They had your luggage too?"

"I was heading off-planet after what I did to Saige and Lariah, so I'd sent my luggage to the spaceport early that morning. Then Lio got me with the Controller. They impounded my luggage, waiting for me to come looking for it, and it was still there. Yours was with the luggage of the other missing women. Saige said that as soon as we know the names of the other two women, she'll contact the spaceport for their things as well."

"I never thought I'd see any of my belongings again," Summer said. "Come and have some coffee with me."

"No thanks, I've had enough coffee this morning," Darleen replied.

"Come sit then," Summer urged, "I want to talk to you."

Darleen hesitated, but after a moment she crossed the room to the chair beside the bed and sat down.

"Before you ask, I want to tell you that last night Faron and Saige asked me not to discuss Arimas or anything else of that nature with you. They said it's a private matter, and should be discussed between you and the Katres. I told them that I understood that, and that because I owe them, I would try to do as they asked. But I also told them that right now, my first loyalty is to you. You freed me. And we have a deal. So, if you want me to tell you, I will, but I think that if Faron and Saige wanted it to be kept between you and the Katres, then they probably have a good reason for that."

"That isn't what I was going to ask you first, but I admit that I was going to ask you that eventually. But now I won't, so don't worry about it."

"What were you going to ask me then?" Darleen asked curiously.

"Yesterday Saige told me that if we find out where more women are, that they would help us with getting to them, and freeing them."

"Well, that's good. It could be a problem for us, especially if they are on another planet," Darleen pointed out.

"That's true," Summer agreed. "Also, Faron is setting up a meeting today to interrogate Lio. What I wanted to discuss with you is, what if they decide to leave us behind and go free the women on their own? There's a lot to be said for that. We aren't warriors, and it could be dangerous. I doubt that anyone will think twice about it if we stayed here and let them handle it."

"No," Darleen said at once. "I have to be involved Summer. I just have to be. There is something inside of me that needs this." Darleen looked down for a moment, then raised her eyes to Summer's again. "I would understand if you would prefer not to go."

Summer shook her head. "No, I have to do this too. I just wanted to be sure you felt the same way."

"Great," Darleen said with obvious relief. She reached out and snagged a piece of toast off of Summer's tray and started nibbling on it, her face turning thoughtful. "You know Summer, I lived here on Jasan for about a year before Lio got me. I learned quite a bit about Clan Jasani in that time and they are very alpha men. If they can find a way to keep us here on the sidelines while they rush off to save the day, they will."

"Yes, that's just what I was thinking too," Summer said. "But we have access to information that they don't."

"As soon as you let Lio answer all of their questions, they will have the information they need," Darleen pointed out.

"Yes, well, we will just have to see about that," Summer said. "You and I paid a very large price for that information, and I don't see any reason for us to give it away for free."

"You're gonna bargain, aren't you?" Darleen asked.

"Well, it's either that or lie, and I don't lie too well." Summer said.

"Is it true that they can't ask Lio questions themselves?" Darleen asked.

Summer grimaced. "Yes, I'm afraid it is. I didn't mean to make that happen, but I was in a hurry when I did it, and I fixed it too good. Unless I can figure out how to reverse what I did, he answers only to my mental commands."

Darleen shrugged. "It doesn't matter. In fact, its better this way. If I could, I would order him to do a lot of really horrible things to himself."

"I don't think anyone would blame you for that Darleen," Summer said. "But I think it would be a bad thing for you. He's caused you enough damage." Summer smiled as she took in the short growth of blond hair on Darleen's head, her pale, but normal complexion, and her clear eyes. "It appears as though Doc has done a good job reversing some of it though."

"Yes, he certainly has," Darleen agreed, her eyes lighting up a little at the mention of Doc. "He's started me on a series of injections for the malnutrition, and I feel better already. He said that when I get a little stronger, he'll be able to fix my hip. He's already done so much more than I'd even hoped for, and he says there is a lot more he can do about...well, other things."

"I'm very happy for you, Darleen," Summer said, making a mental note to thank Doc herself. She finished her coffee and hopped out of bed. "Okay, there is one thing I have to make sure is still here," she said as she reached for the largest suitcase. "If it is, and it's still in one piece, then nothing else really matters."

"What is it?" Darleen asked as she watched Summer lay the suitcase down on the floor and open the latches. The top popped up and Summer flung it all the way open.

"You'll think it's silly," Summer said as she removed a couple of layers of folded clothing, exposing a bundle wrapped in what looked like a section of quilt.

"Maybe," Darleen admitted. "But tell me anyway."

Summer smiled. Darleen was always honest, and she liked that about her. "It's a music box," she said, unwrapping the bundle carefully. "My great-grandmother left it to me when she died. I was seven years old at the time."

"Why would I think that was silly?" Darleen asked.

Summer opened the last fold of the quilt, exposing a black cloth bag. She dropped the quilt into the suitcase and climbed back onto the bed with the much smaller bundle, holding it reverently.

"My parents thought it was silly," she said. "They didn't understand why it was so important to me. Why it's always been so important to me. To be honest, neither do I. I just know that the first time I laid eyes on it, I knew I had to have it. I felt as though it was *supposed* to be mine." Summer shrugged again and began working at the knot in the drawstring at the top of the bag. "Whenever we visited my great-grandmother, she would ask me what I wanted to do, and every single time I told her I wanted to see the music box. She always smiled and got it out for me. When she died, she left it to me in her will. I've always felt as though it were the most important thing I owned."

The knot in the thin cords came loose beneath her patient fingers and Summer opened the bag. She hesitated a moment. "Okay, here's hoping it isn't damaged," she said before reaching into the bag and pulling the music box out.

"Its perfect," she breathed as she turned it around in her hands. She felt a little foolish about it, but she had missed this thing over the past year, and had often worried about what had happened to it. The idea of it being chucked out into space with the rest of her luggage had nearly made her physically ill on several occasions. But here it was. As perfect as the day she had packed it.

In spite of the size of the original bundle, the music box itself was small enough to sit in the palm of her hand. It was round, and covered with little, intricately cut pieces of stained glass in a rainbow of colors. In the center was a porcelain figure of a girl with dark hair dressed in a pink ballerina costume, standing on her toes, her arms up over her head in a graceful pose. Around her sat three golden panthers, each on a golden pedestal.

Summer turned the little key in the bottom of the music box and set it carefully on the nightstand beside the bed. A soft, hauntingly beautiful tune began to play as the ballerina slowly turned, the golden panthers seemingly watching her intently.

"What is that tune?" Darleen asked. "It's beautiful, but I don't think I've ever heard it before."

Summer smiled. "No one has ever heard it before. That was one of the things that bothered my parents about it. They asked everyone who came to the house for years to listen to it, but nobody ever recognized it. They finally just gave up." Summer frowned. "I made up words once, when I was really little, to sing along with the tune. My mother hated that, though I don't know why." She shook her head. "I quit singing them because it upset her."

"Well I think it's a wonderful little music box," Darleen declared. "Not in the least bit silly."

"Thanks, Darleen," Summer said. She watched the music box for a few more moments, happy that it was safe and sound after so much time. When the music ran down, she got up again.

"I guess I better see what clothes I have in here," she said as she went back to the suitcase. "Then I'll take a shower and we'll get this day started.

Chapter 22

"You may disembark now, Mrs. Katre-Hiru."

Mara started to frown, remembered herself and smiled for the cabin camera that she knew was trained on her instead. "Thank you, Captain," she said politely as she stood up and began gathering her things. She hated the name Katre-Hiru even more than she hated having to catch flights with these young, wet behind the ears pilots. She had waited hours to catch a ride on this flight, which had taken most of the night. But it was the only way she could get to the Dracon's ranch without having to pay her own way. And she was not going to spend her own money on this venture. She had three very high-ranking sons, and the Jasani Military Air Transport Command could darn well ferry her across the planet to visit them. They owed her that much at least. Which reminded her.

"Captain, will you be going back to Berria soon?" she asked sweetly.

"No, Mrs. Katre-Hiru," the disembodied voice said over the cabin speaker. "I expect to be here for several days, at minimum."

Mara gritted her teeth hard enough to crack them. What she really wanted to do was tell the stupid Clan Gryphon to stop calling her Mrs. Katre-Hiru. She knew her Clan rank had dropped from first female to third after the death of her male-set. She didn't need to be reminded of it every single time someone said her name.

Mara took a slow, deep, calming breath. It could have been worse, she reminded herself for the thousandth time. If not for the fact that her eldest sons were Consuls of Clan Katre, her rank would have dropped down amongst the lowest in the Clan. She was lucky it had dropped only to third, and even luckier that she had been promised that rank for the remainder of her life.

She looped the handles of a couple of bags up over her shoulders, picked up another with her free hand and began making her way towards the exit. Since this was a troop ship, not a passenger liner, there were no luxuries or amenities on board. Nobody to serve her drinks or snacks, nobody to help her with her bags. In the beginning, when she'd first started making these trips, some of the young males had helped her on and off the transports, offering to carry her luggage for her and other such things. But, for some reason, they had stopped doing that recently. Now, if she wanted her bags off of the transport, she darn well had to carry them herself.

Mara had to turn sidewise to get through the cabin door with all of her bags hanging around her. She nearly stumbled on the top step of the metal staircase someone had rolled up to the transport for her, but strong hands caught her. "Here Mother, let me help you with some of those," Ran said as he began sliding the straps off of Mara's shoulders.

"Thank you, Ran, honey," Mara said. "I am so glad that someone came to help me. Otherwise I'm not sure how I would have managed, though I'm sure I would have fallen down these horrible stairs and broken my neck. Not that anyone would have noticed. I don't think any of the crew came back to check on me even once the whole trip. I could have jumped out the window or fallen over dead and nobody would ever have known, but that's the price I pay in order to come and see my sons. I just never know how any of you are as you never vox, never vid, and I'm all alone now with your fathers gone so if I want to know how my sons are doing I have to come here to see for myself. Of course I'm sure that you are all very busy doing important things and don't have time to stop what you're doing and let me know how you are, but that's fine, I don't mind coming here to see you. That's what a Mother is for, isn't it? To fly half way around the world every few weeks to make sure her sons are well and eating right and taking care of themselves? I don't know if anyone would even tell me should anything happen to you. I suppose not, I don't matter after all, I'm just a widow now, nobody of importance, so if I want to know how you are I have to come and see with my own eyes, don't I?"

By the time Mara stopped talking they were down the stairs and across the field to the ground-car that Ran had brought out when the incoming transport Captain had radioed ahead to let him know his Mother was on board. Ran didn't bother trying to halt his Mother's tirade, or attempt to correct any of the more outrageous things she was saying. He just let her go on, listening with half of his attention as she talked. When they reached the ground car he opened a door for her and helped her in before unloading her bags and satchels into the trunk.

The moment he opened the driver's side door she began talking again, rambling along in essentially the same vein as before. Ran started the vehicle and pulled onto the graveled road, wondering idly how long it would be before the engineers got around to paving the road. It was getting so much traffic now that the gravel wasn't holding up well at all. He drove past the cluster of new buildings that housed the rotating male-sets stationed on the ranch for guard duty, the armory, barracks, cafeteria, training facilities, medical center and armory before turning off on a smaller side road that led to a group of guest houses meant for important visitors and higher ranking warriors.

"Don't tell me that I am to be delegated to a guest house again," Mara said angrily. "I just don't understand it. I called that silly little Vulpiran several times, what's his name, the one who handles guests, and I told him specifically that I did not want to be put in a guest house. I'm a widow now, and I don't like being put out here all on my own. I told him straight out that I expected to be given a room in the main house. Why am I being treated this way? I've been here several times now and you can't tell me that there is no room in the Dracons' home for me. It's just rude, that's what it is. That little upstart redheaded piece may be good enough in bed to keep the Dracons happy, but it's more than clear to all and sundry that she hasn't got any manners at all."

Ran was shocked. He was used to his mother's wagging tongue, and she was often unkind, but this went too far.

"Cease," he growled. His growl was soft, but there was something in it that silenced Mara immediately.

"You speak treason Mother, and I will not abide it," he said. "Princess Lariah is a very kind and generous woman, and does not deserve your insults. You have never even met her, and have no cause to insult her.

"Further, you speak nonsense. The guest houses are specifically set aside for important people, and it is an honor that you are offered one every time you visit. Other family members are assigned beds in the guest barracks, or must make their own arrangements in town. As for the Vulpiran Quartermaster, he does not take orders from civilians, he is not a hotel manager, nor is the Dracons' home a vacation resort."

"Well, I did not think that it was," Mara said huffily. "And since when does my own son take sides against his mother?" she demanded.

"When she commits an act of treason, punishable by banishment at the least, and death at most," Ran snapped. "I sincerely hope you did not insult the Quartermaster when you spoke to him. He is a respected veteran and not in the least bit *silly*."

Mara suddenly realized she had gone too far. Never had Ran spoken to her in such a manner. He was the gentlest and most understanding of all her sons. Clearly she had crossed a line with him, and she knew him well enough to know that if she didn't fix it quickly, he would not soon forgive her.

"I'm sorry, Ran honey," she said contritely. "I know I should not have said such things. It's just been a very difficult day for me. I was thinking about your fathers on the flight over here, and how long it's been since the accident. It's not easy for me to be alone after living with the three of them for so many years." Mara reached into her pocket for a handkerchief and dabbed her dry eyes gently.

Ran sighed. "I know it's been difficult Mother. It's been a hard year for us all. But there are some things you cannot say, no matter the reason. You are lucky I am the only one who heard you."

"I know Ran honey, and I appreciate that. Sometimes my mouth runs away with me and I don't even know what I'm saying. Please forgive me."

"Of course I forgive you Mother," Ran said. "And please, stop crying. Here we are, you get the biggest guest house this time, the one you like with the best view, remember?"

Mara sniffled a few times, patted her eyes again and put her handkerchief away. "Yes dear, it's lovely," she said. "Perfectly lovely."

An hour later Mara stood at the door of the guest house and watched as Ran drove away, waving gaily to him until he turned out of sight. Then she stepped back inside and slammed the door shut as hard as she could, causing the front windows to rattle alarmingly.

She stomped across the wide, lavishly furnished living room of the Dracons' best guest house, then turned and stomped back, before turning and retracing her steps again, and again. She was so angry, so frustrated and so worried she didn't know what to do.

This was her tenth trip to the Dracon's ranch in as many months and she had counted on staying in the Dracons' home this time. She had worked on that damned Quartermaster for weeks, but clearly it had done no good at all. She didn't know how she was going to manage her end of the bargain with Winkie if she couldn't get closer to the Dracons' than a damn guest house. She might as well have not bothered coming at all.

When she had turned to Winkie for help she had known that he was a powerful and ruthless man. Otherwise, why would she have gone to him? Her mistake had been in thinking of him as her sweet little baby brother who would, eventually, give in to her wheedling. Do the thing she had asked, and forgive the debt. That was what she'd expected. That was what she had counted on. But now she knew that it wasn't going to work out that way. Not this time.

No, she thought to herself, she could not return empty handed again. No matter what, she had to find a way to get what she had come for. And she wasn't going to leave again until she had it.

Slightly breathless from her pacing, but feeling better for having burned off the worst of her rage, Mara selected the cushiest chair in the room, kicked off her shoes and sat down. She wiggled around until she was quite comfortable and put her feet up on the needlepoint ottoman. Then she put her head back, closed her eyes, and began to plan.

Chapter 23

Summer and Darleen left the med-lab together after Summer and Saige had healed the second of the three women from the slave compound. Her name, they discovered, was Trina Evans and, like Rebecca from the previous night, she appeared to be groggy from the sedative Doc had administered, but otherwise fine.

Summer hadn't suffered the same collapse as the night before, but the effort had been tiring for her. Since she still had to get through the interrogation with Lio, Saige had agreed to heal the third woman later in the afternoon or early evening.

When they entered the house Summer was surprised to find the Katre brothers standing in the hall, apparently waiting for them. Summer's stomach did a little flip at the sight of them. She frowned in annoyance at her own reaction. Secretly she thought they were extremely handsome men, and she couldn't help her physical attraction to them. Even if Maxim was stuffy and temperamental.

Maxim bowed to her, which still made her a little uncomfortable.

"We thought to escort you to the meeting room," he said. "Faron and the others are waiting."

"All right," Summer replied. "We need to get Lio first."

"No need, he is already there," Maxim replied.

"How?" Summer asked in surprise. "Did he follow someone else's commands?"

"No," Maxim replied with a shrug. "We merely picked him up and carried him."

Summer grinned. She couldn't help herself.

"I would have liked to see that," Darleen said. "The great Lio Perry, lugged around like a bag of dirty laundry."

Maxim arched a brow. "I am not sure how *great* he is, but dirty laundry is a rather apt description. Perhaps after the meeting we can take him down to the barn and hose him off."

Summer laughed at the mental image. She would not do such a thing to the man, but she had to admit that she was sorely tempted.

Maxim stepped aside and bowed again, waving Summer and Darleen forward. They headed down the hall, the Katres falling into step behind them. There was something almost familiar about the sensation of the three men walking behind her, almost like déjà vu, but not quite. Summer saw the door to the meeting room loom ahead and she shook her head clear of such strange thoughts. She was going to need a clear head for what was to come.

Faron Lobo rose from his seat as Summer, Darleen and the Katres entered the meeting room.

"Good morning Summer, Darleen," he said. "I trust you are feeling a bit better after a good night's sleep?"

"Yes, much better, thank you," Summer replied as she and Darleen took the seats that Faron indicated with a wave of his hand. She noted that Lio was standing in one corner of the room facing the wall, then put him out of her mind. She would see to it that he was properly fed and bathed after this meeting, she promised herself.

She was a little surprised that the only people in the room aside from herself and Darleen were the Lobos, and the Katres. She had gotten the impression from Faron that there would be more people here. Apparently Faron read the expression on her face.

"We thought it would be easier for you if there weren't too many more unfamiliar faces here," Faron said. "Eldar Hamat Katre will be joining us in a moment, but that is all."

"Thank you for that," Summer said. She had been a little nervous at the thought of an entire room full of Clan Jasani asking her questions. She relaxed a little bit, but not much.

"We would like to begin with questions about the Xanti," Faron said. "We have almost no information on them at all, so almost anything he can tell us will be helpful. Shall we just ask him questions directly?"

"I have to mentally order the Controller to force him to listen to your questions, and then answer them truthfully," Summer said. "The problem is going to be knowing which questions are the right ones to ask."

"How do you mean?" Faron asked.

"The Controller responds to specific commands, specifically. If you ask a question such as *What can you tell us about the Xanti?,* it won't work. It's too general. On the other hand, if you ask *What is the name of the Xanti you work with*?, then you will get an answer."

Faron frowned thoughtfully. "That makes things a little more complicated," he said. "If we don't know enough to ask about something in particular, we won't learn about it. Is that correct?"

"Yes, I'm afraid it is," Summer replied.

"Excuse me," Darleen interrupted softly. All eyes went to her at once, which made her nervous, but she clenched her fists in her lap and continued as though she didn't notice.

"Yes, Miss Flowers?" Faron asked.

"I spent a year in Lio's office listening to every conversation he had," she said. "I think I might be able to help give you some indications of what to ask him about. If you think it would help. And please, call me Darleen."

"Yes, it would help," Faron replied. "Thank you, Darleen." He paused a moment to think. Obviously Darleen was in very poor health, so now was probably not the time to put her through an interrogation. As eager as he was to learn as much as possible about anything and everything Lio Perry knew, he was going to have to exercise some patience.

"Darleen, if you would not mind, it would be helpful if you could begin a list of what you believe may be important questions for us to ask Lio. When you are a little stronger, we will work together on this. Then we will question Lio further. Would that be acceptable to you?"

"Very much so," Darleen said eagerly. "I'll begin at once."

Faron smiled, impressed by how much the woman had changed for the better. "Thank you," he said. "In the meantime, we will question Lio about matters we are more certain of. Such as the slave routes, compounds and names of people and ships who are involved."

A while later Faron was beginning to realize just how important Darleen's information was going to be. So far, Lio had not been able to answer any of their questions with answers that did them any good. The Xanti had covered themselves too well. Lio knew only code names for the ships, captains and locations of those involved in the slavery ring. The real information was all in the computers, which was another problem in itself.

"The only slave compound whose true location I know is located on Li-Hach-Cor," Lio said in response to Summer's silent command.

"Damn," Faron said softly. "That's not good news."

"Why not?" Summer asked in surprise.

"Because the Li-Hach are an extremely problematic species," Maxim replied. "We have cordial relations with them, but that is the best that can be said of it. They are very territorial, and will not agree to our entering their system for any purpose without extensive and, in all likelihood, lengthy negotiations. Even then, I doubt that they will allow it."

"But he did not say Li-Hach," Summer pointed out. "He said Li-Hach-Cor."

"What is the difference?" Faron asked.

"Li-Hach-Cor is a terraformed moon in the Li-Hach system, but quite distant from Li-Hach."

"Nevertheless, if it is a part of their system, the same applies. They will not agree to our presence easily or quickly," Maxim said.

"Not if it's an overtly military presence," Summer said. "Otherwise, I doubt they will care, so long as nobody goes closer to Li-Hach than Li-Hach-Cor."

"Why do you say that?" Faron asked curiously, shooting Maxim a quelling look when it was obvious he was going to argue further.

"The people of Li-Hach are, as Maxim pointed out, very territorial and war-like," Summer replied. "However, about two hundred years ago a faction of the population, which had been rather small up until then, began to grow larger and became too much of a *distraction* to the rest of the population. This faction called themselves Li-Hach-Aki, which, in their language, means The People of Peace.

"At the time, Li-Hach had just signed the Intersystem Convention for Law Enforcement and Counterintelligence, which has a Sentient Species Bill of Rights, so they couldn't exterminate the thousands of Li-Hach-Aki without severe political consequences. So it was decided to remove them from Li-Hach altogether. They had already begun terraforming a moon at the outer edge of their system, which they called Cor, for agricultural purposes. The Li-Hach-Aki were sent there to live, and handle the agriculture as well."

"So, only these peace lovers live on Cor?" Faron asked.

"Yes," Summer replied. "It is a small population, I believe about eight to ten thousand altogether. They have a small settlement, and make generous use of technology provided by their Mother World to aide them in growing a large percentage of the produce consumed by Li-Hach. But they only cultivate one relatively small portion of the planet. It is easy to imagine someone setting up a compound on the far side of their world that would go undetected for a long time."

"How do you know so much about them?" Dav asked. "To my knowledge we do not have half that much information in our data banks on Li-Hach."

Summer hesitated, glanced quickly at the Katre's and lifted her chin. She wasn't really sure why Maxim seemed to be angry with her again, and she had no real wish to make him any angrier. But, if he decided to dislike her even more because of how much she knew, then that was his problem.

"My mother is a Sentient Species Specialist," she said. "She's written many books on the subject, and I've read them all."

"Your mother?" Eldar Hamat asked, frowning thoughtfully. "Miss Whitney, do you mean to say that your mother is Kandria Whitney?" He spoke the name with obvious respect, which Summer was used to.

"Yes, she is," Summer replied. She liked this Katre. He seemed kind and soft-spoken. Unlike his nephew, Maxim, he hadn't glared at her once during the entire meeting.

"With as many books as she has written, I find it startling that you remember so much of one species," Eldar Hamat commented.

Summer looked down at the table, wishing she could just be rude and refuse to respond to Eldar Hamat. But she couldn't. "I have a somewhat special memory," she admitted.

"Yes?" Hamat asked.

"I remember everything I've ever read, heard or seen," she said in a rush.

"And you hesitate to admit this, why?" Eldar Hamat asked gently.

"Because people tend to think badly of me for it," she replied honestly. "They see me as a know-it-all, or a freak. I've spent most of my life pretending to know nothing about anything."

"My memory is much like yours," Eldar Hamat said, much to Summer's surprise. "It is perhaps a bit different, but I understand your problem. However, if I may say so, anyone who does not accept and appreciate you fully for who and what you are does not deserve your consideration."

Summer smiled. "Thank you Eldar Hamat," she said. "That is very kind of you to say, and I will try to remember it."

"If you are the daughter of Kandria Whitney, then you are also the daughter of Admiral Quentin Whitney," Faron said.

"Yes, I am," Summer replied, not at all surprised that these people were familiar with her parents.

"I don't understand why your parents did not come to Jasan in search of you when you went missing," Eldar Hamat said.

Summer again dropped her eyes to the table in front of her. "Probably because they have no idea that I was missing," she said softly.

She looked up at the confused expressions around the table and sighed inwardly. "My parents and I had a bit of a falling out a few years ago. We have not spoken since that time."

"We sent the names of the missing women to Earth," Faron said. "Your parents should have been informed at that time."

Summer hesitated, then lifted her chin. "My parents no longer live on Earth, and I no longer use the name they gave me," she said with a note of finality. She had no intention of discussing that issue further.

Faron cleared his throat, evidently taking the hint. "As your father is who he is, I imagine you have more than a little military knowledge."

"Yes, I have some," Summer said.

"In that case, I am hoping you won't mind going to Li-Hach-Cor on a military vessel," Faron said. "We don't have the time to engage in political games with Li-Hach. Therefore, a military ship with a minimal crew which just happens to visit Li-Hach-Cor out of curiosity seems the best way to go."

Summer grinned. "Sounds like a good idea to me."

"I do not like it," Maxim said.

"Why not?" Summer asked with a frown.

"I see no reason to send you into danger," he said. "That is what military personnel are for."

"Well, happily, what I do is not your business," Summer replied sweetly.

"You are our Arima," Maxim snapped.

Summer laughed. "Yes, so I overheard someone say. But you have not told me that, nor, by your request, has anyone bothered to explain to me what an Arima is. Therefore, it means nothing to me. And if it did, that still does not give you the right to tell me what I can or cannot do. In spite of everything that has happened this past year, I am not owned. Furthermore, I will do whatever I am able to see to it that the other women who were abducted are freed."

By the time Summer was finished speaking she was no longer smiling, but barely holding her voice down, she was so angry. How dare this man think to dictate her actions? He didn't even like her.

Maxim opened his mouth but Faron rose from his chair and held up a hand.

"Enough," he said softly. Maxim turned angry eyes to Faron, but Faron ignored him. "This is not the time or the place for discussion of these deeply personal matters."

Maxim clamped his jaw shut and turned away, embarrassed by his inability to control both his temper and his mouth with Summer Whitney. What in the stars was wrong with him? he wondered. She had not, in truth, said a single thing wrong during the entire meeting. Yet, every time she spoke, he grew tense, as though waiting for something rude and embarrassing to come out of her mouth. If she would just show her true colors and be done with it, then he could relax, he thought to himself. Well, that and getting away from her scent, he amended. The aroma of sun warmed grass and spring wildflowers filled the meeting room, causing his body to react in a very uncomfortable manner.

Faron turned to Summer. "There is a specific reason that we would ask you to go to Li-Hach-Cor," he said.

"Yes?" Summer asked curiously.

"You mentioned yesterday that you are able to mentally control computers," Faron said. "How much control do you have over them?"

"I've been able to control basic functions since I was a kid," Summer said. "The only time I ever tried to stretch that ability was when I discovered the Controller in my own head. I have certainly been able to do a lot more with the nano-bots than I ever did with a computer, but I don't know if that means I can do more with computers or not."

"Would you be willing to try?" Faron asked. "To do more with a computer, I mean."

"I suppose so," Summer replied. "But, why?"

"We confiscated the computer system in Lio's office, and the system at the compound as well," Faron replied. "Our tech experts had no problem logging into either system, but, unfortunately, once in, there was nothing there. Both systems were completely wiped clean. Council scientists determined that both computers were equipped with a bio-metric recognition device. The moment a non-authorized person touched them, they erased themselves."

"I've never even heard of anything like that," Summer said. "And I'm sorry, Faron, but I really don't think I can do anything to recover wiped information. I will try of course. Whatever I can do to help, I will do. I just don't think it will work."

"I thank you for your offer of help, Summer Whitney," Faron said with a smile. "It is very much appreciated. However, we do not want you to try to recover wiped information. We want you to try to access a system before it is wiped."

"You think that if I can control the computer telekinetically that it will bypass the bio-metric system," Summer guessed.

"Yes, that is what we think," Faron said. "Or rather, that is what we hope."

Summer frowned thoughtfully. "All of those questions you asked earlier about ships and captains and routes that Lio couldn't answer, you think that information will be in a computer system."

"Yes," Faron said, "we do. What Lio has given us is, I believe, a code key. If we can get a computer system with the matching information for the codes, we can break this slavery ring."

Two hours later Summer and Darleen left the meeting room with Lio following obediently behind them. Summer felt wrung out from the long ordeal, but she had gotten what she and Darleen wanted without having to bargain, and Lio had provided at least some useful information.

"I'm sorry Maxim is angry with you again," Darleen said, surprising Summer.

"Why?" Summer asked. "It's not really my problem how the man feels. I have no idea why he keeps getting so angry with me, and I have even less understanding of why I should care about it. . I don't even know the man, though from what I've seen so far, he's bullheaded and stubborn."

"Well, whatever Maxim thought, Ran certainly seemed amused," Darleen said.

"Yes, he certainly did," Summer agreed with a grin. "I don't really understand that any more than I understand Maxim's anger, but I did think Maxim was going to smack him there for awhile."

"Yes, I thought so too," Darleen replied. "Whatever had Maxim angry with you, I think Ran's snickering had him even angrier."

"Do you know where the kitchen is around here?" Summer asked, changing the subject. "I'm starving. Then I suppose we need to clean Lio up some. He really is getting a bit ripe."

"Yes, the kitchen is this way, and as for Lio, I think the barn idea Maxim had earlier was a good one," Darleen replied, tossing an unreadable look at Lio before turning and leading the way down the hall.

Chapter 24

"Faron told me that you claimed Warrior Rights, and that Maxim Katre acknowledged your right to them," Saige said over lunch. Summer and Darleen were both a little nervous about eating in front of others, but as only Saige had joined them in the kitchen for lunch, they soon relaxed.

"That's true," Summer said. "But truthfully, I only did it as a means to keep Darleen and Lio with me. Maxim wanted to take them both away and I was afraid to let that happen."

"Even so, Warrior Rights is a serious business," Saige said. "I can't believe that Maxim would have granted them unless he believed you to be worthy of them."

"She handled the pain baton as though she knew how to fight with it," Darleen said. "The way she moves is...warrior like."

Saige narrowed her eyes at Summer. "Yes, I can see that," she agreed.

"The closest I have ever come to any weapon before yesterday was reading the books in Father's library," Summer insisted. "I know a lot about weapons because of that, and I know a lot about how they are used, but that's all."

"I think there is more to you than you know, Summer Whitney," Saige said cryptically. "However, the important point here is that you requested Warrior Rights, and they were granted. Therefore, you are required, by Jasani custom and law, *to go armed as the warrior you are*."

"What does that mean exactly?" Summer asked warily.

"It means that you have been granted warrior status, and as such, you must always be ready for battle, and must carry your chosen weapon or tool of battle with you at all times."

"How do you know this?" Summer asked.

"Because I have been granted Warrior Rights," Saige replied.

"But you don't carry a weapon," Summer pointed out. "At least, I've never seen you with one."

"I am proficient in the art of *tiketa*, a form of acrobatic kick-fighting. I do not need to carry a weapon with me because my body itself is my weapon," Saige explained. "Since Clan Jasani are shifters, they don't necessarily need to carry a weapon either, as their alter forms are quite dangerous enough. However, most Clan Jasani will carry a favored weapon on their persons at all times, and all humans in the Jasani military do so as well. Is there a weapon you favor above others?"

Summer shook her head slowly, wondering how she was going to bluff her way through this one. The closest she had ever come to handling a real weapon had been the pain baton the previous day.

"How about you Darleen?" Saige asked.

"Me?" Darleen squeaked in surprise.

Saige smiled. "From what I understand, you also have been granted Warrior Rights, through the Battle Bond," she said. "So yes, you need to carry a weapon as well."

"I have never used a weapon in my life," Darleen objected. "I don't know the first thing about them."

"I suggest that you two take a walk down to the armory this afternoon and see if you can find something that appeals to you. It really is very important that you honor the status granted you by carrying a weapon."

"Just because Maxim agreed to something I asked for on the spur of the moment?" Summer asked doubtfully.

"Maxim Katre is one of the highest ranking officers in the Jasani Military, Summer," Saige said. "If he granted you Warrior Rights, the only person I am aware of who might dare to contradict him would be High Prince Garen, and even he would not do so without good cause."

My name is Alice and I've just fallen down the rabbit hole, Summer thought. *I don't know which potion to drink, or which pill to take, but I wish someone would wake me up before I have to decide.*

"Okay, where exactly is this armory?" Summer asked, knowing she had little choice in this unless she wanted to risk offending a lot of people. People she needed to help her rescue those women on Li-Hach-Cor.

A short time later Summer and Darleen left the Lobos' residence and, following Saige's directions, took the graveled path downhill until it intersected with a wider path obviously intended for vehicles. There was a narrower path alongside it so the women followed that until they topped a low rise and saw a cluster of long, stone buildings in a shallow valley before them.

"So much has changed in the past year," Darleen commented.

"Yes?" Summer asked as they stepped off the path and cut down the slope to the valley floor, wading through the tall grass rather than following the path half way around the valley to the road.

"None of this was here a year ago," Darleen said. "This was all cow pastures. The only buildings that are familiar are the main barn which you can barely see in the distance just south of here, and the Dracons' house which you can just see the roof of over that hill north."

"Wow, that is a lot of changes," Summer said. "It almost looks like a small town in the middle of this valley. Is all of this to protect the Dracon Princes?"

"I think it's to protect Lariah and Saige, and their daughters," Darleen replied. "They each have three now. They are the first female Jasani to be born in thousands of years, and from what I overhead in Lio's office, the Xanti would love to get their hands on them."

"That's awful," Summer said softly, trying to imagine what it would be like to need so much security in order to protect your children. She shuddered at the thought. How did Saige deal with such fear and worry?

Darleen and Summer reached the valley floor and headed for the cluster of buildings. Just as they reached the first building at the far end of the cluster, a side door opened and about a dozen men filed out into a large cleared area. Darleen and Saige slowed their pace as they watched the men organize themselves into neat, orderly rows. A small man wearing a loose robe tied with a sash followed a moment later and took up position in front of the group, facing them. There was something about the man with his dark gray hair and solemn face that drew Summer's attention. She stopped walking without actually realizing it, and stood motionless, unable to take her eyes off of the man.

He spoke rapidly in a language that sounded vaguely familiar to Summer, addressing the class before him. When he was finished speaking he bowed at the waist and waited for his students to copy him. He then removed a long stick that was stuck in the sash at his waist and held it up with both hands at the hilt, his feet shifting into a fighting stance. Every one of his students did the same, until all stood there with their wooden practice swords at the ready. The man then began leading the class in a series of movements that, to Summer, were mesmerizing.

Suddenly, Summer felt as though she were standing outside of herself, watching as another took over her body and mind. This was not frightening, like the Controller, but spiritual and beneficial in some ethereal way that she neither understood nor questioned.

The teacher finished his last movement and Summer felt herself move forward, approaching him with measured steps. When she was only a couple of feet from him, she bowed, her hands together before her in an attitude of prayer.

"May I help you, Miss?" the man asked, speaking Standard.

"Watashi wa Nintai no tame ni kita," Summer said, wondering at herself even as the words left her mouth. She was speaking in Japanese, a language she had only heard spoken a few times in her life, and had never spoken herself. Yet she understood what she had said. *I have come for Patience.*

The teacher...*sensei*, her other self insisted...stared at her for a long moment with his brilliant black eyes. When he spoke, he used Japanese as well.

"Nintai wa, go tochaku no tame ni nagaiai matte iru," Sensei replied. *Patience has waited long for your arrival.*

"Hai, sumimasen. Jikan wa, kappu de sokutei sa reteimasen. Anata wa watashi o tesuto suru ka?" Summer said with another short bow of apology. *Yes, I'm sorry. Time is not measured in cups. Shall you test me?*

"Sore ga hitsuyodesu," Sensei replied, returning her bow. *It is required.*

Sensei turned and spoke to one of the waiting students who raced forward and offered Summer his practice sword. Summer took it, feeling as though she were in a dream, while at the same time knowing she was not. She held the wooden sword in her hand, testing the weight, the balance, the feel of it before gripping it lightly, but firmly, with both hands. Her body turned slightly, her feet shoulder width apart, her balance on the balls of her feet, knees slightly bent.

Sensei moved first, and Summer watched outside of herself with awe as her body met his movement and responded with a counter move. She flowed back and forth across the ground, attacking, defending, advancing, retreating, each movement a part of the one before it and the next to come without a misstep or hesitation. It was a dance unlike anything she had ever seen, and she could barely believe it was her body performing it. After several minutes Sensei ceased moving, and so did Summer, neither of them the slightest bit out of breath from their exertions.

Sensei slipped his wooden sword into his belt and bowed, Summer copying his actions exactly, slipping her wooden sword into the leather belt at her waist as she was not wearing a sash. She then bowed to Sensei in return.

"Please follow me," Sensei said, speaking Standard again.

Summer nodded, feeling once more in full control of her body as she followed the man off of the practice field and into the building, Darleen at her side.

Just inside the doorway Sensei stopped and called out to someone deeper in the building. A thin young man hurried forward, and spoke to Sensei in the same language Summer had used earlier. Only now she did not understand a word either of them were saying. She stood patiently, waiting for whatever was to come, not knowing what it was but aware that something important was taking place.

The assistant took off running and Sensei turned back to Summer.

"What is your name, if I may ask?"

"Natsu," Summer replied without thought. She gave her head a little shake, wondering where that had come from. "Summer," she said. "My name is Summer Whitney."

Sensei smiled, a tiny curving of the corners of his mouth. "I should have guessed it would be such," he said. Summer did not understand his comment, but felt it would be rude to say so.

"Do you know of the double headed dragon?" he asked, his tone mildly curious, but no more.

"No, I'm afraid not," Summer replied.

Another tiny smile. "Again, I should have known. But one day, you shall know, and when that day comes, we shall meet again."

As Sensei finished speaking the young man came running back holding a long, thin package wrapped in what appeared to be red silk. He knelt on the floor and held the package up, balanced across his palms, toward Sensei.

Sensei unwrapped the silk carefully, almost reverently. Summer noticed that he was careful not to touch the object beneath the silk which, she soon realized, was an ancient Japanese sword. When the sword was completely revealed, but still lying on its bed of silk across the young man's palms, Sensei stepped back and waved her forward.

"Patience," he said. "As you have sought her, so she is here, awaiting you these many centuries."

Chapter 25

Summer could hardly tear her eyes from the sword.. *katana* whispered the voice in her mind that she had thought gone. It was so beautiful. The sheath...*saya*...was red lacquer, inset with white jade designs that Summer knew had meaning, though she did not know what the meaning was. She waited a moment to see if the voice would whisper their meaning to her, but this time it remained silent.

She reached out for the katana with both hands, lifting it carefully, understanding that this was an important moment, but not knowing why.

She pulled the katana from the saya just enough to reveal a short expanse of mirror-bright steel blade, razor sharp even after centuries of waiting. She slid the blade home again, shifted it to one hand and bowed deeply to Sensei, holding the bow for a long moment. When she straightened again, Sensei smiled.

"Until we meet again, Miss Summer Whitney," he said softly.

Summer nodded, then turned and left the building, Darleen hurrying to catch up with her. The moment she stepped outside the students, still standing in their formation, bowed to her. Summer returned their bow solemnly, knowing somehow that failing to do so would be a grave insult to them. When she straightened, she removed the wooden practice sword from her belt and returned it to the young man who had loaned it to her. That required some more bowing, but she did it with as much grace as she could muster. When she turned to leave the area, she was startled to find Maxim, Loni and Ran standing a few yards away, watching her.

She wanted very much to turn her back on them and walk the other way. Much had just happened to her that was surprising and confusing, and she wanted time to think about it. But if she turned around now it would be blatantly rude, and once again, much as she wanted to, she couldn't bring herself to do it. She approached the Katres, her step now reluctant.

"Hello," she said, feeling self-conscious with the katana in her hands.

"You are most skilled," Maxim said. "It was a joy to watch you dance with Sensei."

"You must have studied most of your life to attain such skill," Ran said.

Summer felt her face heat. She wanted to tell them the truth, which was that she had never even seen a katana before in real life, let alone practiced with one. But she didn't think they would believe her after what they had just witnessed. She wasn't sure she would have believed it herself.

"We would accompany you to the armory, if you don't mind," Maxim said. "We would be honored to assist you in selecting and fitting a back harness for your katana."

Back harness? Summer thought. She automatically began flipping through her store of weapons knowledge, but quickly gave it up. She was too overwhelmed and confused at the moment. She would just wing it.

"Okay," she said.

Maxim stepped aside, indicating the correct direction, and Summer started walking. Again she had that strange sense that walking with the Katres in this way was close to normal, but not exactly right.

"What was that all about?" Darleen asked in a low voice as Summer headed toward what she thought was the correct building.

"I'm not altogether certain," she admitted as they walked past a long building that, from the aromas pouring from it, she thought must be a cafeteria.

"Yooo-hooo!" Summer turned toward the high-pitched voice coming from the doorway of the cafeteria and was surprised to see a large woman with frizzy brown hair hurrying toward them at a fast waddle. Summer had never seen such a large woman before and was shocked by the sight. She had read about the disease of obesity which had once plagued humans centuries past, but it had been treatable through basic metabolic management for so long that it rarely occurred any more. She schooled her features and admonished herself not to stare as the woman reached them, breathless and red cheeked from her short trip.

"So there you are," the woman said, ignoring Summer and Darleen completely as she planted her hands on her ample hips and addressed Maxim. "I've been waiting for you to join me for lunch, and here I see you sniffing after these two females like adolescent boys instead. Well, I'm sure they're no better than they should be, so just you let them go on their way and you come and sit with me now."

Summer's breath caught in her throat at the woman's rudeness. She turned to look at Maxim, Loni and Ran, wondering who the woman was, and whether they would stand for being ordered about like errant children.

Ran and Loni were stony faced, but did not seem particularly shocked by the woman. Maxim, on the other hand, had the strangest expression on his face as he looked from the woman to Summer, then back again. Without thought, Summer reached for Maxim's emotions and was surprised to discover that his strongest feeling at the moment seemed to be deep confusion.

"Well, are you going to keep me standing in the street all day while you just stare?" the woman demanded. "Let's go now."

"Do not presume to give me orders, Mara," Maxim said, his voice low, but blade sharp.

"Do not call me Mara," the woman retorted, not in the least bit cowed by Maxim's tone. "I am your mother and you will address me as such."

Summer nearly gasped at that. This woman was their mother? Summer looked at her more carefully, but saw no resemblance at all.

"It you will excuse me, I have other matters to attend to," Maxim replied coldly. He turned to Summer.

"Shall we continue?" he asked politely, ignoring Mara's retort that she did not, in fact, excuse him at all.

"Um, yes, of course," Summer stammered. She glanced at Mara, whose face was white with rage, then turned and headed for the armory, her head buzzing with questions that she knew she couldn't ask.

She heard Mara's voice behind her, but could not understand anything the woman was saying. Considering what had already left the woman's mouth, she wasn't really all that interested in hearing more anyway.

Summer stepped onto a long, narrow porch of the building she was fairly certain was the armory, wondering why they didn't put signs out for those new to the place. She reached for the door, but Maxim was faster. He turned the knob and pushed the door open for her, then stepped back.

"Thank you," Summer said.

Maxim bowed his head and Summer stepped through the door, Darleen right behind her. She paused a moment for her eyes to adjust to the dim interior, and couldn't help but overhear Maxim as he spoke softly to a man who was standing just inside the doorway. She was not altogether surprised that Maxim was telling the man to prevent Mara from entering the building, but she still found it difficult to believe.

"Gardez donc," Summer exclaimed softly as her eyes became more attuned to the light, surprised at the number and variety of weapons laid out before her. There were hand guns, rifles and even field artillery of

every size and description from those that shot particle beams and lasers, to those that fired projectiles and darts. There were knives, swords, and axes, as well as batons, staffs, bows, spears, pikes, halberds and such a wide variety of throwing weapons that she couldn't take them all in.

In spite of the number of books she had read on the subject of weapons, there were still many of them that were totally unfamiliar to her. Some items were similar enough to others that she could make a guess as to their usage. Others she could only wonder at.

"I suppose the best thing for me would be a hand laser," Darleen said doubtfully. "Something simple that I can learn to use quickly, but which won't require skill to operate."

"That would be wise," Maxim said politely. He looked up and waved a hand, calling a human clerk forward.

"Greetings, Lord Commander," the man said with a polite bow. "How may I be of assistance?"

"Greetings," Maxim replied. "If you would, please assist Miss Flowers in the selection of a hand weapon. Something light-weight and suited for her small hands."

"Of course, Lord Commander," the man replied. "It would be my pleasure."

"Summer, if you will come with me, I will assist you in selecting a back harness for your katana," Maxim said.

"You okay?" Summer asked Darleen.

"Yes, of course," Darleen replied with a nod. "You go ahead."

Summer turned to Maxim. "Lead the way," she said.

Maxim turned and headed for a different section, Summer at his heels. She smiled when they turned into an aisle that held racks of katanas, sabers, swords and knives, as well as a variety of harnesses, scabbards and belts designed to hold them. Maxim studied a display of such things for a few moments, then reached for one that was a deep, midnight blue with a design stitched along the shoulder straps. He held it up and Summer reached out to run one finger along a strap.

"I think this is a phoenix," she said as she studied the design closely.

"I am not familiar with that bird, but I think it suits you," Maxim said quietly. "If you like it?"

"Yes, I like it very much," Summer replied.

Maxim smiled, an expression that nearly caused Summer to gasp aloud. She was glad that he chose that moment to begin adjusting the straps on the harness and was not looking at her, as it took her a few moments to wipe the shock from her face.

"I think this will do," Maxim said, holding the harness up. "Turn around, please," he said. Summer turned and allowed Maxim to put the harness on her, holding out her arms as he requested while he made some final adjustments.

"Now, raise the katana over your head and slip it into the harness, the blade facing your left," he said.

Summer followed his instructions, missing the loops meant to hold the katana the first two times she tried it. Maxim made further adjustments until she could slip the blade into the loops in one smooth motion, and remove it just as easily.

"Try that a few more times, and let me know if anything catches in the slightest degree," Maxim suggested. Summer nodded and did as he said, practicing the movements repeatedly until she could both draw the katana, and sheath it in one easy move.

"I think it's perfect," she said finally, as she looked up to find Maxim nowhere in sight. She turned around and spotted him further up the aisle, standing before an array of giant battle axes. Summer joined him, watching as he reached out and stroked the handle of a slender, almost graceful looking axe with a recurved blade and a carved wooden handle.

"This was no axe," Maxim murmured softly.

Summer frowned at the axe, then looked to Maxim. "What is it then?" she asked.

Maxim's gaze flew to her as he withdrew his finger from the axe. "Excuse me?" he asked, clearly startled by her presence and her question.

"You said it was not an axe," Summer said. "I just wondered what it was."

Maxim smiled faintly. "I owe you an apology, Summer Whitney," he said.

"For what?" Summer asked.

"Mara," he said, his teeth clicking together as though he had to bite the word to get it out.

"Why should you apologize for another's actions?" Summer asked.

"She is our mother."

"That does not make you responsible for what she does or says. It does not appear as though you have a very good relationship with her," Summer said, unable to prevent herself from fishing just a little.

"No, I do not," Maxim replied. Summer thought she caught a note of sadness in his voice, but from the cool expression on his face, she was sure she was mistaken.

"I'm sorry," Summer said.

Maxim frowned, opened his mouth as though to speak, then closed it again. Summer suddenly understood.

"She is the reason you do not like me, isn't she?" she asked.

"I do not dislike you," Maxim argued. "But, I admit that she is the reason I have been so critical of you."

Summer nodded. "You think that I am like her."

Maxim opened his mouth but Summer held up a hand. "No, please do not deny it," she said, her voice gentle in spite of the sudden sharp pain in her heart. "I am who I am, Maxim. If I were able to continue pretending to be someone else, perhaps you would feel differently about me. But I cannot."

Summer swallowed hard around the lump in her throat and blinked against the sudden sting in her eyes. "I thank you, Maxim Katre, for assisting me with the harness. It was most kind of you. If you will excuse me, I must leave now."

With that, Summer turned and walked almost blindly back down the aisle to the front of the armory. She barely noticed Darleen standing by the door waiting for her. She fished around in her pocket for the transaction card she had found in her luggage that morning, and offered it to the young man who had assisted Darleen.

"There is no charge to you, ma'am," the man said politely. Summer wanted to ask why but knew that if she spoke, the dam would break and the tears would flow. She could only nod as she turned toward the door and hurried out of the armory, shoving the card back into her pocket as she all but ran through the cluster of buildings, back across the valley toward the gravel path, and some semblance of privacy.

Chapter 26

Mara watched Ran and Loni as they followed the tall, dark haired woman with their eyes as she raced by.

"I sincerely hope that you are not going to tell me you want to mate with that female," she said snidely. Her sons tore their gazes from the other woman and looked back at her in surprise, as she had intended.

"She is too skinny, too tall, and her hair is so long it looks positively uncivilized. Besides which, her face is ugly. Especially her nose with that great lump in the middle of it. What is wrong with it anyway? Is she deformed? I have no wish for ugly grandsons. If you must mate, you had better pick someone at least passably pretty. I warn you now that I will not tolerate any offspring from that female."

"When did you become so foul, Mother?" Loni asked, his voice calm as always, though his eyes warned her that she had, again, gone too far. First Ran, then Maxim, now Loni. What was wrong with her? she wondered. She seemed unable to curb her tongue at all lately. Well, that is what stress will do, she thought.

She opened her mouth to again call on her loneliness as an excuse, but Loni shook his head. "Good day, Mother," he said shortly.

With that, Loni offered her a short bow that was the bare minimum of politeness and strode away without a backward glance, Ran at his side. She watched them in surprise until they entered the armory. Well, she told herself, at least they had not followed after that woman.

Thinking of the dark haired woman caused her to turn and look after her, noting with satisfaction that she was still moving quickly out of the valley and had nearly reached the gravel path back to wherever she had come from, the black cloaked figure limping along at her side. Mara wondered who the woman was, and why her sons seemed to be interested in her, then decided it did not matter. Should they try to mate with the woman, Mara was fully confident in her abilities to drive her away. With that happy thought, she put the matter out of her mind.

She stood there for a few moments, trying to decide what to do next. She had been trying to come up with some idea to get herself into the Dracons' home all morning long, and so far she had failed. In the end, she thought perhaps another lunch would help her to think so she turned to go back into the cafeteria. She glanced up once more to see that the dark haired woman was nearly out of the valley, and caught a glimpse of something in the distance as she turned. She turned back and gasped aloud. Finally, her luck was in.

Just there, strolling through the grass and heading in her direction, were several figures. One, a petite woman with long red-gold hair was walking behind three toddling children. Behind them paced a gigantic dog with black and gold stripes in his fur, harnessed to a small wooden wagon. Surrounding the group were three warriors, all alert, but obviously enjoying their duty as they watched the children toddle along in the grass.

Mara was afraid of the dog, Tiny, but as he was harnessed to the wagon, she thought she would be safe from him. She knew that the children often rode in the wagon and that the dog pulled it, which she personally thought was outrageous. Just a fancy show for the upstart princess and her oh-so-precious daughters. Even from where she stood, Mara could see that all three of the children had their mother's ugly red hair. Ugh. If she'd been born with red hair, she'd either dye it, or go bald, Mara thought disdainfully.

Mara studied the small procession carefully as it grew closer to the double row of buildings, noting with some concern that they were not, apparently, going to visit any of them. Instead, they appeared to be skirting the more populated area, and the crowd of people gathering to watch politely from a distance. Mara realized that they were only cutting through the valley, probably on their way to the Lobos' home on the other side.

She began walking casually toward the building at the far end, keeping the Dracon children in sight as she went. Before long she was slightly ahead of them, and noted with some relief that they would actually pass quite close to the building where she was headed. She reached into her pocket and felt the familiar object she had been carrying on each visit to the ranch for nearly a year as she reached a spot just beyond the corner of the building. From her position she could see the children, but would not be easily seen herself. She slipped the cap off of the object in her hand with a practiced motion, and gripped it carefully between her fingers. Then she waited.

Lariah Dracon laughed as her youngest daughter, Tani, tumbled head over heels in the thick blue grass. The little girl sat up, lifted her face to the sky and laughed happily. Nothing ever seemed to bother Tani. She always found joy in everything her world had to offer.

Lariah's vox beeped softly in her ear and she reached up to tap it, still grinning as her eldest daughter, Salene, toddled over to Tani and tried to help her littlest sister to her feet.

"Yes?"

"Have you guys left yet, Lari?" Saige asked.

"Yes, we're about half way through the valley now," Lariah replied. "Something wrong?"

"No, just curious," Saige said. "I think I'll come down and meet you half way."

Lariah opened her mouth to reply when several things happened at once. First, she noticed that her middle daughter, Rayne, had wandered a bit far from the rest of the group, nearing the back of one of the new buildings. The guard who would have normally herded her back was helping Salene and Tani get back to their feet after Salene's attempt to help had landed them both in a tangled, giggling pile.

The next thing she noticed from the corner of her eye was a very large figure darting away from the building toward Rayne, just as Tiny began growling furiously, sending her a mental warning of danger. Lariah spun toward Rayne and the figure, which she now realized was a large woman, just as the woman grabbed hold of Rayne, causing the usually calm child to scream.

Lariah's dracon burst forth at the terror and pain in her daughter's voice. One second she was a human female, small and delicate, the next she was a fifteen foot long dracon with a mouth full of sharp teeth whose only reason for not incinerating the offending woman instantly was that her daughter was too close to avoid harm.

The woman released Rayne, dropping her carelessly to the grass as she started to turn back toward the building, only to freeze when she looked up to see a gigantic, leopard spotted dracon standing over her. When the woman started to take a step back, Lariah lifted her head and roared her fury into the sky. The woman stilled, her heart racing so fast that Lariah's sensitive dracon ears had no problem hearing it.

A fraction of a second later, the scent of Rayne's blood reached the dracon's sensitive nose, enraging it to the point where Lariah had to struggle to hold it in check. It wanted nothing more than to bite the woman in half. Instead she stood close to the woman, her fangs bared, growling softly as a warning to the woman not to move.

"We are on our way sharali," Garen said into Lariah's mind. *"What has happened?"*

"A woman has harmed Rayne," Lariah replied, unable to provide further details. She was too angry to think in words at the moment. The sound of racing paws reached Lariah and she was glad to know that Saige was on her way as well. Lariah had managed to hold the dracon in check so far, but she still wasn't altogether certain she was capable of forcing it to allow the woman to live.

"I'm sorry," the woman said, but neither Lariah, nor her dracon, wanted to hear a word. She growled furiously, loud enough to cause the ground to shake. The woman shut her mouth and said nothing more.

Three soft popping sounds announced the arrival of Lariah's men, Garen, Treyen and Valen, the Royal Princes of Jasan.

"Please return to human form," Garen said softly. Lariah's dracon growled again, but did as her mate asked. As soon as she was back in her human form Lariah bent to pick Rayne up off the ground, cuddling the sniffling child close to her. She looked to her other two daughters, relieved to see that Trey already had Salene in his arms, and Val had Tani.

"Explain to me why my daughter's blood scents the air," Garen commanded the woman, his voice a rumbling growl of anger.

"I have no idea what you are speaking of," Mara said. "I just meant to pick the child up when that crazy woman of yours started...."

Garen threw his head back and roared with fury as he shifted from human to dracon, then back again. "You dare to insult the Princess to my face?" he demanded as soon as he was back in his human form.

Mara swallowed hard. "I apologize, High Prince," she said. "I am frightened, and when I get frightened, my tongue gets carried away."

Mara's eyes widened as a gigantic, black and white striped wolf wove its way through the gathering crowd as it stalked toward her, its pale green eyes fixed on her face. Mara knew that somehow, that animal could see right through her. She started to take a step back when another voice growled from behind her. "Do not move," Maxim warned.

Mara spun around to face her eldest son, ignoring his warning. "Maxim, explain who I am," she ordered him imperiously. "This is getting ridiculous. I am being treated like a criminal and I've done nothing wrong."

Maxim placed large hands on his mother's shoulders and, gently but firmly, turned her back around to face her accusers. "Do not move again," he said softly, his voice so cold that Mara actually shivered.

This was not going well. She had thought she could bluster and bully her way out of this, but she had underestimated the Princess. She had never guessed the little snip of a thing could, or would, show such rage.

And she had certainly never imagined that the Princes themselves would show up over the matter of one squalling brat.

"Rayne has a spot of blood on her arm," Lariah said. "Check that woman for needles."

Mara blanched. "That's..." Mara fell silent at Garen's upheld hand.

"If you speak again I may rip out your tongue," he growled.

No, Mara thought, this was not going well at all.

Maxim reached for her wrists and held them up in a loose, but unbreakable grip. Mara didn't bother to struggle. She knew there was no use in it. Instead she waited for her son to find the tiny device still tucked between the fingers of her right hand that she had not had a chance to hide.

Her mind raced, grasping for an excuse, an explanation, anything that would get her out of this current mess, but she could not think of a single thing to say in her own defense. She looked up, her gaze meeting the clear eyes of the huge wolf once again as Maxim carefully removed the collection device from her hand and held it out to High Prince Garen.

"A blood collection device," Garen growled softly as he took the device from Maxim. "Now, I wonder, why would you want a sample of Princess Rayne's blood?"

The giant wolf suddenly began to shrink until it became a woman with short brown hair, and the same green eyes as the wolf. Mara suddenly hated the eyes, the wolf, and the woman.

"This woman's heart is foul," Saige said as she approached, her gaze never flinching from Mara's. "It is filled with jealousy, envy, greed and hate. She has no kindness in her, nor any compassion." Saige walked around Mara slowly. When she was once again facing her she frowned. "She has not always been as she is. But her choices have set her feet upon a path that can not be recalled, and she is far past redemption."

Saige looked beyond Mara, her gaze resting on Maxim for a long moment before she turned to Garen. "High Prince," she said, her voice ringing clear for all to hear, "It is with sorrow in my heart for your loyal subjects, Clan Katre, that I must tell you there is no good remaining in this woman. She is as a viper at your back." Saige bowed to Garen, then turned and bowed to Maxim. "I am sorry, Lord Commander," she said softly.

To the surprise of all, Maxim offered Saige a sad smile. "Do not feel sorrow, Arima Lobo," he said. "You cannot change the heart you see."

He released his mother and stepped away from her before turning to Prince Garen. "High Prince, I ask that we be granted permission to perform *moztu-oku* on this one who was once a Mother to us."

Garen glared at Mara for another long moment, then turned his gaze to Maxim. "Clan Katre has ever been noble and loyal," he said. "For that reason, your request is granted."

Maxim, Lonim and Ranim all bowed to High Prince Garen in gratitude. Then, turning so that they formed a triangle, each facing the other, they began speaking in the ancient tongue.

This was the *moztu-oku*, a ritual of denouncement that, once complete, was irreversible. All present remained silent out of respect for the Katres, and this most serious and solemn ritual. Almost all.

Mara turned to watch her sons with narrowed eyes. "No, not that again," she hissed, "stop that right this moment." But they continued as though they did not hear her, as though they did not even see her.

When the ritual was complete, Maxim called forth a Falcoran male-set from the crowd. "Please arrest this woman, now called Amara Winicke, and place her in a holding cell. She is to speak to no one, nor is she to have visitors, nor access to any communication device. She is charged with treason for her attack on the Royal Daughter, Princess Rayne Dracon, and is to be held for trial."

"Maxim, what are you talking about?" Mara said, using her best wheedling voice since her objections and protests had not worked. "I did not attack that child. This is all just a misunderstanding. I only..."

Maxim turned his back on the woman who had once been his mother and walked away, Ran and Loni each a half pace behind him, Ran on the right, Loni on the left, as always. He wasn't sure where he was going. He only knew that he had to get the three of them away from Mara. Everything else, he would deal with later.

Chapter 27

Summer watched the scene below with growing horror. She had just reached the top of the low rise at the edge of the valley when Lariah's roar caused her to turn back in surprise. She had been so shocked to see what looked like a dragon in the valley below that, at first, she hadn't realized that the person the dragon was standing over was Mara. It had to be Mara, she told herself, as Mara was the only woman of that size she had ever seen.

"Darleen, please tell me that you see a dragon down there too," she said weakly.

"Not a dragon," Darleen said. "A dracon. That's Lariah Dracon, if I'm not mistaken."

"Lariah?" Summer asked. "Do you mean the Princess? That Lariah?"

Darleen nodded. "Oops, the Princes just arrived as well," she said. "I don't know what that woman did, but she's in deep now."

Summer shook her head at the sight of three huge men with long, blue black hair suddenly appearing from out of nowhere. Then the dragon...or rather, dracon, shrank into the form of a petite woman with red-gold hair who bent down to pick up a small child. Then one of the men suddenly exploded, taking the shape of a dracon that was much larger than the first one had been. The dracon roared angrily, then returned to human shape.

Summer's knees gave way in shock and she sat down suddenly on the blue grass. What the heck is going on here? She wondered. She felt a rapid vibration in the ground beneath her and looked up in time to see a gigantic wolf race by not twenty yards from where she sat. Well, she thought, it sort of looked like a wolf. If a wolf was eight feet tall at the shoulder and had black and white stripes.

If the Red Queen wanders by yelling "off with their heads," I am in big, big trouble, she thought.

The striped wolf ran across the valley, slowing only when it reached the crowd of people collecting around Mara and the Princes. Then she saw Maxim, Loni and Ran make their way toward Mara. She felt their fear for their mother, and their worry.

Summer turned her gaze back to the wolf in time to see it transform into Saige. She gasped aloud. "Okay, what the hell is going on here?" she demanded.

Darleen sat down next to her. "I take it you didn't know that Clan Jasani are shifters," she said calmly.

"Shifters?" Summer asked faintly.

"Yes, shifters," Darleen repeated. "There are seven Clans. The Dracons are the royal family, and turn into what you called a dragon. The Lobos turn into that big striped wolf you just saw Saige transform from. There are also the Bearens, the Falcorans, the Gryphons and the Vulpirans."

"And the Katres?" Summer asked.

"Yes, the Katres as well," Darleen said. "I cannot tell you what they look like when they shift because I have never seen them, but I believe it is a large cat-like animal."

Ah, the Cheshire cat makes its appearance," Summer thought. *I wonder when the rabbit will show up?*

Summer gave her head a sharp shake and turned back to watch the scene in the valley below. Gradually, the emotions she sensed from the Katres changed from fear and worry to anger, then sorrow and, finally, resignation. Their mother had done something horrible. Something really, really horrible. Her heart grew heavy as it filled with tears for them.

As they continued to watch, the Katres stepped away from Mara and formed a circle, then they all appeared to be speaking at once. It looked like some sort of ritual to Summer, but she was too far away to be sure.

"How is it that Lariah and Saige shift?" Summer asked a few moments later as she watched the Katres turn and leave the scene below. "I know that Saige was human when I met her." She thought about that a moment, then sighed. "Actually, I don't know that at all. I assumed it. She could have been part bat for all I know."

"I honestly do not know," Darleen said. "Very little is known about such things outside of the Clan Jasani themselves. I do know that, in thousands of years, only Saige and Lariah have ever given birth to daughters. And I know that Lariah was the first Arima to be found in millennia, just as Saige was the second. I believe you are the third."

"But you cannot tell me what an Arima is?" Summer asked hopefully.

"I could, but I have said I wouldn't," Darleen replied slowly. "At the same time, it doesn't appear that anyone else is going to tell you, and I think you have a right to know. Frankly, I'm torn on that one."

"Do not worry, Miss Flowers," Maxim said, startling both of them. They leapt to their feet and spun around, Darleen stumbling over the whirling folds of her cloak and losing her balance. Loni leapt forward so quickly that Summer barely saw him move, catching Darleen before she tumbled backward down the hill.

"Thank you," Darleen said breathlessly.

When he was certain she had her balance back, Loni bowed and stepped back with his brothers.

"We apologize for startling you," Maxim said. "And I thank you, Miss Flowers, for not telling Summer what you, rightly, felt she should know. I assure you, we will not keep her in the dark any longer."

"I imagine you would prefer privacy for this," Darleen said.

"If you would not mind," Maxim replied.

Darleen looked to Summer, who hesitated. She reached out for the Katres' emotions and discovered that they were all a little sad, but not angry.

"It's all right, Darleen," she said. "You go on back to the house and I will meet you there later." Darleen turned and left, her uneven footsteps on the gravel fading quickly to silence.

"I don't know exactly what happened down there," Summer said, "but it appears to have involved your mother, and I am sorry for that."

"She is no longer such to us," Ran said sharply. He immediately looked contrite. "I apologize," he said. "I have no cause to speak to you in such a manner."

Summer shrugged, a tiny lift of her shoulders. "It's okay," she said. "I didn't know it was possible to sever a relationship with your own mother though."

None of the Katres seemed willing to discuss that matter, so Summer changed subjects. "I know you have something to tell me, but before you do, may I ask you a question?"

"Certainly," Maxim replied, his tone agreeable enough, though his golden eyes looked wary.

"Apparently most of the people around here are shifters of one sort or another. Are you?"

"Yes, we are," Maxim replied. "Our alter form is an animal we call the katrenca. It is much like what I believe you would call a feline."

Summer snorted. "Somehow, I don't think you turn into fluffy white Persians," she muttered.

Maxim cocked his head slightly. "I do not know what a *fluffy white Persian* is, but if you like, we can show you our alter form now."

"Yes, please," Summer replied. "If you wouldn't mind."

Maxim turned to Ran and Loni. Ran shrugged and stepped several feet away. He smiled briefly at Summer, and called his katrenca.

Summer's eyes widened as Ran quickly expanded, his shape changing from that of a tall man to a gigantic cat. He was easily ten feet tall at the shoulder, and perhaps twenty feet long, not counting his tail. He had thick, golden fur and large golden eyes, the same color as his hair and eyes when he was in his human form. But, though he had the coloring of an Earth lion, he looked more like a panther to Summer. Well, with the exception of the long fangs and the short, sharply pointed horns set just above his ears.

Summer walked toward him slowly, reaching out to run her fingers through the thick, silky fur on his foreleg. His paws were far larger than her head and spiked with long, scimitar-like claws, but for some reason, she felt not the slightest hint of fear. She knew he would never harm her, or allow her to be harmed. In fact, she was so certain of that, that it never crossed her mind to wonder about it as she reached out with both hands to rub Ran's thick fur.

After she had a few minutes to drink her fill of him in his katrenca form, Ran shifted back to human.

"I am glad that you felt no fear of me," Ran said.

Summer smiled at him, but could not think of a single thing to say that was remotely appropriate, so she said nothing at all.

"Summer, there are many things that we must discuss with you," Maxim said. "However, before we begin, there is one thing in particular that I wish to clear up first."

"All right," Summer said, feeling wary herself now. It seemed to her that whenever Maxim had something to say to her, it was unkind or angry.

"Earlier, in the armory, you misunderstood my meaning when I spoke of Mara, and left before I had a chance to explain. I wish to explain now, if you will allow me to do so."

"Of course," Summer said nervously.

"I did compare you to Mara," he said. "As you guessed. And, as I am certain you noticed, she is not a kind woman. She spent five hundred years making our fathers miserable with her sharp tongue. When we met you yesterday morning, and you argued with me about Darleen and Lio, I became convinced that you were the same as Mara.

"However, the moment I saw the two of you together, I realized how wrong I was. You are not remotely like Mara. It was my worry, and my imagination, that got the better of my common sense, and for that I apologize to you most profusely."

Summer shook her head in shock. Maxim sighed and took a step back. "I suppose I cannot blame you," he said.

Summer frowned. "For what?"

"For not forgiving me," he said.

"I do not understand why it would matter to you what kind of person I am," Summer said, "nor do I understand why I seem to care what you think of me. But, that aside, I have to admit that, while I did not see much of your...er...Mara, from what I did see, I can't say I blame you for your concerns. So, of course I forgive you."

"Then why were you shaking your head?" Ran asked curiously.

"Because I thought Maxim said that Mara made your fathers unhappy for five hundred years," Summer explained with a smile. "Obviously I misheard you."

"No, you did not," Maxim said. "As I said, we have much to discuss with you. If you do not mind, we would prefer to do it inside."

"Inside?" Summer asked.

"Yes. It is growing cold and I think you would be more comfortable indoors."

"Okay, inside sounds good to me," Summer agreed. "Should we go back to the Lobos' home?"

"We can, if that is what you wish," Maxim replied. "We also have a house nearby which we would prefer to use, if you do not object."

"You have a house here?" Summer asked. "I thought this was the Dracons' ranch."

"It is," Ran said. "We are honored to be distantly related to the Princess, Lariah Dracon. As a courtesy to Clan Katre, our Princes built a house for us, and our great-uncle, Eldar Hamat, to use when we visit."

Summer thought that she should be hesitant to be alone with these men in their own home, but she wasn't. Just the opposite, in fact. She didn't think there was any other place on Jasan where she would be more safe. And she was curious about the change in feelings she sensed coming from all three of the Katres, especially Maxim.

"All right, let's go there then," Summer agreed, shivering a little as the wind began to pick up.

"We can travel much faster if you will allow one of us to carry you," Maxim offered.

"That super-speed thing that Loni did when he caught Darleen?" Summer asked, grinning.

"Yes, that *super-speed thing,*" Maxim replied with a grin of his own, the first one she had ever seen on his face.

"Sounds like fun," Summer said.

Maxim stepped forward and lifted Summer into his arms, pulling her close against his chest. Summer felt a thrill of arousal rush through her body at his touch and ducked her head, hoping to hide her sudden blush.

"Are you sure I'm not too heavy for you?" she asked, wondering nervously if he had the senses of a cat while in his human form. If he did, if *they* did, then she thought it likely they could scent her arousal. Oh well, she thought, not much I can do about it if they can.

"No, you are not heavy at all," Maxim replied.

He pulled her even closer against his chest and suddenly, the strangest sensation came over her. It was so strange that it took her a moment to identify the feeling. She felt connected somehow. Cared for. She gave her head a tiny shake, reminding herself that, up until the past hour or so, this man holding her close against his body had given every indication of disliking her intensely. She mentally reviewed every harsh look and sharp comment he had directed at her, but it didn't change a thing. The strange, good feelings remained.

"Are you ready?" Maxim asked.

Summer opened her mouth to answer him but found she couldn't speak. Her emotions were simply too overwhelming at the moment. She nodded instead, hoping that would suffice. Evidently it did as Maxim turned around until they were facing away from the Lobos' house, and then took off running. He moved so fast that Summer saw nothing but a blur as they moved past grass, trees and, she thought, a couple of buildings. Within seconds Maxim slowed down, then stopped altogether.

Summer took a deep breath, realizing that she hadn't breathed at all while they were moving.

"Oh my goodness*!*" she gasped. "How do you move so quickly? Is it part of being a shifter?"

"No," Maxim replied as he set her down on the front porch of the house the Dracons had built for the Katre's use. "It is part of being Clan Jasani."

Summer lifted a brow and waited for more. This time, Maxim took the gesture for what it was. She was not being demanding, she was merely curious. As a Katre with a katrenca alter form, he understood curiosity very well. It was a universal trait for those of his Clan.

"Katrencas are exceptionally fast, to begin with," he explained. "In addition, all male Jasani are born with the ability to use magic. We happen to be strongest in Air and Earth magic. It is the Air magic that allows us to greatly increase our natural speed."

Summer thought about that as she followed Ran into the house, then waited until Loni turned on the lights before moving further inside.

"As I understand it, true magic is the control of the four elements, Earth, Air, Fire and Water," she said as she gazed around the living room. Summer was not very domestic, but the overstuffed furniture and the warm glow of polished wood gave her a feeling of instant comfort.

"That is correct," Maxim replied as he guided her to a chair near a large stone fireplace and helped her to remove her katana harness. Ran set a thick log on the grate in the fireplace, stepped back and waved his hand. The log burst into flame, providing instant warmth. Summer smiled.

"I guess that's a fairly good indication of your ability to control fire," she said. Summer fell silent for a long moment which caught the Katres' attention. She seemed to be simply sitting there, gazing blankly into space, but Maxim had the sense that the distant look in her eye indicated intense focus. After a few moments, she proved him correct.

"According to Mother's books, she was only able to prove magical ability in two species, and one of those was questionable," she said as though she hadn't paused at all.

"What were you doing?" Ran asked curiously.

"Oops," Summer said softly. "I'm sorry. I don't usually do that in front of people."

"Do what?" Maxim asked, as curious as Ran.

"As I said earlier today, I remember everything I've ever read, seen, heard or said," Summer replied. "But, I've read a LOT of books on a very wide variety of subjects. Sometimes I have to sort of...leaf through them to find what I'm looking for. When I do that, it's like I'm actually seeing the books in my mind, so I kind of glaze over a bit."

"What's it like to be able to remember everything?" Ran asked.

"What's it like to be able to wave your hand and start a fire?" she asked back.

"Point taken," Ran replied with a grin."

"Which species did your Mother prove had magic?" Maxim asked.

"There is a population of humanoids on Sauria 2 who are apparently able to manipulate Fire and Earth to some extent. However, since they cannot control Air or Water, Mother believed that theirs was more likely a telekinetic ability than a magical one.

"The other species are known only as the Spellcasters of Warneb. They are very secretive and won't reveal their true names to out-worlders. They use a lot of magic in their everyday lives, and shun technology."

"She did not list the Jasani as users of magic?" Loni asked quietly.

Summer felt Loni's curiosity, and his deep inner calm, though neither trait showed on his face. On the surface, he looked as though he felt nothing at all.

"No, she did not mention the Jasani," she replied. "She did say that there is very little known about Clan Jasani, and she was right. I originally came here as a Candy Bride, and I did a lot of research both before and after I made that decision. I didn't find much information, and I never came across a word about magic, or shifters."

Maxim's brows rose in surprise. "That is interesting," he said. "There are many aspects of our history, and our lives, that we keep to ourselves. But we do not hide the fact that we wield magic, nor the fact that we are shifters. To try to do so would be impossible since we regularly encourage human women to come here to mate with our male-sets, and of those who come, few remain."

"Do you usually inform the women that you're shifters before they marry?" Summer asked.

Maxim's brows lowered instantly. "Now, don't get angry," Summer said quickly. "I am not trying to be insulting. I have a reason for my question."

Maxim shook his head at himself. He didn't understand why he was so quick to lose his temper with Summer when he normally rarely lost his temper at all. No, he amended. Now that he thought about it, he realized that over the past year he had grown very temperamental.

"Yes, females are always told the truth before mating," he answered. "That is the reason the majority of them change their minds about mating and leave Jasan."

"That really doesn't make much sense," Summer said with a frown.

"I assure you, it's true," Maxim replied a little stiffly.

Summer glanced at Maxim in surprise, replaying the last comments in her head. "I'm sorry Maxim, that isn't what I meant," she said quickly, wondering if they would always have such trouble understanding each other. "What makes no sense to me is, why isn't it common knowledge that Jasani are shifters? You guys tell a potential mate that you're shifters, she freaks and hops on the next liner home, and then...what?

She never tells anyone about it? *None* of them ever tell anyone about it? *Ever*?"

Maxim was stunned. Why had none of them ever realized this before? It seemed so simple and obvious now that Summer had pointed it out, yet none of his people had ever once considered it.

"We must be a species of fools that we never realized that before," he said, shaking his head.

"I do not think you are fools," Summer argued. "I think that you live here, on Jasan. What is, or is not, common knowledge on other worlds is not exactly the most important bit of information in your daily life."

"Nevertheless, it is a very important fact that we never noticed," Maxim said. "And it is also troublesome."

"Yes, I agree," Summer said. "Do you keep records of the women who come here, and then leave?"

"To some extent, yes," Maxim said. "We will contact the council in the morning and discuss this matter at length. For now however, we would like to get back to the reason why we brought you here."

"All right," Summer replied hesitantly. This time Maxim understood, and did not take offense.

"Do not worry," he said. "I give you my word that this subject will be addressed with all seriousness. I will not forget."

"Thank you," Summer replied. "And yes, I would like to know more about why you brought me here."

"I think I should tell you about our history first," Maxim said slowly. "Things that we do not generally tell those who are not Clan Jasani."

Even as he spoke, it suddenly occurred to Maxim that if Summer did not like the things he was about to tell her, she could simply stand up and walk out of their lives. Forever. And there would not be a single thing they could do to stop her. He had been so busy trying to decide whether they should accept her, it had not occurred to him that she might very well refuse to accept them. It was a very humbling thought and it caused him to fall silent for a long moment as he struggled with it.

"Is something wrong?" Summer asked after a moment.

Maxim shook his head quickly. "No, nothing," he said. "I apologize, I was...thinking where to begin."

"Okay," Summer replied slowly, wondering why he was lying to her. "You said your history."

"Yes of course," Maxim said. He cleared his throat, feeling nervous all of a sudden. "Over three thousand years ago, our home world was destroyed," he began. "There was barely enough time for some of our people to escape in pods, which were sent out in hopes that at least some might survive.

"Several pods landed here, on this planet that the survivors named Jasan. Unfortunately, all of the survivors were male. There was not a single female among them, and, for a time, it was thought that our race was doomed after all. A few males who were still very strong in magic were able to travel to other worlds. They split up, a few of them searching for survivors, the others searching for females of a race compatible with our own. They found what they were searching for on a distant planet called Earth, and convinced a number of human women to return with them to our new world."

"Until today I never gave much thought to the question of compatibility between human females and Jasani males," Summer said. "But now that I know you are shifters, I find it surprising."

"Human women are not completely compatible with us until after the mating ritual is performed," Maxim explained.

"Mating ritual?" Summer asked. "And, what exactly does that entail that it would cause one's biology to be altered?"

"Summer, I will answer your questions, this I promise," Maxim said patiently. "But I ask that you let me tell you this in my own way."

"I'm sorry," Summer said. "I tend to jump ahead. Please, go on and I will try not to interrupt."

"I do not mind your interruptions," Maxim assured her. "I just wish to give you the information in what I believe to be a logical order so that it will make more sense."

Summer smiled, glad that Maxim was working so hard to be patient with her.

"Jasani babies are born in threes," Maxim said. "Either all males or all females, never both at the same time. In males, the three share one soul. In females, each has their own soul, but that soul is destined to be paired with the soul shared by a male-set. When the female's soul is matched with her male's soul, the four of them become linked together. What we call *soul-linked*."

Summer felt a strange warmth fill her as she listened to what Maxim was saying. There was something almost familiar about it. And that was a thought that startled her.

"How does any of that work with human women?" she asked, trying to shake off the strange sensations. Of course this wasn't familiar. How could it be? She'd never heard of anything like this before and, as she remembered everything she had ever read or heard, she was positive of that.

As Maxim began telling her about their mating fangs, how they were used, and how the serum in them was altered for use on human women, Summer began to have that weird, down-the-rabbit-hole feeling again. But, she admitted to herself, what Maxim was telling her was no stranger than what had happened to her earlier with the Sensei and the katana.

"And an Arima?" Summer asked when Maxim finished with his explanation of how human women were altered in order to carry male Jasani babies. "What is an Arima?"

"An Arima is the female Jasani who mates with a male-set and links them all together," Maxim explained.

"But you just said that there are no female Jasani," Summer pointed out. "And I know for a fact that I'm not Jasani. I'm human. So how can I be an Arima?"

"We don't really understand it all," Maxim admitted. "We do know that some of the women who escaped the destruction of Ugaztun made it to Earth because we share a familial genetic connection with Princess Lariah. Both Lariah and Saige have been transformed into true Arimas by their male-sets. As our Arima, you can be transformed into a true Jasani as well."

"Do you mean to say I would be a shifter?" Summer asked. "I'd change into a big cat, like you guys do?"

"If we perform the soul-link triad together, yes," Maxim replied.

Soul-link triad? Summer wondered. One thing at a time, she decided. "But how do you know this? How do you know I'm this Arima thing?"

"From the moment we scented you in that building, our mating fangs descended," Ran said. "There is nothing other than a true Arima who could cause such a response in a male-set without using the potion."

"So, because of this biological response the three of you had, you are what? Stuck with me?" Summer asked. "You guys don't even like me."

"That is not true," Ran said.

Summer shook her head. "Okay, let's leave that part alone for the moment. What happens if I don't want to be your Arima? What if I don't want to change into a giant cat?"

"Then you don't," Maxim said, forcing himself to keep his face calm, though his heart was in his throat. He had been wrong to prejudge her, and he knew it. He would not make things worse by trying to force her into this.

"You will just let me walk away?" Summer asked.

Maxim took a deep breath and forced himself to think carefully before he spoke. "Summer, please do not misunderstand me," he began. "We are not asking you to make a commitment to us right now and frankly, we are not ready for that either. What I want, what *we* want, is for all of us to take the time to get to know one another. But yes, to answer your question, if you wish it, we will let you walk away. Whatever else you may think of us, we would never attempt to force any woman to do anything, least of all mate with us against her will."

Summer didn't know what to say, or what to think, or how to feel. There were too many things happening that made no sense to her. She needed time to sort things through.

She was trying to think of a way to say that without being rude or abrupt when the vid on the wall beside the fireplace lit up and beeped softly. Ran stood up and reached over to hit the button accepting the call. Faron's face appeared on the screen.

"I am very sorry to interrupt you," he said, "but we have a situation here."

"What is it?" Maxim asked.

"I'm afraid we need Summer," Faron said. "Doc says that the last woman with a Controller is in bad shape. We're going to lose her if something isn't done fast."

Summer leapt to her feet. "Why?" she asked. "What's happening?"

"Never mind," Maxim said as he hurried to Summer and picked her up. "We're on our way right now," he told Faron before heading for the door. Ran opened the door for them while Loni picked up her katana. Then Maxim was outside with Summer in his arms, and they were moving so quickly that Summer again saw nothing but blurred images. When they stopped, they were on the gravel path in front of the med-lab.

Maxim set Summer on her feet and reached for the door. "Thank you," Summer said breathlessly, realizing she had again forgotten to breathe while they were moving so fast. She stepped inside and paused at the feeling of barely controlled panic in the room.

There was someone lying on the exam table and Darleen, Doc, Saige, Dav and Faron were all gathered around it.

"What's going on?" Summer asked as she hurried to join them.

"We aren't really sure," Doc said. "This woman's heart is beating so fast, and so irregularly that it will fail very soon, but I cannot determine why. Without knowing the cause, I cannot stop it."

"It's the eppy," said a soft, weak voice from the corner of the room. Summer turned and saw the familiar face of Keeper Tesla, a little pale and tired but obviously alive, lying on a bed with lines running to various machines behind her.

"What's an eppy?" Doc demanded.

"Every five days all of the women get an injection," Tesla said. "They said it's to keep them from deteriorating, that if they don't get them, they can die. The injections are called *eppys*. They were due yesterday afternoon. We were prepping them when everything went...bad."

Doc frowned in thought. "Oh hell," he said softly as he spun around and hurried across the room to the drug cabinet. He grabbed a blood sample tube and hurried back. With a couple of quick gestures he had a sample of the woman's blood, which he carried over to another machine. A few short moments later he swore again and went back to the drug cabinet.

"These damned Controllers separate mind and body from each other," he said as he opened the cabinet and reached for several different bottles. "They lock the conscious mind into a perpetual nightmare, which triggers the fight or flight response. That's a real, physical response that is intended to last for seconds only, a stimulation event in the brain meant for survival. It's like being constantly stimulated to run for your life. Before long it's going to take a toll on the body."

Doc prepared a syringe and hurried back to the table and began preparing an injection site on the inside of the woman's arm. "So, they give them eppys once every five days. That has to mean some kind of epinephrine and norepinephrine antagonist, to suppress the fight or flight response."

Doc slipped the needle in carefully and began injecting the drug slowly, watching the vital readouts on the display over the exam table carefully. After a moment his shoulders relaxed a little.

"Yep, that's doing the job," he said with relief. He withdrew the needle and continued monitoring the vitals for a few more minutes, but clearly the crisis was over.

"I am going to take a guess here and say that these women have a life span of about five years," he said as he disposed of the injector and began putting the drugs back in the drug cabinet.

"Between five and eight, if they're lucky," Tesla said sadly.

Summer studied the woman for a long moment. "Tesla, I do not understand why you risked your life to save your prisoners."

Tesla sighed and relaxed back against her pillow. "I couldn't let them be killed like that," she said. "It was wrong."

"It was also wrong to inject them with a device that took away their minds," Summer pointed out.

"Is that what was done to them?" Tesla asked. "I didn't know that."

"What did you think?" Summer asked, trying not to sound accusatory. "You must have known something was wrong with them. All of those women who didn't so much as move an inch without an order to do so."

"Yes, I knew something was wrong with them," Tesla admitted. "During all of the months I was there I tried every day to find out what was done, but I failed. The other women who worked there didn't really know any more than I did from what I could tell."

"I don't understand," Summer said. "Are you saying your reason for being there was to find out what was being done?

"Yes," Tesla replied. "In part. The real reason I was there was to find my sister."

"Sister?" Summer asked, shocked.

"About two years ago my sister entered into a bride contract with a Jasani male-set and left Earth," Tesla explained tiredly. "We never heard from her again. We tried to contact the men she was supposed to marry, but we never got a response from them. So, I came to Jasan to find her myself. I tracked her down to the slave compound, but by the time I got there, she was...gone. She died there, I believe. I insinuated myself into the place as a Keeper and tried to discover what had happened to her. Why she ended up there, and how she died. I never did learn what really happened to her, but I couldn't leave. There were so many women there who needed someone to help them. So I stayed."

"How did you manage to track her to the compound?" Faron asked. "We have been trying to locate the missing women for many months and have never been able to learn anything."

"My sister and I had a...connection. We were twins. I could always find her, and she could always find me."

"Why didn't you contact the authorities?" Summer asked. "You knew something terrible was happening there."

"Because I thought the authorities were a part of what was happening," Tesla said tiredly. "My sister signed a bride contract on Jasan, and then disappeared on Jasan. I thought the Jasani were behind it. Until now. Now I am confused because I have no idea who was behind it."

"That's enough now," Doc said as he eyed his patient carefully. "This woman needs to rest. You can speak with her more tomorrow."

"All right," Summer said. She reached out and touched Tesla lightly on the shoulder. "Tesla, I wish to thank you for protecting those women that you could, and also for taking care of all of us. You are a brave woman."

Tesla shook her head weakly. "I should have done more."

"Rest now," Summer said. When Tesla's eyes closed, Summer turned back to the exam table and the woman now lying peacefully on it. "Can we Heal her now?" she asked Doc.

"Yes," Doc said. "Unless there is some reason you need her to be conscious, now would be a good time."

Summer looked to Saige who nodded and took up a position on the other side of the table. Summer reached out to touch the woman, then closed her eyes and focused.

It had been a very long day for Summer. So much had happened that was both confusing and emotionally draining, and she had already healed one woman earlier in the day. She found she had to strain to get a good mental grip on the Controller. Once she was certain she had it, she reached out with her other hand to tap Saige.

She sensed the bright, cleansing light of Saige's Healing power flash through the woman's brain as she had before. As soon as it faded, Summer pushed with all of her energy to destroy the Controller, reaching deep inside of herself for the strength to do it. Realizing she had expended too much of her own energy, she still managed to hold on long enough to be sure she had accomplished her part of the Healing process. Only then did she allow herself to slip away into darkness.

Chapter 28

"Za-Linq, report," Xaqana-Ti commanded.

Za-Linq glanced over at the comm panel, took a moment to collect himself, then rose from his chair and strolled casually across the room.

Za-Linq was not nearly as enamored of his Ruling Female as his predecessor had been. Za-Queg had always had a soft spot for Xaqana-Ti. Not that Za-Linq blamed him. Xaqana-Ti was exceedingly beautiful with her large, gently rounded curves, her mesmerizingly graceful movements, and her scent so richly enticing it was enough to draw any male to her, whether of her brood or not. And her voice. Her voice was acknowledged far and wide as the most beautiful, the most dulcet, the most melodious in living memory.

"Za-Linq, report at once," Xaqana-Ti snapped.

Well, Za-Linq thought to himself with some amusement, her voice *was usually* the most beautiful. When she wasn't angry about something.

Za-Linq reached for the comm panel and paused, careful to ensure no hint of his amusement would sound in his voice. Then he hit the correct button.

"I apologize, Most Glorious One," he said, panting slightly for effect. "I came as quickly as I could."

"I have just received your report that the Jasani slave compound was purged," Xaqana-Ti said without preamble. "Please explain the meaning of this."

Za-Linq bit back a sigh of frustration. If she would read the report, then she would have her answer and he would not be interrupted in the middle of his *makina* maintenance to explain it to her, he thought testily.

"The human male that Za-Queg utilized as his agent for the Jasani strand went missing," he explained, careful to hide his impatience. "He made some mistake and fell into Jasani hands. I had no choice but to exterminate him. Since the Jasani military had full access to his office, I felt it prudent to purge the slave compound as well."

"His computer system would have self-wiped the moment an unauthorized person touched it," Xaqana-Ti said.

"You are, as always, entirely correct, Beautiful One," he said, using just the right notes of subservience without being too obvious. "However, there was no telling what information the human may have left lying around his office for the Jasani to find. Humans can be so careless. There is nothing to worry about though," he added. "The new compound is complete and in a far more secure location than the old one anyway. I have not yet replaced the human agent, but notifications have gone out to all of our captains informing them that operations for the Jasani route will begin again shortly. The new compound will soon be filled. Everything is in order."

Xaqana-Ti hissed, shocking Za-Linq greatly. He had never heard such unguarded distress from her before. "Everything is *not* in order," she spat. "There was a *berezi* in that compound. The *berezi* we have only just allowed the Brethren to know we have. And they have already paid a very large price for her. When word gets out that we have lost yet another *berezi*...." Xaqana-Ti broke off, but the faint skittery noises coming through the speakers told Za-Linq just how close to the edge she was.

Za-Linq was stunned. He'd had no idea that there was a *berezi* in the slave compound. He opened his mouth to say so, but quickly realized how foolish an error that would be. Jasan was his territory, and his responsibility. That included the slave compound and everyone in it. For him not to be aware of a *berezi* in his own territory was tantamount to dereliction of duty.

His mind raced as he tried to decide how to handle this crisis. Suddenly, he remembered something he had noted when reviewing the compound's files after the extermination. He decided to gamble.

"I apologize most profusely for this upset," he said, sincere this time. An emotionally out of control Xaqana-Ti was not good. Angry, yes. Frustrated, maybe. But distressed enough to reveal her true fear and worry? No, absolutely not. In this state, she might very well order her entire brood exterminated, and there would be no stopping it. Za-Linq quickly adjusted his attitude.

"Xaqana-Ti, most Beautiful Lady, may I assume you are referring to the *berezi* whose human name was...." he hesitated a moment, trying to pull the strange name from his memory. What was it? What was it? Oh yes. "The one called *Sum-myr-whin-tey*?"

There was a sudden silence through the speakers. "Why do you ask this?" Xaqana-Ti asked.

"Because she was removed from the compound early yesterday morning and transferred to Badia for shipment," he said.

There was a long silence which, Za-Linq guessed, was due to his Ruling Female's need to search her records for the *berezi's* name.

"Yes, that is what she was called," Xaqana-Ti said finally. "What is her current location?" she demanded.

"I am still attempting to locate her," Za-Linq replied, thinking quickly. "The human handled the details of this transaction." Za-Linq realized that Xaqana-Ti must have gone behind his back and worked with Lio on this secretly. Therefore, she knew very well that Za-Linq had no knowledge of it. But that was not going to get him off the hook for this. Strictly speaking, Lio was *his* human, and he was directly responsible for everything the man did, or did not do.

"That is a serious problem. For you," Xaqana-Ti said with something closer to her usual calm. "I suggest you find her, and see that she is delivered as promised."

Za-Linq struggled for the correct response. He wanted very much to ask how he was supposed to find a female he'd known nothing about up until this moment, and where she was supposed to be delivered. But, from Xaqana-Ti's current state of upset, it seemed obvious that she did not know the answer to the latter question, and the first was irrelevant.

"I have all of my resources on this matter," he lied smoothly, though he was fully aware that Xaqana-Ti knew he was lying.

"How long will it take you to obtain the information?" Xaqana-Ti asked.

"Since the Jasani have certainly caused a full system wipe of Lio's computers, I will have to contact our main buyers individually for the information. It will take time, perhaps as long as two Standard weeks," he said, pulling a number from nowhere.

"You have ten days," Xaqana-Ti replied shortly. The connection was closed with a sharp click and Za-Linq had to struggle to remain on his feet, such was his combined fear and relief.

He stumbled back across his quarters and all but fell into his chair. He simply could not believe how quickly his situation had changed. After all of his careful work, he was in a worse spot than even Za-Queg had been in, and it was through no doing of his own.

He did not blame Xaqana-Ti, of course. As Ruling Female, she had the right to go behind his, or anyone's back whenever she wished. Ruling Females did such things all the time to keep their brood in line and it was not for him to question her, or her reasons. No, he was not angry with her. He was, however, furious with Lio Perry. The little human had betrayed him. He, Za-Linq, was Lio Perry's superior, and Lio should have informed him of the negotiations concerning the *berezi*. Therefore, Lio Perry was directly responsible for the position Za-Linq now found himself in. Za-Linq wished with all of his being that Lio Perry was still alive so that he could make the human pay for his disloyalty.

It took Za-Linq several long minutes to calm himself enough that he could think. Now all he had to do was find the missing *berezi*, and deliver her to whomever had purchased her. Za-Linq shook his head. How was he supposed to do either of those things with no information, and no Lio Perry?

But, he did have information, he realized. He got up and hurried to the vid terminal in his quarters and pulled up the compound's files that he'd uploaded before the purging. After a few moments, he found the notes he'd seen earlier concerning...ah...Summer Whitney was the name. Well, who could keep track of humans and their strange sounding names?

The compound had received a missive from Lio indicating that the *berezi* had been purchased, and ordering them to send her to him for off-world shipment. The file showed that they had complied with the order, sending the *berezi* to Lio early the previous morning. Za-Linq searched carefully, but there was no further information. They had not known who the purchaser was, or even when the *berezi* was supposed to be shipped out. The only other notation on the file was made by the Keeper who had logged in after returning from delivering the *berezi.*

Za-Linq realized that the *berezi* must have been delivered to Lio at about the same time Lio was supposed to have been attending his *board meeting*. So Lio had not had a chance to ship the *berezi* off-world. Such shipments were always made at night. Therefore, the *berezi* must have been taken away with Lio by the Jasani. He wondered briefly if Lio's pet female had also been taken, then decided it didn't matter. Only the *berezi* mattered.

Za-Linq began pacing his quarters, remembering the previous day. After he'd finally been retrieved by his ship, he had spent some time working off his frustration on his chief engineer. By the time he had finished with that little diversion and returned to his quarters, he'd discovered that the tracking device on Lio indicated he had been taken straight to the Dracons' ranch.

Za-Linq had felt somewhat pleased with that course of events. He finally had a valid reason to dispose of Za-Queg's human. In fact, it was required of him.

Of course, once Lio had crossed onto the Dracons' property the tracking signal had been lost, but that didn't matter. The force field around the property that disrupted the tracking signal blocked outgoing transmissions, but did not disrupt the short phased digital pulse that triggered the sub-dermal explosive device. He had activated the explosive without a moment's hesitation, and no small amount of satisfaction.

Za-Linq stopped pacing and smiled, very pleased with himself. The *berezi* had certainly been taken to the Dracons' ranch along with Lio. He was sure of it. With the current state of heightened security around the ranch, it seemed plausible to conclude that she was still there. There was nowhere else on that whole miserable planet that they could take her and be sure of her safety. The only question now was, how was he going to get her back?

The female certainly had a Controller. That was a given. And since she was a *berezi*, she had the Prime Controller. He tried to think of a way to use that knowledge in order to get his hands on the *berezi,* but as far as he knew, the only thing he could do from a distance was set off the self-destruct program, but he did not want to destroy the *berezi*.

Somehow, he had to find a way to get that *berezi* off the Dracon's ranch and onto his ship. He didn't know how he was going to do that, but he had managed to figure out where the *berezi* was, so his confidence was back. One way or another, he would get that *berezi*. He had no intention of ending up as his predecessor had. No matter what.

Chapter 29

Summer awoke slowly, enjoying the feel of soft warmth surrounding her. She snuggled closer to the hard body beside her and sighed contentedly.

Hard body? She stiffened as her eyes flew open in shock. Yep, definitely a hard body in the bed with her. She leapt from the bed, relieved to discover that she was still fully dressed even as her mind struggled to remember what had happened, and why she was in bed with...who?

She spun around, her eyes widening in shock to see Ran lying in her bed, his head propped up on one hand as he smiled up at her.

"What?" she demanded, unable to actually form a full, coherent sentence.

"What?" Ran asked, his smile fading as his brows lowered in confusion.

He was confused? Summer thought. Well, huh.

"What are you doing in my bed?" she demanded.

"You expended too much energy Healing the last woman," Ran said as he sat up and swung his legs over the edge of the bed. "Maxim caught you before you hit the floor and we brought you here to rest. We thought it would be best for one of us to keep an eye on you."

"How does that explain your presence in the bed?" Summer asked.

"You seemed cold," Ran said with a grin. "I thought I should warm you up."

"That is what blankets are for," Summer said coolly.

"I suppose you have me there," Ran admitted, though he was still smiling.

Summer gave up. "Okay, I am awake, I am fine, and I thank you for your concern. You can go now."

"Actually, I was hoping for a chance to talk with you for a moment, if you don't mind," Ran said. Summer frowned as she studied Ran's face, but he seemed serious now. More than that, she sensed his feelings, and knew that he really was serious, and worried.

"All right," Summer agreed reluctantly. "What is it?"

"I believe that you are able to sense our emotions, at least to some extent," Ran said. "Am I correct?"

"Yes, that's true," Summer said. "How did you know?"

"Because it's normal for an Arima to do that," Ran replied. "I also believe that's why you think that we do not like you."

Summer sighed and sat down in the chair be the bed. "As you just confirmed that I can sense your emotions, then you already know the answer to that."

"You did not feel dislike from me, Summer, nor do I think you felt dislike from Loni," Ran said gently. "I am sure you felt us withdraw from you, but there is a reason for that, and it is not about you."

"Go on," Summer said warily.

"The relationship between the brothers of a male-set is in some ways complicated, and in other ways simple. Basically, the eldest of any male-set is the leader. Not just because they were born first, though they always are, but because they are born with that quality in them. The next brother is the second-in-command, and then the third."

"So you're low man on the totem pole?" Summer asked.

Ran smiled. "I don't know what a *totem pole* is, but I think I get your meaning. And no, that is not what it means. We are not human, Summer. We look very human. But we don't have any human DNA.

"We share one soul between us. That means that we need to be together. We need to work together, live together, do almost everything together. It is not a choice we must make, but a necessary part of who and what we are. One of us must be the leader, and the others *need* to follow that lead. Loni and I have no problem speaking up if we disagree with something Maxim says, or a decision he makes. We are separate individuals with separate brains and we each have our own personalities, ideas, feelings and opinions. But in many ways, we are also three parts of one whole. In order for the whole to work, we must cooperate with one another."

"That is a very difficult concept for me to grasp," Summer said.

"I understand that, but even if you don't grasp it entirely, it's important that you are at least aware of it."

"Why?" Summer asked.

"So that you can understand, at least a little, what's happening with us," Ran said. "You asked if we wanted you only because you are our Arima, but in reality, the opposite is true. Maxim wished to be careful and go slow, even though he knew that you were the one woman in all of the universe meant specifically for us. He did not want us to end up in the same position as our Fathers *only* because you are our Arima. Maxim was worried, very worried, that you could be like Mara. Neither myself, nor

Loni, agreed with him, but at the same time, we have no desire to be with a woman like Mara either. So we agreed to go slow, as Maxim wished.

"Because of that, we made an effort to hold our feelings back from you. We know that you, as our Arima, can sense our emotions. We could not let you feel how much we wanted you. It would have been unfair to you, and difficult for us."

"All right, I understand that," Summer said, trying to ignore the growing relief she felt at Ran's explanation. There were other problems, she reminded herself. "Maxim did not like me, and that you cannot deny."

"I cannot explain my brother's feelings, nor his actions," Ran said. "He has said he does not dislike you, and if he said it, then it is true. I admit that there is something going on with him that neither Loni nor I understand. But it is nothing to do with you. Whatever it is, it has been rubbing at him for many months now."

Summer already knew that Maxim did not dislike her, not now at least. When he had told her that earlier in the armory, she had felt his sincerity. Just as she felt Ran's sincerity now. Because of that, she had to believe that what Ran was saying was true.

"There is one other thing that bothers me," she said. "Actually, there are several things that bother me, but this is the only other really big one."

"If you tell me what it is, I will try to help you with it," Ran said.

"Well, it's about Mara," she said. "I only met her once and no, she was not very nice. And I assume that whatever she did today was really bad. It looked bad even from where I was sitting. But still, I don't understand how you guys could sever your relationship with your own mother. I don't have a great relationship with my mother, but I don't think I could ever do what you did. That bothers me, Ran."

"I don't blame you for being bothered by it," Ran said sadly. "She really is not a good person, Summer. I wish I could say otherwise, but I can't. And it is no exaggeration at all that she made our fathers miserable for five hundred years."

"I don't understand that either," Summer said. "If they were so unhappy with her, why not divorce her?"

"Because there is no such thing as divorce for Clan Jasani," Ran replied. "Once mated, whether it be to an Arima or a chosen human female, there is no going back. Jasani males can only mate once, Summer. They can only have sexual feelings for one woman, can only have children with one woman. Once a choice is made, it cannot be unmade."

"Wow," Summer said softly. "That's...well, I don't know what that is. It certainly makes Maxim's desire to go slowly even more understandable. But if your fathers were that unhappy with her, wouldn't it have been better to end the relationship even if it meant no more sex or children? If they wanted children that badly, there are other options. They could have adopted."

"Perhaps," Ran said. "But there is no option for ending such a relationship in our culture. You make your choice, and you live with it. There is no going back."

"But you said earlier today that Mara was no longer your mother," Summer pointed out. "Obviously you did something to sever that relationship."

"Yes, but that is different," Ran said. "When one does something so wrong, so far against all rules and customs, breaking faith with not just one or two people, but with our entire society and race as a whole, then there is a ritual, *moztu-oku,* which is used to sever all ties with that person. It is rarely done, and only as a last resort in extreme situations."

"What Mara did was that bad?" Summer asked.

"Yes, it was," Ran said.

"What did she do, Ran?" Summer asked softly. "I would rather hear it from you than from someone else."

Ran hesitated. He did not want to admit what Mara had done. But Summer was right. It would be better for her to hear it from him than someone else. "She stole a sample of Princess Rayne's blood," Ran said reluctantly.

"Why?" Summer gasped.

"That is not yet known," Ran replied. "But it cannot have been for any good reason."

"No, I can see that," Summer replied.

"Even so," Ran said, "what you need to understand is that we performed the *moztu-oku* for Mara's sake."

"How was that for her sake?" Summer asked doubtfully.

"The penalty for the crime that Mara committed, assaulting a child of our royal family, if she were Clan Jasani, is instant death," Ran said. "Even though Mara is human, she was, before the *moztu-oku*, by our law, deemed to be Clan Jasani because she was legally mated to a Jasani male-set, and gave birth to Jasani sons. By severing our ties with her, it is as though she was never Clan Jasani at all. She is, at best, Citizen Jasani."

"And what is the penalty for her crime as a citizen?"

"Like any other citizen, she will be tried by a jury made up of Citizen Jasani who will then decide her fate. Since she was caught in the act, and no real harm was done to Princess Rayne, it is not likely she will be sentenced to death. She will instead be sent to a prison planet, or perhaps she will be sent to the mines for a specified period of time. After that, she will be banished from Jasan for the remainder of her life. But she will still have her life. "

"Won't your Prince be angry with you for manipulating the situation that way?" Summer asked.

"He would be if we did such a thing behind his back, and rightly so," Ran replied. "But we did not do that, nor would we. Maxim asked High Prince Garen for permission to perform the *moztu-oku*. Prince Garen was kind enough to permit it, and don't think for a moment that he did not fully understand the reason for Maxim's request, or the consequences of it.

"No matter what kind of a person Mara is, she is still our mother. Her life was the only thing we had to offer her, and Prince Garen granted our request for that." Ran paused for a moment, then smiled sadly. "Mara will never understand that what we did, we did for her. But we know it, and it is ourselves we must live with."

Summer sat quietly for a few minutes, going over everything that Ran had said. She realized something, but wanted to be certain. "That was Maxim's idea, wasn't it?" she asked. "To sever Mara so that she would not lose her life."

"Of course it was," Ran said. "He is not the monster you seem to think him, Summer."

"I do not think him a monster, Ran," Summer objected. "I do not know him at all. But I am beginning to know you a little. I was wondering why it was that you were going behind Maxim's back to talk to me. But now I realize, you aren't, are you? He knows you are here."

"Of course," Ran said. "We discussed what we believed to be your biggest concerns, and agreed that one of us should try to explain things to you. We thought it would be easier for you than having all three of us trying to convince you to give us a chance at the same time."

"Is that what you are doing?" she asked with a smile. "Convincing me to give you a chance?"

"Yes," Ran replied with a grin. "Is it working?"

"Oh, excuse me one moment," he said as he reached up to tap his vox. "Yes?"

"Yes, she's fine," Ran said. "We will be there in just a moment."

Ran reached up to tap the vox off. "That was Maxim. He asks that we go down to the meeting room. Faron wishes to speak with us."

"All right," Summer agreed easily, standing up. "Let's go."

Ran opened the door for her and guided her out of the room and down the hall, wondering what Faron wanted. Maxim's voice had given away nothing. Well, he would soon find out.

Chapter 30

Summer pulled her long, thick braid over her shoulder out of the way and slipped her arms through the katana harness, securing it in place without really thinking about it. She was getting used to walking around with it all the time, though she hadn't tried to use it since that first day. She looked around the guest room she had used for the past several days, and ran through a mental checklist. Satisfied that she had not forgotten anything, she opened the door and stepped into the hall.

"You about ready?" Darleen asked as she too stepped into the hall from her room next door.

"Yes, I think so," Summer replied. "You?"

"Absolutely," Darleen replied. "I'm excited to finally be going. All of this waiting around drives me a little crazy."

"It's only been a week," Summer said. "And a very busy week at that."

Darleen nodded. "Yes, that's true. Between trying to remember, and write down, everything Lio did and said over the course of a year, and working with you on getting Lio to sound normal when he speaks the words you put in his mouth, and Doc's treatments, it has been very hectic."

"Yes, but in my opinion, out of all of that, the most important things have been Doc's treatments," Summer said, studying her friend closely. Darleen's hair was a couple of inches long now thanks to Doc, the scars on her face were fainter than they had been, and the dark circles beneath her eyes were almost gone. "You look so much better. Still too thin, but much better. And you aren't limping at all now."

"I never thought anyone would be able to do half as much as Doc has already done," Darleen said. "I am very grateful for all of his help." Darleen shrugged. "But, I am happy today is the big day."

"Yes, me too," Summer agreed as they turned and headed up the hall toward the kitchen. "I wish I had been more successful with some of the things I've been working on though."

"The computer control stuff isn't going so well huh?" Darleen asked.

"Yes and no," Summer replied. "I can do all of the usual things. I just can't get them to upload system files to a remote data retrieval device without setting off system alarms unless I know where the alarms are beforehand."

"Summer," Darleen said softly, stopping in the middle of the hall and waiting for Summer to stop and look at her.

"Yes?"

"Without you, none of this would be happening right now," Darleen said. "The slave compound you were in would not be closed. The women who were saved, would not be on the way home to their families. I would not be here right now. The Jasani would still be looking for a break in the slave ring, instead of having its primary human agent on Jasan in custody, along with all of the information in his head. We would not be ready to board a ship for Li-Hach-Cor in an effort to free even more women from another slave compound.

"So, if you are not able to get through the Xanti's computer system, well, that's too bad. Another way will have to be found. You cannot do everything."

"That is exactly what we have been trying to tell her," Maxim said from behind them. "But she won't listen to us. Hopefully, she will listen to her friend."

Summer turned around and smiled at Maxim, Loni and Ran. Ever since her conversation with Ran a week earlier, she had started to see Maxim in a different light. That had been the same night that Faron had announced the plans for the upcoming rescue mission to Li-Hach-Cor. Since then, everyone had been too busy for much in the way of personal conversation. Summer was glad of that as it had given her exactly what she'd wanted most. Time to work through things in her own mind, in her own way.

"I understand what you guys are saying," she said as the Katres caught up with them and bowed. She was even starting to get used to all of the bowing. "And I appreciate it. But these computers are important. We need to get the information that's in them or we won't be able to find the other compounds."

"We will," Maxim said. "Don't worry about it so much. Right now, it is most important that you both eat some breakfast before we leave."

Summer rolled her eyes at Maxim, but she was no longer offended by his imperious tone. She had spent a lot of time working closely with the Katres over the past several days, and had come to realize that was actually his *concerned* voice. She was also getting better at understanding the emotions she was feeling from the three of them.

"Okay, okay, we are going to eat right now," Summer said. "Are you guys coming with us?"

"No, we've already eaten," Maxim replied. "When you are finished, there will be a ground-car waiting outside to drive you to the airfield."

"How much time do we have?" Summer asked.

"As much time as you need," Maxim replied smoothly.

Summer shook her head and turned to Ran, who grinned.

"As long as we are out of here in the next hour, we will reach the spaceport in time for the shuttle to keep its schedule," he said. "On the other hand, if we are late, they will wait. So as Maxim said, you have as much time as you need."

"We will not need an hour," Summer said. "Twenty minutes, tops."

"I do want to take a moment to thank Saige," Darleen added. "But that won't take long."

"Very well, we will meet you at the airfield when you are done," Maxim said with a short bow before turning and heading back down the hall with Loni and Ran behind him. Summer stood there for a long moment, watching the three men as they walked away from her, unable to tear her eyes from the sight.

Darleen cleared her throat. "Let's go get some food," she said, turning toward the kitchen.

"Yes, um, good idea," Summer replied, though she waited until the Katres turned the corner out of sight before turning around and catching up to Darleen.

When Summer and Darleen reached the kitchen they were pleased to see Saige already there, sitting at the table with Eldar Hamat.

"Good morning Saige, Eldar Hamat," Summer said, smiling at Eldar Hamat, whom she liked very much. She now knew that he was the eldest of all of the Jasani, and had actually lived through what they referred to as the *Dark Time*. Since Jasani did not age, he didn't look old, but he did look worn and tired, though his eyes were usually bright and lively. This morning however, they looked a little sad.

"Good morning Summer, Darleen," Saige replied. Eldar Hamat looked up and smiled warmly at them both.

"Darleen, it's so wonderful to see you walking without a limp," Saige commented. "How are you feeling?"

"I feel great," Darleen replied. "No pain at all. I think Doc is a miracle worker."

Saige smiled and waved them toward a couple of chairs. "Come and sit down," she said. "There's plenty of food, so help yourselves."

Summer took a seat and began filling her plate. "Eldar Hamat, are you well?" she asked. "You seem a little unhappy today."

"I am well enough," Eldar Hamat replied. "I am just old, and it seems that my responsibilities take a greater toll on me now than they once did."

"Your responsibilities?" Summer asked.

"Eldar Hamat will be handling the interviews with Mara Winicke," Saige answered. "It will be difficult for him. I'm trying to convince him to let someone else handle the matter."

"I see," Summer said, realizing at once who they were talking about even though she'd never heard the woman's last name before. "It's none of my business, but I agree with Saige. Why not let someone else handle it?"

Eldar Hamat sighed heavily. "I cannot," he said. "It would not be right."

Summer opened her mouth to ask why not, but a short, sharp shake of Saige's head warned her to leave it be. She closed her mouth, nodded and began eating her breakfast though she hardly tasted it.

"Saige, I want to thank you, and your Rami, for your hospitality," Darleen said. "You have been very kind to allow me to stay here. Especially after all I did in the past."

"Yes, I add my thanks as well," Summer said. "You and your family have been very generous, and I am very grateful to you."

Saige smiled. "It has been our pleasure to have you both," she said graciously. "For all that the two of you have already done, and are still doing to help in our fight to stop the abductions, it is the least we could do. Without you, we would not have known about the slave compound here on Jasan, let alone the one on Li-Hach-Cor."

"I would like to ask you something, if you do not mind," Darleen said hesitantly.

"Certainly Darleen," Saige said. "You may ask what you will."

"That day, that bad day, when I did...what I did," Darleen began, struggling to find a way to express herself without actually naming the things she'd done.

"Yes?" Saige said, letting Darleen off the hook.

Darleen's shoulders relaxed and she gave Saige a grateful look. "That pendant you wear all the time, the heart?"

Saige nodded as one hand rose automatically to touch the large heart-shaped pendant that never left her neck.

"I touched it that day, held it in my hand for a moment," Darleen said. "Do you remember that?"

"Yes," Saige replied, keeping her voice gentle for Darleen's sake though the memory of that day was always one that made her angry.

"Well, I think something happened to me when I touched it," Darleen said. "And I was just wondering if you could explain it to me."

Saige's brows rose in surprise. "I'm not sure," she said. "Can you tell me a bit more? What happened to you?"

"Well, first, I felt dizzy and cold, then scared. More scared than I'd ever been in my life up to that moment. All I wanted to do was get away from you and that pendant as fast as I could. But when I drove away, I had this strong feeling that if I didn't turn around and go back and free all of you, something really bad was going to happen to me."

Darleen fell silent for a long moment as she stared at the table in front of her. Summer, Saige and Eldar Hamat waited patiently, knowing that she had more to say. When she raised her eyes to Saige, she looked sad and confused, but determined.

"Well, of course something bad did happen to me," she said. "But the part that is strange to me is that the whole time I was there, in Lio's office, I kept thinking that I deserved at least some of what was happening. And that if I ever got free, I had to do something worthwhile with my life." Darleen sighed. "The thing is Saige, you met me. You know those are not thoughts and feelings that I would normally have. Regret and altruism were never a part of Darleen Flowers' makeup.

"Don't get me wrong, I am glad that I feel differently now. I actually kind of like the person I am now. But I would like to know if it was the pendant that changed me."

Saige considered Darleen carefully as she thought about everything she had said. She knew that this was a very important matter for Darleen, and she deserved a real answer.

"Darleen, this pendant gives me the ability to see the true hearts of those around me," she said. "Whether or not it caused a change in you when you touched it, I cannot say. However, I see that this is an important matter for you. If you like, I will try to summon Riata, and ask her."

Darleen paled. "Riata?" she whispered.

"Do not worry so," Saige told her. "Riata has no anger toward you."

"All right, but please, tell her for me that I am so very sorry for that day," Darleen said, her blue eyes bright with sudden moisture. "I promise, I never meant such a thing to happen."

"All right, I will tell her if she comes," Saige promised. "Now, if you will give me just a moment."

Saige bowed her head and closed her eyes, sending herself quickly to the place of gray fog. She looked around, but there was nothing to see but the dry gray wisps. She was about to close her eyes and go back when suddenly Riata stepped out of the fog and bowed to her.

"Greetings, Saige Lobo," Riata said.

Saige returned her bow, and her smile. "Greetings Riata," she replied.

"I am concerned for Darleen," she said, assuming that Riata knew the reason for her visit.

"Yes, as am I," Riata replied. "I thank you for telling her that I hold no anger toward her."

"You are most welcome," Saige replied. "Do you think that the pendant caused Darleen to change?"

"I think that the pendant showed Darleen her true self more clearly than any mirror ever could," Riata replied. "But the decision to react to knowledge must be made by the one who learns the knowledge, not the knowledge itself."

"Thank you, Riata," Saige said, relieved. She hadn't liked the idea of the pendant making people change who they were, whether it was for the better or not. People had to make up their own minds about such things, make their own choices.

"I appreciate you taking the time to help with this small matter," she added.

"If it were a small matter, I would not have come," Riata pointed out. "Darleen has her own part to play in events to come. But first, she must grow into the woman she was meant to be."

Saige wanted to ask what that meant, but she was learning a few things about these visits with Riata. She could ask the question, but she would not get an answer. "I will refrain from sharing that with Darleen," she said.

"Of course you will," Riata said with a grin. "Otherwise, I would not have told you."

Saige laughed softly as Riata faded away, liking the woman greatly. Then she closed her eyes and returned to her kitchen.

When she looked up at Darleen, she could see the worry and fear in her eyes more clearly than she had before.

"Be easy, Darleen," she said. "Riata has answered our question, and no, the pendant did not change you. It only gave you knowledge of yourself. The decision on how to use that knowledge was yours alone."

Darleen blew out a long, slow breath of air, her entire body seeming to relax as she did so. "Thank you Saige, more than I can say."

"You are most welcome Darleen," Saige replied. "I would add one thing myself though, if you do not mind."

"Of course not," Darleen said calmly, though her shoulders tensed again.

"You were wrong, Darleen," Saige said gently. "You did not deserve what was done to you. No one deserves what was done to you."

Darleen nodded her head slowly, though she didn't look particularly convinced. "Thank you Saige," she said again. "For everything."

Summer cleared her throat, breaking the long silence that fell after Darleen last words. "We best get a move on," she said. "We don't want to keep the Katres waiting too long."

Darleen nodded and reached for her fork. A few minutes later Darleen and Summer finished their breakfast, said their last goodbyes to Saige and Eldar Hamat, and hurried out to the ground-car, eager to be on their way at last.

Chapter 31

Slater watched the welfare ship from a short distance, waiting for just the right moment. There was a part of him...a very big part...that wanted to stay on Onddo and use the sugea to destroy the village and all of those who had turned on him. But mostly he just wanted off of Onddo. He did not like sleeping in the wild. He did not like worrying about his safety. He did not like feeling hunted.

So here he stood, as he had years earlier, waiting for the right moment to sneak aboard the welfare ship and escape from those who wished to kill him. He watched as the small group of people who had been gathered near the entrance to the ship wandered away at last. One more quick look around to be sure the area was clear and he transformed into the figure of a male human he had devoured long ago on the Jasani skyport.

"So, you're going to sneak aboard the welfare ship and leave again, are you?"

Slater jumped at the sound of the voice and spun around, already reaching for the sugea. He froze in shock when he saw who had spoken.

"No, don't pull out the sugea," Magoa said. "That would bring all sorts of attention that neither of us wants."

Slater was so surprised that the great Magoa was standing there talking to him that he couldn't decide what to do. So he did nothing.

"Good," Magoa said as though Slater had agreed with him. "I think it would be better if you did not leave just now, Slater."

Slater blinked. Had the great Magoa actually addressed him by name? And how did he recognize him?

Magoa sighed. "You have the most potential of all of my offspring," he said. "Unfortunately, you are not the brightest of the lot." Magoa shrugged. "Well, one must use the tools one is given. And right now, you are an important tool. Therefore, I cannot let you leave Onddo at this time."

"Offspring?" Slater repeated, unable to think beyond that one word.

"Yes, yes, offspring," Magoa said, waving a hand dismissively. "Now, when I arranged for you to run off on the welfare ship the first time, I did it for a reason. I had no idea it would take you so long to return with a little help for your home world, but that's fine, that's fine, it took as long as it took. The point is you learned a lot and you came back as you were meant.

"It's too bad that you brought Xanti back with you. I'm not sure what possessed you to do such a thing, but again, it is what it is. The Xanti have brought the future to Onddo and that is what I wanted, so I won't complain. Those damn welfare ships bring nothing but platitudes and a little food. We needed much more than that and now we have it. But, boy, you can't run off now when you are about to become really useful."

Slater shook his head slowly, struggling to understand what Magoa was talking about. But there had been too many revelations. Magoa was his sire? Magoa had arranged for him to leave Onddo? Magoa had meant for him to do the things he had done? It was planned?

"I know you aren't following all of this, but you take some time and think on it, and you will. That's one of your strong points. You're not fast, but you do tend to get where you need to go eventually.

"Right now I'm in a bit of a rush. So, get this straight Slater, my boy, you are not to board that welfare ship and leave. You go back out into the wild and you wait for me to come to you. It's going to take me a few days, maybe even several days. I am very busy after all and I have that damned Xanti following me around every minute of the day so I'll have to shake him off first. Now, are we clear? Do you know what you are supposed to do?"

Slater blinked again. Do? he wondered. What was he supposed to do?

"Come on now son, don't make me wait, we are out of time," Magoa said impatiently.

"Um, yes, I am to stay on Onddo and wait for you," Slater said, not quite certain, but vaguely aware Magoa had something like that.

"That's right," Magoa said. "Now, you stay here for a bit until I'm gone, and then go back to that cave you've been holed up in these past few days. I'll come see you soon."

With that, Magoa turned and slipped away into the brush. One moment he was there, the next gone.

Slater remained frozen for long minutes after Magoa left, his brain filled with wonder and awe. The great Magoa had not only spoken to him, but had known his name. The fact that he was also Slater's sire was simply too much for Slater to process so he set that aside for later.

Finally he realized that he was still holding the form of the crewman, which was draining energy he might need to get back to the cave. He released the form and leaned back on his tail for a moment, trying to think. It wasn't easy to do with so many surprising things rolling around in his head.

After awhile he decided to focus on the moment. He looked around, saw that the area was clear, and began working his way back the way he had come earlier that morning. He forced himself to think of nothing other than his surroundings and getting out of the area without being spotted. Only when he was back in his cave, safe and sound, would he pull out all of the astounding things that Magoa had said to him and try to understand them.

Chapter 32

Summer was amazed at not only the sheer size of the *Vyand*, but also the beauty of it. Everything about it was big, clean and soothing, with muted colors and matte textures. She would have guessed a military transport such as the *Vyand* would be all shiny metal surfaces and bright flashing lights, but that was not the case at all. Even her stateroom, which was easily several times the size of the third-class compartment she'd had on the *Cosmic Glory*, had the look and feel of a high end hotel room. Especially the bed. She had never seen such a huge bed in her life.

She wondered briefly if she were getting special treatment. Surely this was a room meant for important people, such as visiting dignitaries, or high ranking officers. She decided she didn't care. So they gave her a nice, big room. What was she gonna do? Complain about it?

After she finished putting away the few things she had brought with her, she went back out into the passageway, then paused uncertainly. Ran had mentioned that they would be in rooms near hers, but she didn't want to start knocking on doors. As she stood there a door opened next to hers and Maxim stepped out into the hall.

"Do you like your stateroom?" he asked.

"Yes, I do," she replied. "It's very beautiful, but I am a little worried that I might get lost in that bed."

"Oh, lets hope not," Maxim said softly, a faint smile playing around the corners of his mouth. Summer spent a long moment staring at his mouth before she realized what she was doing and jerked her eyes away. She struggled to find something to say, but came up empty.

"Would you like a tour of the ship?" Maxim asked.

"Yes, I would," Summer said quickly. Anything's better than standing here thinking about that sexy mouth, she thought to herself just as Ran and Loni both joined them in the hall. Three sexy mouths, she thought, followed by mental images that made her want to run back into her room and try out that gigantic shower. With just the cold water.

"Summer would like a tour of the ship," Maxim told them. Loni tilted his head the tiniest bit, but Summer felt his smile.

Maxim placed one hand lightly on Summer's elbow and guided her down the long, curving passageway towards the elevator. "We won't be able to give you a tour of the entire ship," Maxim said. "There are some areas that are off limits to civilians, such as the fighter bays, armories, and ammunition stores. We could show you the engine rooms, but I doubt that would be of much interest to you."

Maxim looked at Summer questioningly, and she shook her head. "No, I don't really need to see that," she agreed.

Ran reached out and waved his hand over the sensor to call the elevator. "The areas for military personnel are not, strictly speaking, off limits, but I don't think the barracks or crew mess hall are of interest either. Therefore we will stick with the bridge, the rec deck, and other common areas."

"Rec deck?" Summer asked, smiling. It seemed strange to hear a slang word coming from Maxim.

The elevator doors slid open and the four of them stepped in. "There are five decks on this ship," Maxim said. "We are currently on level two. This is where officer quarters, guest quarters, meeting rooms, the situation room and map room are located. Deck three is the rec deck, which holds the activity rooms, training rooms, cafeteria, ship's library and store. Deck one is the bridge, transport room and the science labs. Deck four is medical and crew, deck five is engineering, ammunition, fighter and shuttle bays. We will start with the rec deck, then move up to the bridge."

Ran pressed the button for Deck 3 and the elevator hummed softly. A couple of seconds later the doors slid open and they stepped out into another passageway. This one was brighter than the previous one with shiny flooring instead of carpet, lots of large plexi-glass viewing windows into various game and training rooms and a more relaxed feel.

"As you can see, the passageways curve, following the shape of the ship," Maxim explained as they walked down the hall. "Running along the outside edge of the deck are the cafeteria, several game rooms and training rooms, the laundry facility and, in the center, the Roar Room."

"Roar Room?" Summer asked. "What is that?"

"Its official name is the Shift Chamber," Ran said with a grin. "A few years ago some of the human crew members dubbed it the Roar Room and it stuck. We like it, so we have come to use it as well."

"Oh, its a room where you can go to shift into your alter forms then," Summer guessed. "Is that something you have to do often?"

"It really depends on the Clan," Maxim replied. "In general, we all prefer to shift regularly. Since we shift into such large creatures, it is necessary to have a large enough space for them included in the design of our vessels."

"Can I see it?" Summer asked.

"Certainly," Maxim replied. "I warn you though, there isn't much to look at. It is just a very large room with thick padding on the floors and walls."

"Why padding?"

"To protect the floors and walls," Maxim replied. "Clan Jasani alter forms have claws, talons, fangs, horns, and a lot of strength. The padding is replaced regularly. It is much easier to replace padding than it is to replace floors and walls."

"Where is Darleen's room?" she asked curiously, wondering why she hadn't asked that before. Once they had boarded the ship from the skyport, Darleen had gone off with Doc, and the Katres had shown her to her room.

"We offered her a room near yours," Maxim said. "But Doc asked that she be given a medical personnel berth near his own as he wants to continue treating her injuries. Darleen agreed, so she is on the med-deck."

"I'm curious. Why is it that Doc is here?" Summer asked. "I thought he worked on the Dracons' ranch."

"He requested that he be included for a number of reasons," Maxim replied. "Partly because he knows the most about Controllers and is therefore best equipped to care for any women we recover. Partly because he wants to continue treating Darleen. And partly because he has his own personal issues with the Xanti."

"Oh. Well, for Darleen's sake, and the women we rescue, I am glad he came with us. What about Lio?" she asked, feeling a bit guilty that she hadn't thought of him since coming aboard either.

"He's fine for the time being," Maxim replied. "He has a bunk in the crew quarters and they will keep an eye on him. Since the Controller can now allow him to go to the bathroom when needed, and sleep when needed, the crew can just pick him up and move him if they need to."

Summer nodded, glad that she had figured out how to get the Controller to allow those necessary physical functions, while still restricting other movements. It had gotten to be such a pain always worrying about Lio that she had considered disabling the Controller and just turning him over to the council. Every time she had thought about doing that she'd gotten the strongest feeling that it would be a mistake. Now, thank goodness, it wasn't a problem.

After touring the recreation deck, the Roar Room, the bridge and a few other interesting areas of the ship, Summer was ready for a break.

Maxim must have realized she was getting tired and hungry because he led them back down to the rec deck and, much to her relief, to the cafeteria. After a big meal and a couple of cups of coffee, Summer felt much better.

"Hello, Chandler," Ran said to a dark haired teenager who was clearing a table near them.

"Hello, Mr. Ran," Chandler replied happily.

"I did not know you were working on the ship," Ran commented.

"Well, Mom wasn't thrilled about it," Chandler said with a wry grin, "but Mrs. Lobo said it was only for a short trip while school is out, and promised I would be safe, so she gave in. After all, I'm just a mess steward, its not like I'll be piloting fighter jets or anything. Yet."

"Everyone has to start somewhere," Ran said.

"Yeah, but that's okay with me," Chandler replied. "I'm just excited to be on a real ship." Chandler put the stack of dishes he was holding into a nearby bus cart and wiped his hands on his apron. "Would you like me to get you some more coffee or water or something?" he asked.

"I would like some more coffee, please," Summer said with a smile.

"I apologize," Ran said. "Summer, this young man is Chandler Petrie. He and his Mother own the hardware store in Granite Falls. Chandler, this is our Arima, Summer Whitney."

"Its very nice to meet you, Chandler," Summer said.

Chandler bowed, his face flushing red with sudden embarrassment. "Its nice to meet you as well, Miss Whitney," he said, suddenly feeling shy. "I'll um...I'll go get that coffee," he said, then sped away for the coffee pot. Summer noted that he limped slightly when he walked, but he obviously didn't let it slow him down.

Maxim could not help feeling mildly surprised at Summer's reaction to Chandler. He knew that she was nothing like Mara. He had determined that many days earlier. But it was still a nice surprise to him when she smiled at the boy and spoke to him so politely. Mara would never have tolerated being introduced to *the help*, and she would have had some very scathing things to say about the boy's limp.

Maxim sighed inwardly. Every time he thought about his mother something dark and ugly rose up inside of him. And it wasn't just because of what she had tried to do to Princess Rayne either, though that had made it worse. He had been angry at Mara for many months now and while he understood his feelings of suspicion toward her, he did not understand the depth of his own anger. That he had transferred some of that anger to Summer from the moment he'd met her was something he wasn't sure he would ever fully understand either. Or forgive himself for.

Maxim smiled to himself as he watched Chandler blush before hurrying away for the coffee pot. He watched as the boy took a moment to select the fullest, freshest pot, then hurried back, obviously trying to hide his limp. He silently agreed with the boy. Summer was definitely worth the effort to impress.

Even as fast as he was, Maxim could do no more than watch with surprise as Chandler stumbled just as he reached the table. He didn't fall, or drop the pot, but the hot coffee did slosh out over the rim of the pot and splatter on the table, the floor, and Summer's arm.

Summer jerked her arm out of the way and stood up quickly. She reached for a napkin and dabbed at the coffee on her arm, her face calm, though Chandler looked horrified. Maxim rose from his chair and reached for Summer's arm, relieved to see that there were only a few small pink areas. Though Summer gave no sign of it, Maxim was sure that the mild burn had to hurt. He glanced up to see that her attention was on Chandler, not herself.

Chandler grabbed a towel from a pocket in his apron and began mopping up the coffee from the table. Maxim noted with some concern that his face was nearly white. He was babbling apologies over and over so quickly that it was difficult to understand much of what he was saying.

"Chandler, its all right," Summer said gently. "Please calm down. There is no harm done, its just a little spilled coffee."

Chandler looked up at Summer, an expression of horror on his face. "But I burned you," he said plaintively. "I am so sorry, Miss Whitney, I am such a klutz! I can't believe I did that, I *burned* you."

"It was only a little accident Chandler," Summer said. "And I'm not hurt, see?" she held her arm out for Chandler to see. "So stop worrying, please, and calm yourself. Everyone has accidents."

Chandler shook his head. "No, this was no accident," he said. "This was clumsiness. I'm so sorry."

Ran felt bad for Chandler and was trying to think of the best way to handle the situation when suddenly he sensed danger. He glanced at Maxim and understood at once where the danger was coming from. He could hardly make himself believe that Maxim would go into a blood rage over such a small accident. Summer was not badly injured, nor had Chandler deliberately tried to harm her. Nevertheless, his eldest brother's eyes were glowing brightly, and that meant there was no time to wonder about the why of it.

"Chandler, please go to the kitchen and get a clean towel for Summer," he said, using his sternest command voice in an effort to cut through the boy's rambling. It worked. Chandler fell silent immediately. He looked up at Ran in surprise, then followed Ran's gaze to Maxim, gasping at the sight of the Katre's glowing, golden eyes. Glowing eyes on a Clan Jasani was a bad sign, and Chandler knew it. He immediately turned and hurried away, his heart racing with fear. He felt terrible about splashing Miss Whitney with the hot coffee, but he didn't want to be killed for it.

Summer frowned as she watched Chandler practically run away from the table. She turned her frown on Ran, wondering why he had spoken so harshly to the boy, then turned her attention to Maxim when she heard him begin to growl softly. She didn't understand the meaning of his glowing eyes, but instinct warned her to be careful.

Maxim spun around abruptly and headed for the exit. Summer glanced at Loni and Ran in confusion. What was going on here? She wondered. Was all of this just because of a silly little accident?

Ran hurried around the table and took Summer by the elbow. "Come on," he said as he guided her toward the exit, Loni taking up position on her other side.

"What's going on?" she asked, struggling to keep up with their long strides as they followed after Maxim.

"We aren't sure," Ran replied, his voice low and tight with tension. "All we know right now is that Maxim is on the verge of a blood rage."

"Blood rage?" Summer asked. That didn't sound good.

"When Jasani males get angry, especially if something happens suddenly that we aren't prepared for, we can go into what we call a blood rage," Ran explained. "The first sign is glowing eyes. Right now, Maxim is fighting hard to maintain his human form until he gets to the Shift Chamber."

"And this is because Chandler stumbled and sloshed a little coffee?" Summer asked in disbelief.

"That's what it looks like," Ran replied doubtfully. "But it doesn't really make much sense. It usually takes something really extreme to send someone of Maxim's age and experience into a blood rage."

"Are you badly burned?" Loni asked. Summer glanced up at him and shook her head.

"No, not at all," she replied. "Only a few drops landed on me and it just stung for a bit. I'm fine, really."

They rounded the wide bend at the end of the corridor and stopped at the door to the Shift Chamber. Loni reached out to hit the panel to open the door when they all heard a loud, deep, bone shaking roar come from within. Summer's mouth went dry and her eyes blurred with sudden tears. There was such anger in the sound, and sorrow. Deep, heart-wrenching sorrow.

The door slid open and Ran guided her into the ante room before releasing her. They all stepped up to the thick viewing window and watched as Maxim, in his katrenca form, raced around and around the huge room, moving so quickly he was almost a blur. Again he roared, and again Summer felt his sorrow. And his rage.

"This is not because of Chandler," she said. "It can't be. Its something else."

"Yes, I agree," Ran said. "We need to go in there to find out what the problem really is."

Summer glanced up at him. "How will you find out anything from him while he's in that state?"

"When we are in our alter form, we are able to communicate with each other telepathically," Ran explained. "We need to go in there and shift. Then we can hear from him what is happening."

"Is it dangerous?" Summer asked worriedly. "What if he hurts you? What if he attacks you before you get a chance to shift?"

"Do not worry," Loni answered her. "We would never attack one another for any reason. Nor would any of us ever attack you. You are our Arima and it is not possible for one of us to cause you harm. Not even during the deepest of blood rages would such a thing be possible."

"All right," Summer said. "But please, find out what is going on and then one of you come back and tell me."

"We will," Ran said. "Wait here for us."

"Okay," Summer agreed. Ran and Loni moved to the narrow door that led into the Shift Chamber and opened it without hesitation. They stepped through quickly and closed it behind them. Summer turned to look through the viewing window again, watching as they both shifted into their alter forms. She could not help her gasp of wonder at the sight. It was so beautiful to watch, and they were so magnificent in their katrenca forms.

Ran crouched down low to the ground and focused on Maxim as he continued to race around and around the room. Loni stood motionless next to Ran, neither of them moving a muscle for several long moments. Then, suddenly, Ran leapt to his feet and both he and Loni opened their mouths wide and roared just as Maxim had. Summer was stunned to feel the very floor beneath her feet vibrate with the sound. She spared a moment to wonder if the ship would break beneath the power of the three huge animals, then shrugged. If it did, it did. There wasn't much she could do about it. Besides, she told herself, this room and this ship were built with just this sort of thing in mind. She doubted it would split open from a few roars.

She looked back through the viewing window and her mouth fell open in surprise when she saw that all three of the Katres were now racing around the big room. What the hell was going on? she wondered.

She heard the door slide open behind her and turned to see Doc and Darleen step into the anteroom.

"What the hell is going on?" Doc asked, as though he'd heard her thoughts.

"I don't know," Summer said, turning back to the viewing window. She quickly explained what had happened in the cafeteria. "Then Ran and Loni went in there to find out why Maxim was so upset, and now all three of them are running around roaring."

"I can't believe that they are all in a blood rage over a little spilled coffee," Doc said. "But we're not gonna find out what the problem is till they either burn it off, or you stop it."

Summer looked at Doc in shock. "Me?" she asked. "How in the heck am I supposed to stop that?"

"There are only two ways to stop a full blown blood rage in a mature male-set," Doc explained. "The first is they burn it off. Race around like they are until they get it out of their system or their tempers cool down. The second is for their Arima to sing them out of it."

"Sing?" Summer asked, wondering if this was some kind of a joke. "Are you saying I am supposed to go in there and *sing*?" Summer glanced at Darleen to see if she was in on this joke too, but Darleen's face was as solemn as Doc's.

"Yep," Doc replied as he continued to watch the katrencas through the view window. "Either that, or let 'em work it off. The way they're going, it looks like they're good and mad about something. It'll probably be a couple of days before they cool down."

"A couple of days?" Summer exclaimed. "Are you telling me they could stay in there, running around like that for a couple of days?"

"Oh yeah, easy," Doc replied. "Or, like I said, you could sing 'em out of it."

Summer glared at Doc, then Darleen, but neither one of them smiled or laughed at her. They must be serious, she thought.

"Okay, I'll go in there and sing," she said in resignation. She knew she was going to feel silly, but she couldn't let them stay the way they were for days. She could sense their anger, and if that had been all she sensed, she might have been able to let them run it out of themselves. But aside from the anger, bigger than the anger, was pain. Real, heart breaking pain unlike anything she had ever experienced herself. And she felt it coming off of all three of them in waves. *That* she could not ignore.

"What exactly am I supposed to sing to them?" she asked Doc.

"That's something only you can know," Doc said. "It's something only an Arima can do, and only she knows how to do it."

"Well, that's not much help," Summer replied testily. "I'm sorry Doc, I'm just a little worried. But that's no reason to snap at you."

"Think nothin' of it," Doc said. "Just remember, there's nothing for you to be scared of. There's nothing that could ever make any of them harm a hair on your head. Anyone else goes in that room, they'd be lucky to live long enough to wonder why they'd done somethin' so stupid. But you, you'll be as safe as a baby in its mother's arms."

"Ran told me they wouldn't hurt me," Summer said. "I guess I have to trust in that."

"We'll be leaving now," Doc said. "Whatever has them in such a state ain't nothin' any of you need an audience for. I'll get someone to stand outside so's nobody else can come in."

Summer watched as Darleen and Doc left and the door slid closed behind them. Then she turned back to the viewing window. She watched Maxim, Loni and Ran as they continued to race around the room with no sign of slowing down, and wondered what she was supposed to sing to them. She didn't even know many songs, she realized. Aside from a few Christmas carols she'd learned as a child, and even those she wasn't all that sure of. She supposed she could make up words as she went along.

Summer gasped as that thought led to another. "Could that be it?" she asked herself softly. But even as she asked the question, she was moving toward the door, knowing deep down that she was right.

She pushed open the door to the Shift Chamber and stepped inside, afraid that if she hesitated she would talk herself out of what she was about to do. Even though she believed both Ran and Doc when they told her that the Katres would not harm her, she couldn't help the relief she felt when they all ran right past her without slowing.

She closed the door behind her and walked to the middle of the room, stumbling a little in the thick padding that covered the floor. When she reached the center of the big room she knelt down, paused a moment to ask herself if this was the smartest thing to do, ignored her own answer to the question, and opened her mouth.

She sang softly at first, her voice a clear, high soprano that even she could barely hear over the pounding of racing paws. She sang louder, the words she had made up to the strange tune of her music box coming to her as though she had last sung them days before, rather than years.

"*Ares tu, ami katrenca, ares tu ami maite*," she sang. "*Lasai, lasai ami katrenca, lasai ami maite*."

As she sang, Summer suddenly understood what the words meant that she was singing. She had always thought the words were meaningless, made-up sounds to go with the unfamiliar tune on her music box when she was a child. But now, those made-up sounds made sense. *What is it, my katrenca, what is it, my love? Calm, calm my katrenca, calm my love.*

Summer continued to sing, lifting her voice higher and higher until she realized that the katrencas were no longer racing around the room. They had gradually slowed until, within a few minutes, they all stood watching her, the only sound in the room now her singing and their breathing.

First Maxim, then Loni, and then Ran released their katrencas and retook their human forms. Her singing stuttered to a stop when she realized that all three of them had tears on their faces. They walked toward her and knelt in front of her on the thick matting, their eyes never leaving her face.

Summer said nothing to break the silence. She simply waited. After a little while she inched forward and reached up to wipe the tears from Loni's face, then Ran's, then Maxim's. As she withdrew her hand, Maxim caught her wrist and held it. She froze, uncertain what he meant to do. He waited until she lifted her eyes to his, then he slowly brought her hand to his mouth and pressed his warm lips against her palm in a lingering kiss.

Summer felt an electric thrill race from the palm of her hand straight to her pussy, making her instantly wet. She swallowed hard, not knowing how she was supposed to act, or what she was supposed to do. She had never felt anything remotely like the arousal she felt now, and she really didn't think this was the right moment for exploring such feelings.

Maxim, however, seemed to have other ideas on that matter. He lifted his mouth from her hand and tugged gently on her arm, urging her to move closer to him. Summer complied, unable to stop herself. She liked the way he was making her feel and, common sense and logic aside, she wanted this. She wanted to know what this felt like and she wanted to know what came next.

She inched forward on her knees until her thighs touched his, still gazing deeply into his golden eyes. Maxim released her hand and, moving very slowly, as though afraid to startle her, he wrapped his arms around her shoulders and lifted her up as he lowered himself into a sitting position on the mat. He lowered her into his lap and her legs wrapped around his waist as though she'd done it a hundred times. Her arms went up and around his neck almost of their own volition, but she barely noticed as Maxim lowered his mouth to hers and kissed her.

The kiss started out light, gentle and slow, coaxing her patiently until she parted her lips for him. Then his tongue caressed her lips so slowly, as though memorizing her taste and feel. Summer hardly dared breathe as her entire being focused on this moment, this sensation, the feel of Maxim's tongue against her lips, the scent of him, the taste of him. When he slipped his tongue between her lips and into her mouth, she sighed with pleasure and opened her mouth wider for him.

As the kiss deepened Summer lost herself in the pure eroticism of it. The sensation of Maxim's lips against her lips, his tongue against hers, inside of her mouth, then her tongue inside of his, the feel of his body against hers, his hands pressing her closer, the heat and taste and feel of it all was so new and so intensely delicious. When Maxim broke the kiss, gently lifting his mouth from hers, she found herself panting with excitement, her entire body zinging with sensations unlike anything she had ever imagined.

She felt Ran move up behind her, his hands, so hot she was surprised they didn't burn her as he placed them at her waist. She felt another set of hands, Loni's she knew, reach over and carefully lift her hair away from her neck so that Ran had access to it. He immediately leaned forward and pressed his lips against a spot just behind her ear that caused her entire body to shiver. Ran rewarded her shiver by rubbing his teeth lightly against her skin. Her body jerked at the intensely pleasurable sensation and she moaned softly. Ran's mouth worked its way to the nape of her neck and she tilted her head forward to give him better access. He licked a spot just at the top of her spine, then nipped it carefully. Her body shuddered uncontrollably, her pussy so wet that she knew they could not help but scent her.

Maxim placed a finger beneath her chin and she responded to the light pressure, lifting her eyes to his, her belly tightening at the heat in his golden eyes. "We want you, *kilenka*," he said, his voice hoarse with his own passion. "We want you more than anything, right here, right now."

Summer hesitated in spite of her own need. "I have never done this before," she said.

"Nor have we," Maxim replied.

"You have never had sex before?" Summer asked with a frown. "In over 500 years?"

Maxim smiled and leaned down to kiss away her frown. "We have had sex," he said. "Not in several hundred years, but we have experienced it."

Summer wondered briefly why they had not had sex in so long, but put that question away for another time.

"What we have not done is make love," Maxim continued, "which is what we wish to do with you."

Summer smiled, though tears stung her eyes. She was a little surprised to hear Maxim say something so romantic, but everything in her knew that his words were honestly felt. And not just by him. She felt Ran and Loni's emotions too, as strongly as she felt her own.

"What if someone comes in?" she asked, unable to keep herself from worrying about that. She did not want a sudden audience for this.

"Do not worry," Ran said into her ear. "I have used air magic to lock the outer door. None shall enter and disturb us."

Summer took a deep breath, her eyes still locked with Maxim's. "All right," she said softly, feeling a new thrill of excitement rush through her at her decision.

"No," Loni said suddenly. They all froze and looked to Loni, Summer suddenly afraid of what he was going to say.

"No, beautiful one," he said, smiling at her gently. "I only think you deserve better than to have our first joining here, in this public chamber, rather than the privacy and comfort of a bed in a locked room."

Summer smiled at him. "Thank you Loni," she said, "but this is fine."

"No," Maxim said. "He is correct."

"Yes, he is," Ran agreed as he released her. Maxim stood up while still holding her, seemingly without effort. "You do deserve better," he said. "You deserve better than much of what you have received from me so far." Summer smiled up at him and he bent to kiss her lightly on the nose. "Hold on tight *kilenka,*" he warned, "we will move quickly now."

Summer tightened her arms around Maxim's neck, though she knew that there was nothing that would make him drop her whether she held to him or not. Suddenly the world around her blurred in that familiar way that told her they were moving almost too quickly for the human eye to see. Before she knew it, they were all standing before her stateroom door.

"What about the elevator?" she asked curiously. She had thought they would have to stop moving for that, but they hadn't.

"We took the stairs," Ran replied with a grin. "Much faster."

"We ask that we be invited into your room," Maxim said, his tone a little more formal than usual.

"My room?" she asked.

"Yes," Maxim replied. "We gave you the room designed for a male-set and their mate in hopes that you would eventually accept us."

Summer laughed. "So that is why the bed is so big! I wondered about that." She shook her head at her own naiveté. She should have figured that one out, but it simply had not occurred to her. "Of course you are invited in," she said.

All three of the Katres smiled and Ran reached over to open the door. A moment later they were all in her stateroom, the door closed and locked behind them. Only now Summer felt a little shy.

Maxim set her on her feet and studied her carefully. "Do not worry, *kilenka*, we will reignite your passion in just a moment," he said.

"What does that mean, *kilenka*?" Summer asked as she watched Ran and Loni turn down the covers on the huge bed.

"It means *little cat*," Maxim said. "Or, *kitten*."

Summer lowered her brows in a mock frown. "I am not little," she said. "Nor am I a cat."

Maxim grinned. "Happily you are not any smaller than you are or we would be terrified of breaking you," he replied. "And we can only hope that, one day, you will agree to the mating ritual, and become our little cat in truth."

Summer really did not know what to say to that, but apparently Maxim did not expect a response as he picked her up and carried her to the bed.

"I can walk you know," she said, trying not to sound snippy, but feeling a bit uncomfortable with all of this carrying around stuff.

"Yes, you certainly can," Ran said, his tone very suggestive, but of what Summer did not know. She arched a brow at him in question as Maxim lowered her to the bed, setting her on the edge of it so that her feet were on the floor.

"Watching you walk is one of the most joyful things I have done in centuries," Ran said as he climbed onto the bed behind where she sat.

Summer started to laugh at him, then remembered herself watching the three of them as they had walked down the hall that morning. Okay, she thought, I get that.

Maxim ran his hands from her waist down over her hips, and down her legs, leaving a tingling path of heat behind. He lowered himself to the floor and began removing her shoes as Ran lifted the hem of her shirt very slowly until he reached the level of her breasts.

"Raise your arms, *saritu*," he whispered softly into her ear. She silently complied, again feeling nervous but at the same time, so curious as to what would come next.

She felt Loni climb onto the bed behind her with Ran, and suddenly wondered why it was she did not feel in the least bit strange having three men about to make love to her. But then, she had always thought that three men sounded more normal to her than one. That was why she had chosen to come to Jasan to begin with.

Ran lifted her shirt off over her head and tossed it aside as Maxim did the same with her shoes and socks. She felt Loni fumble a moment with the catch on her bra, then felt it suddenly loosen and slip down her arms. She automatically folded her arms across her chest, feeling shy again.

Ran and Loni coaxed her to lie back on the bed, Loni moving to her left and Ran to her right as Maxim began unfastening her jeans. Loni and Ran gently unfolded her arms and slipped her bra off. She felt her nipples harden in the cool air and shivered a little.

"Are you cold?" Loni asked.

"No, I don't think so," she said. "I'm not really sure what I feel just now."

Ran smiled, then leaned down and kissed her softly on the lips. She shivered again, but this time she knew it was not from cold. Ran's tongue slipped into her mouth so slowly and sweetly that it almost brought tears to her eyes. Within moments the soft, gentle kiss soon became deep and hot. Summer's hands came up and buried themselves in his mane of golden hair, pulling him closer to her, wanting more. Ran gave her what she wanted, plunging his tongue into her mouth over and over again.

The kiss was so intense, so passionate, that Summer barely noticed when Maxim slid her pants off of her, then lifted her legs up over his shoulders. When his hot, slightly rough tongue took a long, slow lick of her pussy she groaned helplessly into Ran's mouth. Ran raised his head and smiled down at her.

"You are so exquisitely beautiful," he said as he ran his fingers lightly over one breast, his eyes drinking her in. He had never seen a woman who came close to Summer in beauty. She was long limbed and graceful, with a tiny waist and sweet, perfectly shaped breasts tipped with deep pink nipples. Nipples that were, at the moment, long and hard, beckoning him to taste. It was an invitation he could not ignore. He bent his head to curl his tongue around one, smiling to himself when he felt it harden further beneath his tongue. He opened his mouth and sucked the long, hard nipple into his mouth, lashing it gently with his tongue. Summer arched her back, pressing her breast toward him in a silent plea for more. He set his teeth carefully at the base of her nipple and sucked harder, his cock throbbing painfully against his jeans when she moaned in reaction.

Loni leaned down to kiss Summer, his lips meeting hers lightly and gently at first. She reached up and slid her fingers into his hair, urging him closer, needing him to kiss her hard and deep. She loved how different each of them tasted, how different each of them felt when they kissed her, how differently they each touched her. Even though they looked exactly alike, she knew she would never confuse them with each other. Even their scents were unique.

Loni moaned softly and Summer's body reacted instantly to the sound with a new wave of arousal. She slid her hands down Loni's shoulders to his chest, then his waist. She gripped the hem of his shirt and began tugging it up, wanting to feel his bare skin against her, but not wanting to break the kiss to ask for it.

Loni broke the kiss anyway, lifting his head just enough to look into her eyes. "Do you want me to take off my shirt?" he asked.

"No," Summer said, nearly gasping for air she was so aroused. "I want you to take off everything. All three of you."

Loni smiled and rose up on his knees to comply with her request. A moment later Ran and Maxim did the same. In seconds Summer was gazing at the three most incredibly beautiful male bodies she had ever seen. They were all long, lean muscle covered with warm golden skin that looked so smooth and velvety that she couldn't wait to run her fingers over them.

Maxim resumed his position between her legs and began licking the insides of her thighs with long, slow strokes of his tongue. Ran lay down beside her and began licking her as well, tracing the long line of her ribs with his hot, slightly rough tongue. Loni bent down started nibbling at her neck, working his way slowly down to her shoulder.

At first, Summer was a little tense with the idea of being licked all over, but the hot, long licks were so erotic that she could not help but relax into it. After a few moments, she began to feel something new, something incredibly soft and long was being stroked over the skin of her other leg. She opened her eyes and raised her head to see that it was Maxim's tail lock. A moment later Ran's tail lock began drifting lightly over her stomach, and Loni's reached over and began brushing over her breasts and teasing her nipples.

The contrasts between the hot, rough tongues and the soft, cool tail locks caused Summer's arousal to spike so high she began shivering, her skin pebbling, her nipples so hard they almost hurt. When Maxim finally worked his mouth back to her pussy, she nearly climaxed with his first long, slow lick.

Loni and Ran both shifted position at that moment, each of them taking one of her long nipples into their hot, moist mouths, causing her to arch with a new wave of intensity. Again she almost climaxed, but not quite. Summer moaned softly, her head turning from side to side in distress. These sensations were too strong, too intense, and she was feeling too much. She wanted to push them away and pull them closer, both at the same time and couldn't do either. A soft whimper escaped her that she wasn't aware of. But Loni, Ran and Maxim all heard it, and understood her problem.

Summer felt Loni's tail lock wrap around one wrist, and at the same time Ran's wrapped around her other wrist. They both tugged gently but firmly, raising her arms high above her head until they were stretched out above her. They held her wrists in place against the bed while at the same time, Maxim slipped two fingers into her tight sheath and began stroking them in and out of her, going deeper and deeper as he stretched her gently.

Summer's initial reaction to her wrists being held above her was surprise, but her body reacted with excitement. Her pussy tightened, releasing a rush of fluid around Maxim's fingers. Her entire body ached with need, her muscles tense and trembling. Then, as though hearing some silent signal, Ran and Loni tightened their tail locks around Summer's wrists while at the same time sucking hard on her nipples as

Maxim pressed his fingers as deeply as he could into her pulsing sheath, breaking her hymen, and at the same time carefully nipping her throbbing clit.

Summer screamed as her entire body exploded in orgasm. She arched up off the bed as every muscle, nerve and fiber shook and trembled helplessly beneath wave after wave of intense, erotic pleasure. Just as her body started to relax enough that her back was once more on the bed, Maxim rose to his feet and placed the large, hot head of his cock at her entrance.

Summer looked down, her eyes meeting Maxim's. The expression of raw desire on his face made her belly tighten and her pussy pulse wetly against him. His golden eyes flared with heat as he clenched his jaw and arched his hips, pressing his cock slowly into her welcoming channel. Summer arched her hips in an effort to pull him in faster, harder but his hands held her in place, forcing her to accept him at his pace.

Her head fell back against the bed as another rush of heat rolled through her, causing her to whimper with need. Without thinking, she tugged at her wrists and was stunned at her body's response when both Ran and Loni tightened their tail locks and tugged her wrists firmly back in place. She gasped at the intense thrill that raced through her, heating her blood, causing her pussy to clench tightly around the head of Maxim's cock.

Maxim was struggling to hold himself back. This was Summer's first time, and he meant to be careful and not hurt her, even if it was the most difficult task he'd ever set himself. But, when he saw his brothers tighten their grip on Summer's wrists, and her response to it, it was all he could do not to come right then and there. As it was, he was helpless to stop himself from slamming his cock into her hot, moist depths to the hilt, causing Summer to scream out in pleasure as she climaxed. The feel of her soft, hot flesh clenching around him was too much. He pulled out, then thrust back in as deeply as he could, over and over until he too roared out his pleasure as his hot seed jetted deep within her. He held himself deep inside of Summer until he had given her every drop and her orgasm released her. Then he withdrew and bent down to kiss her deeply.

Maxim stepped back and helped Ran and Loni to move Summer further up on the bed and turn her over. Maxim traded places with Loni, and he and Ran gently coaxed Summer up onto her hands and knees on the bed. Loni knelt behind her and placed his throbbing cock at her entrance, then grasped her hips and slowly entered her. He groaned softly as her hot, wet sheath gave way to his thick, hard cock until he was fully seated. He used his tail lock to stroke Summer's back and buttocks in a soothing motion and nodded to Ran. Ran moved around until he was kneeling in front of Summer, his cock bobbing before her. She reached out with one hand and stroked the long, velvety length with gentle fingers, then lifted the head to her mouth.

Ran watched, mesmerized as she reached out with the tip of her tongue and delicately licked away the tiny pearl of fluid at the tip of his cock. He clenched his fists in an effort to hold himself still as she explored the slit for more fluid before giving the head a long, sweet lick. She lifted it closer to her lips and kissed it, then opened her mouth and slipped it slowly between her lips. Ran threw his head back and gritted his teeth with pleasure as Summer's hot, wet mouth engulfed his hard, sensitive cock. He forced himself to remain motionless as she experimented, taking him in as far as she could before tightening her lips around him and pulling back until just the tip was between her lips, then taking him deep again.

"Do you want to take all of him?" Maxim asked as he watched Summer explore Ran's cock with her mouth.

Summer slipped Ran out of her mouth, causing him to emit a soft moan. She looked at Maxim and smiled. "Yes," she said. "I would like that very much."

Maxim smiled and ran one finger lightly over Summer's bottom lip. "Take him into your mouth again," he said.

Summer lifted Ran's cock to her mouth and opened her lips, taking him as deep as she could.

"When he thrusts into your mouth and goes deep, you need to swallow," Maxim said, watching Summer's face intently. "Swallow just like you're drinking water, all right?"

Summer nodded, a tiny movement but clear enough. "Ran's going to thrust almost all the way in, but not all the way, so you can try it. All right?"

Summer nodded again and Maxim looked up at Ran.

Ran pulled his cock almost all the way out, then slowly thrust back into Summer's mouth until he felt her starting to swallow. He stopped, then pulled back out again. He gave her a moment, then repeated the movement several times.

"Good girl," Maxim whispered to her, his excitement climbing again as he watched Summer's luscious lips tighten around Ran's cock.

"This time, he's going to go all the way into your throat," Maxim said. "When you swallow, he will go into your throat for just a moment, and them pull back out. All right?"

Summer nodded again, her breathing picking up with excitement. She felt Loni beginning to thrust in and out of her with short movements and she arched her back, trying to urge him to do more.

"All right, now," Maxim said, bringing Summer's attention back to the cock in her mouth. Ran thrust forward slowly and Summer swallowed, thrilled when she felt Ran's cock press all the way into her throat with a soft popping sensation. Her pussy tightened around Loni's cock and he groaned in unison with Ran.

Ran pulled back out of her throat and held himself still for a moment, struggling not to come.

"Was that all right?" Maxim asked.

Summer nodded again, then pressed down, urging Ran's cock deeper into her mouth. Ran took the hint and thrust deeply once more, groaning with pleasure as his cock filled her tight hot throat, the swallowing motions causing her muscles to ripple around his throbbing length. Maxim stroked himself as he watched Summer's throat fill with Ran's cock, and used his tail lock to reach out and caress her throat gently.

Summer moaned, setting up a vibration that had Ran again fighting not to come. He withdrew his cock and looked to Loni, giving him a short nod. Loni pulled out of Summer's sheath and slammed himself deep with a moan of his own, then out, then in again, setting up a hard, fast pace. Ran thrust into Summer's mouth, shivering with pleasure when she swallowed him down. He held himself there for a moment, then withdrew, giving her time to breathe before thrusting back in again.

Summer's entire body was trembling with the need to climax with Loni pounding into her hard and fast, and Ran fucking her throat long and deep. Every time Ran went deep into her throat and held himself there she felt her body wanting to come, but she just couldn't quite get there. She whimpered softly as Ran pulled out yet again, and she took a fast breath and pressed forward, almost frantic to get him deep in her throat again.

Maxim looked up at Ran, then Loni, then back at Summer. Clearly she needed a little extra help to climax, and Maxim struggled to figure out what it was she needed. Ran gasped and Maxim glanced up, realizing that Ran and Loni were both about to come.

"Do you want Ran to come in your throat?" he asked Summer. She nodded, her eyes almost frantic as she looked at him briefly before closing them again. "Take a deep breath next time, and if he's in your throat too long, tap me, all right?"

Summer nodded again, and took a deep breath through her nose. Maxim watched, nearly frantic himself with the need to figure out what it was she needed. As Ran thrust deeply into her throat and Loni roared as he buried himself deep at the same time, Maxim's cat spoke to him, and he realized at once what Summer needed. He leaned over, brushed Summer's long hair out of the way, and, just where her shoulder met her neck, gently but firmly clamped onto her with his teeth.

Summer immediately bucked hard against Loni as her body exploded once again in a muscle wrenching orgasm. Ran withdrew from her throat and finished coming against her tongue as Loni emptied himself into her womb. Maxim continued to hold with his teeth, careful not to break the skin even as he shook and trembled with his own release.

Loni and Ran both gently withdrew, and Maxim released Summer's shoulder, licking tenderly at the area to soothe any hurt he might have caused. Then they carefully lowered her to the bed and curled themselves around her. When their hearts had slowed and their breathing returned to normal, Loni got up and went into the bathroom. He came out a few minutes later with some warm cloths and the three of them spent several minutes cleansing their Arima as she dozed sleepily.

They enjoyed this time together, the three of them caring for their woman after loving her for the first time. Maxim wondered how he had ever imagined they could simply walk away from her. He did not regret that they had taken things more slowly than was usual for a male-set who had found their Arima. The long years of watching their fathers put up with Mara's constant verbal abuse had left its mark on all three of them, and they had needed to go slowly whether Ran and Loni had recognized that or not.

But now they knew her well enough to be sure of her character, and Maxim realized that the legends were true. Summer had been made just for them, and they for her.

When they had finished cleaning Summer, and checking to be certain that she was well, they all curled around her once more. Maxim's heart seemed to swell within his chest when Summer rolled over in her sleep and wrapped her arms around his waist. He reached down to lightly stroke her silky hair and closed his eyes, feeling more at peace in that moment than he had in many years.

Chapter 33

Za-Linq was beside himself with worry and indecision. There was also more than a little anger in the mix, which made for an interesting reaction from his crew members as he stormed back and forth through his ship. Every single time he felt the need to lash out at someone, there was a distinct absence of potential victims within reach. Za-Linq growled with frustration as he turned and stomped back toward his quarters.

He had awakened that morning after a troubled night's sleep with the knowledge that it was the seventh day of his ten day allotment for finding and delivering the *berezi*, and he was no closer to accomplishing his task than he had been on day one. He had crawled wearily out of his sleeping chamber and donned his *makina*, grimacing at his reflection in the mirror. His appearance was far below regulation.

He bent to the task of grooming himself, feeling strangely soothed by the familiar routine even though he didn't particularly like his appearance. He found it difficult, if not impossible, to understand what it was that humans found so appealing about his looks. The long, shiny blonde hair, the white iridescent skin, the clear green eyes, even the pale red lips all seemed garish and gaudy to him.

As he worked washing and brushing and combing himself, he tried to come up with some new plan for getting the *berezi* back. So far he had sent eleven human agents to the Dracons' ranch, all of them with strict orders to learn as much as possible about the *berezi* and, if possible, to get her off the property. He had not really expected that any of them would really be able to get the woman off the ranch, but it never hurt to try.

Only two of the agents had managed to gain access to the ranch, one of those being Lio's old assistant, Elliot. Worse, the news they had returned with had not been good. Apparently the *berezi* was not only working with the Jasani on some plan that nobody seemed able to uncover, but she was never alone. She slept in a high ranking Jasani's home, and was always surrounded by more Jasani during the day. She had not left the ranch even once since her arrival.

Za-Linq despaired of ever getting his hands on her. So much so that a few days earlier he had sent out carefully crafted inquiries as to the possible discovery of another *berezi.* After all, one *berezi* was the same as another. Even though it had taken years to find just two of them, he felt it would be easier to find a third than it would be to regain the one currently holed up on the Dracons' ranch.

Finished with his grooming duties, Za-Linq decided to check his vid terminal. Perhaps a substitute *berezi* had been found somewhere and the news was just waiting for him to open up and read. With that happy thought, he sat down at his desk and activated the terminal. As the screen came on a small green light began flashing in the corner. Za-Linq frowned at it in confusion. He mentally went over his actions of the previous few days but no, he had not implanted any new tracking devices on anyone. And he had most certainly not reassigned any existing devices to the status of the one currently blinking on his screen.

Still frowning, he reached out and pressed the screen over the blinking light. The screen flashed brightly, then displayed a map of the Jasani system, with the small green light's current position. A position that was moving rapidly away from Jasan into deep space. He tapped the icon representing the ship, causing the ship's identity, course and speed to appear on screen.

Za-Linq stood up so quickly his chair fell over backwards behind him, but he didn't notice. He saw another light flashing on the bottom of the screen, this time a blue one, indicating an incoming message. He reached down and accepted the message, listening to it with growing fury as he continued to stare at the green light moving across the screen.

"Mr. Za Linq, Sir, this is Elliot, Sir, and I got some news for you, Sir, I just saw the *berezi* get into a VTOL and take off Sir, with Mr. Lio's toy Sir, and you aren't going to believe this but I also saw, I mean I think I saw, or at least it looked like it might have been Mr. Lio on the VTOL too, Sir. I don't know where they're going, I'm sorry, Sir, but nobody seems to know or won't say. I'm sorry the news is a little late, Sir, but I had to get off the ranch first, Sir, you know that, not sure why I'm telling you, Sir, but now the *berezi* is gone, Sir, so I guess I will go back to Badia now. Sir. Um...Okay bye."

Za-Linq roared with fury. Not only was Lio Perry not dead as he was supposed to be, he was in league with the Jasani! A traitor! How could Za-Queg have been duped so completely by a mere human? It wasn't possible. Za-Queg was too smart for that! Obviously Lio Perry had been working for the Jasani all along. Yes, that had to be the explanation. Only that could explain how the human had fooled Za-Queg. Of course. And that meant that the human Za-Queg had trusted so much had been the cause of his downfall, and his death. And now, somehow, the backstabbing, squishy little human had possession of the *berezi*. The *berezi* that he, Za-Linq, had only three days to get back or he was going to go the same way Za-Queg had!

No no no no no! He was NOT going the same way Za-Queg had. He was going to get that *berezi* back, and he was going to destroy Lio Perry at the same time. He had no idea how he was going to manage that, especially after learning that the *berezi* and Lio Perry had boarded a full size Jasani Assault Transport. He could not do anything against a ship that size with his comparatively small vessel.

He ordered his captain to follow the Jasani ship in full stealth mode, and not to lose it during a jump on pain of a slow and painful death. Then he stormed back to his quarters and sat down at his vid terminal. Somehow, he had to figure out where the Jasani ship carrying Lio Perry and his *berezi* were heading. If he could do that, he could get there first and be waiting for them.

And then the game would be his.

Chapter 34

Summer awoke the next morning to find herself wrapped around a lean, hard, male body which, she knew instantly, belonged to Loni. She smiled and stretched languorously, not in the least bit startled or uncomfortable. She had been trying to stop herself from dreaming up long hot sexy scenarios with the Katres for a week now. She was glad she no longer had to struggle against it, or dream about it. Especially since her dreams had come nowhere near reality.

"Good morning *kilenka*," Maxim said softly.

She lifted her head from Loni's chest and looked toward the door to see Maxim standing there holding a tray.

"Good morning," she replied with a smile. She turned her head to look up at Loni, then bent to press a kiss against his chest.

"Good morning to you as well," she said.

Loni responded by pulling her gently up his body so that he could reach her mouth with his own and return her kiss with one of his own. "Good morning, beautiful one," he whispered against her forehead before kissing her again. He then helped her to sit up in the bed, pulling the sheet up for her so that she could cover herself modestly.

"Coffee?" she asked Maxim hopefully as he held a steaming cup out to her.

"Of course," he replied. "With cream and a touch of cinnamon, as you prefer."

Summer smiled, pleased that he had taken the trouble to learn something so mundane as the way she preferred her coffee. "Thank you, Maxim," she said as she took the cup. She took a sip and sighed. It was perfect.

"Where is Ran?" she asked, unable to prevent the quiver of worry she felt at not being able to see him. Just then the bathroom door opened and there he was, smiling at her.

"I'm right here, *saritu*," he said as he reached for a cup from Maxim's tray and settled himself on the bed.

"Good morning," she said primly as Maxim joined them on the bed, snuggling up close against her other side and coaxing her to lean back against him a little. "What does that word mean that you keep calling me? Sartu?"

"*Saritu*," Ran corrected. "And I am not telling you that unless you tell us what that funny expression you use all the time means."

"What expression?" Summer asked, then smiled. "Do you mean *gardez donc*?"

"Yes," all three of them said together. Summer laughed.

"You first," she said playfully.

"*Saritu* means graceful one," Ran told her. Summer bent her head and sipped her coffee, trying to hide her blush. Ran gave her a moment, and then said, "Your turn."

"*Regarde donc* just means wow, or look at that," she said. "It's an expression of amazement."

"What language is it?" Maxim asked.

"Cajun French," Summer replied with a smile. "My maternal Great-Grandmother was one of the few remaining old Cajuns on Earth. Like most distinct Earth cultures, the language, customs and food of the Cajuns have faded into the past. But Great-Grandmother taught me a few words here and there. I use them as she did, without really thinking about it."

"Is Cajun French anything like Japanese?" Maxim asked.

Summer looked at him in surprise. "Not at all," she replied. "Why do you ask that?"

Maxim shrugged. "You have some features similar to Sensei," he explained. "Your golden tan coloring, the shape of your eyes a little, your black hair."

Summer nodded. "That's because I have some Japanese blood as well," she said. "My paternal grandmother was half Japanese, but I never knew her. She lived on Nippon-2, and died when I was still a baby. I have quite the mix of old Earth nationalities, but then, so do most humans who still live on Earth. Many cultures have gone out into the stars and settled on their own worlds, carving out a way of life that is a mix of the old and the new. But those of us on Earth are pretty much melted together now. Just generic humans."

While she was talking Maxim had handed her a plate with some sliced fruit and bread on it before handing one to Loni, then Ran, and taking one for himself. He took her coffee cup from her so that she could eat.

"This is just a snack to tide you over for a little while," he said. "Then we have a little surprise for you. After that, we'll go get a real breakfast."

Summer looked at him curiously, but didn't ask questions. Instead she nibbled on the unfamiliar fruit, tasting it carefully before taking a bite from it. "This is wonderful," she said as she reached for another piece.

"I would ask you a question, if you do not mind," Loni said, much to Summer's surprise. He almost never asked questions.

"Certainly," she said. "What would you like to know?"

"Why did you decide to come to Jasan as a Candy Bride?" he asked.

Summer popped another piece of fruit into her mouth and chewed slowly as she thought about her answer. After a few moments she shrugged. "I'm not really sure," she admitted. "I was lonely, and had been for a long time. I wanted to get married, and have a family of my own. But nobody knew the real me, and I wasn't going to pretend my way into a marriage.

"One day I was reading the news, and I saw this ad for contract brides on Jasan. I just had this instant feeling that going to Jasan and marrying a male-set was the right thing for me to do. The perfect thing for me to do. Partly because I thought I could be my real self, and they wouldn't care since Jasan was desperate for women. But mostly, it just *felt* right.

"At the same time, I knew that signing a bride contract sight unseen was not the right thing to do. So I did a little searching and discovered Bride House."

Summer smiled up at Loni. "I guess the answer to your question is that I was just really tired of being alone and I wanted a family."

"Do you still want a family?" Loni asked.

Summer dropped her eyes to her plate and shrugged again. "I suppose, eventually," she said. "Right now the thing I need to do most is free as many enslaved women as I can."

"And we are pleased to be able to assist you," Maxim said.

Summer smiled up at him in thanks, and finished her fruit.

"Okay, what's the surprise?" she asked with a studied indifference that fooled none of them. Maxim chuckled as he returned the remaining dishes to the tray and stood up.

"I can see that patience is not really your strongest quality," he said as he bent down and slipped his arms beneath Summer, picked her up with no effort at all and cradled her against his chest. He stood for a moment, gazing down at her.

"You are so beautiful," he said, his voice hoarse with emotion. Summer raised her head up and kissed him on the lips, lingering for a long moment before relaxing back into his arms. He pulled her a little closer and followed Loni into the bathroom and through a door that Summer hadn't noticed before. Her eyes widened in surprise at the sudden cloud of steam that roiled through the doorway as they entered the sauna, her skin pebbling at the sudden change in temperature from cool to hot.

"Wow, you guys really live it up on these ships, don't you?" she asked, delighted with the private suana.

"Yes," Ran said as he spread a clean towel on a wooden bench for her. "Once we tell everyone else what to do, we just sit around in the sauna and relax."

Summer laughed as Maxim set her carefully on the towel covered bench. "I won't tell anyone since I get to use it too."

"That's a relief," Maxim said as he sat down next to her. "Otherwise, we'd have a mutiny on our hands."

Summer shivered. "What's wrong?" Maxim asked. "you can't be cold, can you?"

"No, I just remembered reading about a mutiny in one of my father's books," she explained. "It was definitely not something a seven year old should have read. It gave me nightmares for a long time."

"I'm sorry," Maxim said, wishing he could kick himself. He seemed to have a talent for always saying the wrong things to Summer.

Summer reached over and lightly brushed his cheek with her fingertips. "Don't be," she said. "You said nothing wrong."

"How are you feeling?" Maxim asked. "If you prefer, we could run a hot bath for you instead."

"No, I'm fine and this is wonderful," Summer said as she leaned back against the wall and relaxed, closing her eyes as she let the heat seep into her. After a while, she opened her eyes and looked through the steam at Maxim, Ran and Loni. They were all just sitting there watching her, and none of them looked the least bit relaxed.

Summer sat up and looked at each of them again. She didn't want to ruin things by bringing up an unpleasant subject, but this was important. She didn't know why, but something inside of her told her it was.

"What is it?" Maxim asked.

"I think we need to discuss what happened last night," she said.

Ran grinned. "We all made love and had many orgasms. If you do not remember it, I think we can be talked into a repeat performance."

Summer rolled her eyes. "Yes, I'm sure that's true," she said. "Maybe later we will give that a try. But that isn't what I meant."

"You are correct *kilenka*," Maxim said. "We should discuss what happened." His face lost its smile and his eyes grew distant. "It is not a pleasant story."

"I figured that much," Summer said. A thought occurred to her and her face flushed pink. "I'm sorry," she said. "I just assumed...I mean, if you don't want to tell me, I really have no right to...:"

"No, you need to know this," Maxim said. "I only hesitate to tell you more unpleasantness about our family. I have no wish to run you off for good."

"I hope I'm not that shallow," Summer replied. "Please, don't worry about what I might think. This is not about me."

Maxim leaned in to kiss her lightly, wondering how he could have ever thought for even a moment that she was anything like Mara. He had been such a fool. He promised himself that he would spend centuries, if necessary, trying to make it up to her. He leaned back against the wall, and wondered where to begin.

"About a year ago a tragedy occurred in our family," he said, his voice low and sad. "Our younger brothers, who were pilots, were flying our fathers from their home in Berria, which is on the far side of Jasan, to the Dracon's ranch. The air transport exploded in mid-air. All aboard were killed."

Summer sighed softly. She had been worried he was going to tell her something bad, but she had not imagined it would be this bad. Their fathers and their brothers, all gone at once. She could not begin to imagine how painful that must have been for them.

"No definitive explanation for the explosion was ever discovered," Maxim continued. "There were speculations and theories, but the destruction of the air transport was so complete that there was not enough left of it to examine.

"As you know, when we are in our alter forms we are able to communicate with each other. Usually that only applies among an individual male-set but, occasionally, there are exceptions. I was able to communicate with our eldest father when he was in his human form, and I was in my alter form. It was an oddity, but useful at times."

Maxim hesitated a moment, looked at his brothers and then back to the floor in front of him.

"At the time that the accident occurred, I was in my alter form," he continued. "There was no particular reason for it. I simply felt like taking a run that afternoon. Suddenly, out of nowhere, I heard Father say, *Look to Mara, this is no axe*."

"This is no axe?" Summer asked, remembering when Maxim had uttered those same words in the armory. "But what does it mean?"

"I did not know," Maxim said. "I did not tell Ran and Loni about it because I wanted to understand what it meant first. I didn't learn until later that day that the air transport was destroyed. I suspected that it happened just as he sent me that message. That he used Mara's name rather than referring to her as our Mother as he normally would have made me suspicious of her. But I could not understand what he meant about the axe. His favorite weapon was an axe, so I thought he was talking about that. But what did he mean that it was not an axe? If it was not an axe, what was it?"

Maxim shook his head. "I thought I would go crazy trying to figure that out."

"When Chandler stumbled in the cafeteria, and you said it was just an accident, he said, it *was no accident*. And suddenly I knew, that was what Father had meant to say to me. He did not mean to say *this is no axe*, he meant, *this is no accident*, only he didn't get a chance to finish the word. That must have been when the transport exploded. His message was actually *Look to Mara, this was no accident*."

Summer gasped. Mara had killed not only her husbands, but her own sons as well? How could anyone do such a thing? Why would anyone do such a thing? Could there ever be a reason good enough to explain such a horrible action?

"So when Loni and Ran went in to find out why you were in a blood rage, they got the full story from your head," Summer said. Maxim nodded.

"I am sorry, my brothers," he said. "I would not have had you learn of it in such a way."

Ran shrugged, a tiny lift of his shoulders, and Loni nodded. "There is no good way to deliver such news," he said quietly.

"Why would she do such a thing?" Summer asked, unable to stop the question from slipping out.

"As we told you, Mara and our fathers spent over five hundred very unhappy years together," Maxim said. "It is a bigger mystery that such a tragedy did not take place sooner."

"You think that your mother murdered your fathers *and* your brothers, her sons, in a fit of anger after five hundred years?" Summer asked incredulously. "That makes no sense whatsoever."

"What difference does it make?" Maxim asked softly. "Whatever her reason, the result cannot be changed."

"It makes a great deal of difference," Summer insisted. "For a woman to do such a thing to her own children, she must have had a reason. Not a good reason. I am sure there can be no good reason for her actions. But at least a strong one. Something that made her feel she had no choice. Something really bad."

Maxim merely shrugged. Summer wanted to reach out and shake him.

"Why were they going to visit the ranch?" she asked. "Did you know they were coming?"

"No," Maxim replied, lifting his gaze to hers. She was relieved to see a spark of interest in them. "We had no idea they intended to come, no idea they were on their way."

"Was that usual?" she pressed. "Did they normally make surprise visits to you?"

"Never," Ran said. "They always told us when they were coming because there was always a good chance we would be traveling. Our duties are such that we are rarely in the same place for long."

"Nor did they ever travel without Mara," Loni put in. Summer was relieved to see that all three of them were showing interest now.

"When Mara was caught trying to get a sample of Princess Rayne's blood, did she offer any explanation for it?" she asked, hesitant to bring up yet another unpleasant incident, but sensing it was important.

"We didn't let her give one," Maxim replied.

"I have a feeling the two events are connected," Summer said. "Don't ask me why, because I don't know. Maybe its because it seems so unbelievably foolish that anyone would try to do what Mara did in full daylight with guards all around. It makes no sense at all. Unless she was desperate. People who are desperate sometimes do desperate things."

Maxim's eyes widened. "Oh, *squilik* shit," he said, causing Loni and Ran to look at him in shock. Maxim never swore. Not ever. And most especially not in front of a lady.

"You're right, Summer," he said. "Mara must have done something. Something bad enough that our Fathers immediately called Liam and the boys to give them a lift to the ranch. Not to see us, or they would have called first. They were going to talk to the Princes. For them to do that, whatever Mara did was something very bad, and something of extreme importance."

"Mara knew of the *moztu-oku*," Loni said suddenly. "When we spoke it after she attacked Princess Rayne. She said, *no, not that again*."

"Our Fathers renounced her," Ran said, his eyes wide with shock.

"That is why Father called her *Mara* when he spoke to me that last time," Maxim added.

"What kind of actions would cause them to do that?" Summer asked.

"Betrayal," Maxim said at once. "There are other reasons, but the only one that seems as though it could possibly apply in this case is betrayal."

"Yes," Ran said, "you're right. And whatever it was she'd done, Mara was scared. So she contacted someone with enough power to obliterate the air transport. Someone with the ability to hide their presence in Jasani space."

"The Xanti," Loni growled. "It had to be, there is nobody else with that power."

Maxim and Ran both nodded in agreement. "But the Xanti don't do things for free," Maxim continued. "So Mara had to make a bargain with them. That is why she suddenly started visiting the ranch every few weeks. It must be."

"That is why she got so mad the other day when I picked her up and drove her to the guest house," Ran said. "I could not understand it at the time. She was furious that she had not been invited to stay in the Dracons' home."

"Thank the stars that she wasn't," Loni said.

"What could she possibly have done that would make your fathers feel it was necessary to hop on an air transport straight to the Dracons?" Summer asked.

"I can not imagine," Maxim replied.

"She had to have contacted the Xanti almost as soon as they left the house," Ran said. "The explosion took place about an hour and a half into the flight."

"She must have been working for them," Maxim decided. "I cannot think of any other explanation."

"Working for them doing what?" Summer asked.

But that was a question that stumped them all. After a long silence, Maxim shrugged. "We will soon learn," he said. "I will send a message to Eldar Hamat."

Maxim rose and held out a hand to Summer. She reached up and took it, letting him help her to her feet.

"I would ask you a question, if you do not mind," Ran said as he and Loni stood up as well.

"Sure," Summer replied as she pushed open the sauna door and stepped out, breathing in the cool air with relief after the heated steam.

"How is that you knew to sing to us last night?"

"Doc told me that the only way to calm your blood rages was to either wait for you to run them off in a couple of days, or to sing to you. So, I sang," Summer replied. She headed straight for the shower and reached in to turn on the taps.

"I mean, how did you know what to sing?" Ran asked.

"I have this music box that my Cajun Great-Grandmother gave to me when I was a child," she explained. "I made up words to go with the tune, which nobody seemed to know. I hadn't thought about the words in years, though I still have the music box. For some reason, it just came into my head that I needed to sing those made-up words. So I did."

"I would like to see this music box some time," Maxim said.

"Okay," Summer replied easily. "It's in my luggage at the Lobos' right now." She stepped into the shower and sighed as the cool water poured over her. A moment later Maxim, then Loni and Ran all joined her.

Summer stepped beneath the shower and turned her face up into the cool spray with a sigh of pleasure. A moment later, she felt a hard body, still hot from the sauna, press up behind her. The contrast between the hot flesh behind her and the cool water caused her skin to pebble and her nipples to harden. She shivered as a pair of large, warm, soapy hands reached around from behind and ran slowly over her breasts, squeezing gently, as a soft, warm tail-lock wrapped loosely around her neck and rubbed lightly against her throat. She leaned her head back against Loni's shoulder and closed her eyes, just letting herself feel. Ran stepped in front of her and ran his hands down her body as he knelt down on the shower floor. He gently spread her legs wider, then leaned in for a long, slow lick of her throbbing pussy, his rough tongue increasing the friction against her most sensitive flesh causing her to shiver helplessly.

Maxim chose that moment to take one of her long hard nipples into his mouth, nudging Loni's hand aside, while Loni carefully pinched her other nipple between his fingers, as he licked and kissed her neck.

So many intense sensations all over her body at once had Summer racing toward orgasm almost before she knew it. She moaned softly, her body tensing as it neared a climax that she couldn't quite reach. Summer shook her head in growing frustration. They had to stop. It was too much. She placed her hands on Ran's head, ready to push him away when all at once he nipped her clit gently, while at the same time Loni nipped her neck, and Maxim her nipple, throwing her up and over the peak into a body shuddering orgasm that went on and on. Summer screamed her pleasure, her fingers gripping Ran's hair tightly as she jerked and shivered, bright lights flashing behind her closed eyes.

Loni, Maxim and Ran eased back as Summer's orgasm faded, their caresses more soothing than exciting now. It was long moments before Summer opened her eyes and realized that without the three of them holding her, she would be a lump on the floor. She smiled as her body shuddered with another aftershock of pleasure, and waited for it to pass before standing up on her own again.

Maxim lifted his head and Summer stretched up to kiss him. It was a long, slow kiss of exploration, the first she had initiated. She loved the way his lips felt against her own, the way his breathing sped up when she ran her tongue lightly over them. She slipped her tongue delicately into his mouth, and shivered as the taste of him flooded her senses.

She left his mouth and trailed kisses along his jaw, down his neck to his chest and shoulders, taking her time, licking and tasting as she went. She found his flat, male nipples and spent a few moments exploring them, enjoying the differences between them and her own, as well as the similarities. She moved further down, kneeling on the floor as she explored his belly button with her tongue. Her hands wrapped around his hard, thick cock, and she caressed it gently, loving the contrasts between the silky soft skin over the hot, hard flesh. She bent her head and licked the tiny slit at the top, taking the pearly drop of moisture into her mouth with a soft moan. She circled the head with her tongue, then the ridge beneath, then traced the pulsing veins, memorizing every inch of him, his taste and scent and texture.

When she was sure she had explored him thoroughly, she took him deep into her mouth while reaching out on either side for Ran and Loni. Their cocks were almost the same as Maxim's, but now she knew each ridge and bump, and her sensitive fingers felt the differences.

She stroked Loni and Ran with her hands as she took Maxim as deep as she could, then swallowed as he had taught her. The feel of him popping deep into her throat caused a new wave of arousal to race through her and she shuddered again. When she could not hold her breath any longer she pulled back, then took him deep once more. Again she waited until she needed to take a breath, the sound of Maxim's groan of pleasure cause her pussy to gush hungrily.

She lifted her mouth from Maxim and turned toward Loni, taking him as deep as she could in one stroke, swallowing as he reached the back of her throat. Loni groaned at the sudden, intense pleasure of being deep inside of Summer's hot throat, struggling hard not to climax instantly.

Summer pulled back, then took him deep again, and this time Loni could not stop himself. He roared his pleasure as he came, straining to hold his body motionless in an effort to prevent himself from pounding deeper than he already was.

Summer felt Loni's seed pour into her throat, and held herself still for as long as she could before pulling back for a breath of air. She spent a few moments licking and kissing Loni's sensitive cock, memorizing his taste and scent and texture as she had Maxim's.

She moved back to Maxim, and took him deep again, still stroking Ran with one hand. Maxim gritted his teeth at the intense pleasure of being inside of Summer's mouth. He had very nearly climaxed at the sight of her taking Loni into her throat, and now he knew he was not going to last. Summer pulled back to breathe and rested a moment as she ran her thumb over the head of Ran's cock, causing it to harden further in her hand.

"Take him deep again," Ran said hoarsely. Summer glanced up at him, the intense grimace of arousal on his face causing her pussy to spasm. She smiled slowly, then stuck out her tongue and gave Maxim's cock a long, slow, deliberate lick. Ran shivered in her hand as he grew even harder, and more come seeped from him.

Knowing that Ran was watching her intently as she licked Maxim sent her arousal spiking to new heights.

"Deep, baby, take him deep," Ran said again, and this time she obeyed. She opened her mouth wide and took Maxim deep, swallowing just as he touched the back of her throat. Ran groaned with pleasure at the sight and Summer stroked his silky cock faster as she pulled back, then plunged Maxim all the way into her throat once more.

"Oh yes," Ran gasped as Maxim roared, his cock jerking and pulsing in her throat as he came, Ran's seed spurting over her hand at the same time. It was too much, too intense, too hot for Summer and, much to her surprise, she felt herself climaxing along with them. It wasn't the same kind of bone-wrenching orgasm as she'd had before, but it was intense and delicious in a different way, coming with Maxim in her throat and Ran in her hand.

She pulled back and let Maxim slip from her mouth, resting her head against his hip as she panted and shivered. When she caught her breath she looked up and smiled at her men, who were all gazing down at her with something warm and gentle in their eyes.

Maxim reached down and lifted her up off the floor. She hadn't realized her knees were sore until she was off of them. But she didn't mind in the least. Just thinking about it caused her to shiver again.

Maxim gave her a gentle kiss. "That was beautiful," he said.

"Hmmm...," she replied, not quite able to form whole words yet.

Maxim chuckled and turned her around to face the shower. "Now you just relax, and we will do the rest," he said as Loni reached for the shampoo and Ran the soap.

Summer's immediate thought was that she did not need them to wash her. Then she realized that as limp as she felt at the moment, maybe she did. Curious, she reached out for their emotions, and smiled to herself. They were not doing it because she needed it. They were doing it because they enjoyed it. And they were enjoying it very much indeed. She sighed softly and allowed herself to relax and enjoy it as well.

Chapter 35

Summer finished brushing out her hair and set the brush down on the dresser. She gazed into the mirror for a long moment, watching Maxim, Ran and Loni's reflections as they watched her. It seemed so normal to her to be in this room with these three men. Even if the feeling of normalcy itself seemed odd, which it did.

Summer shook her head at herself, then turned around, her eyes catching on the katana leaning against the wall.

"A lot of really strange things have been happening to me," she said as she eyed the intricate designs in the saya. "Things that I do not understand."

'What sorts of things?" Ran asked.

"For one thing, stuff keeps popping into my head. I seem to just *know* if something is wrong or right, or needs to be done a certain way or discussed. Like about Mara, I just knew you had to talk about it more, that what you were thinking wasn't quite right."

Summer shrugged. "I know, that's not very specific, but its weird and it seems to be happening more and more. Then there's the thing with the music box. How is it that I made up words to that as a child, and then they turned out to be real words in a language I don't even know? Words that were needed to stop your blood rages."

"Lariah and Saige have both said that they had dreams of their male-set as children," Maxim said. "Lariah had dreams of dracons, and Saige dreamed of the Lobos in their human forms. You are made for us, Summer, as we are made for you. Perhaps some part of you worked to prepare you for this when you were young.

"I don't know why, but I'm actually going to go along with that," she said. "It just feels right, and there, see, its happening again. Why does it feel right? And then there's the thing with the katana."

"What thing with the katana?" Maxim asked.

Summer sighed. She didn't want to admit this because she knew it was going to sound more than strange. It was going to make her sound like a lunatic. But she had to tell them.

"Before the day I met Sensei and he gave me that katana, I had never in my life held one," she said. "I've never even seen one used. The closest I've ever come to one was a picture in a book."

"We saw you with Sensei," Ran said. "You not only moved with great skill, you held your own against him, and he is a master. I have never seen anyone wield a katana as you did. It was as though you were born with one in your hand."

"And while it was happening, I felt like I was standing outside of myself, watching," Summer said. "I have no idea where it came from, or where it went."

"Went?" Loni asked.

"Yes, went," Summer replied. "I very much doubt that I could repeat whatever it was I did that day."

"Lets find out," Maxim said.

Summer gazed up at him in surprise. "How?"

"We will go to a training room and experiment," he said.

"I'll probably cut my arm off," Summer muttered to herself, though she was already reaching for the katana.

"We won't use the real thing," Maxim said. "We will use *bokken*, wooden practice swords."

"That's a relief," Summer said as she slid her arms into the back harness. Without even realizing she was doing it, she reached back to check the katana's position, and made a small adjustment to the harness. "You guys ready?" she asked, wondering why they were all standing there staring at her.

A few minutes later the four of them were in a practice room. Summer shrugged out of the back harness and laid the katana carefully on a bench at one side of the room. She ran her fingers over the jade inlay, amazed at the workmanship.

"It is quite beautiful," Maxim said.

"Yes, it is," Summer agreed. "Do you know what these markings mean?"

"No, I'm sorry, I have no idea," Maxim said. "We can research it if you like. What did Sensei say to you when he gave it to you?" Maxim held up a hand as Summer opened her mouth.

"Wait," he said. "If it is something you are supposed to keep to yourself, please do not feel you need to tell me."

"No, I don't think it's a secret," she said. "Besides, Darleen was there, too."

"Good, then would you mind telling me?"

"Of course not," Summer replied. "It was very weird though. I spoke Japanese, which I've heard a couple of times, but have never spoken, and he spoke it back to me. And somehow, I understood all of it."

Summer repeated everything that both she and Sensei had said that day outside of the dojo, word for word. When she was finished Maxim, Ran and Loni were all frowning down at her.

"What?" she asked.

"You said, *time is not measured in cups*?" Maxim asked.

"Yes, whatever that means," Summer replied. "Why?"

"I've heard that before," Maxim said. "I just can't remember where." Maxim looked at Loni who shook his head, and Ran, who shook his head as well.

"You don't remember?" he asked Ran in surprise. Ran usually remembered such things.

"No," Ran said, still frowning. "I can't even remember *when* I heard it. It could have been when we were children for all I know."

"Perhaps it will come to you later," Maxim said, still frowning. Ran shrugged, though Summer had the sense that his inability to remember bothered him a great deal more than he showed.

"Here," he said, holding up a wooden practice sword that he had selected for her. "This is about the same size and weight as your katana."

Summer smiled her thanks and accepted the bokken from Ran. She hefted it experimentally, hoping that the familiarity would come over her again like it had that day in front of Sensei, but it didn't.

She wasn't even sure how to hold it.

Ran, Maxim and Loni watched her carefully as she wrapped her hands around the hilt. It was obvious that she had no knowledge of how to properly hold it.

Maxim walked over to the rack of bokkens and selected one for himself. He walked back to Summer, stopped a few feet from her and bowed formally.

Summer watched him, a small frown on her face as she wondered what he was doing. He straightened from his bow, then took up an offensive stance, holding the sword in an attack position. Summer watched him carefully, feeling as though the world around her had suddenly slowed to a crawl as Maxim raised the bokken and sliced it toward her. Without thinking, her body reacted, blocking the blade while stepping forward into it, letting his blade slide along her own as she allowed hers to swing down and around in a circle, coming up to slice across his thighs. Had he been a fraction slower, and had the blade been real, it would have been a severely disabling cut, if not a fatal one.

Summer followed through, bringing the bokken up to complete the arc as she turned, swinging the bokken around towards his abdomen.

Again Maxim had to block quickly, abandoning his own offense in order to prevent a strike.

The two of them flowed back and forth across the training room, neither of them holding back, both putting their all into each blow and parry. Maxim was amazed by Summer's sheer speed. He knew that without his katrenca agility and magically enhanced speed, she would have struck him half a dozen times in the first few moments. Several minutes later they each came to a stop. They stood facing each other, their bokken held high, panting slightly from their efforts. Then, as though on some silent signal, they each lowered their bokken and slid them into their belts, then bowed solemnly to each other.

When Summer rose from her bow she suddenly noticed that there was a crowd of people gazing through the viewing window at them, and that they seemed to be cheering, although she could not hear them.

Summer frowned and looked to Maxim, Loni and Ran in confusion.

"They are applauding your skill, *saritu*," Ran explained. "As well they should. I have never seen a more dangerously beautiful and graceful display as what you just showed us."

Summer shook her head slightly. She did not know how she had done what she'd done, and it felt wrong to take credit for it. It had come to her from nowhere.

"Bow to them," Maxim said softly as he approached her. "No matter where it came from, it was you, and it was stunning to behold. It would be rude to ignore their acknowledgement."

Summer turned to face the viewing window and bowed solemnly as Maxim had suggested. She felt a little silly doing it, but Maxim was right. It would be rude to ignore them.

The people standing at the viewing window all returned Summer's bow, then began to drift away. Summer crossed the training room to the rack where the bokken were stored and returned hers to its place. Then she retrieved her katana, but hesitated before putting the back harness on.

"What is it?" Ran asked. "Would you like some help with that?"

"No, thank you," Summer replied. "I just had this idea that I should wear it at my hip for awhile."

Ran raised his brows and shrugged. "That's easily done," he said. "It would be better to use a wide sash than your belt though."

"Is the back harness uncomfortable?" Maxim asked as he removed his own sash and folded it in half before wrapping it around Summer's waist.

"No, not at all," Summer said. "Do you know what the word *battojutsu* means?"

Maxim finished tying the sash and stepped back. "Yes, I do," he said, looking at her curiously. "Why do you ask?"

"Because the word just popped into my head, and I do not remember ever having seen it or hearing it before," Summer said. "Like I said, strange things keep happening to me."

"Well, *battojutsu* is not strange," Maxim assured her. "It is a method of fighting with the katana that focuses on defending against surprise attacks. For example, it teaches methods of attacking your attacker during the act of unsheathing the katana."

"I wish I knew where all of this stuff was coming from," Summer said as she slid the katana into the sash.

"I wouldn't worry about it too much," Maxim said. "Perhaps one day you will find the answer. In the meantime, what would you like to do now?"

"I think I need to eat," she replied a little shyly. She'd been eating like a horse ever since she'd gotten free.

"Of course," Maxim replied. "I am a bit hungry myself after that. You stretched my skills wonderfully, and I thank you for it."

Summer shook her head as Maxim took her hand in his and began leading them out of the training room. "What bothers you?" he asked.

"What if I actually need to use that skill sometime and its not there?" she asked. "Since I'm walking around with the thing on my hip, eventually someone is going to think I know what to do with it. Or, what if during this raid I actually have to defend myself?"

"I do not think it is something you need to be concerned about," Maxim told her. "I think that the moment your life is threatened, your hidden talent will come to the fore and protect you. Just as when I swung the bokken at you in the practice room. Before that, you didn't know how to hold it. Then, suddenly, you were dancing with me as though it was something you have done since birth."

"Yes, that's true," Summer said, brightening a little. "But, I sure would feel better if I knew I could count on that."

"We still have a day and a half before we reach Li-Hach-Cor," Ran said. "We can experiment."

"That's a great idea," Summer said, smiling at Ran. "Only, maybe we could find a training room that doesn't have a viewing window?"

"If you wish," Ran said with a grin.

"Actually, I think it would be a good idea to surprise you with a sneak attack now and then," Maxim suggested. "That way we could see what your reactions would be in a sudden, unexpected situation."

"That sounds good," Summer agreed. "Only, we need to get another one of those bokken for me to carry around. I don't want to accidentally hurt someone with the real thing."

"Of course," Maxim replied. Summer was very pleased with the plan and her step lightened considerably as they neared the cafeteria. Until they passed by the windows and she saw how many people were in there. And noticed that many of the faces were familiar from the viewing window of the training room.

"Um, maybe we can eat later," she said. She'd had more than enough public attention for one day.

Maxim followed her gaze and understood her at once. "There is no need for that," he said. "We will use one of the private dining rooms."

"Private dining rooms?" Summer asked. "Where are they?"

"Just a bit further up this way," Maxim said, leading them beyond the cafeteria to an unmarked door. He opened the door and guided her into a waiting area. Maxim pressed a call button beside another door and then turned back to Summer. "In general we all like to eat in the cafeteria for social reasons," he said. "But there are times when a more private setting is desired. For that purpose, there are several private dining rooms. The food is the same as that in the cafeteria though."

"I think the cafeteria food is good, so that's fine with me," Summer said.

The door opened and a small, thin man dressed in white from head to toe stepped into the waiting area. He bowed low and held it for a long moment. "Greetings, Lord Commander," he said.

"Greetings, Roberto," Maxim replied. "Is the Star Room available?"

"I am pleased to say that it is, Lord Commander," Roberto replied. "If you will follow me?"

He bowed again and then led the way through the door and down a long, dimly lit hallway. Summer noticed that they passed several doors, all with a name stenciled on them. Roberto stopped at one, opened the door and stepped out of the way, bowing them through.

Summer stepped into the dimly lit room and gasped in surprise. The room was large enough to hold a round dining table with six chairs set around it, as well as several upholstered chairs set here and there with small tables between them. But Summer barely noticed any of that. What caught her attention was, strictly speaking, the decor.

The walls, floor and ceiling were all covered with a gigantic holographic image of their current location in space. It was not a stationary image, but rather a projection of their real position as seen by optical scanners on the ship's hull. The data was actually collected and used for more serious purposes than decorating a dining room as a mini planetarium, but someone had thought it would make for interesting decor, and it did. Summer felt almost as though she were standing in space as she gazed around the room in wonder.

"This is magnificent," she breathed softly.

"It does not bother you?" Maxim asked.

"No, not at all," she said. "Why would it?"

"Some people tend to have a bit of vertigo when they enter this room," he explained.

"Happily, I am not one of them," she said.

Ran gently insisted that Summer take a seat at the table, as she was so enthralled with the view that she hadn't moved since entering the room. Maxim ordered for her when she indicated with a wave that he should do so. But when the food came, Maxim had to threaten to turn off the projections if she didn't eat her food.

"All right, all right," Summer laughed as she tore her gaze from the ceiling and walls. "I'm sorry guys," she said as she shook out her napkin and put it in her lap. "Its just so amazing."

"There is no need to apologize," Maxim told her. "We wanted you to enjoy it, and your pleasure is our pleasure. We just want you to eat your food as well."

"No problem, my appetite is back now," she said as she picked up her fork and started eating. Her eyes kept straying to the stars and planets on the walls as she ate. She had never seen anything so beautiful.

"This is a wonderful gift," she said softly. "Thank you all so much."

Maxim, Loni and Ran all paused uncertainly. "This is just a small surprise," Maxim said. "Not a real gift."

Summer looked at him, then Ran and Loni, her head tilted to the side as she considered them. "A gift is something that one gives to another that is meant to bring happiness and joy. It does not need to be something one wraps up in pretty paper, or something that is purchased with money. This was a gift that you gave me, and I will always remember it as such."

"You give us too much honor," Loni said.

"No," she argued gently. "I give you as much honor as you deserve."

Maxim's heart was filled with warmth and happiness as he turned back to his own meal.

"May I ask a question?" Summer said, the hesitancy in her tone catching all of their attention.

"You may ask anything of us that you like," Maxim said.

"The other day, when you told me that your home world, Ugaztun, was destroyed, you did not say how. I was just wondering, what happened to it?"

"Are you sure you want to hear this?" Maxim asked. "It is not a pretty story."

"Yes, I would like to hear it," Summer said. "If you don't mind telling me, of course."

"No, we do not mind," Maxim replied. He picked up his glass and took a sip of wine as he considered where to begin.

"Our ancestors lived on a planet which they called Ugaztun, as we have told you. The people were strong in magic and used it for many things, including exploration among the stars. It was soon discovered that we had a sister planet. The inhabitants of that planet were very much like those of Ugaztun, yet very different. The main difference being that we were mammalian, and the people of Narrastia were reptilian.

"The two peoples clashed from the first meeting, beginning a war which was to last for centuries. Like us, the Narrasti were adept at controlling the forces of Air, Earth, Fire and Water. We were evenly matched, too much so, such that neither side could gain a serious foothold against the other.

"Then, the Narrasti developed a method of harnessing their magic in such a way that it meant the destruction of our world, Ugaztun. Whatever had been done could not be stopped, so we did the next best thing, which was copy what they had done and send it to their world so that they, too, would face destruction.

"After that, there was nothing to be done other than try to create enough pods to evacuate as many of our people as possible before the end."

"And both planets were destroyed?" Summer asked.

"Yes," Maxim replied. "All that is left of them now are two gigantic asteroid belts."

"What kind of magic could destroy an entire planet?" she asked, horrified by the thought of such power being used in such a manner.

Maxim shrugged. "Nobody knows the answer to that question," he said. "Even then, while it was happening, that was a question everyone wanted an answer for. But none of those who survived and reached Jasan knew the answer, nor have any been able to understand it in all the years since. It is a question who's answer has been lost in time."

"I don't think its possible," Summer said without knowing she was going to say it.

"You don't think what is possible?" Maxim asked.

"I don't think its possible for the magic of a world to be used against that world to such an extent that the world is destroyed," Summer said.

"Why not?" Maxim asked.

"I don't know," Summer said. "I don't even know where the thought came from, but I think it's true. Think about it for a moment. When you wield magic, you are using the four elements, Earth, Air, Fire, Water. Those are elements of power which come from the world itself. It doesn't make sense that you could use the power of a world to destroy that world."

"Yes, but we did not use the magic against our world," Maxim argued. "Nor did they use their magic against their world."

Summer started to argue further, but changed her mind. What was the point? It had all happened so long ago. Three thousand years! The civilizations of Earth were in their infancy then. Some didn't even have the written word yet.

Summer froze as a memory popped into her head.

"Maxim, where exactly are those two asteroid belts?" she asked.

There was something in her voice that caused Maxim to glance at her sharply, but she only stared back intently.

"What was once Ugaztun now orbits the star commonly referred to as Zeta Reticuli B," he said. "What was once Narrastia now orbits Zeta Reticuli A."

Summer gasped, dropped her fork onto her plate with a clatter and rose to her feet in one fluid motion. She began pacing the floor, her brows drawn down in concentration. "Can you tell me exactly how long ago it was that the planets were destroyed?" she asked.

"Three thousand, two hundred, sixty four Standard years," Ran replied.

Summer took a long deep breath, spun around and stood looking at all three men. "Okay, here is the big question," she said. "Assuming magic was used to destroy both planets, what kind of magic would it most likely have been?"

Maxim shook his head. "Nobody really knows, Summer," he said. "It has been speculated that, if enough males with strong Earth magic combined their energies, it might be possible to crack a planet's core."

"All right, lets say that happened. The planet's core was cracked. Would that cause the planet to explode in a brilliant ball of fire?"

"I don't think so," Maxim replied uncertainly. "Ran?"

"No," Ran said. "The gravitational forces, and the heat from the core would most likely sterilize the entire surface of the planet."

"When the planet cooled, would it be an asteroid belt?" Summer asked.

"No, it would probably solidify once more into a planet," Ran replied.

Maxim frowned. "Summer, it would take an extraordinarily large amount of external force to cause a planet to explode as you describe, and also break it into pieces. But Ugaztun and Narrastia did not explode. They broke up into asteroid belts, yes, but as the result of strong magic of some sort, not as the result of explosions."

"No Maxim, I think you are mistaken," Summer said hesitantly. She did not want to argue with Maxim when things had been going so well between them. But she had to tell them what she knew.

"I think that those two planets were destroyed by an external force which caused them both to explode simultaneously. I am just a little uncertain about the locations."

"I don't understand," Maxim said. "How could you possibly know such a thing?"

"When I was a child we traveled a lot," she said as she began pacing once more. "Between my Mother's research and my Father's military duties, every school break and holiday was spent on some new planet. When I was twelve, we spent a couple of weeks on Sheara 3. Father was overseeing a Joint Forces Command College symposium at the base there, and Mother was working on her latest book. That left me with a lot of time to wander around the base looking for something to do.

"I came across this little museum that had a lot of local artifacts related to space and the stars. There was a scroll there, very old and very beautiful. The writing looked more like elaborately drawn scrollwork than letters. Next to the scroll were translations in several languages, including Standard.

"The scroll spoke of a double explosion of brilliant white light that flared into the heavens so brightly that it blotted out the stars for a full night. The exploding stars, or planets, were close together, but the light from one did not touch the other. Now here's the interesting part. The scroll was dated, and the date was converted into the Standard calendar on the translation sheet. Taking into account the number of years that have passed since I saw it, and the distance between the Zeta Reticuli and Sheara systems, that double explosion took place three thousand, two hundred and sixty-four years ago. The only thing I am not certain of is the location of the planets, but then, how many planets explode at the same time?"

"But Summer, our world did not explode," Maxim pointed out.

Summer stopped pacing and turned around to face Maxim. "How do you know that?" she asked.

Maxim opened his mouth, then closed it. He sat thinking for several moments. Finally he sighed and looked up, meeting Summer's gaze. "I don't know that," he admitted. "It has always been said our planet was destroyed by magic. But there is still one of the original pods in existence today and I have seen it. It does not contain windows or viewports. Whether Ugaztun and Narrastia exploded or not, nobody aboard an escape pod could possibly know."

"Wait," Ran interrupted, "are you saying that both Ugaztun and Narrastia were destroyed by an outside force? Not magic?"

"That's what it looks like," Summer replied. "I can't say that for certain of course, and I would want to review that scroll to be sure I haven't made an error."

"Have you ever made such an error before?" Loni asked.

"No," Summer admitted. "But considering the importance of this subject, I think it warrants a careful check of that scroll, and its translation."

"I agree," Maxim said. "If what you say is correct, then someone else destroyed both worlds, and made it seem as though we did it to each other."

Chapter 36

Za-Linq stripped off his soiled clothes and left them in a pile on the floor before stepping into the shower. He turned his face up into the spray, letting the warm water rinse away the worst of the blood that covered him. After a few minutes he reached for the soap and began a more thorough cleansing of his skin and hair. He tried to remember the last time he had made such a mess of himself during clean-slice, but couldn't. But then, this really hadn't been a game of *xafla* anyway, so it didn't really count. It had started out that way, but his rage had overcome his reason.

For good cause, too, he consoled himself as he worked the suds into his hair. He had warned his crew that incompetence would not be tolerated. Then that useless navigator had gone and lost the Jasani ship. How such a thing was possible was beyond Za-Linq's comprehension. The ship was gigantic. Laziness. Incompetence. Worthlessness.

Za-Linq stilled, the water beating down over his head as he worked to rein in his temper. He needed to think. There had to be a way to find that blasted ship and as he was surrounded by a crew of incompetents, it was clearly up to him to figure it out.

His temper under tight control, he finished cleansing himself and turned off the water. He reached for a towel and began to use it as he mentally traced the Jasani ship's route up to the point where it had been lost. But no, his concentration was not what it should be. He needed to look at a map to see this. He dropped the towel on the floor, reached for a robe and left the bathroom. He considered calling on one of his officers to plot the course for him, but decided that he really could not afford to kill any more of his crew. After all, they were needed to run the ship. For now.

He sat down before his vid terminal and began pulling up astrometric charts. A couple of hours later he stood up and began pacing his quarters. The maps weren't helping, the plots weren't helping, nothing was helping and tomorrow was the tenth day. If he didn't have that *berezi* by then....

Za-Linq shuddered. He didn't want to think about it. It was bad enough he dreamed of it each night. If only he knew where the damn *berezi* was supposed to be delivered.

Za-Linq froze. How could I be so dim? He wondered. *Berezi* are sold only to Brethren. That was their only purpose, the only reason the Xanti searched for them to begin with. That reduced the possible buyers of his *berezi* to only a small few. And of those, only one was in this end of the galaxy.

Za-Linq smiled. Then frowned. What if Lio was not taking the *berezi* to the buyer? What if he was going somewhere else?

Well, he decided, it didn't matter. He had only one option right now, and that was to bank on Lio's greed. He would not get paid if he did not deliver the *berezi* as promised. For Za-Linq's purposes, that meant the buyer had to be William, on Li-Hach-Cor.

It had to be. If his guess was wrong....

No, he would not think of that. He was right. He knew it. He had to be.

He reached for the bridge comm and gave orders to plot a new course. Then he settled down to wait. And worry.

Chapter 37

Summer, Darleen, Doc and the Katres stood on the bridge and stared at the many different views of Li-Hach-Cor displayed before them. It was quite obvious that there was only one large settlement on the planet, and that it was set amidst a very large green land mass in the southern hemisphere. Exactly as Summer had explained days earlier in the Lobos' meeting room.

"According to the data," Maxim began, "there are about ten thousand people living on that planet and they are all either in that settlement, or scattered throughout that land mass. For so few people to cultivate such a large area, they must make use of massive amounts of technology."

"And the rest of the planet?" Summer asked.

"It appears as though the rest of the planet is barren," Maxim replied.

"How is it possible that one quarter of the planet is green, and the rest is barren?" Darleen asked.

"Terraforming," Ran replied. "They probably terraform more land as they need it, a bit at a time. Eventually, the entire planet will be viable, but right now it appears that only this one land mass has been made livable."

"Yes, that is how it appears, but I have my doubts," Maxim said. Summer looked at him in surprise.

"What are you thinking?" she asked.

"When we went to the slave compound on Jasan, all of our instruments indicated that there was nothing but forest below us for miles in every direction," he explained. "Obviously, that was not the case. They were using a very sophisticated camouflage system unlike anything we had ever seen before. I have a feeling that the slave compound is really there, and is using the same type of system. We were able to spot it using our katrenca vision from the air. Once on the ground, the camouflage system was not an issue. Apparently it is designed to prevent detection only from above."

"Then how can we find it?" Summer asked. "There is too much planet down there for us to cover on foot, or even in a ground-car. It would take us years."

"Perhaps the Li-Hach-Aki can help us," Darleen suggested. "Summer said that the Li-Hach-Aki are peace lovers. If that's true, then I doubt that they would condone slavery. At the same time, as peace lovers, they can't force the intruders to leave themselves."

"Good points," Ran approved. "Perhaps we can get the Li-Hach-Aki to aid us in this. If they know that we are here to free the women being held captive, and shut down the compound, maybe they will be willing to tell us where it is."

"If they know where it is," Maxim said.

"Yes, if they know," Summer agreed. "But we are going to have to handle this carefully. If we go storming in there demanding answers, or even if we go in armed, we may not get anything out of them."

"True," Maxim said. "What if we take one shuttle down to the planet with just the six of us, and have another go down with an armed squad? They can land some distance away so that the natives won't know they are there, but close enough to help if we need it."

"No, I don't think that's a good idea," Summer said. "I think we need to go down alone, and have a squad stand by here."

Maxim gazed at Summer for a long moment. "Perhaps the high level of technology the Li-Hach-Aki use for their agriculture is indicative of other technology as well," he said thoughtfully. "If we try to sneak a ship full of military personnel past them, they may very well know it, and be offended by it."

Summer stared at Maxim in open shock.

"When I am not being bull-headed and temperamental, I'm not altogether dense," he said with a grin. Summer felt her face heat. "I'm sorry," she began, but he stopped her with a gentle finger against her lips.

"Don't be," he said, gazing into her eyes for a long moment. He removed his finger and kissed her lightly on the lips.

"Come on," he said. "Let's get ourselves down there and see if the natives will help us out."

Calnic watched curiously as the two human women approached on foot. He was fully aware that a Jasani male-set watched and waited from the ground-car beyond the Sentinel Line that bordered their land, but he did not mind. They had not been threatening or demanding. They had, in fact, been very polite.

They had approached the outer tower slowly, showing themselves to be unarmed and nonthreatening. They had respectfully requested a meeting with a settlement representative. They had then waited patiently for him to arrive, and had followed all of the official requests for the meeting without scoffing or sneering. They had not acted anything at all like the Other.

Thoughts of the Other caused Calnic to shiver, his pale, blue-grey skin darkening slightly with worry and fear. They had lived peacefully on Li-Hach-Cor for many years until the Other had come. Now, they were always worried. Always afraid. The Other made many demands of food and water that their settlement was hard put to fill. They dared not miss the quotas set by Li-Hach, so they were forced to pay the demands from their own food stores. Many people went hungry now. Hungry, though they worked amidst such plenty.

Calnic hoped that these visitors meant to remove the Other from Li-Hach-Cor. The thought gave him a vague thrill such as he had never experienced before in his life. He wondered if it was wrong for him to hope such a thing.

He shrugged his narrow shoulders. Whether he hoped it or not meant little. He would see what these human females wanted and, if it was not against their beliefs, he would aid them as he could. Such was they way of the Aki.

The women stopped in the appointed place, a circle marked on the well-worn path running through the forest surrounding their village, as requested. They were very calm, Calnic observed. That was a good sign. Taking another long look around to be sure this was not a trick such as the Other sometimes played on them, he stepped out of the small border hut hidden amongst the trees and approached.

Like all Li-Hach, Calnic was very tall, perhaps ten Standard feet. Everything about him was long and slender, including his head. He wore a long blue robe, belted around his waist with a yellow sash to indicate his status as a messenger of Aki, and nothing else. He had very large eyes that matched the blue-gray tone of his skin, a thin, flat nose and a lipless mouth. Li-Hach did not have hair, though they did have a row of thin, spiny protuberances that began in the center of the forehead and ran all the way down their backs.

As Calnic approached the women he noted that they both had five fingers on each hand, as did the Other. He always wondered how they managed to manipulate things with so many fingers. Calnic, like all Li-Hach, had one thumb-like appendage on each hand, and two long fingers. That was quite as many as anyone really needed, Calnic thought. Five seemed quite excessive to him.

Calnic smiled at his own wayward thoughts as he stopped in the circle several feet from the women and bowed his head slowly.

"Greetings, human women," he said, pleased at the opportunity to use Standard. He so rarely had the chance to use it, and it had taken him so long to learn.

"Greetings, Li-Hach-Aki," the tallest of the women said, most politely. "I am Summer. This is my friend, Darleen."

"I am most pleased to accept your names," he said. "I am called Calnic."

"We are most pleased to meet you, Calnic," Summer said.

"How may the Aki assist you?" Calnic asked, hoping the woman would not be offended by his abruptness.

"There is, we believe, a compound on this world that should not be here," Summer said.

Calnic blinked in surprise. He had hoped, but not believed. He must be careful, he decided, lest his hope lead him astray.

"This is a truth," he said carefully.

"It is a bad place, where many are held as slaves," Summer said.

"This is also truth," he said, nodding his long, thin head slowly.

"We would free those who wish to be freed," Summer continued.

Calnic froze. Had his prayers been answered at long last? If so, he would have to do his part. All blessings required a tithe. Otherwise, it would be withdrawn. This was a very important moment. He thought carefully, taking his time.

"The Aki would be pleased to learn such a thing has been done," he said, speaking far more clearly than he felt safe, but deciding it was worth the risk.

The woman was silent for a long moment, and Calnic's hope grew. She, too, was being careful.

"Li-Hach-Cor is a large world," she said at last. "To search for such a place would take much time."

Ah, Calnic thought sadly, his hope shrinking. The Other's camouflage system prevented them from finding what they sought.

Calnic wondered what to do. For a Li-Hach, it was a simple matter to see right through the technologically generated camouflage. But, as Calnic was aware, humans did not possess the ability to manipulate such things with their minds. That was a Li-Hach trait.

He shook his head slowly and regretfully. "It would be an unkindness to tell you what you wish to know," he said, throwing caution to the winds. "You cannot see through the camouflage, and will be upon the compound before you are through it. By then, the Other will have terminated your lives."

"Can you see through the camouflage?" Summer asked.

"Yes," Calnic replied, "but I cannot go with you. It would be against Aki for me to do so."

"How is it you can see through it?" Summer persisted.

"It is a simple matter to manipulate such things for Li-Hach," Calnic said. "If it were not so, we would not be able to control the many machines required to cultivate such a large amount of land."

"You control the machines with your mind?" Summer asked.

"Not precisely," Calnic replied. "We control the computerized components in the machines with our minds."

"I can do that as well," Summer said, surprising Calnic greatly.

"It is so?" he asked. Suddenly his skin flushed an odd purplish color. "That was rude of me," he said with a slow, deep bow. "I apologize most profusely for implying doubt of your word."

"No offense was meant, and none was taken," Summer replied politely. "And yes, it is so. Could you teach me how to see through the camouflage as you do?"

Calnic straightened up and thought hard. What he was considering was forbidden. But it was forbidden by Li-Hach law, not Li-Hach-Aki law. It was a fine line, and he knew it. He also knew the punishment would be severe, should anyone find out. This was a very high tithe to pay indeed. But it would be worth it if....

"What of the Other?" he asked suddenly.

"The Other?" Summer repeated blankly.

"He who is master over the compound you speak of."

Summer fell silent for a long moment. Calnic waited patiently. Such thoughts and decisions could be complicated, he knew.

"The Other has caused problems for the Aki," Summer said. She made it a statement, not a question, so Calnic did not have to respond to it. Nevertheless, he dipped his head slowly in acknowledgement.

"We will do all we can to rid the Aki of the Other," she said. "If we are not successful, know that we will have done all we could. Know also that the Other shall never know of this meeting from us."

Calnic dipped his head again. He could not have asked for more. The Aki needed to be free from the Other. This was their first hope of that in all of the years since the Other had come to Li-Hach-Cor. It was a risk, but it was a worthy risk.

"Would you approach me please, Summer?" Calnic asked, pronouncing the woman's strange name carefully.

Summer bowed politely, then walked forward until she was only a couple of feet from Calnic. "I give you my promise that you shall not be harmed in what I do," Calnic said softly.

Summer smiled. "You have my trust, Calnic."

Calnic returned her smile, then bent forward, reaching out slowly with both hands. He very gently, very lightly, placed one finger of each hand at Summer's temples and closed his eyes to focus. He was pleased to discern that Summer did indeed have the ability to connect with computer processors as she'd said. In fact, she had far more ability than she knew. Calnic smiled to himself. He had made a wise decision. This was a very unique woman. She was most worthy of the gift he was about to bestow.

A few moments later he lifted his fingers from Summer and bowed to her.

"Go in peace, Summer Whitney, Mind of the Jasani, Sister of the Soul, Sister of the Heart, Slayer of the Double-Headed Dragon, and Harbinger of Peace to the Thousand Worlds."

Calnic straightened and smiled at the expression of surprise on Summer's face. "The Aki have been blessed to bring aid to you this day," he said. "Long shall you be remembered." Calnic dipped his head once more before turning around and walking slowly back to the border hut, and the growing contingent of his brothers waiting anxiously for his return. He paused and looked back just once to see the women getting into the ground-car. He raised one hand in farewell, knowing he would probably never see Summer Whitney again. But he did not mind. He would feel her strength and courage in his heart for all time.

Chapter 38

That appeared to go well," Maxim said as Summer and Darleen got back into the ground-car.

"Yes, I think it did," Summer agreed.

"When you approached him, I nearly broke our agreement to remain in the vehicle," he said.

"You are not overly patient either, are you?" Summer asked with a smile.

"No," he agreed easily. "Patience is not a common trait of the katrenca. So what did he do when he placed his hands upon you?"

"I think he changed me," Summer said thoughtfully. "He said a few things that I did not really understand, but of one thing I am certain. The Aki want the slave compound gone from their world. They fear one that he called *the Other*. I promised that should we fail, the Other would not learn from us that we had met with the Aki."

"Your word will be upheld," Maxim said. "Now, if you would, please explain your comment that he changed you."

"As you know, I can control computers to a certain extent telekinetically ," Summer said. "Now, I am sensing the computer components in this ground-car and I've never been able to do that before. I could stop them all if I wanted to. I'm not sure how, but I know I can." Summer frowned for a moment, then gave her head a little shake and looked back at Maxim. "Calnic told me that they, the Li-Hach, could see through the camouflage. I asked him if he could show me how to do the same. I think he gave me the power to do it." She turned her gaze to Ran. "Would you please pull up the planetary views from the ship," Summer asked.

"The images?" Ran asked.

"No, I think I need the live views for this," Summer said.

Ran complied. Summer leaned forward and watched the views as Ran scrolled through them. "There," she said suddenly, pressing her finger against the screen.

Ran blinked, and bent to look more closely at the screen but as far as he could tell, the spot she was pointing at was no different than the rest of the image. There was nothing to see but barren land surrounded by more barren land.

"Are you certain?" he asked.

"Oh yes, I am certain," Summer said with a grin. "Mark this point."

Ran did as she asked, marking a point on the opposite side of the planet. "It's a large complex, perhaps twice the size of the one on Jasan," Summer said as she continued to look at what no one else in the ground-car could see. "It's rectangular, with what appears to be a large open courtyard in the center of it. The main structure is surrounded by a high wall set back about twenty yards, and there are about a dozen concentric rings of electronic security that begin about a mile away from the outer wall, but no guards."

Summer continued to stare at the screen. "I think that whoever is in that complex already knows that we are here," she said. "I also think that we are going to need to use Lio."

Maxim stared at Summer for a long moment. She was a warrior, whether she knew it or not, and her instincts were good. Far better than she realized.

"What do you have in mind?" he asked.

Summer turned and looked at Darleen. "Do you wish to be in on this?" she asked. "There is no shame in saying no."

Darleen tilted her head. "Would you say no?"

"I cannot," Summer replied.

"Nor can I," Darleen said.

"Very well," Summer said and turned back to Maxim.

"This is what I propose," she said.

"JCX-2089er, this is HJ RL Perry, please respond on this frequency," Lio said into the mic with just exactly the right amount of exasperation in his voice, just as Summer had ordered. "Dammit, I can't float around out here forever, William. Answer me."

"Hello Lio," said a deep voice. Everyone in the comm room froze for a moment. They had been at this for hours now, and had almost given up on the plan. Now that they had gotten a response, it took them all a moment to register it.

Summer sent a command to Lio, who opened his mouth and began speaking. "About damn time," he said irritably. "I need you to guide me in. I had to borrow this ship from Jasan and it does not have the decoders for the Blind Sight system."

"Why didn't you get the locals to tell you where I am?" the voice asked.

Lio snorted. "Those tall skinny, blue things without brains?" he asked contemptuously. "According to them, you don't exist. Evidently they lied to me."

"Ah, did they?" the voice asked.

"Perhaps I shall go back down there and teach them some manners," Lio said with a hint of amusement in his voice.

"No," the voice said at once. "I have no desire to have the Li-Hach searching for the reason their crops have been destroyed."

"That is unfortunate," Lio said. "I am yearning for something to destroy. I have not had a good week. Now how about those coordinates? Or shall I head off for Seti Rendora with your special package instead?"

"You have my package?" the voice asked, clearly excited now.

"Of course," Lio replied. "I bring yours, and one of my own."

"Very well," the voice said. "Come on down Lio, but be certain that there are only the three of you. I would not want any unpleasant misunderstandings."

"No problem," Lio said easily. "I will have one crew member pilot the shuttle down, drop me and the females in a ground-car, and then return to the ship. Will that suffice or must I pilot the shuttle myself?"

"And risk all of your lives?" the voice said with amusement. "I know what a terrible pilot you are, Lio. I think you best let someone else handle the shuttle."

"I do not need your insults," Lio said coldly. "I've spent hours trying to raise you, and I grow bored. Perhaps I shall go to Seti Rendora after all."

"You are so touchy, Lio," the voice replied. "I've sent the coordinates to your ship. For your sake, you better really have what you say." The connection closed and Summer took a deep breath and blew it out shakily.

"Well, that worked," she said.

"Yes, it did," Maxim agreed.

"How much time do we have?"

Maxim turned to Ran. "About two hours before we are in position to reasonably launch the shuttle."

"That's not very much time," Maxim said.

"It's enough," Summer said. "Don't worry Maxim, I know I can do this."

"I know you can as well," he replied. "I have every faith in you. But it is very difficult to let you walk into danger without us. I don't know how we are going to be able to do it when the time comes."

"It's the only way Maxim," Summer said patiently. "You know that. We cannot get through that security by force without a long battle, and that risks the lives of the women held prisoner down there. Not to mention the high probability of drawing the attention of the Li-Hach. Our presence here in a military ship could trigger a diplomatic incident. An ugly one. A sneak attack is our best chance. As soon as we are close enough to the compound for me to sense the computer systems, I can start shutting them down. It'll be easy. We've already proven that."

Maxim grinned ruefully. She had completely disabled two shuttles and three ground-cars before they had conceded her ability. He had no idea what it was going to take to fix them, but he had a feeling it was going to be expensive. Not that he cared. It was worth it for him to be certain she could do what she planned.

"The only thing I'm worried about is how to hide the katana," she said. Maxim smiled.

Chapter 39

"Darleen, which would be more like Lio?" Summer asked as they prepared to climb into the ground-car on the shuttle. "Would he prefer to drive himself, or would he have one of us do it?"

"Definitely one of us driving," Darleen said. "He likes being waited on. We should both sit in the front seat and he should sit in the center of the back seat."

"All right, but I hope you can drive," Summer said. "I have to focus on the electronic surveillance and alarm systems, as well as the camouflage and anything else they might have."

"I can drive," Darleen said.

"Good, because I'm not a very good driver anyway."

"By the way Summer, great outfit," Darleen said seriously. "Where did it come from?"

"Apparently the Sensei sent a package to Maxim the day we left the ranch," she said looking down at herself. "There was a note that said only, *battle dress*."

Darleen frowned as she took in the long, full navy skirt, the short navy jacket and halter, the matching knee high boots and wrist guards, all decorated with a swirling design. "Battle dress?" she asked. "I don't get it."

Summer pulled the katana from its place hidden within the folds of the skirt and held one wrist guard against the blade. When she was sure Darleen was watching, she slid the razor sharp blade along the wrist guard.

Darleen gasped and reached out to stop her, but there was no need. The blade did not so much as scratch the wrist guard.

Darleen ran one finger over the spot where Summer had sliced the blade and smiled her feral smile. "Looks like cotton, wears like...steel?"

"Close enough," Summer said with a laugh as she slid the katana back into place.

"Okay, let's get moving here," she said as she went back around the ground-car and ordered Lio into the back seat before climbing in the front passenger side. Darleen took the driver's seat and spent a moment going over the instrument panel.

"You ladies all set?" Maxim's voice asked in Summer's ear.

"Yes, I think so," she said. "How much time do we have?"

"Just a few more minutes," Maxim replied. "We will set down just long enough for you to drive out, then we will take off again as soon as you're a safe distance away."

"Okay," Summer said. She hesitated a moment, glanced sideways at Darleen and decided to hell with it. She was not ashamed of her feelings and she didn't care who heard her.

"I love you," she said. "I love all three of you, Maxim, Loni and Ran. I just wanted to be sure you know that."

There was a brief silence, then she heard Maxim clear his throat. "I love you too, Summer," he said his voice sounding a little hoarse in her ear.

"I love you too, Summer," Ran broke in excitedly. "And thank you so much for telling us."

Summer waited for Loni to say something, but there was nothing but silence. "Um, Loni?" she asked, her stomach suddenly feeling tense. Maybe....

Her thoughts were interrupted as the door beside her flew open and strong hands reached in and lifted her out of the ground-car. Summer barely had a chance to gasp before Loni pulled her against his chest, lowered his mouth to hers and kissed her. The kiss was long, hot and deep, and by the time Loni raised his head, Summer was breathing hard and feeling a bit disoriented. She opened her eyes and gazed up at him, letting herself get a little lost in his golden eyes for a moment.

"I love you," Loni said, "more than I can tell you."

Summer blinked the sudden sting out of her eyes and smiled.

"Thank you," she said. Loni grinned, a real, honest to goodness grin that made her laugh with happiness to see. Then he returned her to her seat in the ground-car, closed the door, gave her one last long look, and sped away.

"Thanks guys," Summer said once she had composed herself a little. She risked a glance at Darleen and was surprised to see her grinning, with one eyebrow cocked.

"Its about time," she said archly.

"Oh, be quiet and drive," Summer replied with a mock scowl.

"You better not let anything happen to you, Summer," Maxim warned sternly. "I mean it. Not a single scratch."

"Aye, Commander," Summer said with only a tiny trace of sarcasm.

Maxim chuckled softly and closed the connection. Summer leaned her head against the seat and went over everything in her mind. There were a lot of ifs and maybes in this plan. But she thought it would work. If they were careful.

"Summer, I have a question," Darleen said.

Summer turned to look at Darleen and saw the little frown of worry. "What is it?"

"I know you need to reactivate my Controller, and I'm okay with that since the only one that will be able to control it is you," she said. "But, if something happens to you, will I be stuck like that forever?" She shook her head. "I know, its a terrible thing to ask, and I'm selfish for thinking of it, but I can't help it. I just need to know. I won't change my mind, I promise you that, I'm with you all the way on this. I just need to know what will happen to me."

Summer reached over and patted Darleen gently on the shoulder. "It is not selfish, it is not terrible, and I am very sorry I didn't think to explain it better to you before. Of course you are concerned about what will happen to you Darleen, and there is no reason you shouldn't be. But don't worry, I got it covered."

Darleen looked up. "Really?"

"Yep," Summer replied "I'm going to put a timer on it. I'll activate the Controller for a specific time frame, say, one hour. After that, it will just shut off and you'll be as you are now."

"Are you sure it will work?" Darleen asked.

"I don't see why not," Summer said. "But we can try it now if you like."

Darleen nodded so Summer reached out and took hold of Darleen's Controller, noting that it was far easier to do now than it had been before whatever Calnic had done. She activated it to her mental commands, then ordered it to deactivate in thirty seconds.

Darleen went very still all of a sudden and Summer shivered at the dull, blank look in her friend's eyes. She hated that look. Had seen it on too many women this past year, including herself.

Suddenly Darleen blinked and her eyes lit up with life once more.

"That worked perfectly," Summer said.

"Yes, it sure did," Darleen said. "Thank you, Summer."

"No problem," Summer replied, noting that the shuttle, and the ground-car, began to vibrate just slightly. "Won't be long now," she said.

"Nope," Darleen replied. "What about Lio?"

"What about him?" Summer asked.

"If something happens to you, what about him?"

"I'll order his Controller to follow you in my absence," Summer said. "That should help if anything goes wrong. I think there is still some valuable information in that head of is, so its worth saving if possible. But Darleen, if it comes to a choice, just remember that you are more important than he is."

"All right Summer, but do me a favor, will you?"

"If I can," Summer replied.

"Don't let anything happen to you."

"I'll do my best," Summer promised.

Chapter 40

William sat at the desk in his office and watched the Jasani shuttle touch down in the precise area he had indicated. A panel opened at the bottom of the shuttle and a large black ground-car exited slowly. The car continued straight ahead, aiming directly toward the compound. When it was a safe distance away, the shuttle lifted off the ground and shot back into the sky.

His gaze moved to another of the many monitors set up around the room, checking to be sure that the shuttle was, in fact, going back to its ship. He smiled when he confirmed that it was, revealing a row of sharp, pointy teeth.

He switched his gaze to another monitor, and watched the ground-car as it continued at a steady pace toward the compound. It would be a long, slow drive through several miles of barren wasteland between the shuttle landing site and the compound, with nothing to look at other than rocks and sand. He didn't think the females would mind since they certainly had Controllers, and he didn't care what Lio thought.

He reached over to yet another monitor and made a tiny adjustment to one dial. A moment later he had a close-up view of the ground-car. It wasn't a particularly good view, but it was good enough for him to identify two females in the front seat, and at least one figure in the rear seat. That jelled with what he knew of Lio Perry. Always had to show off the help.

William chuckled, a harsh, croaking sound that did not in any way resemble a laugh. He did not understand why Lio was delivering the woman himself, or why he was using a Jasani transport ship, or why the delivery was being made two days late. Nor did he really care about the answers to those questions. So long as one of those females in that ground-car was his *berezi*, nothing else really mattered. If neither of them were *berezi,* then things were going to get very ugly for Lio.

He turned to check another monitor and did some rapid calculations in his head. At the ground-car's current speed, it should arrive in about eleven minutes. William reached into a drawer in his desk and removed a control panel. He keyed in a password and, using his talons, he began typing in commands to disable outlying security rings so that the ground-car could pass through them safely as it approached.

The huge amount of security he used around the compound did cause some inconveniences, but William never considered removing or deactivating any of it. His father had drilled into him how important security was at all times, and anything the great Stalnek had thought important, was engraved in stone as far as William was concerned.

Which was why he did not have guards. Every guard was a security risk because every guard was another person that he had to trust. And William trusted no one. Instead, he used Falasian females to look after the slaves and keep the compound clean. Falasians were smaller than humans, with pink skin, pink eyes and white hair. The males of that race were larger and sturdier than the females, and very war like. The females, on the other hand, were generally passive and shy. Which made them perfect for William's use. They made sure that the slaves were cleaned, fed, exercised and groomed and he never heard a word from any of them.

William had no interest in the slaves themselves other than the money they brought in to the family coffers, which was needed to fund the Brethren back on Earth. This was simply a processing center. A place where new slaves were brought and injected with Controllers before being transferred elsewhere for training. Occasionally slaves were sent here for a short time to await pick-up from a buyer. But the females themselves held no interest for William. He did occasionally wander through the compound and check the new slaves, just in case, by some accidental fluke, one of them might turn out to be a *berezi*. But none of them ever had been.

William felt a strange, trilling sensation in his stomach which, after a few moments, he identified as excitement. He had been stuck on this rock managing the slave distribution compound for several years now and he was bored. The idea of the long awaited *berezi* finally arriving was, therefore, exciting. He tried to imagine having a child of his own at long last, and couldn't do it. His duty to find a *berezi* and impregnate her in order to bring back the true blood of the Brethren had been instilled in him at a young age. It was the sole purpose of his existence, and he had spent his entire long life striving to accomplish it. And so far, he had failed. Until now.

"William, this is Za-Linq, please pick up."

William frowned toward the vid terminal. He did not like coincidences. Lio arriving and Za-Linq contacting him at the same time made him suspicious.

"Pick-up, William," Za-Linq repeated.

William cocked his head. Was it his imagination or did Za-Linq sound distressed? Interesting. He had never heard a Xanti sound anything other than calm and cool. But, he didn't really have an imagination either.

He set the control panel down and reached for the vid terminal. As soon as he accepted the call, a somewhat harried looking Za-Linq filled his screen. The skin was the usual white iridescence that irritated William's eyes if he had to look at it too long. But the long, flowing hair that always seemed to float gently around his face in a cloud of soft, golden curls was messy, and the Xanti's shirt was buttoned incorrectly.

"Za-Linq," he said cautiously. The changes in the Xanti's appearance caused his spines to lift.

"Why did it take you so long to answer my call?" Za-Linq asked irritably.

William tilted his head slightly, but did not answer. He was in business with the Xanti, but he did not answer to them.

"Never mind," Za-Linq said. "According to my tracking signal, Lio Perry is on his way to you right now."

"Yes, he is," William replied.

"He is a traitor and cannot be trusted," Za-Linq said. "You must destroy him at once. Or if you wish, I will do it. I believe he is in that ground-car heading toward you right now, but all of that damned security you insist on using has my screens jumping around so I'm not sure. Is that his location?"

"Yes it is, but do not destroy that ground-car," William growled. "It contains my *berezi*."

Za-Linq froze for a long moment. "Are you certain of this?" he demanded.

William shrugged. "I am certain a male is in the ground-car with two females," he said. "As soon as they arrive, I will know more."

"He stole that *berezi*," Za-Linq said. "He took her to the Jasani Princes and stayed there for several days. I only just discovered that he was not dead as he was supposed to be and tracked him here. It is good that he is bringing you your *berezi*, but do not trust him. He is certainly trying to trick you."

William tilted his head the other way. "To what end?" he asked.

"I do not know!" Za-Linq screamed in frustration. "I only know that Lio is disloyal and traitorous and not to be trusted! He could be trying to pass off a fake *berezi!*"

"He cannot pass off a fake *berezi* on me," William said calmly. "The moment I am within a few feet of her, I will know if she is, or is not, a *berezi*."

"I want him destroyed William," Za-Linq yelled as though William had not spoken. "I want him destroyed at once."

William shrugged. "So, destroy him then," he said. "But not until after I get my *berezi*."

"If he really has her with him," Za-Linq snapped.

"He better have her," William said softly. "Your Ruling Female promised her to me two days ago. I paid her price. She did not come. If she is not here now, in that ground-car, I will transmit to all who wish to listen that the Xanti cannot be trusted to deal fairly."

"I am coming down there," Za-Linq said. "I will personally see to it that you get your true *berezi*, and that Lio Perry is destroyed for the traitor that he is."

"Fine," William said, now bored with the conversation.

"You must delay Lio's arrival," Za-Linq said, apparently a bit calmer now that he had William's agreement. "I cannot get there for another half hour."

"No," William replied. "I will wait no longer than I must. You may come when you wish. Good-bye." William reached out and disconnected the call. He shook his head and sighed. That was one confused Xanti.

He turned and checked on the ground-car's progress. Just a few more minutes. He stood up and strode over to the mirror hanging on the wall near the door. He looked into it briefly, gazing at his orange eyes and green scaled skin. He bared his teeth to check that they were clean, and used one talon to scrap away a bit of meat. There, he thought. Perfect. He smiled at his reflection, then headed out to the inner courtyard to meet his bride.

Summer sensed the security systems as they went down right before the ground-car reached them, then went back up as they passed through. She quickly disabled them, while altering the main system just enough that it would appear that it was still active. She had to work quickly, focusing hard on what she was doing to the exclusion of everything around her. When Darleen made a soft hissing noise in the seat beside her, it took her a moment to realize the other woman was trying to get her attention.

Summer looked straight ahead and realized with a little start that they had arrived at the compound. She quickly activated Darleen's

Controller, and then her own, just as Darleen drove through a gate between two buildings, and into a large courtyard. Darleen stopped the car and cut the power, then sat motionless while her Controller awaited further orders.

Summer silently ordered Lio to speak.

"Summer, Darleen, get out of the car and come around and open my door," he said, his tone so arrogant that Summer winced inwardly. Darleen had insisted that was the way the man often sounded, and Summer hoped she was right. According to Lio, he had never actually met William in person, or even seen him on a vid for security reasons. They had only spoken a couple of times. Hopefully that meant William wouldn't notice if Lio sounded a little off.

Darleen and Summer both moved at once as though in response to his command, though Summer was the one actually controlling all three of them. She stood next to the door while Darleen opened it and stepped aside. Lio climbed out of the car slowly, then reached up to straighten his tie and run his hand through his hair as he looked around the courtyard with mild curiosity. Darleen closed the door, then moved so that Lio was standing between the two of them, and they all had their backs to the ground-car.

Summer heard heavy footsteps approaching long before she saw the creature that owned them. She was very glad that her Controller was activated as she would never have been able to pretend she was anything other than horrified at the sight of William.

William was about eight Standard feet tall, and had to weigh at least 300 pounds, all of it muscle, bone, fang and talon. He had green skin, orange eyes and a broad nose with thin slits that fluttered slightly as he breathed. His mouth was large, wide, and filled with long, sharp teeth. There were long rows of fin like growths down the backs of his arms and legs and along the top of his head. Summer had a difficult time believing that something that looked so much like a mutated dinosaur could actually talk like a human.

"Hello, Lio," William said as he approached them. Lio gazed up at William calmly.

"Hello, William," he replied.

"I see you did bring my *berezi*," William said. "Za-Linq did not think that you would."

Summer thought frantically. Za-Linq was the name of the Xanti Lio told them he worked for. Were the Xanti here? She had to find out more.

"Za-Linq?" Lio asked. "What has Za-Linq to do with this?"

"I don't really know," William said. "And I don't really care. So long as you brought her, whatever problem you have with the Xanti is your own."

"Is Za-Linq here?" Lio asked.

"No, but he indicated he would be soon. Now, excuse me a moment." William leaned down toward Lio and, much to Summer's surprise, sniffed him. He then leaned over and did the same to Summer and Darleen. When he straightened up again he shook his head.

"Yes, I thought so," he murmured softly.

"You thought what?" Lio asked.

"Well Lio, it seems to me that all three of you have Controllers," William said in a conversational tone. "Which begs the question, who is controlling your Controllers? I am wondering if Za-Linq is playing some sort of game with me. But I can't quite figure it."

"I don't know what you mean," Lio said testily.

"Be silent, Lio," William said. "I can smell the Controller on you, as I can on the women."

William turned his back on the three of them and paced away, his reptilian nose lifted into the air. As he walked slowly around the courtyard, keeping Summer, Darleen and Lio in the center of his circle, Summer thought rapidly, trying to decide what to do.

It wasn't easy. Her mind kept going back to the realization that this...this *thing* was what, or who, had bought her and if not for Lio's moment of carelessness in leaving her alone in his office that day, this is where she would have ended up. She almost felt a touch of gratitude toward Lio for a moment.

The other thing she couldn't get past was that William had somehow scented the Controllers. How was that possible? she wondered. Ah, she thought, the Controllers must somehow alter brain chemistry, maybe by triggering an immune response. Or maybe the nano-bots have waste products. Whatever the case, he must scent them somehow.

When William had turned his back on them and walked away, Summer had come very close to pulling out her katana and attacking him. But, she had decided against it. Darleen and Lio were both standing very close to her, and they were both helpless to defend themselves. And there was also the issue of the Xanti, Za-Linq. William had said he was on his way, which meant she could easily find herself fighting two opponents.

What would Father do? Something tactically smart. If she could hold out a little longer, reinforcements in the form of Maxim, Loni and Ran would arrive. They would certainly stand a better chance of defeating

William than she would. Yes, she decided. That's what she had to do. Wait for the guys to show up and save the day.

That decided, she relaxed a little bit. After all, if William knew they all had Controllers, there wasn't any reason she could think of for him to harm them. They should be perfectly safe until the guys showed up. So, when William finished his circle and walked back to them, she was completely shocked when he folded his thick arms across his chest and said, "Well, looks like I'll have to kill one or two of you in order to flush out whoever's Controlling you."

William tapped one fang with a sharp, curved claw, looking back and forth between Lio and the spare female. From the looks of her, Lio'd had her for awhile. He'd heard Lio was hard on his *toys*. It was obviously true. Well, of the three of them, she was certainly the most expendable. He wouldn't mind killing Lio, but he thought it might be worth the effort to try and get information from him first. Information was always valuable. Of course, there was no way in the nine hells he was going to harm his *berezi*.

"Very well," he said, his decision made. "Whoever is Controlling these three, you might as well show yourself. Otherwise, I am going to have to dismember this skinny little female first, then I suppose I'll have to do Lio." William sighed heavily as though he were being much put upon and slowly turned around again, just in case someone was out there beyond the wall about to show themselves. As he turned back to face the three humans, he reached out for the skinny blonde, and froze in shock.

Ah hell, Summer thought as she quickly sent a command to Darleen's nano-bots, then another to Lio's before ordering her own to deactivate. Since she was almost certain that William scented the Controllers only when they were active, it was risky to deactivate hers, but it was a risk she had to take. She forced herself to remain motionless, not allowing her eyes to move or her breathing to change, waiting for the right moment. As soon as William started to turn, she sent a silent command to Darleen to grab Lio and run. She'd already sent a timer command to Darleen's Controller which would release her in about thirty more seconds, and Lio had orders to follow Darleen.

As she reached for the katana hidden in the folds of her skirt, she saw Darleen out of the corner of her eye as she reached out and grabbed Lio's arm, then turned and ran. A scant second or two later, William finished his turn with his arm out, reaching for Darleen. Perfect, Summer thought, as she unsheathed the katana in a long, upward arc that sliced right through William's thick arm at the elbow.

As William stumbled backward in shock, Summer took the opportunity to get away from the ground-car. With it at her back, she was at a distinct disadvantage. She wanted to look for Darleen and Lio, to make sure they were safe, but she didn't dare take her attention from William for a moment.

"Controller, cease movement," William snapped, ignoring the greenish yellow blood pouring from the stump of his arm. Summer glanced quickly at the wound, wondering if it would bleed enough to weaken him.

William's eyes narrowed as he caught her glance and he lifted his nose in the air and sniffed. Then he smiled. With all of those long sharp teeth, it was not a particularly joyful expression.

"Ah, I am glad that you are now aware," he said calmly, as though she hadn't just sliced his arm off. "I am William Wade Winicke, your new husband, and you are my bride."

Summer's eyes widened in surprise as she glanced quickly at his face, and then back to his still bleeding arm. "Don't worry, my little *berezi*," William said. "The limb will grow back in a few days, and our children will self heal even faster than that."

Summer fought to keep her face blank, but the thought of having children with this thing made her sick to her stomach. William must have seen something of her feelings in her face because he started growling angrily.

"Controller, activate!" he ordered, clearly thinking that as her Controller was now deactivated, he should be able to activate it. Only it didn't work.

"Fils de putain," Summer spat with contempt, deliberately goading him. "What makes you think I would wish to mate with such *chierie* as you?"

I don't know who is Controlling you, but I will have their head for this," William roared as he lunged toward Summer.

It was just such an unguarded move that Summer had been hoping for. She stepped forward and to the side, bringing the katana up high, then swinging it downward with all of her might just as William's left leg stretched out toward her as he lunged. The katana cut through his thick, reptilian hide with only the slightest resistance.

Summer stepped back out of William's reach as he went down on his other knee, roaring so loudly her ears hurt. She turned sideways again and brought the katana around in a swinging arc aimed right for William's thick neck. This time there was no resistance whatsoever as the whistling blade cut cleanly all the way through, sending William's ugly big head flying several feet before it fell to the ground with a solid thunk.

"Grow that back, lizard boy," Summer said archly.

Chapter 41

Summer turned at the sound of approaching footsteps and was happy to see Darleen hurrying towards her, Lio ambling along in her wake. Summer bent down to wipe the katana's blade on William's pants, then sheathed it before turning to Darleen for a relieved hug.

"I can't believe you did that," Darleen said.

"Neither can I," Summer admitted. "But its done. All we have to do now is call Maxim and the others, and then we can release the prisoners."

She heard a noise behind her and turned to see the most amazingly beautiful being she had ever laid eyes on. He was tall, lean, broad shouldered and graceful as he walked into the courtyard and stopped a dozen feet away from them. His skin was white, and sparkled brightly in the sun as he moved. His hair was long and golden and flowed gently around his shoulders, and his smile was so perfectly gorgeous it was hard to tear her eyes away from it. But the more she looked, the more she realized there were little things wrong. The golden hair was mussed and snarled, causing a huge clump of it to hit him in the cheek as it flowed forward every few seconds. His shirt was buttoned incorrectly, and one eyelid twitched constantly.

Summer took in all of this in a flash, going from shock at the man's beauty to suspicion, then wariness all in the space of a second. She reached for her katana, but the newcomer was faster. He raised one hand and shot Darleen with a hand laser, hitting her in the leg. Darleen fell to the ground at Summer's feet with a short yelp of pain.

"Do not move again or I will be forced to kill your friend," the man warned her.

Summer released the katana, and the man smiled. "You are smart for a human," he said. "I am Za-Linq, your new master now that William is dead. I am sure that we will have no trouble reselling you so long as you behave yourself and don't force me to damage you."

Summer made no move, though she was thinking furiously.

"Good human," Za-Linq said as though she had agreed to obey him. He then turned to look at Lio. "Now, Lio, before I take my leave, I would like you to explain to me how you thought you could get away with betraying me the way you betrayed Za-Queg."

Summer sent a silent command to Lio's Controller, directing him to answer the question truthfully, but in as many words as possible. As Lio began talking, Summer focused on the Xanti. From the moment her initial shock had worn off at his unexpected appearance, she sensed that the being before her was more machine than anything else. Perhaps she could do some damage to it while it was occupied with Lio.

She reached carefully for the machine, using a light touch, and was pleased to discover that it was bio-mechanical. Were the Xanti even living organisms? she wondered as she probed the body carefully, searching for its main processing center. After a few moments, she realized that there didn't seem to be one. This was little more than a robotic shell. If that was true, where did it get its orders from, she wondered. How did it speak and move?

Summer pondered the question as she began shutting down systems within the bio-mechanical shell.

This one looks like a limb movement translator. Off it went. Life support regulation. Off. Communications. Off.

She wasn't always sure what it was she was shutting down, but she figured that even hit or miss, she would eventually shut down something of importance that would effect the Xanti's ability to control the thing.

Navigation. Offline. Was that a processor for atmosphere exchange? Shut that puppy down.

"You are not making any sense, Lio," the Xanti was saying. "Not that it really matters I suppose. All that matters is that I win. Now, I will kill you, and the extra female, and take my *berezi*."

Summer paused when she discovered a set of functions that would not allow a full shut down. She searched for a few moments and smiled inwardly when she found alternate methods of cutting them off.

Internal emergency lighting system. Disable. Emergency breathing apparatus. Locked out for maintenance. Automatic Perimeter Defense System. Frozen due to proximity to Ruling Queen.

Ruling Queen? she wondered as she continued shutting down anything and everything she could find.

For the first time in days, Za-Linq felt calm. He had the *berezi,* Lio was about to be dead for certain, and all in time to meet Xaqana-Ti's deadline. That William was dead was a bonus that Xaqana-Ti would enjoy, as it meant she could sell the *berezi* to the Brethren a second time.

He pointed the gun at Lio and started to pull the trigger when suddenly his hand stopped responding to his commands. He looked down at it and tried again to pull the trigger, but the hand would not obey him. Za-Linq growled softly. He had just performed the routine maintenance on his *makina* a few days earlier. There was no reason for the hand to stop functioning. He tried to lift his other hand in order to operate the gun with it instead, only to discover that neither hand would move.

Za-Linq was so focused on the problem of getting his limbs to respond to his commands that it took him a moment to realize that his air intake system had ceased to function. He hit the switch to activate the self-contained emergency air system and froze in fear when nothing happened. He hit it again. Still nothing.

By this time he was beginning to see spots before his eyes and he knew that if he did not get air soon, he would lose consciousness, and then he would die. In a panic, he hit the emergency evacuation switch and again nothing happened. Za-Linq scrambled around, his vision nearly gone now, searching for the manual evac mechanism. He caught it mostly by accident and pushed on it with all of his remaining strength, grateful for the cool, fresh air that filled his lungs as he tumbled to the ground.

Summer watched the Xanti carefully as it struggled to move, saw the beginnings of panic come over its glittery face. Then nothing. The Xanti stood there, apparently frozen in place for several long moments. Summer continued to seek out and shut down as many different components as she could find within the mechanical shell, her worry growing as the thing continued to stand motionless.

Suddenly there was movement beneath the Xanti's shirt in the area of its chest. A small movement at first, then a larger one as something seemed to be pressing out against the fabric The shirt ripped with a harsh tearing noise and two doors popped out, followed by a large, black object which tumbled out through the opening and onto the ground.

Summer gasped, horrified by the sight of the thing lying on its back in the dirt at the Xanti's feet. It was black, shiny, and segmented into three distinct sections with ten long, spindly legs, five on each side. It had big red eyes, wide glistening mandibles and a long stinger on its back end. It was, without doubt, the biggest, ugliest spider Summer had ever seen in her life. She shuddered with revulsion as she watched it wriggling its legs in an effort to flip itself over.

Summer reached down and grabbed hold of Darleen's hand, yanking her to her feet without taking her eyes off of the huge spider. Instinct told her to get away from the thing, and she meant to obey it. Darleen evidently had the same instincts because she was up on her feet and moving backwards as fast as she could in spite of the injury to her leg.

Suddenly the spider managed to flip itself over. It turned around to face them, standing on the tips of its ten legs. Summer and Darleen froze. As ugly as the thing was, they didn't dare take their eyes off of it for a moment. It rose up, its legs straightening as it got higher and higher, then it lowered itself, bending its legs till its belly almost touched the ground, then up again in a slow, rhythmic motion. Then it reared up on its back two legs, its remaining legs held stiffly in front of it. It looked at Summer and Darleen with its bright red eyes for a long moment, and Summer's mouth went dry with fear. Then it turned its gaze on Lio. With a high pitched squeal of fury, the spider dropped to all ten legs and leapt for Lio. Summer instantly ordered Lio's Controller to run, but it was already too late. The spider leapt into the air with surprising agility and landed on Lio's back, wrapping its long spindly legs around him.

Summer turned her head. She didn't want to see what was coming next. Then she realized that if she wasn't watching, she wouldn't see the spider when it came for them, which she was sure it would do as soon as it finished with Lio. She reached for her katana, the thought of touching the giant spider even with the blade making her stomach lurch in disgust.

The sudden low, buzzing sound of a particle rifle brought her head up and around, the katana held ready as she moved protectively in front of Darleen. She smiled with relief when she saw Maxim, Loni, Ran and Doc, and knew that she did not have to look at Lio and the spider after all.

Chapter 42

Summer slid the katana back into its sheath as Maxim strode toward her, his expression stern and forbidding. But she understood him better now. She took two steps toward him before leaping into his arms, her arms wrapping tightly around his neck as she buried her face against the warmth of his throat. The feel of his strong arms holding her tightly against him, and the rapid beat of his heart served to enforce what she already knew. He had been worried and afraid for her, and he was relieved that she was alive and unharmed.

"You are well?" he asked, his voice low and deep, his breath as he spoke tickling her ear.

"I am well," she said, raising her head to gaze into his golden eyes. "And I have made a decision."

Maxim raised a brow. "A decision?" he asked.

"Yes," she said. She turned to make sure that Loni and Ran were close by, and they were exactly where she'd thought they'd be. Ran close on their right, Loni close on their left.

"Move in here a little guys," she said softly. Both men did as she asked until the four of them were touching each other, all of their heads together.

"When I was down here, alone, fighting that...that thing over there," she said, nodding towards William's remains, "I suddenly realized how horrible it would be if I were to die without having first known what it was to be mated with the three of you. And I knew that, no matter what else happened, I had to stay alive so that I could do that. I promised myself that I would not go another day without doing whatever it is we need to do to make me your Arima."

Maxim, Loni and Ran all stared at her in stunned silence for a long moment. Then Maxim squeezed her tightly, bent his head and kissed her hard and deep. They heard a long, loud whoop of joy that was so startling to them both that they broke their kiss and stared in shock at Loni, who grinned back at them before reaching for Summer. Maxim released her into Loni's arms and he bent to kiss her long and deep as well. When he raised his head, Summer was touched to note that he had tears in his eyes.

"Thank you, Summer, for accepting us," he said softly. "I promise you that I will treasure you every moment of our lives together."

Summer smiled, blinking back her own tears as Ran reached for her, anxious for his turn. He spun her around a couple of times, then kissed her deeply. "I love you," he said simply.

"As I love you," she replied.

"Um, I hate to interrupt, but I think that bug is wiggling," Darleen said hesitantly.

Ran put Summer down at once and spun around to face the Xanti, his particle rifle out and aimed. Summer stared at it for a moment, but she didn't see any movement. She did sense...something though. She reached out tentatively and was surprised to find an electronic component in the thing's body giving off a signal of some sort. She wasn't sure what it was, but she immediately disabled it. She then focused her attention on the robotic shell and found another one, which she disabled as well.

"I just deactivated what I think were homing beacons in both the...bug...and the shell," she said.

"The *bug* is, I believe, a Xanti," Maxim said. "We have never known the Xanti's true nature until now. Probably because they retrieve the bodies of their fallen. Thanks to you, they won't be able to do that this time. But, just to be on the safe side, lets wrap it up."

Maxim focused on the Xanti, and Summer shuddered again as its legs slowly unwrapped themselves from around Lio's body, then rose into the air and settled a few feet away.

"I've encased it in a block of solid air," Maxim said. "I want to get it up to the ship and in a stasis bag as soon as possible though. This will be very important to our council scientists."

"What about Lio?" Darleen asked as she stepped up next to Summer. Summer turned to look at Darleen's leg, which Doc had bandaged.

"How's your leg?" she asked.

"It'll be fine," Doc answered for her. "Just a deep graze. I'll have it fixed up good as new as soon as we get back on the ship."

Darleen sent Doc a shy smile that Summer pretended not to notice.

"We'll put Lio a stasis bag as well," Maxim said, answering Darleen's question.

"So, he's dead then?" Darleen asked. Summer and Maxim both glanced at Darleen sharply. There had been something a little strained in her tone.

"Yes, Darleen," Maxim said. "He is dead."

Darleen sucked in a deep, shaky breath and blew it out, and Summer understood. Even though Lio had been under complete control these past several days, there had been a part of Darleen that was still afraid of the man. After all that he had done to her, Summer didn't blame her. She reached out and hugged Darleen tightly, surprised and pleased when Darleen hugged her back.

"It's over now," Summer said softly.

"Yes," Darleen replied hoarsely. "Finally, it's really and truly over."

"The Xanti certainly came from a ship that we are unable to detect," Ran said as Summer released Darleen and stepped back. "But if we can get the body out of here and on our ship quickly, we should be able to get it back to Jasan with us."

As Ran spoke, Loni was already on the comm with the ship, calling for two shuttles to land nearby. Summer had shut down all of the security devices including the camouflage, so the shuttles had no problem selecting landing sites.

"Did you have any idea that the Xanti were spiders?" Summer asked, not even trying to hide the disgust in her voice.

"No, none at all," Maxim said. He turned to take a closer look at William. "I have no idea what this is though."

"Maxim," Summer said hesitantly. Something in her voice caused all three of the Katres to instantly center their attention on her.

"What is it, *kilenka*?" Maxim asked.

"Did Mara have any Winicke family that you know of?"

"None still living," Maxim replied. "Why?"

"Because that thing, whatever it is, said his name was William Wade Winicke."

It took several hours to free all of the women imprisoned in the compound, dismantle all of William's security and strip everything from William's office, down to the desk and chair. Summer had been able to get a partial upload of data before some security program she had not detected shut things down. She was disappointed, but, as Ran kept telling her, it was better than nothing at all.

The Falasian females were extremely helpful in getting the fourteen women out of their cells and prepared to leave, once they understood that the intent was to rescue, not kill their charges. When Darleen asked them if they would like to accompany them back to Jasan, and help care for the prisoners on the way, they had asked only if they would be slaves.

When the answer was an emphatic no, they instantly agreed and lined up, ready to go.

Summer double-checked everything in and around the compound to make certain she hadn't missed any of William's security devices. She didn't want anyone getting hurt if they happened to stumble upon the place. Only when she was satisfied it was completely safe did she return to the ship. She went straight to the bridge and sent a message to the Aki to let them know that the Other was now gone and would bother them no more. Once that was done, she headed for her stateroom, wanting nothing more than to wash away the scent of Li-Hach-Cor.

When she left the bathroom, feeling much better after a long hot shower and some clean clothes, she was not surprised to find Maxim, Loni and Ran in the room. She had sensed them drawing close a few minutes earlier and knew they would be waiting for her.

"We have ordered a meal to be served in the Star Room," Maxim said as he crossed the room to kiss her. "If you prefer, we could have it delivered here though."

"No, lets go to the Star Room," Summer said. "I love that room. Its so relaxing."

"That is what we hoped," Maxim replied as he took her hand and led the way out of the stateroom and up the hall toward the elevator, Loni and Ran right behind them. As they got into the elevator, Summer finally noticed that all of them had solemn expressions on their faces.

"What's the matter?" she asked. "You all look so serious. Is there something wrong?"

"No, there is nothing wrong," Maxim assured her. "It is only that we have a few important things to discuss with you over dinner."

"And we are concerned and confused by William," Ran added. "I remember clearly Mara talking about her baby brother William when we were children. She always called him Winkie though. She never mentioned him after we got older. I assumed that he had eventually grown old and died as humans do not have the same life span we do."

The elevator opened and they stepped out into the hall and headed toward the private dining rooms.

"He was certainly not human, whatever he was," Summer said. "But Mara must be human, otherwise how did she have you guys?"

"We don't really understand it ourselves," Maxim replied. "We have already sent a message to the council informing them of this rather strange development, and asking them to take some samples from Mara.

Doc has already taken samples from William's remains and sent the results. All we can do now is wait."

Maxim opened the door into the private waiting area and ushered Summer through before pressing the call button. Roberto appeared almost at once and, after greeting them, led them to the Star Room. Summer spent several minutes gazing at the stars before Ran coaxed her attention away from the view and back to their meal.

Summer ate heartily, hungrier than she'd thought after the long and busy day. When she had satisfied the worst of her hunger she turned to Maxim. "So what is it that you guys need to discuss with me?"

"We want, more than anything, to perform the mating ritual and the soul-link triad with you," Maxim began. "But before we do, there are a few things that you should know. If, after we tell you these things, you change your mind, we will understand."

Summer placed her fork carefully on the table beside her plate and put her hands in her lap beneath the table, her heart suddenly pounding with fear. The way Maxim was talking, he was going to tell her something really bad and she wasn't altogether sure she wanted to hear it.

"Do not worry so," Loni said gently, placing a comforting hand on her shoulder. "What we must tell you is not so bad. Just information you should own before making your final decision."

"All right," Summer said, feeling a little relieved. "Lets have it."

"As Loni said, it is not so bad," Maxim said. "But it is important. The first thing you should know is that there is a prophecy that, we believe, mentions you."

"Prophecy?" Summer asked. Whatever she had been expecting him to say, it was not this.

"When the first pod of survivors reached Jasan, there was a seer among them. Actually, there were three, a Katre male-set. Eldar Hamat was one of them. His brother, Semat, was severely injured and dying. Before the end, he spoke a prophecy which he was unable to finish before he died. That prophecy spoke of an Arima who would one day come to Clan Dracon. Lariah was the Arima spoken of.

"Then, a year ago, Saige came. The second Arima. During her transformation, she learned that Riata, the Alverian Empath and Healer that we told you about, was to be her Spirit Guide."

"Yes, Saige told Darleen and I a little about that," Summer said.

Maxim nodded, glad she was aware of that much at least. "When Riata came to her, she revealed the portion of the prophecy that Semat was unable to finish. We call it *The Lost Prophecy of Semat*."

"And that's the part you think talks about me?" Summer asked.

"Yes," Maxim replied. "Rather than explain it, Ran will recite the prophecy to you in its entirety now."

Summer turned to Ran who took a sip of his water to give himself time to pull the prophecy out of his memory. He set the glass down and met Summer's gaze with his own.

In the fullness of manhood, the patience of the royal sons of the third generation beyond this day, shall be met with their soul's fulfillment in a daughter of a distant sun.

Have they faith in the three, by the three shall all be blessed.

Radiant with the glory of lau-lotu shall they descend from the sky in flame before the people, and the people shall be renewed.

Shall faith be denied, so the people shall be lost, forevermore.

Shall the people have faith, so shall the people be blessed with a chance for renewal.

The renewal of the people shall begin with the Soul,

Who shall call to the soil of her distant home for she who shall be the Heart, and she who shall be the Mind.

And these shall be the Three.

Have they faith in the Three, by the Three shall all be blessed.

By the Three shall be found new knowledge

Of shadowed truths,

Of enemies born to be brothers,

Of Dark Deceivers

Of schemes from beyond the Veil of Stars to cast the peoples of the suns numbering a hundred times ten into the eternal deep.

Have they faith in the Three, by the Three shall all be blessed.

Shall the Three endure, the people and their brothers shall banish the Dark Deceivers from the Veil of Stars forever.

Shall the Three perish, so shall the people be lost, forevermore.

Summer listened carefully to every word Ran spoke, committing every nuance to memory. When he was finished she sat silently for a few moments, considering it.

"It seems obvious, from what I already know, that Lariah Dracon is the Soul. Saige then, must be the Heart, and you guys think that I am the Mind." she said.

"Yes, we do," Maxim replied. "But Summer, what is most important to us is that you understand we did not consider that when we met you.

Nor after we met you. We did not even think of the prophecy at all until today when you said you wanted to become our Arima in truth. We do not want you to think it is the reason we want you."

Summer smiled. "Maxim, I know your true feelings. I am happy that you told me this now, but I would never believe you only wanted me because of the prophecy."

All three of the Katres seemed to sigh in relief, though none of them actually made any sound. Summer acted as though she didn't notice, though she smiled inwardly.

"Do you think that the *Dark Deceivers* are the Xanti?" she asked.

"We suspect that they are, but we are not entirely certain," Maxim replied. "The only parts of the prophecy that we are sure of are those that speak of Lariah, Saige and, we believe, you."

"How do you know that any of the prophecy is real?" Summer asked. "It could be all just fevered imagination."

"Yes, that was always a possibility," Maxim said. "However, as of now, a good deal of the prophecy has already come to pass. That would seem to indicate that the remainder of it is real as well."

"I am not altogether sure that I like the idea of being one of the *three*," Summer said. "The idea of being in the spotlight does not appeal to me. On the other hand, it is not even close to being a good enough reason for me to rethink wanting to be mated with you guys. I cannot change what is. I can only make my choices the best I can and deal with whatever comes next as best I can."

Maxim, Loni and Ran all smiled at her, but she felt the flood of relief and excitement pouring from them in spite of their calm expressions. "So, what was the other thing?" she asked.

"The mating ritual itself," Maxim said. "We have some concerns about it that we must discuss with you."

"Haven't you guys been doing this ritual thing with women for centuries now?" Summer asked in surprise. "Why is it now a problem?"

"We have been doing a form of our mating ritual with human women," Maxim agreed. "But the full ritual we must do to make you our full Arima, so that you can soul-link us all together, has been done only twice. Once with Princess Lariah, and once with Saige Lobo."

"Oh," Summer said. "Well, since those two women seem to be perfectly fine, happy and healthy, it can't be that bad."

"For the most part, it is not," Maxim agreed. "There is one portion of the process that is, we are told, exceedingly painful. Our Princes possess enough healing ability that they were able to send Lariah into a very deep sleep during that portion of the ritual. They were also available to perform the same service for Saige Lobo."

"But they are not here, and you guys do not possess that ability," Summer finished.

"That is correct," Maxim said.

"Can't Doc give me something for the pain?" Summer asked.

"No," Maxim replied. "That part of the ritual causes your body to undergo a complete change from human to Jasani. There is no drug that can ease the pain of that."

"Well, what about an anesthesia then?" Summer suggested. "He could put me into a deep sleep, like the Dracons did with Lariah and Saige."

"Unfortunately, that will not work either," Maxim said. "The first part of the ritual greatly increases your regeneration ability. Your body will throw off the effects of any pharmaceutical in moments."

Summer thought hard, trying to come up with another idea. Suddenly, she brightened. "I can activate my Controller and tell it to block pain."

Maxim's brows rose as he considered the idea. "That might work," he said. "Loni?"

Summer turned to Loni, who was frowning in thought. "I do not think it will be enough," he said finally. "If the regeneration process does not destroy the Controller, then it may work up to a point. However, once the transformation process reaches her brain, it will certainly destroy the Controller and she will be fully aware of the pain from that moment until it is complete. And we do not know if the brain is transformed first, or last."

"Excuse me," Ran said as he reached up to tap his vox. He listened for a moment, glanced at Summer, then frowned. "All right Darleen, we will be there in a few moments," he said. He tapped the vox and turned to Maxim.

"There is apparently a show-down occurring in the med-lab between Doc and the Falasians," he said. "The Falasians are insisting that Summer be brought down to intercede for them."

"Very well," Maxim said, rising to his feet. He paused. "I'm sorry Summer, that was rude of me. They are asking for you, so it is up to you whether you wish to go."

"Of course I wish to go," she assured him as she, too rose to her feet. She looked back at her dinner wistfully though. She hadn't gotten to finish. "Do not worry," Ran said. "We will let Roberto know that we will be returning."

Summer kissed him quickly, then let Maxim take her hand as he led the way out of the dining room and down to the med-lab.

Summer and the Katres were all surprised when they entered the med-lab to see what looked like a stand-off between all of the Falasian women, who were circled around the exam table, and Doc, who was standing a few feet away glaring at them. Darleen hurried over to Summer as soon as they entered.

"Doc tested all of the women we took from the compound to make sure they'd all had their eppys," she explained quickly. "He didn't want any of them to suddenly have a heart event like happened to Suzanne."

Summer nodded. That made sense and she was glad Doc had thought of it as she had not. "So what's the problem then?" she asked.

"He discovered that none of them had any in their system at all, so of course he decided to dose them. Only the Falasians surrounded the first woman and will not let Doc near her."

"Why not?" Summer asked in surprise. The Falasians had seemed so meek and mild before. But now she noticed that they were all glaring angrily at Doc with their bright pink eyes. A few of them had even bared their teeth.

"They won't say," Darleen said. "They would only say they wanted you, the *She Warrior*. At least, I guess that means you."

She Warrior? Summer thought weakly. She shook her head and approached what appeared to be the lead Falasian.

"Hello," she said. "My name is Summer. You asked for me?"

The woman turned and bowed to Summer.

"Mahsia Summer," the small pink woman said. "I am Shali."

Summer, more familiar with bowing now, returned the bow without even thinking about it.

"What is the problem?" she asked.

"He will not harm her," Shali said, pointing to Doc angrily.

"He has no wish to harm her," Summer replied in surprise. "He must give her the medication that is needed because of the Controller."

Shali frowned, then looked back at Doc for a moment. "She not needs it," she said, looking back to Summer. "We fix better. Man medicine not good for hers."

Summer thought about that for a moment. "Are you saying that you never give these women their medication?" she asked.

"Man medicine not good for hers," Shali repeated. "We fix poor hers better."

"How do you fix them?" Summer asked.

This question seemed to be a stumper as Shali placed her fist under her chin and frowned hard as she thought about it. Summer was just about to rephrase the question when Shali's brow cleared and she smiled. "We fix mind."

"You fix their minds?" Summer asked, confused.

Shali's expression changed to one of deep sadness. "No can fix tiny machines in mind," she said, shaking her head slowly. "Can only fix mind knowing."

"Ah," Summer said, thinking she understood now. "You use your mind to prevent her mind from knowing what is happening to it."

Shali's face brightened as she smiled widely. "Yes yes, fix mind knowing." She glanced at Doc again, then back to Summer. "Man no hurt hers please," she said. "We care for hers better."

"Don't worry Shali," she said. "Doc does not wish to hurt anyone. He wants only to help them. He did not know you could do it better."

Shali frowned, glanced at Doc quickly once more, then shrugged her delicate pink shoulders. Clearly she didn't trust Doc, but she would wait and see what happened.

Summer looked at Doc who was no longer glaring at the Falasians, but was studying them thoughtfully. "So they have a way of preventing the mind from knowing what is going on in the mind, do they?" he asked.

"Apparently," Summer said. "What do you think?"

Doc shook his head and returned the syringe he was holding to a tray on the counter. "I think that she is correct," he said. "These eppys are not at all good for these women, though they are better than the alternative. Up to now. If the Falasians can keep them stable until we reach Jasan and can get them all Healed, I am certainly agreeable to that."

Summer looked back to Shali, who was looking at Doc in wide-eyes surprise. Obviously she had not thought he would agree to leave their charges in their care.

"Shali," Summer said, getting the woman's attention. "Please be sure to let Doc know immediately should any of the women become ill. If you will promise to do that, we will leave them all in your care."

"Shali promises most truly, Mahsia Summer," she said earnestly. She turned to Doc and bowed slowly. "We shall messenger as promises," she said hesitantly.

"Thank you, Shali," Doc said, returning the small woman's bow.

Shali's eyes widened in surprise and she ducked her head, turning an even brighter shade of pink than normal. She then turned to the other Falasian women and began chattering at them quickly. They all relaxed, offered shy smiles to Summer, ignored Doc, and began urging the woman lying on the exam table to her feet with soft Controller commands that, Summer thought, they did not like using. Well, that said much for them, she thought.

"If that is all, we shall return to our dinner now," Maxim said with a slight bow to Doc and Darleen.

"I'm sorry we had to interrupt you," Darleen began, but Maxim held up a hand.

"Do not be sorry, Darleen," he said. "It was necessary and we do not mind."

"Okay, see you later," Summer said to Darleen and Doc as Maxim placed a hand on her elbow and began guiding her toward the door.

"I will be along in a moment," Loni said. "I wish to speak with Doc."

Maxim looked at Loni curiously but did not ask any questions. Summer wondered about it briefly, but, like Maxim, did not ask. After all, she thought, the man was entitled to go where he pleased without having to explain himself. Nevertheless, she did miss his presence as they returned to the Star Room and their interrupted dinner.

Chapter 43

They had all finished their dinner and Summer had just declined dessert by the time Loni returned. Summer felt his excitement before he reached the Star Room, so her curiosity was already piqued when he entered the room and closed the door.

"I have a solution to our problem with the ritual," he announced as he took his seat.

"Yes?" Maxim asked, instantly alert as he noted the suppressed happiness in his younger brother's expression.

"The Falasians," he said.

Maxim, Ran and Summer all fell silent as they considered Loni's response. Loni waited patiently, giving them time.

"Doc?" Maxim asked.

"We had a very careful interview with Shali after you left," Loni said. "From what she said, and after a couple of experiments, we both believe it will work, and that Summer will feel no pain."

"Experiments?" Summer asked, her eyes narrowed at Loni. "What kind of experiments exactly?"

Loni shrugged, but the set of his jaw told Summer that he was going to be stubborn about this. "What kind of experiments?" she repeated.

"Do you think any of us would experiment with you?" he asked her in a soft voice.

"No," she replied. "But why that makes it okay to experiment on yourself is beyond me."

"I have the ability to regenerate," Loni reminded her. "Any mundane injury to my body will heal quickly. The same is not true of your body. Therefore, it makes sense that I test my theory on myself."

"It worked?" Maxim asked, not just because he was excited by the idea, but also in an effort to divert Summer's frown from Loni.

"Yes, it worked perfectly," Loni said. "Shali was resistant to speaking with us at first, until Darleen explained that it was for you, Summer. Then Shali insisted that she be the one to handle the experiment, and make sure it worked perfectly. She also wishes to be the one to perform her talent on Summer during the ritual."

"So all of this means that we can perform the mating ritual?" Summer asked to be certain.

"Yes," Maxim replied, barely able to believe it himself. "If you still wish, yes."

"Of course I still wish," Summer replied. "Now?"

"You want to do it now?" Maxim asked.

"Yes, now," Summer said. "As I told you earlier today, I do not want to go another day if we can help it. So now."

Maxim grinned, as did Loni and Ran. All three of them stood up, and Maxim lifted Summer into his arms so quickly she barely knew he what he meant to do until they were speeding along to her stateroom.

"Please wait here for a few minutes," Maxim said as he set her on her feet. "We have a few things to prepare, and then we will come back for you."

"Okay," Summer said, suddenly feeling a little nervous. "Is there anything I should do to...prepare?" she asked hesitantly.

Maxim smiled and went o the closet. He reached in, and came back with a garment in his hands which he offered to her. "Before we left Jasan we saw this in a shop window, and thought it suited you," he said as she reached slowly for the gift. "We would be most honored if you would wear it for us."

Summer ran her fingers over the rich, chocolate brown fabric, overwhelmed at their thoughtfulness. "I would love to wear this," she said softly.

"But you have not yet fully seen it," Ran objected as Summer took the garment from Maxim and hugged it to her chest.

"It does not matter," she said. "It is a gift from the three of you. Therefore, I will love it."

Maxim, Loni and Ran all looked at each other, then Summer, then back to each other again. They did not understand. But, she was accepting their gift. That was enough.

"We shall be back very soon," Maxim said, giving her a quick kiss before turning to leave. Ran and Loni each had to have his own quick kiss as well, and then Summer was alone with her gift, and a case of sudden nerves.

By the time the Katres returned a few minutes later, Summer was dressed in her new robe with her long hair braided loosely over one shoulder. The robe was made of some type of soft, silky fabric dyed a rich, chocolate brown that exactly matched her eyes. A design of vines and leaves had been worked in golden thread from the neck all the way down the front to the floor, as well as on the edges of the long, full sleeves. As she gazed at herself in the mirror, Summer had to admit that Maxim was correct. The robe did suit her.

There was a soft, warning knock at the door before it opened and Maxim stepped inside, pausing for a long moment to stare at her. "The robe does you justice," he said. "It is almost as beautiful as you are."

Summer felt her face heat and dropped her eyes, feeling shy. Feeling shy felt silly though, so she took a deep breath, raised her eyes to Maxim's and squared her shoulders. "What next?"

"Now I carry you to the Pleasure Room," he said, smiling.

"Pleasure Room?" Summer asked. "What is a Pleasure Room?"

"It is exactly what it sounds like," he replied as he picked her up and turned for the door. "A room designed for pleasure. There is only one aboard the *Vyand* as it is not often that a male-set brings their mate aboard a military ship."

"I'm surprised that there is even one," Summer said as Maxim turned to lock the door behind them.

"Happily, there is always at least one," he said. "Ready?"

Summer took a deep breath and nodded, knowing that she would likely not breathe once he started moving quickly. A few moments later the blurring stopped and they stood before an unmarked door not far from the training rooms on the rec deck. Maxim lowered her to her feet and opened the door for her. She stepped inside and gasped softly as Maxim followed her in and locked the door behind them.

Summer found herself in a square room that was about the same size as her stateroom only with a very high ceiling. The entire room, floor, walls, and ceiling were covered in what looked like black velvet. She rubbed one bare foot across the floor and nodded to herself. Yep, black velvet. She took a step forward and amended that. Padded black velvet. In the center of the room as a large round bed set low to the floor, covered in soft pearl gray sheets and pillows. The walls had dozens of deep insets, all of which were filled with thick candles which gave off a light woody scent as they burned that was soothing, but not too heavy.

Her survey of the room ended there as Ran approached her, picked her up into his arms and kissed her long and deeply. "You are so beautiful," he whispered when he raised his lips from hers. "We are so blessed, and so honored by you. I would have you know that I will love you all the days of my life and beyond."

Summer smiled as she caressed his face lightly with one hand. "That makes me happier than I ever imagined it was possible to be."

Ran kissed once more, then carried her to the bed and sat her carefully in the center of it. Then he, Maxim and Loni removed most of their clothing, save only their pants, and joined her on the bed.

"The first part of the ritual is that we inject you with our mating fangs," Maxim said. "It will not cause you pain."

Summer shrugged nervously. "I am not afraid of a little pain," she said. "But what will the serum do to me?"

"The first injection will speed up your ability to regenerate," he replied. "It is necessary that you are able to regenerate quickly in order to be able to shift into an alter form. The side effects of that are that you will not age, and you will heal quickly from most injuries or illnesses."

"Most?" Summer asked.

"Magical weapons and nuclear or radiation weapons will not heal as well as mundane injuries," Maxim explained. "Such injuries must heal normally as they do in humans."

"Okay," Summer said. "What do I need to do?"

"Just relax, *kilenka*," Maxim said as he shifted on the bed until he was behind her. "Lie down here."

Summer lay back as Maxim indicated so that Loni was on her left side, Ran on her right, and Maxim near her head. Maxim lowered himself until he too was lying on the bed with his head next to hers. He looked at his brothers, who nodded as they each picked up one of Summer's wrists and raised them to their mouths.

"Easy now, *kilenka*," Maxim said into her ear. "This will only take a moment. Please do not move."

"All right," Summer said, doing her best to relax. She knew that these men would never cause her harm. She knew that they loved her. And she wanted this. She was just a little nervous about the unknown.

At some silent signal that Summer missed, Maxim lowered his head to her neck and at the same time, Loni and Ran lowered their mouths to her wrists. They all sank their mating fangs into her flesh, but she felt only a mild stinging sensation. She focused on her breathing, unable to do anything about the rapid beat of her heart as she forced herself to remain motionless for what seemed like an eternity.

Finally, all at the exact same time, the Katres lifted their mouths from her flesh and she felt them each lick her where their mouths had been, just once. Loni and Ran lowered her wrists back to her sides and Maxim raised his head.

"How do you feel?" he asked her.

"Okay, just a little nervous," she admitted. "Is it done?"

"Yes love, it is done," Loni replied.

Summer took a long deep breath of relief. "That was easy," she said, trying to make her voice sound light.

Maxim and Ran chuckled softly as Maxim rose to his knees. "You are very brave," Maxim said. "Now, how would you like a bath?"

"A bath?" Summer asked in surprise. "Um...okay?"

"Come," Maxim said, picking her up once more before working his way off of the bed. "This part of the process will take about an hour," he explained as they all walked across the room and through a door into a large bathroom that was lit with candles like the bedroom. "Then, you will suddenly begin to feel sleepy," he said as he set her on her feet. Loni walked over to a large tub that, to Summer, seemed more like a swimming pool than a bath tub by the size. He reached in to check the water temperature and nodded in approval.

"What happens after I get sleepy?" Summer asked, as she watched appreciatively while all three of her men removed their pants. Ran caught her gaze and grinned at her. "Sorry *saritu*," he said, we won't be able to indulge ourselves until later."

Summer made a show of sighing heavily. "Too bad," she said as Maxim reached for the belt of her robe and untied it.

"Do not worry, we will get there," Maxim said as he slipped the robe off of her, laid it carefully over a stool, and led her to a set of steps.

"This is the first time I have ever had to climb stairs to get into a bath tub," she said as she walked up the marble stairs, then down more steps on the other side into the warm, scented water. She saw that the edges of the tub were lined with seats so she selected one and lowered herself all the way down, sighing with pleasure. She realized too late that she had forgotten to put her hair up so it wouldn't get wet, flipped her soaked braid back over her shoulder and shrugged. It would dry.

"So, what happens when I get sleepy?" she asked again when all three of the men were in the tub with her.

"You will suddenly fall into a very deep sleep," Maxim said as he reached for Summer's braid, pulled it forward and released the braid with nimble fingers. "That is when your DNA will be rewritten to be Jasani instead of human."

"I remember everything I've ever read," she said, "but I've never read any medical books. My knowledge of such things is very limited, but even so, that does not sound good."

"It is, in truth, the most dangerous part of this process," Maxim admitted, as he released Summer's loose hair and watched it float in the water. "You will sleep for about an hour. When your DNA is finished being rewritten, we will have only a short time to inject you a second time to begin the next step in the process."

"Which is?" Summer asked.

"Your body must change to match your new DNA," he replied. "That is the part that is painful, so we will have Shali here for that."

"Will I be conscious?"

"I do not know," Maxim said, reaching out to run his fingers lightly through her hair. "I know that neither Lariah nor Saige were, but that is because they were put into a deep sleep to escape the pain. I do not know if Shali will do the same thing or not."

"You do realize that my hair is now completely soaked and, since I will be lying down sleeping, it will be a mess of snarls later."

Maxim smiled. "When you go to sleep, we will dry it for you and braid it. Do now worry *kilenka,* you are our Arima, and it is our privilege to take care of you in all ways."

It occurred to Summer to warn them that she was not a doll, and that she was perfectly capable of taking care of herself, but she held her tongue. She reminded herself that they had recognized she was the best one to approach the Aki, and that her plan to go alone into the compound on Li-Hach-Cor was the best one. They wished to care for her, but she didn't think they meant to smother her. And if they did, she would just have to educate them.

"Why do you smile?" Ran asked her, breaking into her thoughts.

"No reason," she said, searching for a change of subject, "By the way, what do you think the explanation is for William? Do you think he really is related to Mara?"

"We will soon find out," Maxim replied. "Did he say anything of import?"

"There were a few things you should know," she said. "The first is, he was able to scent the Controllers in all three of us."

That got a few surprised looks, as she had known it would. "I believe he scented the brain chemistry changes caused by its activity though because when I deactivated mine, he knew it. He tried to verbally reactivate it to Control me, but of course that didn't work."

"That's interesting," Maxim said.

"Yes, I thought so," Summer said. "He thought someone else was using the Controllers and threatened to kill Darleen in order to get whoever it was to show themselves. That's why I had to attack him. When he reached for her, I struck his arm off with the katana."

"Excellent," Maxim approved.

"That's when he told me that it would *self heal* in a few days, but that I should not worry because our children would heal much more quickly."

"Your children?" Maxim asked, shocked.

Summer glanced at Ran and Loni, noting that they too were stunned by that bit of information. So much so that their eyes were beginning to glow. "Don't get worked up," she said. "He's dead now, remember?"

"What else?" Maxim asked.

"He knew that I was a *berezi*, and he said that he was my husband and I was his bride. That's when he told me his full name. Right after that, I decided to see if his head would grow back the way he said his arm would."

"I just noticed something," Ran said.

"What's that?" Summer asked curiously.

"You have a bit of a temper, don't you?"

Summer hit the water with the heel of her hand, splashing Ran directly in the face. "What makes you say that?" she asked sweetly.

Maxim and Loni both chuckled as Ran wiped the water from his eyes.

"What about the Xanti?" Maxim asked. "Did he have anything to say of interest?"

"Not really," Summer replied. "He mostly wanted me, or rather, he wanted the *berezi*, and he said something about selling me again now that William was dead. He also seemed to think that Lio had betrayed him."

"Perhaps he did," Maxim said with a shrug. "I am sorry to lose the information the man may have eventually given us, but I cannot say I am sorry to be rid of him."

"I know," Summer replied. "I nearly turned him over to the Council before we left, and when I knew he was dead, I couldn't help thinking that if I had done that, he would still have his life. But, at the same time, had we not brought him, we would not have been able to bluff our way through the compound's security."

Maxim understood that Summer's regret was for the loss of a life, not for Lio himself, but he did not want her to dwell on it further. So he changed the subject.

"We have something for you," he said.

"Yes?" Summer asked with a smile. "What?"

"The translation of the writing on the saya came in," he said with a grin.

"I didn't even know you requested it," Summer said.

"Of course you didn't," Ran said. "If you had, then it wouldn't have been a surprise."

Summer arched a brow at him and considered splashing him again. But, as he reached over to a shelf near the tub for an electronic pad, she refrained. For the moment.

"The writing is quite old," Maxim said. "Several thousand years old in fact, as is the katana itself."

"I had a feeling it was old, but I had no idea it was that old," Summer said. "What does it say?"

Ran flipped on the electronic pad and scrolled through a few pages.

"The translation is: *In time, with Nintai, shall the double headed dragon be struck down by the heat of Natsu."*

Summer's face paled. "What is it?" Maxim demanded.

Summer swallowed hard. "When Sensei asked me my name that day, I told him it was *Natsu*. Only I don't know what that means, or where it even came from. Ran, can you find out what the word *Natsu* means?"

"Of course," Ran replied as he quickly typed a request into the electronic pad. "According to this, it is Japanese for *summer,"* he said after a few moments.

"I thought it might be," Summer said. "Do you remember I told you that my parents and I had a falling out, and I changed my name?"

"Yes," Maxim said, staring at her intently. He did not like any of this, and regretted getting the translation. But it was done, so now he needed to learn everything about it that he could.

"Well, I didn't change my name because I was angry with my parents," Summer explained. "I did it because I wanted privacy. Everyone knew that the famous Whitneys had one daughter, and her name was Natalie-Sue. But the public never knew that in my family, I was always called Summer. I always thought it was an extension of the name *Sue*. But now I see there was more to it than that. "

"Natalie-Sue, Natsu," Maxim murmured. "Do you think your real name is Natsu?"

"Yes, I think so," Summer said. "I need to contact my parents to find out for sure, but I have one of those strange feelings again, and it's telling me that I'm right about this."

"So the message on the saya is saying that you will fight a dragon if you're patient?" Ran asked doubtfully.

"Not exactly," Summer replied. "Sensei called the katana *Patience*. He used it like a name. I remember from that day when I spoke Japanese that *Nintai* is the Japanese word for Patience. "

"Then it means that you will fight a dragon with your katana?" Maxim asked, shaking his head before he finished the question. "No, I do not think so.

"How about we discuss that if, and when, the time comes?" Summer suggested, hiding her grin. She was a little amazed to realize that only a week or two earlier she would have been offended by both Maxim's words and his tone. Now she knew he was being overprotective and worried, not overbearing and thick-headed.

"We also got a response from Eldar Hamat regarding the *time in a cup* question," Ran said.

"Was he able to help with that?" Summer asked hopefully.

"Yes," Ran replied. "When the first pods landed on Jasan, there was one which contained important artifacts of our old world. Among them is a tiny carved figure of a bird. The figure is called The Owlfen, though there is no record of such an animal having really existed. On the bottom of the carving are the words *Time is not measured by the cup; it is a river that is endlessly renewed*."

"What is that supposed to mean?" Summer asked.

"Nobody really knows," Ran replied. "It is speculated that it means all things repeat themselves in time. But that's just a theory."

Summer yawned widely. "Excuse me," she said, surprised by the yawn. She hadn't felt the least bit sleepy a moment ago, and now she barely could keep her eyes opened. She realized that all three of her men were staring at her and she suddenly realized why.

"Guess this is the next...stage," she said, yawning again.

"Yes," Maxim said, watching her carefully in case she fell asleep and slipped under the water. Faron had told them how Saige had fallen asleep so suddenly in the shower that Ban had barely had time to catch her before she hit the floor.

"Do not worry, *kilenka*," he said. "We will take good care of you."

"I'm not worried about that at all," Summer said, then yawned once more before falling fast asleep.

A short time later Summer was lying on the big, round bed, dressed in the robe they had given her. They had used air magic to dry her hair and had then braided it in one long, loose braid the way she preferred. Shali was now waiting patiently in a room across the hall, and Doc had checked Summer, confirming that she was in the same light coma that Lariah had been in during this stage. He promised to come running if they called for him, then left them to their vigil.

There was nothing they could do now but wait. And check her repeatedly for signs that her breathing, blood pressure and heart rate were slowing. Even though they knew it would be an hour at least, they could not help themselves from checking her every few minutes.

"What do you think William really was?" Ran finally asked Maxim.

"I'm not sure," Maxim said slowly. "I have an idea, but its a troubling one."

"Which is what?" Loni asked as he reached out to check on Summer's vital signs again.

"Well, he was clearly reptilian," Maxim said. "Very reptilian. And Mara is human. So for the two of them to be siblings, they must have one parent in common, at least."

"Agreed," Ran said.

"The problem is, how does a human mate with a reptile?" Maxim continued. "They are not remotely of the same species. Mammals and reptiles do not mix."

Loni and Ran now gave Maxim their full attention, a feeling of uneasiness growing within both of them. "Except?" Ran asked, knowing that Maxim had thought of an exception, though he could not come up with one himself.

"Except when magic is involved," Maxim said. "Strong magic. And do not forget, Summer said that he knew she was *berezi*, and that he expected to have children with her."

Ran frowned as he ran everything Maxim had said through his mind, trying to come to some conclusion. After a moment he shook his head. "I am sorry Maxim," he said. "Wherever you are leading, I am not following very well."

Maxim looked to Loni who gave his head a single shake. No. Loni did not follow either. Maxim wondered if that meant he was going too far afield with his suspicions. He hoped so. But he was worried.

"Regardless of the reason, or the method, Ugaztun and Narrasti both were destroyed at the same time," he said. "If we sent out pods of survivors, it is logical to assume the Narrastia did as well. Some of our survivors reached Earth. Perhaps some of theirs did as well."

"You think that William is a descendent of the Narrasti?" Ran asked in surprise.

"I think it is a possibility," Maxim corrected. "I am troubled that he apparently wanted a *berezi* in particular, and that he was certain of getting children with one."

"Do you think that is why the Xanti are targeting *berezis* for abduction?" Ran asked.

"I don't know, but perhaps," Maxim replied. "It might also have something to do with why *berezis* receive the Prime Controller rather than the one used on other women."

Loni cocked his head. "I do not understand," he said.

"I don't either," Maxim replied. "It is just one more difference that I think has meaning. Unfortunately, I do not know what that meaning is."

Ran turned to check on Summer, and this time, he noticed a change. He looked at his watch, then checked her again.

"It's happening," he said.

Loni used power speed to leave the room and retrieve Shali. He was back in moments with the diminutive female with the strange pink eyes and white hair. Shali did not look directly at any of the men in the room. Instead, she hurried to the bed and reached out to place a pale pink hand on Summer's forehead. She closed her eyes for a moment, then opened them and removed her hand.

"Her mind knows no pain now," she said in her high voice, clearly speaking to the Katres though her eyes remained fixed on Summer.

"For how long?" Maxim asked.

"For until I do right," she replied.

Maxim puzzled over that one for a moment, but still her meaning escaped him.

"She will not know pain until you undo whatever you've done?" Ran asked, much to Maxim's relief.

"This is so yes," Shali replied.

"Will she remain asleep?" Maxim asked.

Shali nodded. "Is better she not here when brain not know body. Is not right for brain." She turned and this time she did dare to meet Maxim's gaze. "It no good to stay," she said sternly. "Brain must know body."

Maxim nodded. That, he understood. "Do not worry Shali," he said. "We will call you back as soon as the pain is passed."

"Her is good," Shali said, turning back to Summer and patting her lightly on the hand. "Her not be for Brethren."

"Brethren?" Maxim asked.

"The Willi-yam man," Shali said. "Brethren be bad bad. Better Brethren dead."

"Shali, did William ever...," Maxim hesitated, not knowing how to phrase what he wanted to say. He grimaced and spit it out. "Did he ever use the women in the compound sexually?"

"No no," Shali replied, still patting Summer's hand. "Humans womens not work for Brethrens," she said matter-of-factly. "He try others, almost like hers, but not. Theys all die." This last was said with sorrow, as though Shali had mourned the unfortunate women.

"How do you mean they were almost like Summer, but not?" Maxim asked, working to keep his voice gentle.

Shali put her fist beneath her chin and frowned, her eyes squinty as she thought hard on the question. After a few moments, she gave her head a little shake. "They is like cousins. Close. Not like sisters. Closer. But not too far. Like humans."

Maxim gave his own head a little shake at that one. "Um, okay Shali, thank you very much," he said, wondering if it was remotely possible that Ran had understood that one.

"Come, Shali," Loni said. "I will escort you back across the hall."

Shali nodded and bowed in Maxim's general direction before moving quickly toward the door. When Loni returned a moment later, they all gathered around Summer, watching her vital signs carefully as they began to slow further.

"Now I think," Maxim said and got up on the bed near Summer's head while Loni and Ran took their positions at her sides. Maxim checked her once more, and nodded. Yes, now was the time.

He extended his mating fangs and lowered his mouth to Summer's neck, took a slow breath, and slid them into her skin. A few moments later, when instinct told him, he removed his fangs and licked the tiny holes on her neck, Loni and Ran doing the same at her wrists.

When they were finished, they all looked at each other, then at Summer. From all they had been told by both the Lobos and the Dracons, this was going to be the most difficult part for them. They were not looking forward to it.

A few hours later, Maxim, Loni and Ran were exhausted with fear and worry. Maxim had never in his entire life witnessed anyone in such pain. The only thing that allowed him to keep his sanity was the sure and certain knowledge that Summer was unaware of the pain her body was experiencing. It was the only thing that kept all three of them from succumbing to blood-rages.

But, finally, it seemed to be ending. Summer's body still continued to twitch and jerk occasionally, but the convulsions that had her body twisting and flailing so hard that she nearly landed on the floor several times were finished.

After Shali had come and undone whatever she had done to Summer, they all thanked her profusely for her help. They had a far better understanding now of just how important Shali's help had been to them.

They had just finished washing Summer's body with warm cloths when her eyes suddenly popped open. She blinked a few times as though trying to assess her current surroundings, then lifted her head and smiled at them. For a long moment, all three of them just stared at her smile, and were grateful for it.

"How's it going so far?" she asked.

"The last part was more difficult than we expected," Maxim admitted. "But it is finished now, and you seem well enough."

"I feel great," she said as she started to sit up. "A little bit sore maybe, but that's all." She looked at the three of them, taking in the strained look on their faces the tight set of their shoulders and mouths. "I'm sorry it was so difficult for you guys," she said softly.

"Do not worry about us," Maxim said. "Seeing you awake and talking is all we needed."

"All right, what happens next?" Summer asked. "Or are we finished?"

"No, not quite," Maxim said. "Now we must perform the soul-link triad."

"And what is that exactly?" Summer asked. Just as she finished speaking her eyes widened and she gasped. She crossed her arms in front of her and bent over at the waist.

"What is it?" Maxim demanded as he rushed to her side and started to pull her into his arms. Summer moaned softly as he placed his hand on her shoulder, so he pulled it back quickly, afraid that he had somehow hurt her.

"What is happening to me?" she gasped, raising her head to look at Maxim beseechingly.

Maxim started to shake his head when the scent of Summer's arousal hit him, along with the reason for her current distress.

"It is the mating fever," he said, trying to remain calm. "This is the last stage."

"Whatever you have to do, please hurry," Summer said, gasping and panting as she rocked herself on the bed. She had never felt anything remotely like this. This was arousal taken to a level beyond pleasure.

"Ran, get the cream," Maxim said. "Loni, pick up these loose things." Ran and Loni both hurried to do as Maxim had asked as Maxim knelt beside the bed. "Summer," he said, and waited for her to meet his gaze. "Let me remove your robe," he said.

Summer nodded and forced herself to move her arms so that Maxim could untie her belt. The silky fabric of the robe rubbing against her skin as he slid it off of her was almost more stimulation than she could stand. She shuddered, uncertain if what she was feeling was pleasure or pain.

Maxim tossed the robe to Loni who turned and ran back to the bathroom with it. He then stopped and stripped off his pants and tossed them in after the robe. Maxim removed the remainder of his clothing as well and tossed it to Loni who put them in the bathroom and closed the door.

"Are we ready?" Maxim asked.

Ran took a look around the room, searching for any loose clothing or other objects they may have missed. Seeing nothing, he nodded and turned to Loni. "Go ahead," he said.

Loni walked over to a panel near the door and, after making certain that the door was locked and sealed, he flipped a switch.

"Hurry up Ran," Maxim urged as Summer began whimpering softly, causing his heart to hurt in sympathy. They had been told this portion of the ritual was difficult for the Arima, and that they would not have much time to complete it, but he had not realized how intense the mating fever would be.

Ran hurried over to the bed, moving slower with each step, though he seemed to be floating a little as he moved. Summer blinked at him, wondering if the intense arousal was somehow effecting her perceptions.

When Ran reached the bed he sat down on the edge, his feet on the floor, and then laid back. Maxim picked Summer up and moved her so that she was over Ran. She understood what Maxim was doing and widened her legs so that she was on top of Ran, straddling his hips. Ran reached down and guided himself into her as Maxim lowered her slowly.

Summer tried to press herself downward, eager to have Ran deep inside of her, but Maxim and Ran both held her back, forcing her to go slowly. She moaned softly as her inner walls stretched to accommodate Ran's thick cock, her pussy clenching wetly around him as though trying to pull him in deeper and faster.

Ran gasped with the effort to hold himself still as Summer's soft, hot sheath engulfed him. The urge to slam himself home was so great that for a moment he was not altogether certain he could resist it. When he was fully seated within her, he grasped her waist gently but firmly and held her still as her body struggled to begin the age old rhythm of pleasure.

When Maxim was sure that Ran had control of Summer he released her and reached for the cream Ran had given him. He opened the jar and scooped out a large dollop, then gently began to apply it to the small pink opening between Summer's cheeks.

Summer flinched in surprise at his first touch, though as he applied the cream and began stretching her carefully, she relaxed and began pressing back against his fingers.

"Why?" Summer asked breathlessly, unable to form a more coherent sentence as her body trembled and ached for more stimulation than Ran or Maxim were allowing.

"We must all enter you at the same time," Maxim said, forcing himself to go slowly and prepare Summer carefully.

Summer whimpered again, her back arching as she gripped Ran hard with her inner muscles, her pussy gushing around him.

"Hurry, please hurry," she gasped.

Maxim gritted his teeth against the urge to give Summer what she wanted, what her body so desperately needed. But he had to be certain he would not cause her any hurt.

"Just one more moment, *kilenka*," he said softly as he scooped another dollop of the cream out and applied it.

"Its so hot," Summer moaned, pressing back against him harder. "Please Maxim," she whimpered. "Please.

Maxim could take no more of her pleading, or his own body's aching need. He put the jar down, then pressed the head of his cock against the carefully prepared opening and pushed. Summer pressed back against him and suddenly, he was inside of her hot, tight channel. He groaned deeply, wanting nothing more than to thrust into her as far and as hard as he could, but made himself go slow. By the time he was fully seated deep within her, sweat was pouring down his face from the effort he had to exert just to hold back.

"All right Loni," he said, his voice hoarse with the strain of holding still as Summer's body continually clenched and shivered around the two cocks buried deeply within her. Loni was already in position, standing on the bed so that his cock was near Summer's lips.

"Summer," Maxim said, "lift your right wrist to Ran and your left to Loni."

Summer immediately did as Maxim asked, willing to do whatever he said as quickly as possible in an effort to get on with this. She wasn't sure how much longer she could tolerate the tension and arousal in her body without screaming.

"Good girl," Maxim gasped. "When Loni is fully in your throat, we will do the final serum injection. You will need to hold your breath for a few seconds, all right?"

"Yes, fine, hurry," Summer replied in a hoarse whisper.

Loni pressed his cock against Summer's lips and she opened her mouth at once, giving the crown of his broad, hard cock one long swipe with her tongue before taking him deep. As soon as he reached the back of her throat she swallowed hard and felt the popping sensation as he slid deep into her throat. The moment he was seated, the intense arousal eased a fraction. Not a lot, but even a little was a huge relief. She found that she could at least force her body to remain still for a few moments as she felt the light sting in her neck and wrists as her men once again bit into her flesh with their mating fangs.

Moments later they withdrew and Summer took a long, deep breath, even though Loni was still deep in her throat. She didn't question it though. Something within her was changing, and she was focused on that until all three men began thrusting in and out of her in a perfect rhythm. For a moment she struggled to find a way to match their thrusts with her own, but she soon realized she couldn't, and just allowed herself to relax instead.

"Wrap your arms around Loni's waist," Maxim gasped.

Summer immediately did as he asked, holding tightly to Loni as he thrust deeply in and out of her throat. Suddenly she felt her body begin to change, and realized that all three of the passages entering her body now led to her womb. She wondered about that for a moment, but was distracted by the oddest sensation. If she hadn't known better, she would have sworn that all four of them were floating weightlessly through the room.

The rhythm of the thrusts sped up and Summer forgot about floating. She wondered briefly how it was possible to feel so much pleasure everywhere in her body all at the same time. Then she sensed something inside of her awakening, something deep within her womb. She focused on that, watching behind her closed eyes as the something grew, then began to open as a flower in the sun, emitting a bright white light. The light grew, intensifying as the rhythm increased until all at once an orgasm rushed through her, through all of them, causing them to arch and strain as their voices rose in a chorus of shared ecstasy and release.

But it was not over yet, Summer knew. She sensed Maxim, Loni and Ran's seed leave their bodies and enter hers, rushing through her passages to her womb where it poured in, mixing together with the bright light. The light grew impossibly brighter and spread quickly back through her passages to her men, beckoning, calling, pulling at them until something within them responded. Something warm and rich and filled with all of the love they felt for her, some part of their essence, poured from them and into her, following the paths of their seed. As that essence reached her womb and mixed together as their seed had, she felt another part of each of them separate and settle into her very skin, fusing to her being even as a part of her essence left her and entered them. The light flared brighter than ever and again they all felt another orgasm rushing toward them, bigger, faster and more intense than the first one had been.

Summer's body tightened and strained until she thought her bones would break as the orgasm slammed into her, causing wave after wave of such intense pleasure that she wondered if it would ever stop. Finally, the orgasm began to ease, and her muscles relaxed. She realized that, even though Loni was still in her throat, she was breathing easily, and wondered how that was possible. Her body jerked with after-shocks, and she again had that strange sensation of floating.

A few moments later all three of them began to withdraw from Summer's body, though they all continued to hold onto her, petting and stroking her gently as they all calmed and relaxed. Summer opened her eyes and leaned her head back away from Ran looking around herself in surprise.

"No wonder I felt like we were floating," she murmured as she looked down at the round bed below them.

Maxim kissed her on the neck, then trailed more kisses across her shoulder. "It is sometimes easier to manage the gymnastics of such a joining without gravity," he said in between kisses."

"I see that," Summer replied as she let her head rest against Ran's hip. "Now I understand why the walls and ceiling are padded."

"Yes, it makes banging into the ceiling more comfortable," Ran said as he stroked her hair lightly. Summer heard the smile in his voice and though she wanted to laugh, she was simply too tired for it.

"Is it finished now?" she asked.

"Yes *kilenka,*" Maxim replied. "It is finished now. You are fully Jasani, and fully Clan Katrenca now. What is more, you are fully our Arima, and we are soul-linked."

Summer sighed softly. "That's wonderful," she said softly. "I am very happy."

"And tired," Ran guessed.

"Yes, I'm sorry," Summer replied as her eyes closed.

"Do not be sorry," Ran said. "Close your eyes and sleep. Your Rami will take care of the rest."

"Rami," Summer said, her voice a low whisper. "I like that."

They continued to float for a while longer, enjoying this time together, holding each other as Summer slept. Finally, Maxim waved one hand toward the door and the artificial gravity switch clicked on. They waited patiently as the gravity in the room took hold once more and they floated slowly to the bed below them. Once they were untangled, they laid Summer out on the bed and drank their fill of the sight of her, their Arima, with the lau-lotu on her shoulders and arms. Never had they thought to see such a sight for themselves, of themselves.

"Shall we take her to the bath or shall we bathe her here while she sleeps?" Ran asked glancing at Maxim as he spoke. His eyes widened as he took in the lau-lotu on his brothers shoulders..

"She is beautiful, our katrenca," he whispered as he raised his own arm to study the image more closely. "I have never seen a katrenca with chocolate eyes before."

"She is stunning in both of her forms," Loni said softly as he ran his fingers lightly over the markings on his arm. "I shall never allow my lau-lotu to fade for any reason," he proclaimed. Maxim and Ran bowed their heads in acknowledgement of Loni's oath, knowing he would never break it, so long as he lived, in either of his forms.

Chapter 44

"Summer, Lehen Arima of the Katres, Mind of the Jasani, you are Called." Summer sat straight up in bed, instantly awake at the sound of the voices in her mind. *"The Triad of the Soul, the Heart and the Mind is complete. Now shall the Nine speak. All shall hear, all shall listen, all shall know. Gather the Clans of the Jasani to Enclave three days hence."*

Maxim, Loni and Ran had come fully awake and alert at Summer's sudden movement. The all sat up, then froze, sensing that they must not disturb Summer at that moment. Only when her body relaxed and she gasped in surprise did Maxim reach for her. He pulled her into his lap as Ran and Loni moved close, all of them worrying if something had gone wrong with the ritual.

"Are you well?" Maxim demanded.

"I'm fine," Summer replied. "I just...well....is it normal for Arimas to hear voices in their heads?"

"Voices?" Maxim asked. "What sorts of voices?"

"Women's voices," Summer said. "Several of them, all speaking at the same time."

"What did they say?" Ran asked.

Summer repeated word for word what they had said to her. "Do you think its a dream?" she asked.

"I don't think so," Maxim said slowly as he pondered what she had told them. "You awoke, then sat up, and then they spoke. I think that leaves dreaming out."

"What do you think it means?" Summer asked. "Who are the *Nine*?"

Maxim looked at Ran, then Loni, but none of them were familiar with that term. "We are not familiar with the *Nine*. But I think that we should do as the voices told you," Maxim said.

Summer's eyes widened. "Oh, absolutely, we must do as the voices said, that much I am certain of. If we don't...," she hesitated, then fell silent.

"If we don't what?" Maxim asked her.

"I don't know for sure," she said. "Something bad. Something very bad."

Lariah Dracon sat on the floor in the living room, her back against the sofa, Trey's hands stroking her hair as she watched their daughters playing with Tiny on the floor. Tiny loved to have the girls climb all over him, and was careful to never move when they were on him so that they did not fall off.

"Princess Lariah, Lehen Nahoa Arima of the Dracons, Soul of the Jasani, you are Called." Lariah gasped softly, closing her eyes to help her focus as the voices continued to speak in her mind. *"The Triad of the Soul, the Heart and the Mind is complete. Now shall the Nine speak. All shall hear, all shall listen, all shall know. Gather the Clans of the Jasani to Enclave three days hence."*

Lariah opened her eyes and turned to face Trey. "Please call Garen and Val," she said. "I have something important to tell all of you."

Trey studied her face for a moment, then nodded and went in search of his brothers without another word.

Saige carefully laid her eldest daughter in her bed, barely daring to breathe in hopes that Varia would not awaken the moment she left her arms as she sometimes did. When she was sure that Varia would remain asleep, she pulled a light blanket up over her, then spent a few moments just gazing at her daughter in wonder. These days her heart was so filled with happiness and love she sometimes wondered how she managed to contain it all.

"Saige, Lehen Arima of the Katres, Chosen of the Eternal Pack, Heart of the Jasani, you are Called." Saige's eyes unfocused as she concentrated on the voices in her mind. It did not occur to her to doubt for a moment that whatever was happening was both real, and important. *"The Triad of the Soul, the Heart and the Mind is complete. Now shall the Nine speak. All shall hear, all shall listen, all shall know. Gather the Clans of the Jasani to Enclave three days hence."*

When she was certain the message was complete, she blinked, blew a kiss to her sleeping daughter, and left the nursery. She had to find Faron, Dav and Ban right away. Then she would vox Lariah to see if she too had received a message, though she was pretty certain she already knew the answer to that.

Chapter 45

Slater sat outside of his small cave, warming himself on the narrow ledge in the weak sunlight. He wondered how much longer he was going to have to stay out here on his own, waiting for Magoa to show up. He had spent a lot of his time during the past week wishing that he was back in his stone hut, getting the low quality meat delivered to him each day. He hadn't really enjoyed either the hut or the nearly rancid meat when he had them, but they were both much better than living in a cold cave and hunting on his own.

He had used his sugea to travel to a distant area of the planet to hunt, and that had been fun. He hadn't realized how big Onddo really was, or how much game there was on other parts of it. The problem was bringing enough meat back to the cave to last him a few days before he had to go out for more. He had spent far too many years living on crowded ships and spaceports where getting food was almost too easy. He longed for that again.

Slater stretched and rose to his feet. He didn't really feel much like moving, but he was growing hungry, and he had only enough meat on hand for one good meal. After he ate that, he would need to use the energy he got from it to transform into the sugea in order to hunt for more meat. It was a cycle he was bored with, but he had to eat.

He turned to go back into the cave and paused when he heard a strange noise. It was vaguely familiar, but he couldn't quite place it. He turned back and looked around, pleased that he had chosen a high cave with a good vantage point for his den. Actually, the sugea had chosen it, but as he was the sugea, he saw no reason not to take credit for it.

He stood still for long moments, seeing nothing out of the ordinary, but hearing the strange sound grow ever closer. He frowned, struggling so hard to place the sound that he didn't even notice the gigantic red beast when it first appeared over the ridge on the opposite side of the valley from where he stood. When he did notice it, for long moments all he could do was gape at it.

A sugea. A huge, red sugea. And it was flying directly toward him. The flapping of its leathery wings was causing the familiar sound.

Slater froze with indecision. Should he transform into his sugea? Or would that make the red one angry? This red sugea was far larger than his own green sugea was. Not to mention the fact that he was not, in truth a sugea. He just transformed into one to make others think he was a sugea. He had a feeling that was something a real sugea would not be pleased to learn.

On the other hand, if he stood there on the ledge and that sugea attacked him, he would die. If he was in his sugea form, at least he had a chance. If nothing else, he could fly away.

By the time all of these thoughts went through Slater's head, the sugea was almost upon him. He turned to go into his cave, having decided to run, and then shift, when the sugea landed on the ledge, transforming smoothly into Magoa.

Slater froze again, this time in shock. Magoa was a sugea? Or was Magoa an adinare?

"Hello, Slater my boy," Magoa said genially, clapping Slater on the shoulder heartily. "Surprised you, didn't I?"

Slater could only nod slowly. Magoa laughed, a deep barking sound that nearly made Slater flinch it was so unexpected.

"I have lots to tell you boy, and not a lot of time to do it in, so listen close," Magoa said.

Slater nodded again, feeling as though he should speak, but quite unable to form words at the moment.

"I don't have time to mince words with you, so I will tell you straight out. Yes, I am a sugea and son, so are you."

Slater gaped. He simply could not help himself. He started to shake his head, then remembered that he was supposed to be pretending to everyone that he was a sugea, so denying it would be foolish.

Magoa chuckled. "I know, you think you are an adinare, am I right?"

Slater didn't know what to say. Yes or no, either way led him into trouble. So he just remained still. That seemed to be fine with Magoa as he continued on as though Slater had answered.

"Well, you are not a shifter that can turn into a sugea, Slater. Nope, not at all. It's the other way round. You are a sugea with the power to shift. And that is a very excellent and rare gift indeed."

Slater started to preen, thought better of it, and remained motionless.

"Now, I know you don't know much about this, but where one sugea has some power, two sugea together have a hundred times that power. I've been trying to get a sugea offspring for years, and you are the only one that's come along. But you needed some growing up, and I needed someone to go out and bring the future back to Onddo. Now that's done, we got to figure out how to get rid of the damn Xanti, and then we can get on with the real planning. You following me?"

Slater started to nod, then started to shake his head, then remained still.

"Well, that's fine, that's fine, you will. Right now, you just need to know that your task while you are out here is to practice the things I'm going to teach you," Magoa said. "That's important Slater. It won't be easy, but you will work at it, won't you?"

Slater nodded, relieved to be able to actually give an answer he was certain of.

"Good boy," Magoa said. "We got us some business to tend to with the Ugaztun, which I hear now call themselves Jasani."

Slater nodded again.

"All right then. Now we'll get on with the lessons. You need to learn how to use your magic Slater. You do what I tell you, it will grow and get stronger. You hear me?"

Slater nodded emphatically. Oh yes, he heard that all right.

"Come on over here then, and we'll get started," Magoa said selecting a spot on the ledge next to the one Slater usually used.

Slater moved to his spot on the ledge, wondering if this was a dream as he settled himself comfortably. As Magoa began to talk, Slater listened, paying very close attention. In the back of his mind though, he knew, glory was coming. Just as he had always believed. He'd doubted there for awhile. But now, now it was back. And bigger than ever.

Chapter 46

Three days later Summer stood before a large round dais in the center of an arena crowded with Jasani. Maxim, Loni and Ran stood close beside her, their presence alone helping to calm her nerves. She looked up, straight across the dais from her, and saw Saige waiting calmly with the Lobos, and the sight relaxed her a little. She had spoken with Saige earlier, just enough to learn that both she and Lariah had received the same message, and that neither of them understood it any better than she did.

A commotion from the other side of the dais drew her attention, and she watched as Princess Lariah and the Dracons took their places. Summer had not yet met the Princess, but she looked friendly enough, and Saige was obviously friends with her. She felt an odd kinship with the petite woman who's eyes met her own across the dais, which she accepted without question. It was same feeling she had whenever she was with Saige.

As she gazed at Lariah, it occurred to her that none of them knew exactly what it was they were supposed to do next. They had gathered the clans and they had agreed to meet by the dais, but beyond that they had not planned.

Even as she wondered what to do next, the answer came to her. She patted Maxim on the hand then turned and stepped up onto the dais, unsurprised to see both Saige and Lariah do the same. The crowd around them fell silent but none of them noticed. They were too intent upon each other as they walked slowly toward the center of the dais. As they came together they each raised their arms, clasping hands to make a circle. The moment they were linked one to the other, a rush of power flowed through them, and they threw back their heads and stared up into the sky as a bright column of sparkling light rose from ground in the center of their circle into the heavens.

The gathered clans watched in silence as the faces of nine women slowly formed in the air above the three Arimas on the dais.

Behold, Clans of the Jasani, the Lehen Triad of Jasan is formed," Summer, Lariah and Saige intoned, though it sounded as though many female voices spoke along with them. *"Through them, we, the Nine First*

Arimas of the Nine Clans of Ugaztun, shall speak to the people. A truth that should not have been forgotten, was forgotten. Before the future can be formed, this lost truth of the past must now be remembered."

"Hear us now, Clan Dracon, Clan Lobo, Clan Katre, Clan Bearen," Lariah said, her voice high and clear.

"Hear us now, Clan Gryphon, Clan Falcoran, Clan Vulpiran," said Saige.

"Hear us now," Summer said in turn, *"as we are not bound by the Covenant of Silence that should never have been made."*

"So shall we speak of the Lost Clans," all three women spoke together, *"of the Owlfen, and the Tigrenca."*

A sudden stillness came over the crowd at the last words, and the very air seemed to hold its breath.

Lost Clans? Garen wondered in shock. His eyes went to the eldest of them there, Eldar Hamat Katre, who met his gaze with a stunned expression of his own. No then, none knew of this. How was this possible? he wondered.

Then, once more, all of the women spoke together.

"Once, long and long and long ago, the Clans were Nine as they were meant to be. But they were not brothers, the Clans, one to another as they are now.

In that time, the Clans fought among themselves, squabbling over land and air and sea as young races often do.

In that time, females had the Right of Choice and fought as they wished, or not, as they wished.

In that time, Enclave was a gathering of females, led by the First Nine Arimas, in part for those women whose time it was to consider the finding of their Rami. All but a few of the women of all the Clans attended.

"The Owlfen and the Tigrenca were at war, each with the other. The heat of their battle ran through the Enclave. In the depths of their blood rages, they noticed not where they were, nor what they did.

"By day's end, all of the Nine were dead, as were all but a few of the other females. Such was the blood rage of the men of the other Clans that the Owlfen and the Tigrenca were both annihilated in retribution.

"Only when the last of the two Clans was destroyed, did the blood rages cool and the males understand what they had done. The Clans were now seven, out of communion with the world and nature. The power of the Clans was broken. There were few women left, and the people were lost.

"In despair, the male-sets of the remaining Clans gathered together in the first male Enclave. They worked together in peace to find a way to save the race of the Ugaztun.

"So it was decided that the women would not go to war, nor would they be taught the ways of war, that the men would guard and protect them.

"So it was decided that the Clans would not war, but become brothers in all things and never again raise hand or claw or fang or talon one to the other.

"So it was decided that the Shame of Ugaztun would remain in the past, and not be spoken of again under the Covenant of Silence.

"And so it came to be, and the Clans kept their covenant and warred no more. In time, the Shame of Ugaztun was forgotten, as were the Lost Clans, as though they had never been.

"Then came the time of the Narrasti. The women were sheltered, coddled, hidden away. The Seven First Arimas tried to come together, to raise the strength they knew should be their own, to warn the Clans of the future which lay ahead on the chosen path. But they did not know they were supposed to be Nine. They did not know the past. Thus they could not raise that which they needed, and it came to pass as they had feared, and all of the women of Ugaztun were lost.

So ends Ugaztun.

So begins Jasan.

Time is not measured by the cup; it is a river that is endlessly renewed. So the remnants of the women of Ugaztun did as they could to keep the blood of the Clans alive among the people of the world they found. Now is the time for those women, the descendents of the remains of the women of Ugaztun, to fulfill their destinies.

So comes the chance to renew the Lost Clans. If the Clans are not restored to number nine as they are meant, so shall the people be lost, forevermore.

"By the energy and the power of the Heart, Soul and Mind are the Jasani now truly joined with the Earth, Air, Fire and Water of this new world. If the Clans heed not the Triad, if they do not abide by their words and warnings, the Clans of Jasan will no more be. If the Clans honor the wisdom of the Triad, there is hope.

So speak the Nine.

So is our task done.

The Bearens' Hope

Book Four of the Soul-Linked Saga
by
Laura Jo Phillips

Available Spring 2012

A Sneak Peek
will be available to read online soon.
Look for it at:
www.laurajophillips.com

ABOUT THE AUTHOR

Laura Jo lives in the Arizona desert with her loving husband, their two children, one very large dog and two *interesting* cats. Laura Jo loves to hear from her readers. Visit her website at www.laurajophillips.com to see when the next installment in the Soul-Linked Saga is coming, and sign her guestbook. Or, email her directly at laurajophillips.books@gmail.com

While you are there, take a peek at the ever growing **Handbook of the Thousand Worlds** which details lots of interesting information about the people, technology, governments, and other interstellar information about the worlds the Soul-Linked Saga takes place in.

Made in the USA
Monee, IL
04 August 2021

74921496R00173